Graham Wallas

The Life of Francis Place from 1771 to 1854

Graham Wallas

The Life of Francis Place from 1771 to 1854

ISBN/EAN: 9783337333331

Printed in Europe, USA, Canada, Australia, Japan

Cover: Foto ©Raphael Reischuk / pixelio.de

More available books at **www.hansebooks.com**

THE LIFE

OF

FRANCIS PLACE

1771–1854

BY

GRAHAM WALLAS, M.A.

LECTURER AT THE LONDON SCHOOL OF ECONOMICS AND
POLITICAL SCIENCE

LONGMANS, GREEN, AND CO.

39 PATERNOSTER ROW, LONDON

NEW YORK AND BOMBAY

1898

Printed by BALLANTYNE, HANSON & Co.
At the Ballantyne Press

PREFACE

THE main sources of this biography are the well-known Place manuscripts in the British Museum, referred to by their number in the catalogue, and the autobiography and letter-books lately in the possession of Francis Place's descendants, to whom, and especially to Mr. Francis C. Miers, I have to express my sincere thanks. I am glad to say that by Mr. Miers' generosity the autobiography and letter-books have now been deposited in the Museum with the other manuscripts.

My own work has, of course, by no means exhausted the interest of these documents. I have confined myself to writing Place's life, and have made no attempt to deal with the materials which he collected for the general history of his time. Within these limits I have tried to make my book useful to any future historian who may deal with the period, by giving references to the original sources for all statements of fact. For the punctuation of quotations from Place's manuscript I am responsible. Place punctuated extremely badly, and his printed works were apparently repunctuated by the printer's reader. He spelt pretty accurately, but made occasional mistakes, which I have not reproduced. I have further, in one or two instances, corrected little grammatical slips where the insertion of a footnote seemed to be pedantic.

It is an important question for the historical student

how far Place's evidence should be accepted on points as
to which (as in the case of some incidents in the Reform
struggle) he is the only witness. My own opinion, formed
after consulting independent evidence in newspapers and
elsewhere for a very large number of Place's statements,
is, that his accuracy on all questions of fact was most
remarkable. His memory seems to have been excellent,
and his description of events after 1820 was written within
a few years or months of their occurrence, and was checked
by the use of a mass of printed documents and original
letters.

Finally, I have to record my gratitude to Mr. F. W.
Galton and Mrs. McKillop for their skilled assistance,
and to many other friends for exhortation and reproof.

GRAHAM WALLAS.

17 JOHN STREET, BEDFORD ROW,
LONDON, W.C., *December* 1897.

CONTENTS

SUMMARY OF CHIEF EVENTS IN PLACE'S LIFE.

1771. Born November 3.

1784–1789. Apprenticed to leather-breeches maker.

1791. Marriage.

1793. Strike of leather-breeches makers. Out of work for some months.

1794–1796. Member of London Corresponding Society. Went to Birmingham (1796) to defend delegates.

1796. Assisted in publication of Paine's "Age of Reason."

1799. Opened a shop at Charing Cross, with a partner.

1801. Recommenced the business alone.

1804. Began to take interest in Lancastrian schools.

1807. First interest in Westminster elections.

1808. Introduction to Bentham and James Mill.

1810. (April) Burdett's arrest. (June) Inquest on Joseph Sellis. Place's estrangement from Burdett.

1810–1814. Acquaintance with Godwin.

1813. Acquaintance with Robert Owen began.

1813–1814. Member of " British and Foreign School Society." Introduction to Hume.

1814. Was instrumental in Repeal of Statute of Apprentices. Gave up politics in Westminster for a time.

1815. Gave evidence before Committee on Mendicity.

1816. Gave evidence before Committee on Education. Apparent maximum of business.

1817. Handed control of business to eldest son. Visit to Bentham at Ford Abbey.

1818. General Election : Romilly and Burdett elected at Westminster.

1819. Westminster election for Romilly's vacancy. Lamb defeated Hobhouse. (August) "Peterloo." (November—
December) "The Savage Parliament."

1820. General Election. Hobhouse and Burdett elected at Westminster : unopposed for thirteen years.

1824–1825. Repeal of Combination Laws.

1827. Death of first wife.

1830. Married Mrs. Chatterley. General Election.

1831–1832. Reform agitation.

1833. Loss of capital. Removal to Brompton Square.

1834. The Dorchester labourers' imprisonment.

1834–1836. Work on : Repeal of Stamp Duty ; Municipal Corporations ; Corporation of London.

1836–1839. Wrote "History of Reform Agitation."

1837. Organised " Working-Men's Association."

1838. Drafted " The People's Charter."

1839. Joined in agitation for Penny Postage.
Imprisonment of Chartist leaders.

1840–1846. Joined in Anti-Corn-Law agitation.

1841. Visit to Manchester for Anti-Corn-Law League.
Health began to give way.

1844. Serious illness.

1851. Separated from his wife. Went to live at Hammersmith.

1853. Removed to Earl's Court.

1854. Death on January 1.

CHAPTER I

EARLY LIFE

On January 7, 1854, an article in the *Spectator* announced that Francis Place had died at the age of eighty-two. " Few men," said the writer, " have done more of the world's work with so little external sign. . . . He was essentially a public man, but his work usually lay behind the curtain. . . . He loved quiet power for the purpose of promoting good ends." [1]

The lovers of quiet power are soon forgotten. The *Spectator* article implies that Place's name, even in 1854, was unknown except to his old political associates. During the forty years which have since elapsed, the " Radical tailor of Charing Cross " has only been known from his friendship with Bentham and James Mill, and, it may be, from Robert Owen's apparently absurd statement that he was the "real leader of the Whig Party." [2] That Place took no steps to secure notoriety during his lifetime, was partly because his power over other men depended largely on his readiness to give them the public credit of the work he planned for them, and partly because indifference to popularity was part of his philosophy. But, fortunately, that indifference did not prevent him from taking a good deal of trouble to make himself known to posterity. He knew by what he had learnt from the scanty records of

1 The *Spectator*, No. 1332, 7th January 1854, p. 13.
2 The " Life of Robert Owen," written by himself (London, 1857), vol. i. pt. i. p. 122.

A

eighteenth-century Radicalism, that history is of great and immediate usefulness to a politician; and being himself a maker of history, he was sensible of a moral obligation to leave authentic records of the public work in which he had borne a hand.   From 1813 to 1850 he carefully kept and indexed his political letters; and in 1823, under the persuasion of Bentham, he commenced an autobiography for publication.   The result was what might have been expected from a man whose sense of the importance of facts made him over-anxious to record every possible detail.   The autobiography, which never was, and never will be, published, branched off into a series of long and unwieldy monographs on the Westminster Elections, the repeal of the Combination Laws, the Reform Agitation of 1830–32, and the numerous other public and private enterprises in which he took part, and was accompanied by huge collections of illustrative documents.   No less than seventy volumes make up in this way the " Place Manuscripts " in the British Museum.[1]   Other volumes are in the possession of his family.   But besides the facts which he was so diligent to collect, these volumes contain the history of an extraordinarily interesting man, who, from 1793, when he became Secretary to the Leather-breeches Makers' Trade Club, to 1838, when he drafted the " People's Charter," was a master in the inception and execution of those difficult and uncertain reforms which we have now come to think of as having been from the first easy and irresistible.

Francis Place was a Londoner; he was born on November 3, 1771, in a " sponging house," or private debtor's prison, in Vinegar Yard, near Drury Lane, kept by his father, Simon Place, who was at that time a bailiff to the Marshalsea Court.   Francis was lucky enough to be sent regularly to some sort of school from the age of four till he was nearly fourteen.   The private adventure schools

---

[1] Additional MSS., vols. 27,789–27,859.

round Drury Lane and Fleet Street in the eighteenth century were not, however, exactly places of education, and he did not learn much until, in his twelfth year, he came under a kindly ineffectual teacher, who lent him books, gave him good advice, and lectured him with the other pupils every Thursday afternoon on the elements of morality. With this exception, the surroundings of his early life were so unfavourable, that in later years he and other believers in the sufficiency of Bentham's " Table of the Springs of Action " were often puzzled to account for the resolution and self-control which he developed.

When Francis Place was nearly nine years old the sponging house was given up, and Simon Place took a tavern with the savings which he had made by legalised blackmail. Place describes his father as a bony, muscular man, about five feet six or seven inches in height, of dark complexion, and very strong. "He was a resolute, daring, straightforward sort of a man, governed almost wholly by his passions and animal sensations, both of which were very strong, and careless of reputation, except in some particulars in which he seems to have thought he excelled. These were few, mostly relating to sturdiness and dissolute-ness. . . . He never spoke to any of his children in the way of conversation ; the boys never ventured to ask him a question, since the only answer which could be anticipated was a blow. If he were coming along a passage or any narrow place such as a doorway, and was met by either me or my brother, he always made a blow at us with his fist for coming in his way. If we attempted to retreat he would make us come forward, and as certainly as we came forward he would knock us down." He was an inveterate gambler, the home being more than once broken up owing to his losses in the State lotteries of the time. On such occasions he would wander away for months, supporting himself by his old trade as a journeyman baker, while his wife kept the family by needlework. Out of school Francis Place, who was short and sturdy, took his full share in that now incredible street life which flourished in London before the new police. He was skilled in street games, a hunter of bullocks in the Strand, an obstinate faction fighter, and a daily witness of every form of open crime and debauchery. In school, however, he became easily head boy, and was regularly employed to teach his fellow-scholars.

Some months before Francis was fourteen years old his father announced that he should be apprenticed to a conveyancer. The boy flatly refused to be "made a lawyer," and declared that he would prefer anything else if it were a trade. "This," he says, "was in the evening, and my father went immediately into his parlour and offered me to any one who would take me. A little man named France said he would, and I was sent the very next morning on liking for a month to learn the art and mystery of leather-breeches making." France was a drunken little wretch, and Place, left to take care of himself, though he worked hard during the day, spent his evenings, as he afterwards unflinchingly confessed, in a sorry enough fashion among his associates in Fleet Street and the surrounding courts. He belonged to a "cutter club"—an eight-oared boat's crew—who used to drink and sing together after the evening's row. The cockswain of the crew was some years later transported for a robbery, and the stroke oar was hanged on a charge of murder. Place, however, did not even at this time go really to the bad. He was less dissolute than his companions, and could not afterwards recollect a single act of dishonesty during his apprenticeship. That this was so was probably due at least as much to a certain dogged personal pride as to the wide views of life which he had learnt at school from the Thursday afternoon lectures on morality.

In July 1789, before he was yet eighteen years old, his indentures were given up, and he became an independent journeyman breeches-maker. He had been working for nine months somewhat irregularly at his trade, when he met, in April 1790, his future wife, Elizabeth Chadd. This was the turning point in his career. His innate toughness of fibre definitely asserted itself, and he became steady, frugal, and industrious. He could, however, save little or nothing. He was a highly skilled workman, but leather-breeches making was a decaying trade, and he could earn no more than fourteen shillings a week. His father, whose health had broken down, had sold his public-house and lost in a lottery all that he had received from the sale, and his mother was working as a washerwoman. But Place was hopeful, and Elizabeth Chadd was unhappy at home. So in March 1791, when he was nineteen and a half, and she not quite seventeen, they were married, and went to live in one room in a court off the Strand. Their joint earnings were under seventeen shillings a week. "From this we had to pay for lodging three shillings and sixpence a week, and on an average one shilling and sixpence a week for coals and candles. Thus we had only twelve shillings a week for food and clothes and other necessaries. Nothing could be saved from this small sum. We however continued to dress ourselves respectably, and were comfortable with each other. As our poverty would not permit us to give anything away, we kept ourselves very much to ourselves, had scarcely any acquaintance, and visited nobody except our parents and my eldest sister. . . . We soon acquired the character of being proud and above our equals. This was the certain consequence of our having no acquaintance with any one, and being better dressed than most who were similarly circumstanced, and we were contemptuously called 'the Lady and Gentleman.'"

As his own trade of leather-breeches making was in so bad a way, he commenced to make stuff breeches, and formed "clubs" of working-men to raffle for his productions. Though he lost money by this speculation he gained experience, and was soon able to get fairly well-paid employment as a stuff-breeches maker, taking work from various master tailors to be done at home. But misfortune was near at hand. In March 1793, two years after his marriage, and a year after the birth of his first child, a strike took place in the leather-breeches making trade. His description of this event is worth giving at some length, as the earliest existing account of a strike written from the inside.

"Some time before I was married I became a member of the Breeches-Makers' Benefit Society, for the support of the members when sick, and to bury them when dead. I paid my subscription regularly, but I never attended at the public-house at which the club was held, excepting on the evenings when the stewards were chosen. The club, though actually a benefit club, was intended for the purpose of supporting the members in a strike for wages. It had now, in the spring of 1793, about £250 in its chest, which was deemed sufficient; a strike was agreed upon, and the men left their work. It was a badly paid, badly conducted trade; a good workman, who was constantly employed, might earn a guinea a week; but scarcely any one was fully employed. It required from an hour to an hour and a half, when two were employed, to cut out and get ready a pair of leather breeches; and as no one master had an arrangement so complete as to have work always ready, and as the whole was piecework, the masters were regardless of the loss and inconvenience the men suffered. The men in the best shops could not therefore earn more than eighteen shillings a week, and in all the others much less. They had therefore resolved to strike for wages, which would put them as to earnings on a level with other trades. So many of them had become makers of stuff breeches that, notwithstanding the trade of leather-breeches making had declined, the proportion of hands to employment was less than formerly, and trade was brisk. The leaders therefore calculated—as they thought securely—on obtaining the advance they demanded. They did not foresee that the masters would represent the strike as unreasonable, and persuade their customers to wear stuff breeches, at least for a time, and that they could get this sort of work done by tailors. As I had not been at the club-house for more than three months, and had now no acquaintance with any one in the trade, I was neither aware of the intention to strike, nor of the strike when it took place. The first I heard of it was from Mr. Bristow. On taking some work home one evening he, instead of giving me more as I expected, gave me my discharge. I asked the reason; he would assign none, and I reproached him with acting unjustly, and in a way I should not have done towards him. He then alluded to the strike, to which he supposed I was a party. I assured him that I had never heard of any intention amongst the men to strike, and had no knowledge whatever on the subject, but that which he had imparted. He was a kind and reasonable man; he told me he was satisfied I had not, and would not deceive him. 'He was,' he said, 'very sorry to discharge me, but that at a meeting of the masters it had been agreed that every leather-breeches maker who was employed to make stuff breeches should be at once discharged, to prevent them assisting those who had struck.' Allison discharged me next day. Thus at once were our hopes destroyed and our views obscured. No chance of employment remained; so I went to the club-house, and here I was informed that every man out of employment was to be paid seven shillings a week from the fund. I found that the number of men was at least equal to the number of pounds the club had in its possession, and consequently there was provision only for three weeks. In the evening, when the men were assembled, I stood up upon one of the tables and addressed them. I pointed out the inadequacy of the sum they had collected, the privations they would probably have to endure. I proposed that as many as were willing should receive one week's pay in advance and a certificate, provided each of them would go on the tramp and engage not to return to London for a month. It was well known that a man who brought a certificate to any leather-breeches maker's shop in the country would be sure of a day's keep, a night's lodging, and a shilling to start again with the next morning, and in some of the larger towns a breakfast and half-a-crown in money to help him along. Many therefore were willing to leave London on the terms proposed. The proposition was adopted, and arrangements made to carry it into effect the next morning. I then proposed that, instead of giving each man seven shillings for his week's subsistence, they should make up Rag Fair breeches,[1] and let as many as would take them have two pairs a week, at four shillings a pair, journeyman's wages. This was a shilling a week more than was proposed to be given, and as the loss on each pair would not be more than two shillings and sixpence, the fund would last more than twice as long as it would if seven shillings were given to each for doing nothing. Besides this, there was another advantage, namely, that every man who could procure any sort of employment could not make, and would not perhaps be desirous to make, two pairs of Rag Fair breeches a week; and if there were men who, having other employment, were mean enough to take money from the fund, this would put an end to any such practice. This proposition was highly applauded, and instantly

[1] *i.e.* leather breeches made of inferior materials.

adopted. A committee of three, of which I was one, was appointed to make the necessary arrangements, and to report on the next evening. I then proposed that a very convenient shop, under the Piazza in Covent Garden, which I had been to look at, should be taken, in which the trade should be carried on. This proposition was referred to the committee, who were empowered to take the shop if they approved of it. I then proposed to them to prepare an address setting forth the reasons for the strike, that it should be printed and circulated. This was also agreed to, and referred to the committee. A report on all these matters was made by me on the next evening, and as my knowledge of Rag Fair breeches-making was well known and duly appreciated, I was unanimously elected sole manager of the whole concern, and the stewards of the club were directed to furnish the money necessary for the purpose. My pay was to be twelve shillings a week, on condition that I would arrange the whole business in a plain manner and conduct it; and those whom I might find it necessary to employ under me in the business should have nine shillings a week each. The business was immediately commenced, and was so managed that legal proceedings could not be taken against us for a combination. Things went on thus until the close of the month of May, when the money was all expended, and the men were compelled to return to their employment without any advance of wages. The masters in their turn punished the men as much as they could; and as the whole number of masters was small, and the whole number of men few, it was by no means difficult for the combined masters to effect their purpose. All who had been in any way active in the strike were not to be employed so long as any other man was unemployed: I and another young man named James Ellis were never again to be employed in any way whatever, by any master breeches-maker."

The terrible description which follows might be written of thousands of families to-day. "During the strike, which continued three months, we expended what little we had saved. Soon after the commencement of the strike our child was taken with smallpox, and died. During the child's illness we, of course, lived and slept in the same room; it was a small one, and it may easily be supposed that our condition was one of extreme chagrin. To my wife it was one of great suffering. Persons who have never been in such circumstances can form but faint ideas of the misery even the best and most frugal of workmen sometimes endure.

"During the next eight months I could obtain no sort of employment, either in my own trade or in any other way. At the commencement of this state of things I contrived so to conduct myself, as to keep away every one who was likely to visit us, and no one excepting my brother ever called upon us; and thus none knew how poor we really were. We visited nowhere except now and then our parents, . . . so we were left alone, which, in our circumstances, was what we desired. • We made many efforts to procure some sort of employment, but were wholly unsuccessful. We suffered every kind of privation consequent on want of employment and food and fire. This is the only period of my life on which I look back with shame. The tricks and pranks of my boyhood were common, and were not thought disgraceful; no one would have abandoned me for what every one did and was expected to do, though the knowledge of it might have distressed my mother. My temper was bad, and instead of doing everything in my power to soothe and comfort and support my wife in her miserable condition; instead of doing her homage for the exemplary manner in which she bore her sufferings; instead of meeting, as I ought on all occasions to have done, her good temper and affection:

I used at times to give way to passion, and increase her and my own misery. The folly and absurdity of giving way to bad temper was always apparent to me, and I never attempted either to palliate or excuse it to myself. I was indeed ashamed of it, and set about to rectify it, and this I soon did to a considerable extent. It is but too common for a man and his wife, whose circumstances compel them to be almost constantly together in the same room, to live in great discomfort. Our disagreements were not, however, frequent, and when they did occur, the fault was always on my side. Nothing conduces so much to the degradation of a man and woman in the opinion of each other, and of themselves in all respects—but most especially of the woman—than her having to eat and drink, and cook and wash and iron, and transact all her domestic concerns, in the room in which her husband works, and in which they sleep. In some cases men and women are so ignorant and brutal that this mode of life is of no moment to them; but to those who have ever so small a share of information, and consequently of refinement, it is a terrible grievance, and produces sad consequences. . . .

"Our sufferings were great indeed. As long as we had anything which could be pawned, we did not suffer much from actual hunger; but after everything had been pawned 'but what we stood upright in,' we suffered much from actual hunger. My wife was a fine, handsome young woman, and I was most affectionately and sincerely attached to her, notwithstanding the ebullitions of temper I have noticed; and when I sometimes looked at her in her comfortless, forlorn, and all but ragged condition, I could hardly endure our wretched state, and know not what mischief or crimes it might have driven me to commit, had not the instructions of my good schoolmaster, and my previous reading, enabled me to form something like correct notions, and to hold to them.

"After about two months' privation I became somewhat reconciled to my condition, hopeless as it at times seemed, and at length I obtained such a perfect command of myself that, excepting commiseration for my wife, and actual hunger, I suffered but little, and bore my lot without much repining. I made up my mind to endure whatever I should be compelled to suffer, and resolved to take advantage of everything which might occur, to work myself into a condition to become a master myself. I never afterwards swerved in the least from this resolution. . . .

"My wife had never been at a pawnbroker's, and could not go. I would not go myself. Hunger at last induced her to request the wife of an old man, a carpenter who lived in one of the garrets, to pawn something for her. This she did, and continued to go as long as there was anything which could be pawned. This woman was about fifty years of age; she was very poor, of quiet manners, and to us, and as far as we could learn, very honest. It is probable that when she was no longer employed to pawn things for us, she concluded we had nothing more to pawn, and communicated her suspicions to our landlord's wife, who, as well as her husband, offered my wife credit for everything they sold; and the wife almost forced bread, coals, soup, and candles on her. And at the end of our privation, notwithstanding we were only half fed on bread and water, with an occasional red herring, we were six pounds in debt to our landlord."

Those eight months of actual starvation had on Place the same lasting influence that the sufferings of his boyhood had on Charles Dickens. Thirty years later, when he was a rich man and had already for four years retired from business, he writes with a pity still keen and fresh of those whom he left behind amid the horrors from which he himself escaped. "The hopes of a man who has no other means than those of his own hands to help himself are but too often illusory, and in a vast number of cases the disappointments are more than can be steadily met; and men give up in despair, become reckless, and after a life of poverty, end their days prematurely in misery. The misfortune is the greater too, as it is only the better sort of persons to whom this happens,—to the careful, saving' moral men and women, who have set their hearts on bettering their condition, and have toiled day and night in the hope of accomplishing their purpose. None but such as they tell how disappointment preys on them; how as the number of their children increases, hope leaves them; how their hearts sink as toil becomes useless; how adverse circumstances force on them those indescribable feelings of their own degradation, which sink them gradually to the extreme of wretchedness. Others there are in much larger numbers, whose views are narrower—they who hoped and expected to keep on in a decent way, who never expected to rise in the world, and never calculated on extreme poverty. I have seen a vast many such, who, when the evil day has come upon them, have kept on working steadily but hopelessly, more like horses in a mill, or mere machines than human beings; their feelings blunted, poor stultified moving animals, working on, yet unable to support their families in anything like comfort; frequently wanting the common necessaries of life, yet never giving up until ' misery has eaten them to the bone,' none knowing, none caring for them; no one to administer a word of comfort, or, if an occasion occurred which might be of service to them, none to rouse them to take advantage of it; all above them in circumstances calumniating them, classing them with the dissolute, the profligate, and the dishonest, from whom the character of the whole of the working people is taken. Yet I have witnessed in this class of persons so despised, so unjustly judged of by their betters, virtues which I have not seen to the same extent as to means among any other description of the people. Justice perhaps will never be done to them, because they may never be understood, because it is not the habit of men to care for others beneath them in rank, and because they who employ them will probably never fail to look grudgingly on the pay they are compelled to give them for their services, the very notion of which produces an inward hatred of them, a feeling so common, that it is visible in the countenance and manners in nearly every one who has to pay either journeymen, labourers, or servants."

Again and again he urges the lesson that the only chance for a working-man in bad times is to preserve, at the cost of however much privation, his own self-respect. "No working-man, or journeyman tradesman," he says, "is ever wholly ruined until hope has abandoned him." He dwells on the necessity of two rooms as a means of avoiding degradation with the insistence which those who have had practical experience of family life in one room always use, and which sometimes seems exaggerated to those who have not. Writing of a somewhat more fortunate time, he says: "The room in which we lived (in 1795) was a front room at a baker's shop. The house had three windows in the front, two in the room and one in a large closet at the end of the room. In this closet I worked. It was a great accommodation to us; it enabled my wife to keep the room in better order. It was advantageous, too, in its moral effects. Attendance on the child was not, as it had been, always in my presence. I was shut out from seeing the fire lighted, the room washed and cleaned, and the clothes washed and ironed, as well as the cooking. We frequently went to bed, as we had but too often been accustomed to do, with a wet or damp floor, and with the wet clothes hanging up in the room. Still, a great deal of the annoyance and the too close interference with each other in many particulars which having but one room made inevitable, were removed happily for ever.

"I have before remarked that the consequences of a man and his wife living in the same room in which the man works are mischievous to them in all respects, and I here add as a recommendation to all journeymen tradesmen and other workmen who are much at home, and even to those who are only at home at meal-times and after working hours, and at other times such as Sundays, and when they have no employment, to make almost any sacrifice to keep possession of two rooms, however small and however inconveniently situated as regards the place of their employment. Much better is it to be compelled to walk a mile or even two miles to and from their work to a lodging with two rooms, than to live close to their work in a lodging of one room. I advise them also to arrange these contrary to the usual custom of those who have two rooms, and to put the bed in the room in which as much as possible of the domestic work is done. A neat clean room, though it be as small as a closet, and however few the articles of furniture, is of more importance in its moral consequences than anybody seems hitherto to have supposed."

At the end of 1793, when there seemed no chance of the boycott upon him being removed, Place determined to leave his trade, and arranged to accept a post as overseer of parish scavengers at eighteen shillings a week. He was to have gone to this work on a Monday, but on the preceding Friday he was sent for by one of his former employers. He refused to go, as another employer had already endeavoured to entrap him into an admission of the existence of the Trade Club, in order to get him prosecuted under the infamous Combination Laws. His wife, however, persuaded him to allow her to go, and "in a short time she returned and let fall from her apron as much work for me as she could bring away. She was unable to speak until she was relieved by a flood of tears." . . . "All difficulty and apprehension vanished on our being again employed by Mr. Allison. We both went to work with a hearty good-will. The carpenter's wife, who was as well pleased as she could have been had she been our mother, was now employed to cook and wash for us, to keep our room clean, and to get our things from the pawnbroker's as fast as we could procure money for the purpose. We now worked full sixteen, and sometimes eighteen, hours a day, Sundays and all. I never went out of the house for many weeks, and could not find time for a month to shave myself. We turned out of bed to work, and turned from our work to bed again. My hair was black and somewhat curled, my beard was very thick, my whiskers large, and my face somewhat sallow, and upon the whole I must have been a ferocious-looking fellow.[1] . . .

"We soon recovered from our deplorable condition, bought clothes and bedding and other necessaries, a good bedstead, and many other things which made us comfortable. We removed to a much more convenient room in a small recently built house near the Angel Inn, in the then open space at the end of Wych Street. We put an iron rod close up to the ceiling, on which ran a couple of curtains. We employed the wife of a hackney coachman who lodged in the garret to cook and wash and clean for us; we had plenty of work, and we worked hard. I bought a stove and had it set on a plan of Count Rumford's. Our little furniture was good enough for our circumstances, and the room was especially neat and clean. There was a small yard to the house and a wash-house, and these

---

[1] He has given earlier another description of his personal appearance. "My complexion," he says, "was dark, my hair very black, and my beard thick. I was rather thin but muscular, was five feet six inches high, and had altogether the appearance of being several years older than I was."

were great conveniences. We had never before been so well off, or had reason to be so well satisfied; I was able also to assist my mother. We used to work later than usual on Friday nights, and earlier than usual on Saturday mornings, so as to finish our week's labour by three o'clock on the Saturday afternoon, and we ceased working on Sundays. I used to clean myself and go to Mr. Allison's to settle with him, and my wife and the coachman's wife used to put the room into the best possible order. We then put on our best clothes if the weather was fine and took a walk. As we scarcely left our work for meals all the week, we had a hot supper on the Saturday, a beef-steak or mutton-chops. Our neat place, the absence of want, the expectation of continuing to do well, the per-suasion that our days of suffering were at an end, and our mutual affection, made us perhaps as happy as any two persons ever really were."[1]

It is one of the most astonishing signs of Place's resolu-tion and courage, that throughout his "out-of-work" months, while constantly faced with hunger and appre-hension, he devoted a great part of his undesired leisure to severe intellectual work. Even as a schoolboy, and during the early years of his apprenticeship, he had done some serious reading. Writing of that time he says: " My desire for information was, however, too strong to be turned aside, and often have I been sent away from a bookstall when the owner became offended at my stand-ing reading, which I used to do until I was turned away. . . . I used to borrow books from a man who kept a small shop in Maiden Lane, Covent Garden, leaving a small sum as a deposit, and paying a trifle for reading them, having

---

[1] Against this may be set an incidental remark in another part of the autobiography : "During several years when I earned my living by sewing I was scarcely ever free from headache, and had often to endure terrible attacks."

one only at a time." During the first year of his married
life he had lodged with an old woman who took charge of
chambers in the Temple, and lent him books borrowed
from the rooms which she cleaned. At that time he says
he had already worked through " the histories of Greece
and Rome, and some translated works of Greek and
Roman writers; Hume, Smollett, Fielding's novels, and
Robertson's works; some of Hume's essays, some translations from French writers, and much on geography;
some books on anatomy and surgery; some relating to
science and the arts, and many magazines. I had worked
all the problems in the Introduction to Guthrie's ' Geography,' and had made some small progress in geometry."

His landlady enabled him to read "Blackstone, Hale's
' Common Law,' several other law books, and much biography." When out of work he read "many volumes in
history, voyages and travels, politics, law and philosophy,
Adam Smith and Locke, and especially Hume's ' Essays '
and ' Treatises.' These latter I read two or three times
over. . . . Reading of Hume put me on improving myself
in other ways. I taught myself decimals, equations, the
square, cube, and biquadrate roots. I got some knowledge
of logarithms, and some of algebra. I readily got through
a small schoolbook of geometry; and having an odd
volume, the first, of Williamson's ' Euclid,' I attacked it
vigorously and perseveringly. Williamson's is by no means
the best book on the subject, yet I am still of opinion that
it is the best book I could have had for the purpose of
teaching myself. My progress was for some time very
slow; I was perplexed between quantity and number, and
could not readily abstract myself from the consideration of
numbers. I suspect that this has its baneful influence on
all who learn arithmetic before they acquire any knowledge
of geometrical figures and definitions of them, which, by
experience, I now know may be taught to children without

much difficulty; and which, being taught, assists the
learner to a great extent when he comes to be taught
mathematics as a science. Often and often did I find
myself at fault, and was as often obliged to turn back
again. I was sometimes brought to a standstill, and at
times almost despaired of making further progress. Williamson's 'Euclid' is preceded by five dissertations; these
I read carefully, working the problems as I went on. I
have no doubt that I should have had less difficulty had I
not been impressed with a persuasion of the great difficulty
of acquiring the information I sought. The volume contained the first six books of Euclid. With labour such as
few would take, and difficulties such as few would encounter, I got through the six books; but not at all to my
satisfaction. I knew no one of whom I could ask a question or receive any kind of instruction, and the subject
was therefore at times very painful."

All this was, of course, put an end to as soon as an
opportunity came to work "full sixteen or eighteen" hours
a day. But this busy time did not last long. After a few
months his employer sent less and less work, and soon he
was again discharged. He then reorganised the Breeches-
Makers' Union, early in 1794, under the guise of a Tontine
Sick Club, became its secretary with a salary of £10 per
annum, and obtained in the spring of 1795, without a
strike, the advance which had been vainly asked for in
1793. This, however, led to the dissolution of the club,
the funds of which were shared out among the members,
and Place lost his office. He was then paid to draw
up articles or rules for various trade clubs, and became
secretary and organiser to those of the carpenters, plumbers,
and others. He spent much of his time in delivering by
hand the printed notices of meetings, and was allowed to
charge postage price for so doing.

The autobiography, till it reaches the year 1794, is curi-

ously individualistic in tone. Place, when he looked back
on the first twenty-three years of his life, and wished to
estimate the conditions under which his character was
built up, remembered almost exclusively the personal
temptations and errors of his boyhood, his intense love
for his wife, his early marriage, and the stern struggle for
regular work and opportunity of knowledge which followed.
The most impersonal intellectual interest to which he
refers is the religious question, and the series of doubts and
fears which were ended when David Hume's "Essays,"
supplemented by a chance copy of Paine's "Age of Reason,"
finally made him an agnostic.

But no young man could have lived as he did in London
throughout the five years which followed the French Revolution, organising trade unions and suffering himself personally from the effects of unjust laws, without being
profoundly influenced by the great message which the
French Republic was proclaiming to the world.   And
indeed when, "at the request of my landlord," he joined
the London Corresponding Society in June 1794, it is evident that this step was the result not of a casual impulse,
but of a steady intellectual development.   Place was never
a man who incurred risk without due consideration, and
the risk involved in what he was doing was sufficiently
obvious.   The English Government had now been for more
than a year at war with France.   Burke, "in one of his
mad rants in the House of Commons,"[1] had denounced
the Corresponding Society by name as "the mother of all
the mischief."   Two delegates of the Society had been
arrested at the Edinburgh Convention six months before
and sent to Botany Bay, and finally, on May 12, 1794, a
few weeks before Place joined, Thomas Hardy, the originator and secretary of the Society, with ten others of the
most prominent members, had been arrested on a charge

[1] 27,808 (4).

of high-treason, and were then awaiting trial. These arrests were the immediate cause of Place's action. "The violent proceedings of the Government," he says, "frightened away many of the members of the Society, and its number was very considerably diminished. Many persons, however, of whom I was one, considered it meritorious and the performance of a duty to become members now that it was threatened with violence and its founder and secretary was persecuted. This improved the character of the Society, as most of those who joined it were men of decided character, sober thinking men, not likely to be easily put from their purpose."

The London Corresponding Society had been founded at the end of 1791, its object being "to correspond with other societies that might be formed having the same object in view, as well as with public-spirited individuals."[1]

The Corresponding Society formed the working-class wing of the Democratic movement of the time. The societies of the "Friends of the People" and "Constitutional Information" were already in existence, and engaged in spreading the ideas of the French Revolution. But their annual subscriptions of five guineas and two guineas and a half respectively excluded working-men from membership. Hardy therefore fixed his subscription at a penny per week, with a shilling entrance fee. The political programme of the Society consisted of the "Plan of Radical Reform"— universal suffrage, annual parliaments, payment of members—which Major Cartwright had advocated in 1776, and which was to reappear more than forty years later as "The People's Charter." The name of the Society proved unfortunate. The British public always believed that it implied an intention of corresponding with the French Government,[2] a serious matter in war time. As a matter

---

[1] 27,808 (3).

[2] *Cf.* a survival of this tradition in Mrs. E. C. Gaskell's "Sylvia's Lovers" (London, 1863), vol. i. p. 298.

of fact, the name had originally no reference to France,
but was due to the fact that the law forbade any federation
of political bodies. A regular exchange of letters between
kindred societies up and down the country was the easiest
way of evading the law, and the term had been used at
least once before by a society formed for a similar object.[1]
Such a correspondence with the provinces did go on as far
as the expense of postage and the interference of Government with the post-office would allow. But the main
strength of the Society was in London. " The Society
assembled," says Place, " in divisions in various parts of
the Metropolis. That to which I belonged was held, as
all others were, weekly, at a private house in New Street,
Covent Garden. Each division elected a delegate and sub-
delegate; these formed a general committee, which also
met once a week; in this committee the sub-delegate had
a seat, but could neither speak nor vote while the delegate
was present. I was soon elected delegate, and became a
member of the general committee. In this Society I met
with many inquisitive, clever, upright men, and among
them I greatly enlarged my acquaintance. They were in
most, if not in all, respects superior to any with whom I
had hitherto been acquainted. We had book subscriptions,
similar to the breeches clubs before mentioned; only the
books for which any one subscribed were read by all the
members in rotation who chose to read them, before they
were finally consigned to the subscriber. We had Sunday
evening parties at the residences of those who could accom-
modate a number of persons. At these meetings we had
readings, conversations, and discussions. There was at
this time a great many such parties; they were highly
useful and agreeable.[2]

---

[1] "Mr. Burke belonged to the Corresponding Society in Bucking-
hamshire" [*circ.* 1780] (newspaper cutting, 27,837–48).

[2] Place mentions an incidental result of these readings upon the
members of the inner circle of the Corresponding Society. " This

"Early in the month of October 1794, a special Commission was issued to try the persons accused of high-treason. To prepare matters for the approaching trials, several committees were appointed. Of one of these I was a member; and when the nine days' trial of Thomas Hardy commenced, I used to attend daily at the Old Bailey from noon till night, go to work when I came home, and again in the morning early till noon; and thus I contrived to do as much as an ordinary day's work. I was very active and useful in directing others, and was well pleased to see the esteem in which I was held by those with whom I acted, who were clever men in circumstances very superior to mine."

Few State trials are more famous than those which followed. Thomas Hardy, Horne Tooke, the old philologist, who, like many moderate men, was supposed to be an extremist merely because he was courageous, and Thelwall, the Radical lecturer, were successively tried and acquitted. Then the prosecutions of the remaining defendants were abandoned. A quarter of a century later Place referred to "the State trials in 1794, the bare mention of which brings to my mind an association of ideas the most exhilarating, and sends me back to the Old Bailey with the most vivid recollections of the men and things of that time. Never can I forget the emotions I felt during the nine days' trial, or the joy in which I partook on hearing the verdict 'Not guilty' pronounced on my worthy and excellent friend Thomas Hardy, on whose inoffensive, upright character the breath of calumny has never breathed from the mouth of any one who ever knew him." [1]

course of discipline compelled them to think more correctly than they had been accustomed to do ; it induced them to become readers of books, and the consequence, the very remarkable consequence, was that every one of them became a master, and permanently bettered his condition in life " (Place to Noble, March 10, 1836).

[1] See the unpublished MS. of the second Reply to Lord Erskine 1819, referred to at p. 143.

The triumphant acquittal of Hardy, Tooke, and Thelwall increased the membership of the Corresponding Society, and by the end of May 1795 it consisted of seventy different divisions, with an average weekly attendance of over two thousand members. Place had from the first been recognised as a capable organiser, and in the summer of 1795 he usually took the chair at the weekly general committee. Some of his decisions are still to be seen in the British Museum,[1] entered in the dirty little minute-book of the Society. The entry for August 27, 1795, is as follows:—" Citn.[2] Place in chair. A citizen said . . . there was a person named Dykes amongst them, as he believed was not a good citizen, as he belonged to the Loyal Britons.[3] Citn. Place said he had once been a Loyal Briton, but he did not think himself any the worse for it, and he said he knew that Dykes, and believed him to be a very good citizen."

On the committee of the Corresponding Society Place advocated the political tactics in which he continued to believe throughout the rest of his life. The majority of the members were always proposing large public meetings with the view of intimidating the Government, so that they might be "compelled to grant a reform in the House of Commons." Place and a very few of his friends had no such expectation. "I believed that Ministers would go on until they brought the Government to a standstill—that was until they could carry it on no longer. It appeared to me that the only chance the people either had or could have for good and cheap government was in their being taught the advantages of representation, so as to lead them to desire a wholly representative government; so that whenever the conduct of Ministers should produce a crisis they should be qualified to support those who were the

---

[1] 27,813 (114).   [2] *i.e.* Citizen.
[3] This was no doubt a friendly society or sick club of some kind.

most likely to establish a cheap and simple form of government. I therefore advised that the Society should proceed
as quietly and privately as possible." Public meetings were,
however, held, and the effect upon the Government was,
not the granting of parliamentary reform but the passing
of the Treason and Sedition Bills, otherwise known as the
Pitt and Grenville Acts, in November 1795. By these
Acts almost every possible form of agitation, or indeed of
political action, was rendered illegal. At the same time
Habeas Corpus was suspended and many reformers were
arrested and sent to prison without trial.[1]

From this blow the Corresponding Society never recovered. "Some thought it dangerous, others thought it
useless, to meet again, and the whole matter fell rapidly to
decay." Great efforts were made by some of the members
to revive the Society, but without much effect. "The
business of the Society," says Place, "increased after its
members fell off. It was necessary in order to keep it
from absolute ruin to appoint deputations from the general
committee to the divisions whose delegates ceased to
attend the district committee, as well as to those which
were sluggish or met in small [numbers. This was an
arduous undertaking. . . . I remember having to attend

---

[1] Place, although he was actively engaged in one of the societies
aimed at by these Acts, and although he and all his friends were
violently opposed to them, was never deluded into the belief that his
own set represented popular opinion. He declared several times that
these Acts were in reality extremely popular. Writing to Harrison on
February 15, 1842, he recounts the events which led to the passing of
the Acts, and says, "Infamous as these laws were, they were popular
measures. The people, ay, the mass of the shopkeepers and working
people, may be said to have approved them without understanding
them. Such was their terror of the French regicides and democrats,
such the fear that 'the throne and the altar' would be destroyed, and
that we should be 'deprived of our holy religion,' that had the knowledge of the grand conspiracy been equal to their desires, they might
have converted the Government into anything they wished for the
advantage of themselves." [27,810 (91).]

in this way as many as three divisions on one evening,
and having to harangue each of them on their neglect,
and to urge them to a state of greater activity. The
correspondence with the country was also very considerable." [1]

In 1796, the Society committed one of the most fatal
mistakes into which a body in want of funds can fall.
Against the urgent advice of Place and his party, a magazine was started. This venture not only increased the
Society's debt, but absorbed the special fund which had
been collected for the defence of the delegates of the
Society, who had been arrested at Birmingham.[2]

Place had been partly responsible for sending them.
"We cajoled ourselves and each other," he says, "with
delusive expectations," that a visit from deputies would
greatly increase the membership of the Society, which,
he adds, "proves us to have been very silly people." [3]

He got more and more dissatisfied with the proceedings
of the Society, and at last took an opportunity of leaving
the committee. "I was out of office at midsummer
(1796)," he says, "and not liking the proceedings of the
executive committee, I refused to be elected to it again,
as I did also to be president of the general committee,
and became simply the delegate of the division to which
I belonged."

In March 1797 he resigned his delegation, and in June
of the same year his membership of the Society. A month
later the Society held a large public meeting in a field near
St. Pancras Church. All who were on the platform were
arrested by the Middlesex magistrates, and after this the
Society "declined rapidly, and by the end of the year was

---

[1] 27,808 (69).

[2] John Gale Jones and John Binns. *Cf.* the very interesting "Recollections of the Life of John Binns," written by himself (Philadelphia,
1854, 8vo). Place was sent to Birmingham to conduct the defence.

[3] 27,808 (72).

in a very low state." But the Society did not actually
come to an end till 1798. In that year O'Quigley, the
Irish delegate to the French Government, was in London,[1]
and an attempt was being made by a few revolutionists
to form a society of United Englishmen to act with the
United Irishmen in organising an armed rebellion. The
Government had nursed the plot by means of spies, and
on April 18th some dozen men were seized, including
Colonel Despard and three others, who against Place's
advice had gone down to dissuade from their purpose the
men who were really in earnest.[2] On the next night all
the members of the committee of the Corresponding Society
were seized. It requires some experience of the amount
of moderation which may be found among advanced bodies
to credit Place's statement that the subject for discussion
that night was the advisability of volunteering in all good
faith for resistance to the expected French invasion, and
that, just before the arrest, it had been "agreed to recommend the members of the Society individually to join some
corps (each) in his own neighbourhood." Place explicitly
denies that the Society had as its object "the formation of
a Republic by the assistance of France." "This is a base

[1] O'Quigley, or O'Coigley, as his name was sometimes spelt, was soon
afterwards caught on his way to France, and hanged for treason.

[2] The members of the London Corresponding Society did all in their
power to dissuade those whom they knew from embarking in the
United Englishmen conspiracy, but without success. At last it was
agreed by Place and others that steps ought to be taken to put an end
to the plot. On this occasion, Place proposed one of those bold steps
which he sometimes took, and which, perhaps, helped afterwards to
produce the notion that he was a spy. "I was for doing this," he says,
"by sending for Evans, B. Binns, and a foolish fellow, their coadjutor,
named James Powell, and frankly telling them we would take means
to stop their proceedings by communicating to Mr. Ford, the magistrate
at the Treasury, who and what they were and what they intended, so
that unless they at once desisted they should be prevented from in-
volving others in mischief and disgrace, and bringing punishment upon
them. This was objected to, especially by Colonel Despard, as it would
appear dishonourable." [27,808 (92).]

lie," he says. "No such avowal was ever made. No proposition of the kind was ever discussed. On the contrary,
it ever was the prevalent opinion of the Society that the
people ought to work out their own regeneration, and that
it was their duty to resist the French if they attempted an
invasion, on whatever pretext it was made. That if this
nation was not wise enough to reform its own government,
the people could not be made free by a foreign power,
but might, as they would deserve, be made slaves. This
was the opinion generally, and indeed almost universally,
entertained by the members."[1] The seizure of its committee finally extinguished the London Corresponding
Society, "which never made any attempt to meet again, not
even, I believe, in any division. The members dispersed,
and wholly abandoned the delegates." Habeas Corpus
was again suspended, and the twenty-eight men who had
been arrested were kept in prison without trial for three
years. For the first eighteen months of this period Place
was left almost alone in the work of collecting and dis-
tributing subscriptions, and pressing for payment of an
allowance to the wives and families of the prisoners, which
was at last granted by the Government.

Towards the close of the year 1796, when he had left
the committee of the Corresponding Society, and for the
time had little public work on hand, Place formed the idea
of publishing a cheap edition of Tom Paine's "Age of
Reason," a book which had much influence on his own
mind. He induced a small jobbing bookbinder and seller
of his acquaintance, named Thomas Williams, to share
with him the expense and risk of publication, and an
edition of two thousand copies was prepared. Within a
fortnight of its publication the whole edition was sold
out, and Williams broke away from the agreement with
Place, and refused to share the profits. Williams then

---

[1] 27,808 (108–109).

produced on his own account another and still larger edition, which was also selling rapidly, when he was indicted for the publication of a seditious and blasphemous libel. After a long delay he was convicted, and sentenced to a year's imprisonment, with hard labour. Place devoted himself to raising means for the support of the convict's wife and family during his confinement.

It was in 1795, while chairman of the Corresponding Society, that Place began to take the first definite steps to raise himself from the position of journeyman to that of employer. He was still poor, but he had gained experience in dealing with men. Above all, his studies had trained his imagination. He could see his future career as clearly as his present difficulties. He could think of society as a whole, and of the processes of trade as being something more than a mysterious iniquity. "It is remarkable enough," he says, "that almost every honest journeyman is deterred for a long time, and some for ever, from making an attempt to get into business, lest he should be 'ruined,' notwithstanding being ruined could only bring him back again to journey-work. This must seem strange to all who have not had practical experience on the subject. The fear of doing injury to others by contracting debts he may be unable to pay is a proper feeling, and when it is not indulged to an extent which prevents a man from bettering his own condition without doing injury to any-body, operates beneficially. But besides this reasonable apprehension, the fear of personal ruin operates to a very considerable extent; it did with me. The reason is, that there is a sort of mystery in the matter, an uncertainty which they who fear to do evil are not willing to encounter. Mr. Godwin's book [1] extinguished this fear in me. It led

---

[1] This reference is to the "Inquiry Concerning Political Justice, &c," by William Godwin (London, 1793, 2 vols.). Place says he learnt to disbelieve in "abstract rights" from Godwin in 1793 (Place to War-burton, May 5, 1839).

me to reason on the matter, and convinced me that a man
might turn others to account in every kind of undertaking
without dishonesty, that the ordinary tricks of tradesmen
were not necessary, and need not be practised. This was
to me the most grateful kind of knowledge I could acquire,
and I resolved to lose no time in putting it in practice."
He began by getting a few private customers, for whom he
could work directly. In this he could have made great
use of his position in the Corresponding Society, but "my
notions of independence," he says, "were somewhat absurd,
and they prevented me from deriving all the benefit I
might have received, and circumstances warranted. I was,
however, afraid of doing anything which might prospec-
tively debase me in my own opinion, and I acted on the
safe side."

His next step was to acquire credit with the drapers and
clothiers. With this purpose he made his purchases on an
elaborate and ingenious system. "I knew that by purchasing materials at two or three shops, however small the
quantities, and letting each of them know that I made
purchases of others, each would sell to me at as low a price
as he could, and each would after a time give me credit.
I afterwards put this mode of proceeding into practice, and
whenever I had two things to purchase, I bought one at
one shop, and carried it under my arm to another shop,
where I bought the remainder of what I wanted. In a
little time credit was offered to me, each wishing to have
the whole of my custom, and each probably supposing it
was greater than it was. From this time I always bought
on short credit; instead of paying for the goods, I put by
the money, taking care always to pay for what I had before
the term of credit expired. I thus established a character
for punctuality and integrity with three mercers and two
woollen-drapers, and, as I foresaw, I should, if I could once
take a shop, have credit for any amount whatever. This

was a work of time, but of less time than I had calculated
upon; I had supposed that it would scarcely be accomplished in less than six years; it was accomplished in less
than four years. . . .

"The number of my customers was small, the prices I
charged were very low, and, what was worse, some few got
into debt with me and never paid their debts. My wife
frequently importuned me to go again to journey-work, ·
and offered to try to procure it herself if I would let her.
I, however, resolutely refused. I insisted upon it that I
should work myself into a condition to become a master
tradesman, and should then be able to maintain my family
respectably; that no hope of my ever being able to do this
in any other way existed, and that nothing should therefore
divert me from my purpose; that our present privations
were by no means so bad as those we had suffered, and
that there was something like a certainty that they would
at no very distant time be ended for ever; that as every
day was a new day, the contemplation of the evils of one
day was as much as we ought reasonably to entertain, and
that it was disgraceful not to bear the evils of one day with
temper. This reasoning often repeated had its weight with
my wife, but it neither satisfied her nor reconciled her to
her condition. Still we were not unhappy; upon the whole
we were comfortable, and at times very far indeed from
unhappiness. There was, however, one bad result of our
long state of probation and privation; it to some extent
destroyed my wife's cheerful disposition, and made her
apprehensive of misfortune; and she never recovered from
this entirely. Her situation was necessarily worse than
mine on account of the two children. . . . Sometimes she
almost despaired of ever being better off in the world, and
at these times she used to complain of my folly in thinking
I should be able to take a shop and commence business;
and as to my succeeding and being able to procure money

enough to live without business, she declared it was sheer insanity. These fits were, however, of short duration, and were always caused by some great privation she and the children suffered. . . . The few good clothes we had left were taken great care of, and when out of the house we always made a respectable appearance, and were generally considered, by those who knew us, as flourishing people, who wanted for nothing. In fine weather on Sundays we usually walked into the fields, taking the children with us. Our walk was frequently to White Conduit House, and the fields beyond it towards Copenhagen House. Both these places were celebrated tea-gardens, and the number of persons who frequented them on Sundays was very great. We carried the children nearly the whole of the way, and returned as we went, never spending a single halfpenny."

From this time forward Place seems always to have thought of himself, not as the half-starved journeyman that he was, but as the prosperous tradesman that he meant to be. He "resolved to give my children the best possible education which my circumstances would afford." With this view he determined to learn French. He and four other members of the Corresponding Society arranged to receive lessons from a "profound and pompous" fellow-member, "who used to talk with great self-complacency of his skill in teaching." Their first teacher did not prove a success, and an emigrant priest was soon secured, under whom the little class rapidly advanced. Place, though he had now left the Corresponding Society, never found any difficulty in borrowing books, and used to stay at home to read Helvetius, Rousseau, and Voltaire for three or four hours every evening. When at work, he fixed his French grammar before him and steadily learnt it by rote. This first-hand acquaintance with the French revolutionary philosophers had an important influence on his political ideas, and in after years his knowledge of French, though never very scholarly, was of immense value to him in his business. A Mr. William Frend of the Temple used also to come and sit with Place at his work, answering his questions and guiding his studies in astronomy and algebra. In the same way the rich and good - natured Colonel Bosville, Colonel Despard till the time of his arrest, and others used to come to talk with a man whose conversation must already have been worth hearing.

Meanwhile his ambition was expanding, and instead of taking a small shop in some Holborn back street as he had originally intended, he entered into partnership with a fellow-workman nearly as poor as himself, and opened a tailor's shop at No. 29 Charing Cross, in the centre of what was then a rapidly improving neighbourhood. The partners took possession on April 8, 1799. The shop was stocked on credit, and their joint cash funds on the day of opening were one shilling and tenpence. But they were both of them enterprising, skilful, and furiously industrious, so that in less than two years' time they had thirty-six men at work, and every prospect of a splendid business. But a sickening disappointment was still to come; Place's partner married a wife with whom agreement was impossible, and having the offer of a large loan, forced the business into liquidation, and bought the goodwill for himself. The effect on Mrs. Place was terrible. "Neither tongue nor pen," says Place, "can describe her anguish. She saw nothing before her but destruction. . . . She was sure we should all be turned into the streets. Industry was of no use to us; integrity would not serve us; honesty would be of no avail. We had worked harder and done more than anybody else, and now we were to suffer more than anybody else." From that time till the day of her death she never lost the apprehension of sudden and undeserved misfortune. "This," Place says, "was undoubtedly the bitterest day of my life." But the crisis was well fitted

C

to bring out his obstinate courage, and the skill in dealing
with men which he had developed in his political work.
At the meeting of creditors he completely turned the tables
on his late partner, and found every one so ready to advance
him money or goods that on April 8, 1801, three months
after his first discovery of the plot against him, and exactly
two years from the day of the opening of the first shop, he
opened a much larger and more conspicuous shop on his
own account at No. 16 Charing Cross. " I put in," he says,
" a new front as elegant as the place would permit. Each
of the panes of glass in the shop front cost me three
pounds, and two in the door four pounds each. . . . Such
shop fronts were then uncommon; I think mine were the
largest plate-glass windows in London, if indeed they were
not the first. . . . Fitting up the shop cost me nearly three
hundred pounds. . . . There were five large Argand lamps
in the shop, besides candles, to make the windows and
every part of it as nearly equally light as possible."

Here for the next five or six years he lived the life
of any one of those successful money-makers whose biographies have been written by Dr. Smiles. He knew well
the method by which money was to be made. Though
a skilled breeches-maker, " I was," he says, " myself no
tailor. I could not cut out a coat as it should be cut, nor
make it up as it should be made up. I never thought it
was worth while to learn to do either. I knew I could
procure competent persons for these purposes, and that
the most profitable part for me to follow was to dance
attendance on silly people, to make myself acceptable to
coxcombs, to please their whims, to have no opinion of my
own, but to take special care that my customers should
be pleased with theirs." The student of Rousseau and
Godwin, and the future disciple of Bentham, shows himself in the reflection, " it was all matter of taste, that is, of
folly and caprice."

During these years he definitely gave up every form of public life. " I never lost a minute of time, was never on any occasion diverted from the steady pursuit of my business, never spent a shilling, never once entertained any company. The only things I bought were books, and not many of them. I adhered steadily to the practice I had adopted, and read for two or three hours every night after the business of the day was closed, which never happened till half-past nine o'clock. I never went to bed till twelve o'clock, and frequently not till one, but I indulged a little in the morning by lying in bed till seven." He had the power of dismissing any train of thought at a moment's notice. " I had long since obtained," he says, " the power of abstraction to a considerable extent. I could dismiss a train of thought at pleasure and take up another, and could leave any business of any kind and go to something else without any reference to the subject I had left, and when I concluded the new thoughts or finished the new business I could revert to the old thoughts or business and take them {up again where I had left them. I used wholly to dismiss all thought of business when it was closed for the day, and could therefore go to my book quite unoccupied with anything else." In time he paid off his own debts to the wholesale houses, and came nearer to the point when he could himself pay cash, and when his ten thousand pounds' worth of book debts represented accumulated profit.

A man of his organising capacity could probably have made money in any business in which he had found himself, and it was an ill chance that made him a tailor. Men are still apt to look upon their tailor as in some sense a menial servant. But eighty or ninety years ago the humiliations of the position were such as a proud man could hardly endure. " How often have I taken away a garment for a fault which did not exist, and which I, of course,

never intended to rectify. How often have I taken back
the same garment without it ever having been unfolded,
and been commended for the alteration which had not
been made, and then been reprehended for not having
done what was right at first. How often have I been
obliged to take back a garment and sell it to a Jew for
not much more or any more than one-third of its price,
because a man or his wife, or his mistress, disliked it when
it was made up. How often on the most trivial or frivolous
pretence have I been obliged to do the same thing, as, for
instance, because there was one button on the front of
a coat or waistcoat more or less than he or she at the
moment thought would make the garment more becoming; how often have I done this, and on a subsequent
order from the same person for a similar garment taken
home the rejected one, which has been highly approved.
How often have I attended, at the command of a customer,
at a distance of two or three miles on a wet day, been kept
waiting in the hall for half-an-hour or an hour, and then
either been told that the customer had forgotten me, or
could not see me, and I must come again at a time named;
and when kept by one person so long that I was five
minutes beyond the time named, been rebuked for negli-
gence by another. In short, a man to be a good tailor
should be either a philosopher or a mean cringing slave,
whose feelings had never been excited to the pitch of manhood. One or the other he must be if he start poor and
hope to succeed in making a considerable business. He
who is neither the one nor the other, will never be anything but a little master, and will probably die in debt.

"I had three things continually in my recollection:—

"The first, and by far the most important, was to get
money, and yet to avoid entertaining a mercenary, money-
getting spirit; to get money as a means to an end, and not
for its own sake.

" The second was to take care that the contumelious treatment I had to endure should not make me a sneaking wretch from principle to those above me, a tyrant to those below me.

" The third was to beware of presumption, that I did not become arrogant. I had no doubt of success, and therefore felt most strongly the necessity of watching and guarding myself, in the hope that when I had realised as much money as I deemed requisite to a state of independence, my habits and manners should not be such as would exclude me from what is called good society, if at that time I should desire such society and should be occasionally cast into it, or should not exclude me from the acquaintance and even friendship of the better sort of men of genius and talent. . . . I, however, still continued to act with the utmost reserve towards my customers, many of whom were men in the public offices. I never made free in conversation with my customers, and when any of them made free with me I always let it pass with as little notice as possible."

Later on as his books accumulated he had to be more and more careful that none of his ordinary customers should be allowed to go into the library at the back of the shop, or to " know anything of me except as a tailor." He complains that on several occasions he lost good customers owing to their learning something of his habits of study, and being perhaps quick enough to guess at the biting scorn which underlay his guarded politeness. " Had these persons been told that I had never read a book, that I was ignorant of everything but my business, that I sotted in a public-house, they would not have made the least objection to me. I should have been a " fellow " beneath them, and they would have patronised me ; but . . . to accumulate books and to be supposed to know something of their contents, to seek for friends, too, among literary and scientific

men, was putting myself on an equality with themselves,
if not, indeed, assuming a superiority; it was an abominable offence in a tailor, if not a crime, which deserved
punishment.   Had it been known to all my customers
that in the few years from 1810 to 1817 I had accumulated
a considerable library, in which I spent all the leisure time
I could spare; had the many things I was engaged in
during this period, and the men with whom I associated
been known, half of them at the least would have left me,
and these, too, by far the most valuable customers individually."   And ten years later he recurred to the same
subject, and noted the very little change which had taken
place in this respect.   "The nearer a common tradesman
approximates in information and manners to a footman,"
he says, "the more certainly will he please his well-bred
customers; the less he knows beyond his business, |the
more certain, in general, will be his success." [1]

In spite of this the business rapidly and regularly increased.   In 1816, when it reached its maximum, the net
profits for the year were considerably over three thousand
pounds.   At the same time, Place's family grew rapidly,
and in 1817, when he retired from business, and handed
the shop over to his eldest son, he had ten children living
out of fifteen who had been born to him.

[1] 27,823 (412).

CHAPTER II

WESTMINSTER POLITICS, 1807-15

Up to the Reform Bill of 1832, borough members of Parliament might, according to the accidents of local history, be elected by a few officials, a close corporation, a body of "freemen" or "potwallopers," or, in a few cases, by all payers of "scot and lot."[1] By far the most important of the "scot and lot" boroughs was the City and Liberty of Westminster, of which Place became an elector when he moved to Charing Cross. Westminster then included the whole of the ancient property of the Abbey, a district stretching from Temple Bar on the east to Kensington Palace on the west, and from Oxford Street on the north to the Thames on the south. At the beginning of the century about half this district had been built over, and the census of 1801 returns the population as 153,272, of whom rather more than 10,000 were rated to the poor-rates for separate houses, and therefore entitled to vote. Many of the streets round the Abbey were extremely poor, and from the description of the voters given in the poll-books, a clear majority seem to have been artisans or very small tradesmen. Outside Westminster the freemen of London City returned four members, but no other Londoner had a vote at all unless he happened to be a freeholder to the annual value of forty shillings, and as such entitled to vote for the counties of Middlesex or Surrey. Until

[1] *i.e.* of the local rates.

1780 the members for Westminster were returned by
the "influence" of the Dean and Chapter in accordance
with the wishes of the Crown. In that year, however,
C. J. Fox, standing as an extreme democrat, succeeded in
winning one of the Westminster seats. Four years later,
after the famous contest in which the Duchess kissed the
butcher, a local arrangement was made, by which the
Tories and Whigs divided the two seats. At the elections
of 1790, 1796, and 1802, Radical candidates came forward,
but with little success.

In the old Corresponding Society days Place had not
concerned himself much with electioneering, and for the
first five years after taking the Charing Cross shop in
1800 he had withdrawn himself entirely from public life.[1]
When at last he again began to pick up the threads of
political life it was not with the Radical independents, but
with the well-to-do Whig tradesmen that he first made
acquaintance. "In 1805, having mastered all the difficulties attending the establishment of a new business, . . .
I permitted several respectable and well-judging men to
come and gossip with me occasionally. They were most
of them electors of Westminster. Mr. Thomas and one
or two others of them were members of the Whig Club,
and great admirers of Mr. Fox, Mr. Erskine, Mr. Sheridan,
&c. I never had any respect for either Fox or Sheridan,
and not much for Erskine. I was satisfied that they were
trading politicians, Tories out of place, who cared little
for the people further than they could be made to promote
their own interests, whether those interests were popular
or pecuniary. Of the dispositions of the leading Whigs I
had proof enough, and with these I used to banter my
new friends. They on their part maintained that Fox and
his partisans were all good men and true, and if an opportunity occurred would redeem in the most perfect and

[1] See p. 35.

complete way all the pledges they had ever given to the people.[1] . . . My opinions of these Whigs and Tories, and more especially of the Whigs, was of course shown only to the few with whom I conversed. I was wholly un-known in Westminster, and knew next to nothing of the electors."[2]

On January 23, 1806, Pitt died, and Fox, in alliance with the Grenvillite Tories, came into office. Fox was at the time the Whig member for Westminster, and a meeting was at once called in Westminster Hall to congratulate the King on the new administration, and to arrange for Fox's unopposed re-election. " I suggested," says Place, " to some of my Whig friends that, among the eulogiums which would be lavished on the Whigs, Parliamentary reform should be included, and that one of the resolutions should declare that the electors relied on the many promises made to them on the subject, and that they trusted the great and important object would continue to receive the support of Mr. Fox and his friends." Fox let it be known that " he should be much obliged if no allusion to Parliamentary reform were made at the meeting, as a separate meeting could be held on the subject."[3] The resolution was omitted, but no reform meeting was held, and after a few months of office Fox died. The Ministers then brought forward Lord Percy, eldest son of the Duke of Northumberland, " a very young man, without pretensions to talents of any kind,"[4] and by putting up Sheridan as a sham candidate, to be withdrawn at the last moment, secured the unopposed return of their nominee.

At this time William Cobbett was attempting in his *Political Register* to revive the democratic movement, which since the coercive laws of 1795 and 1800 had almost ceased to exist. He saw the chance which the Westminster

---

[1] 27,850 (6).   [2] 27,850 (9).
    27,850 (10).   [4] 27,850 (12).

"scot and lot" franchise offered for a representation of the popular feeling of the Metropolis, and on August 9, 1806, a month before Fox's death, published the first of four eloquent " Letters to the Electors of Westminster." In his last letter, written just after the return of Lord Percy, he upbraided them for allowing themselves to be tricked by the Government. "The letter," says Place, "was much read, and was very useful. It produced shame in many and a desire to do something on another occasion; but it did not remove from them the notion, which long practice had confirmed, that a contested election could only be carried by money, money in immense sums; and this prevented me from expecting any extraordinary exertions would be made by the electors for themselves at the expected general election."[1]

On the day of the election the Duke of Northumberland, the façade of whose house was only a few doors from Place's shop, distributed bread and cheese and beer from his steps. Place describes the scene and his own feelings. "My indignation was greatly increased when I saw the servants of the Duke of Northumberland, in their showy dress liveries, throwing lumps of bread and cheese among the dense crowd of vagabonds they had collected together. To see these vagabonds catching the lumps, shouting, swearing, fighting, and blackguarding in every possible way, women as well as men, all the vile wretches from the courts and alleys in St. Giles and Westminster, the Porridge Islands, and other miserable places; to see these people representing, as it was said, the electors of Westminster, was certainly the lowest possible step of degradation, except, indeed, if it be possible, to hear it said, as it was said, that ' the electors of Westminster had been treated by the bounty of the Duke.' Some who mingled in the mob were ashamed of the proceedings, and as the mob

[1] 27,850 (22).

pressed round the butts which contained the beer, suggested that the best way would be to knock in the heads as they stood up on end. This was done immediately. The heads were beaten in, and the coal-heavers ladled the beer out with their long-tailed, broad-brimmed hats ; but the mob pressing on, the butts were upset, and the beer flowed along the gutters, from whence some made efforts to obtain it. It may be possible to imagine something like the disgraceful scene, but it is not possible either to describe it or to excite in the reader the almost uncontrollable feelings of a spectator. I was not the only one who felt indignation. Almost every man I knew was much offended with the whole of the proceedings and with all who were concerned in them."[1]

But the movement in favour of independent action in Westminster soon received a more effectual supporter than either William Cobbett or the little knot of disgusted tradesmen round Charing Cross. Sir Francis Burdett was the most popular political figure in London ; he had entered Parliament ten years before, and had fought hard to improve the treatment of the untried political prisoners in Coldbath Fields Prison. In 1802 the metropolitan freeholders had elected him as member for Middlesex. Since then he had once gained and twice lost the Middlesex seat on petition. His marriage with Miss Sophia Coutts had made him one of the wealthiest men in England ; but having spent nearly £100,000 in contesting three election petitions before the shameless Parliamentary Committees of the time, he had now lost patience with the whole system of party government. In October 1806 he published an address to the freeholders of Middlesex, in which he said, "a double imposture is attempted to be passed on you. The watchword of one party is 'the best of kings,' the watchword of the other is 'the best of patriots'; but neither of these parties will descend to particulars and

[1] 27,850 (19, 20).

inform you what the 'best of kings' and the 'best of
patriots' have already done or will do for you. What they
have done for themselves we know and feel; what further
they will do for us we can only conjecture."¹

A week after the publication of this address Parliament
was dissolved. Burdett refused to stand again for Middlesex, and nominated James Paull as an independent candidate for Westminster. Paull was a poor enough creature'
who had come home from India to carry on in Parliament
an old feud against the Governor-General, but because of
Burdett's influence he was less than three hundred votes
behind the official Whig. It was clear, therefore, that if
strong independent candidates could be brought forward
one or both seats might be carried.

Place had "plumped" for Paull, and towards the end of
the seventeen days' poll had sent him some suggestions as
to organisation. "I now enlarged my acquaintance among
the electors, and constantly maintained not only that the
people had the power to do themselves justice as electors,
but that no more was necessary in the first instance than
that a few men of business and spirit, no one of whom had
any sinister interest, should act together, and hold themselves ready for action when an opportunity offered."² A
chance of action soon came. The Ministry refused to
pledge themselves against Catholic Emancipation, and
towards the end of April 1807 George III. dissolved Parliament and appealed to the country. On the evening after
the dissolution a few independent electors met at Place's
house and decided to run Burdett and Paull. Burdett
refused to come forward as a candidate or spend a shilling
on the election, but promised to sit if elected. Three days
later, and four days before the poll was to begin, Burdett
and Paull quarrelled, and in the duel which followed both
were seriously wounded.

¹ 27,850 (23).   ² 27,850 (21).

The little independent committee, in spite of this tremendous blow, and of the fact that they had no funds to speak of, determined to go on. They dropped Paull, but persisted with Burdett's candidature. At the public meeting which had been advertised for the Crown and Anchor Tavern they could not even obtain a hearing. Paull's friends attached a stout broker's man to each of the committee, with orders to shout " Paull! Paull!" as soon as he began to speak. "I know no word," writes Place, with a lively recollection of the scene, "so well calculated to confound an audience as the open sound Paull." [1]

The committee, however, retired to a small room, collected £34 among themselves in addition to the £50 which they had in hand, and decided to continue their work. "We had," says Place, "a long discussion, in which I put the matter in every form in my power. I offered to give up every other thing and attend wholly to the election till its close. After some time Mr. Brooks and Mr. James Powell agreed to give the whole of their time, and several others agreed to give a considerable portion of theirs. Summonses were immediately issued to some thirty persons who had been active at the last Middlesex and Westminster elections to meet at six o'clock in the evening at the Ship Tavern, Charing Cross. [2] . . . We were all of us obscure persons, not one man of note among us, not one in any way known to the electors generally, as insignificant a set of persons as could well have been collected together to undertake so important a public matter as a Westminster election against wealth and rank and name and influence. I again went over the topics I had urged in the morning, said I would not only undertake the management, but also whatever might otherwise be necessary which others might dislike because it was disagreeable. That as Mr. Brooks had allowed his

1 27,850 (68, 69).   2 27,850 (66).

name to appear in public as chairman and treasurer, no other name need be mentioned in any of our proceedings which any one desired should not appear. That we could not be of any importance as individuals, and it was therefore incumbent on us to make the matter clear to the understandings of the electors, to call upon them to do their duty to themselves, and to leave display and exhibitions of consequence to others. That if we proceeded openly, and acted honestly, failure either from want of money, or from the electors not coming forward to the poll, would be no disgrace to any of us."[1] . . . "It was arranged that no money should be expended on account of the election but by vote of the committee, on a printed form filled up and signed by its order. That there should be no paid counsellors, attorneys, inspectors nor canvassers, no bribing, no paying of rates, no treating, no cockades, no paid constables, excepting two to keep the committee-room doors. That notice of our intended proceedings should be sent to the magistrates, who should be warned to see that the peace was kept.[2]

"At the moment the election commenced some of my coadjutors were exceedingly depressed. We had scarcely any money, nobody had joined us, and we appeared as forlorn as the Whigs and Tories had predicted we should be. Some among us who had borne abuse very well could not bear being laughed at, and the ridicule which was cast upon us almost disabled them from acting."[3]

All those of the committee and their friends who were voters polled early on the first morning, but at the end of the day Burdett had received only 78 votes. On the third day, a Saturday, his poll reached 309. The committee had, however, money enough in hand for another day or two. On Saturday evening they "hired three or four ponies, put decently dressed bugle boys on

---

[1] 27,850 (67).   [2] 27,850 (43).   [3] 27,850 (75).

them, gave each of them a dark blue silk cap, and sent them about the streets to animate the people and distribute handbills." [1]   All Sunday was spent in canvassing. Even Place left the central committee-rooms, and for the first and only time in his life canvassed "some of the courts and lanes in Westminster for about two hours and a half." [2]

On the Monday Burdett received more votes than any other candidate, and on the fifteenth and last day of the poll he was at the head, with over five thousand votes. Lord Cochrane, who had come forward as a Whig candidate with a grievance against the Government, was second, while neither Sheridan, the official Whig, nor Elliott, the official Tory candidate, reached much more than half Burdett's poll. "Sheridan was so far behind that he had no chance of out-polling Cochrane, and as he begged hard to be permitted to make as respectable a show of numbers as he could, Lord Cochrane took his inspectors away, and Sheridan polled whom he pleased, and the same man over and over again as many times as he pleased." [3]

"The moment the election was ended," says Place, "and I had closed my accounts with Mr. Brooks the treasurer, which was at five o'clock in the afternoon, I went home to my business, which I had neglected for nearly three weeks; being from the commencement of the election to its close at the committee-rooms at seven o'clock in the morning, and remaining till all accounts for the day were made up, all the books were posted up, and the business arranged for the next day. This, excepting on the last day, never occurred till after twelve o'clock at night." [4]

The committee continued their existence after the election, and thenceforward were the recognised political authority in Westminster. Every year a public dinner was held to commemorate the victory of 1807, and West-

27,850 (79).   [2] 27,850 (80).
[3] 27,850 (80).   [4] 27,850 (81).

minster meetings in Palace Yard or Westminster Hall
were summoned whenever a chance offered of damaging
the Government or spreading democratic principles. Thus
in March 1809 a meeting was held to denounce the Duke
of York for having allowed Mrs. Clarke to sell commissions
in the army, and in May a dinner was given in honour of
Major Cartwright and Parliamentary Reform.

In the autumn of 1809 the Westminster Committee
found itself mixed up with the celebrated "O. P." riots
in Covent Garden Theatre. This theatre which, with
Drury Lane, enjoyed a licensed monopoly of legitimate
drama, had lately been rebuilt after a fire, and on the
night of reopening prices were raised. The audience
hooted the performance, and called for the "Old Prices."
John Kemble, the lessee, lost his temper, and sent a Bow
Street Magistrate on to the stage to threaten to read the
Riot Act. Next day some of the Westminster politicians
who had been in the pit came to Charing Cross, and
Place made them a mould from "two hearthstones" for
casting the initial letters of their motto. "Powell and
Wall cast about a hundred 'O. P's.,' and as the metal was
fresh from the mould it was very bright, and when stuck
against the crown of a black hat was very conspicuous."
After three months' wrangling in the theatre and police
courts Place was "the means of bringing about a recon-
ciliation, which at the desire of Mr. Kemble was made
at my house on the 23rd of December. Present for the
theatre, Mr. Kemble, Mr. Harris, Jun., and Mr. Este; for
the O. P., Mr. Scott, Mr. Savage, Mr. Powell, and Mr. Willett
as a friend. When the whole affair was settled Mr. Harris
urged me to accept a free admission, which I refused."[1]

In the spring of 1810 a contest began between Westminster and the House of Commons, which attracted the

[1] Henry Hunt in his "Memoirs" (2 vols., London, 1820–22), vol. ii.
p. 385, says that the O. P. riots were a political affair.

attention of the whole country. On February 21 the Commons ordered John Gale Jones to attend at the bar of their House. Jones was the organiser of a debating society near Covent Garden, and had advertised a harmless enough discussion about the exclusion of strangers by the First Lord of the Admiralty during the debate on the Walcheren expedition. Jones came to Place for advice, "a poor, emaciated crazy-looking creature, possessed of considerable talents, but as devoid of judgment as any man well could be."[1] Place strove to make him understand that submission to the House would do him no good, while he had everything to gain as an unflinching martyr in the cause of free speech. Jones promised courage, but repented of his promise. He went to the House, made an abject submission, and was committed to Newgate.[2] On March 12 Burdett moved for his release, and delivered a speech, which he afterwards revised and published in *Cobbett's Register*. This publication was brought before the House as a breach of privilege. The question was debated for three nights, and finally, at seven o'clock in the morning of Friday April 6, a motion to commit Burdett to the Tower was carried by a majority of 38. Burdett instantly came up from Wimbledon, barricaded himself inside his big house in Piccadilly, and announced that he considered the Speaker's warrant to be illegal, and would repel force by force. Huge crowds collected, greater, it was said, than those at the Gordon riots in 1780. The main body were decent orderly people, but small groups of rioters moved about smashing windows and pelting those who refused to cheer for Burdett. The only police force in London was the shifting body of amateur "constables" under the command of the sheriffs, one of whom at least[3] was

[1] 27,850 (158).
[2] "House of Commons Journals," vol. lxv. p. 113, 21st February 1810.   [3] Alderman Wood.

actively hostile to Lord Liverpool's government. The Ministry, therefore, could only keep order by using troops, and on each of the three next nights the Horse Guards were sent to clear the streets. "It was their common practice to ride upon the foot pavement and drive the people before them, pressing on them in such a way as to cause great terror, frequently doing some of them injury and compelling them to injure one another, striking those who could not get out of the way fast enough with the flat of their swords.[1] On the other hand, the people "taking a long ladder from a building, placed it across the street in such a manner as to prevent the horses in the dark pursuing them. They then did all they could to provoke the Guards to charge upon them, and upon their doing so they retreated round the ends of the ladder and under it, and from the other side showered the rubbish they found upon the soldiers."[2] "A rumour was extensively propagated that the utmost hatred existed between the Foot and the Life Guards, and it was said, and believed by vast numbers of people, that the Foot Guards and the 15th Light Dragoons were much more disposed to fight the Life Guards than they were disposed to obey an order to attack the people."[3] "There was a solemn stillness and a gloom half visible which produced on me, as upon inquiry I afterwards found it had done on others, that peculiar sort of feeling which has been represented as being felt by soldiers waiting for the dawn of day to commence a battle."[4]

Burdett wrote to the sheriffs demanding their protection, and the sheriffs with a body of constables "removed the soldiers to some distance each way from Sir Francis Burdett's house. Here they formed across the street and permitted no one to pass."[5]

[1] 27,850 (184).   [2] 27,850 (192).   [3] 27,850 (188, 189).
[4] 27,850 (186).   [5] 27,850 (190).

But the Ministers showed themselves more determined than the City authorities. The volunteers were called out, and "all the troops within a hundred miles of London, both cavalry and infantry, were ordered to march to the Metropolis."[1] At the Tower, guns were mounted on the gates and water let into the ditch.

On the Sunday evening Burdett's brother came to call Place to a council of war. They were admitted into a house in Stratton Street belonging to the Coutts family, and thence made their way by cellar passages through guarded iron doors (the watchword for the evening being "Place") to the great house in Piccadilly. They found Burdett in consultation with the semi-lunatic Roger O'Connor. It appeared that Cochrane, being a hare-brained sailor with a passion for fighting, had "contrived an effectual mode of defence against any force that could be used."[2] Henry Hunt says that Cochrane drove up in a hackney-coach and rolled into the passage a barrel of gun-powder for mining the front of the house.[3]

Place of course saw clearly that this was the kind of step which should only be undertaken by men who seriously contemplate the levying of civil war. "It will be easy enough," he told the conspirators, "to clear the hall of constables and soldiers, to drive them into the street or to destroy them, but are you prepared to take the next step and to go on?"

"This produced instant conviction of the folly of at-tempting any (such) thing. It was all at once, and by all, agreed that nothing should be done in this way, but that as the sheriff had consented to avail himself of the civil power, and as a large number of the inhabitants would probably be collected to attend his orders at nine o'clock

---

[1] 27,850 (193).   [2] 27,850 (199).
[3] See the "Memoirs of Henry Hunt," written by himself (2 vols., London, 1820-22), vol. ii. p. 391.

in the morning, the matter should be left to him."[1] . . .
" I did not then, I do not now (1826), disapprove of Sir
Francis Burdett's notions. Had circumstances been such
as to promise an effectual resistance, not only at the house
of Sir Francis but anywhere else, had there been anything
like a sufficient body organised to have assured the soldiers
that power enough existed to protect them, . . . there
would have been a fair chance in the then disposition of
men, and of no small portion of the army, that a successful
effort at the outset would have given them confidence, and
that many and perhaps nearly all the troops in London
would have revolted. But there was no organisation and
no arms, and to have resisted under such circumstances
would have been madness."[2] Place therefore returned
to Charing Cross to complete the arrangements for using,
as Wilkes had done forty years earlier, the police powers
of the City against the Government.

" It was late in the evening before all our arrangements
were fully made and persons appointed to carry them into
effect. Several were appointed to see as many housekeepers[3] as they could, and induce as many as they could
to assent to go to the Gloucester coffee-house, where the
largest room in the house was taken, to be sworn in as
constables at a quarter before nine o'clock on the Monday
morning. It was intended that a number of these housekeepers, some on horseback, but the principal part on foot,
should attend the sheriff to the officer commanding on the
spot, who was to be desired to withdraw his troops, and
upon his absolute refusal, or on his making a show of
resistance, he was to be taken into custody. If he resisted
this, he was to have notice of an action to be brought
against him, and the same process was to be gone through

---

[1] 27,850 (200).   [2] 27,850 (201, 202).
[3] *i.e.* ratepaying householders, who could be legally called upon to
act as constables.

with any officer on duty."[1] "I was to have the direction of them until they were placed under the command of the sheriff. Bills were printed ready to be pasted on boards to be carried by men on poles, informing the people that the civil power under the orders of the sheriff would keep the peace, and they were desired if necessary to lend their aid, and they were informed that the military were directed to withdraw.[2] . . . Our object was to gain time, to prevent the capture of Sir Francis until after the House of Commons had again met, which it was to do on the Monday afternoon."[3]

On Monday morning Place kept his appointment at the Gloucester coffee-house. Fewer "housekeepers" presented themselves for their extremely risky duties than had been expected, but by half-past nine Place had a hundred men under him. Wood, the reforming sheriff, was late, and on his way to Piccadilly was met with the news that all was over. The [authorities had probably been kept well informed of the proceedings at the Gloucester coffee-house, and the troops had broken into Burdett's house at ten o'clock. They broke up a hastily arranged scene, in which Sir Francis was teaching his son to translate Magna Charta, and carried him off in a coach surrounded by a strong force of cavalry through a yelling mob to the Tower.[4]

Here, from April 9 till the prorogation of Parliament on June 21, Burdett remained in custody. The House did not dare to provoke another Wilkes campaign [by depriving him of his seat, and debated with more anger than dignity the deliberately insolent petitions which came in from Middlesex and Westminster.

While Burdett was still in the Tower, Place was called

---

[1] 27,850 (197).   [2] 27,850 (198).   [3] 27,850 (197).
[4] See the Report of the Serjeant-at-Arms to the House of Commons, "House of Commons Journals," April 9, 1810, vol. lxv. p. 261.

upon to perform a purely incidental duty under circumstances which affected all the rest of his political career.
During the night of May 30, 1810, the household in St.
James's Palace were aroused by cries for help, and it was
found that the Duke of Cumberland had been seriously
wounded.   Half-an-hour later his valet, Joseph Sellis, was
discovered dead, with his throat cut, in a closet not far
from the Duke's room.   The Duke of Cumberland was
already the most unpopular of the King's sons, and a
rumour spread that he had murdered Sellis, and had been
wounded in the struggle.   As the death had occurred in
the Palace the coroner of the King's Household held the
inquest, and the jury consisted of tradesmen and others
living "within the verge of the Court."   Place was summoned, and with his usual attention to detail went down
on the morning of the inquest to the rooms of a barrister
in Lincoln's Inn to read up the law of Coroner's Quest.
He was chosen foreman, and used his morning's studies to
insist successfully that reporters should be allowed to be
present, and that the seventeen jurymen who had answered
the summons should all be sworn.   The King's coroner was
not a very competent person, and Place as foreman seems
to have very largely carried on the inquiry.   "It is my
belief," he says, "that every one of the men who served on
the inquest was prejudiced against the Duke."   But the
jury brought in a unanimous verdict of *felo de se*.   Sellis
was shown to have attacked the Duke with a sword, and
afterwards to have committed suicide.   No one who will
now take the trouble to read the evidence can doubt
for an instant that the verdict was just, but it keenly
disappointed those who had expected the chance of a
scandal greater even than that of Mrs. Clarke.   Place
was promptly accused of having been bribed by the
Court, and the accusation was for the next ten years
continually revived by any one who wished to injure

him.[1] For the moment the chief importance of the incident was its effect on Burdett's mind. One cannot read Magna Charta for ever, and Burdett was not a man who read much else. He had therefore nothing to occupy him in the Tower except the daily gossip of Roger O'Connor and Colonel Wardle. These two men magnified the report against Place, and Burdett came to believe that the sheriff's delay at the storming of his house was due to Place's treachery. Nothing of this, however, was known outside the Tower. The Westminster Committee determined to arrange a triumphal procession for Burdett on his release, and Place, though he hated shows of any kind, consented to become chief organiser.

Parliament was to be prorogued on June 21, and Burdett must necessarily be set free as soon as the House rose. For three days Place never left his post at the Crown and Anchor Tavern, where he prepared the most elaborate printed directions for the marshals, the processionists, and the spectators, at every point on the route. People came over from Ireland and Scotland to see the sight. " Almost every decently dressed person had a blue cockade in his hat. The ladies wore blue bonnets, blue feathers, and blue necklaces made of very large beads manufactured for the purpose ; many wore blue dresses, and all had blue ribbons. Every open space was filled with people, and an immense multitude assembled on Tower Hill. All London seemed to be in the streets." [2]

But Burdett in his rooms in the Tower was every day becoming more fidgety and suspicious, and half persuaded himself that Place might arrange with the Government to have him shot as he rode in the triumphal car. When the

[1] Henry Hunt, for instance, says of this incident : " It is said that since that period Mr. Place has been a very rich man, but that before that he was a poor, *very poor*, democrat.—" Memoirs of Henry Hunt " (2 vols., London, 1820-22), vol. ii. p. 424.

[2] 27,850 (235).

news came by semaphore that the House had risen he crossed the Thames quietly in a boat. Place made the best of the situation, and ordered the procession to go on with an empty car in front, and poor Gale Jones speechifying from the top of a hackney-coach behind. But though the rest of the committee soon got over their disappointment, Place nursed his wrath. Henry Hunt said he called Burdett " a damned coward and a poltroon," [1] which is likely enough. Anyhow, for the next nine years Place and Burdett did not speak to each other.

In 1812 there was a general election, and Burdett and Cochrane were returned unopposed. In 1814 occurred the well-known hoax on the Stock Exchange, for which Cochrane and several others were sentenced to heavy fines and imprisonment.[2] Cochrane's conviction was considered in Westminster to be due to a party intrigue, and he was returned unopposed at the bye-election which followed his expulsion from the House of Commons. Place's name does not appear on the committee which managed either of these elections. He prepared schemes, drew up resolutions, and gave the use of his library for preliminary meetings, but refused to do anything which would require him to go out of his own house.

Meanwhile Burdett's suspicions, under the influence of Henry Hunt and others, were steadily growing, and in July 1814 he sent a letter to the committee of the West London Lancastrian Association, of which both Place and he were members, demanding that " Place and John Richter might be expelled the committee, Place being a spy employed by the Government, and Richter being his tool." [3] Place wrote

[1] See the " Memoirs of Henry Hunt," vol. ii, p. 423.

[2] It was alleged that they had concocted, for Stock Exchange purposes, a plan, in accordance with which several persons dressed as British officers rode up to London from Dover and Sheerness reporting a victory of the allied armies.

[3] James Mill told Place that " in the preceding year, being at Oxford with Mr. Bentham, where they saw Sir Francis Burdett, he told them

indignantly to the committee to offer his resignation. It
was accepted, and he resolved to have nothing further to
do either with the Westminster Reform Committee or the
members for Westminster. In less troubled times this
resolution would probably have been final; as it was, it
lasted about two years.[1] Burdett and Place, however, did not
speak to each other till 1819. As to the accusation itself,
most people seem to have come to think of it as merely
Burdett's way of expressing a passing feeling of irritation.[2]

At this period of his life Place had the ill-fortune to be
admitted to the personal friendship of William Godwin,
and the singularly good fortune to escape from it without
ruin. " In the year 1810," that is to say, as soon as Place's
acquaintance had any pecuniary value, " Mr. William
Godwin sought my acquaintance, and I readily formed a
friendship with him. I had never heard anything alleged
against his moral character. I had heard much in his
praise, and I had benefited in no small degree by his
writings.[3] I was therefore pleased to have him for a friend.
Godwin had, however, a design of no small moment to him
in seeking my acquaintance, and he accomplished his

I was a spy, and he cautioned them against me, and upon Mr. Bentham
desiring some reason for his assertion and advice, he said that, when he
was resisting the Speaker's warrant, I had undertaken on the Sunday
before he was seized to fill his house with people to beat out the
soldiers if they should break in, but that instead of doing so I had
betrayed him." [27,823 (102-103).]

[1] Even in 1815 Place seems to have taken part, probably with some
other organisation than the Westminster Committee, in opposing the
Corn Law of that year. Long afterwards he wrote to Cobden: "I was
one cause of preventing the enactment of the Corn Laws in 1814, and
all but fought against it in 1815" (Place to Cobden, November 15,
1841); and still later he recorded that "this atrocious Bill . . . was
passed behind immensely strong double barricades of timber which
blocked up the streets and other avenues to the Houses under the
cannon of the artillery, the swords of the cavalry, and the bayonets of
the infantry."—"Autobiography."

[2] See e.g. Hunt's remark on p. 55.

[3] See p. 29.

purpose beyond what could have been his most sanguine expectations. It was, however, of no permanent use to him, highly pernicious as it was to several others."[1]

"I soon found that he was uncomfortably circumstanced in his pecuniary concerns, and needed my advice and assistance. Both of these I was willing he should have to the full extent of my capability. I made some inquiries respecting the state of his affairs, and as I went on inquiring saw, as I supposed, a probability of extricating him from his difficulties, and placing him in comparatively easy circumstances. . . . An account was shown to us, and books were brought forward to verify the account. Such a case was shown as induced us to conclude that if £3000 could be raised, Mr. Godwin would not only be placed in a state of comparative ease, but that the business carried on by his wife would, when disembarrassed, repay the loan,

---

[1] Place gives a pathetic little picture of another man whom Godwin helped to disillusionise. "Mr. Godwin's affairs brought me acquainted with a Mr. Elton Hammond, whose father had been a wholesale tea-dealer in the City of London, and had at his decease left a considerable property to his two sons and two daughters. Mr. Hammond was tall and well formed. The contour of his face was very like the imaginary portraits of Jesus Christ as painted by eminent artists, but somewhat thinner and rather longer, or it had the appearance of greater length perhaps from its being thinner. His features were regular and handsome; his countenance was mild, placid, benevolent, yet somewhat sorrowful. . . . Mr. Hammond started in life with enthusiastic notions of the capacity and desires of mankind to become virtuous and happy. To their rapid improvement he hoped to devote himself. He persuaded himself that he should be able to correct their vices and prevent them committing crimes. He set about their reformation with uncommon ardour. How little he was able to accomplish need not be told. He consumed his time and expended his money in the vain pursuit of a phantom, which was perpetually misleading him, and wearied and weakened his intellectual powers before his experience had shown him how hopeless his pursuit was. He was at length compelled to conclude that the progress of mankind towards a state of virtuous benevolence was an almost imperceptible increment; he despaired, and in his despair shot himself. He was emphatically my friend, and I loved him with great sincerity to the moment of his death."

and to this hour (1827) I am satisfied it might, and ought
to, have been so, notwithstanding the accounts laid before
us were not correct accounts, and did not contain a true
statement, but had been fabricated in order to induce us
to procure the money."

Place's letters give the history of the last months of the
acquaintance. On January 2, 1814, he writes to his friend
Wakefield: "Godwin has just left me after his Sunday's
usual visit, and I am happy to find he has visited Sir J.
Mackintosh lately, and that these two men who ought to
have been enemies are perfectly good friends again." On
January 25, after some correspondence as to raising money
from Shelley's post-obit bonds, Place writes again to Wakefield: "Godwin sends you a thousand thanks for your
information. He is in some respects a poor creature. He
fears poverty, not, I think, much on his own account, but
for his family." In September of the same year the
acquaintance ends with an exchange of stern reproaches
from Place, and miserable shuffling excuses and upbraidings
from Godwin. On September 2, for instance, he writes to
Place: "My integrity I thoroughly know; it has always
adhered to me, and it supports me even against such an
attack as this, and from such a man as you. . . . Your
passions carry you so far as absolutely to assert the thing
that is not. You say 'I induced you to go to Lambeth
upon an undertaking that you should be paid.' This is not
so. There my integrity triumphed. You urged me again
and again to undertake for that, but in vain. I said, ' I
will see what can be done, I will do the very best I can.' "
September 3.—"There is nothing more to be lamented
between persons of high worth and rare qualities, than that
they should quarrel. Poor Holcroft used to say that I
should never make him quarrel with or alienate himself
from me; and as long as he remained perfectly the man he
had been, he kept his word. I think I can answer for it, you

shall never make me quarrel with you." September 11.—
"You once told me you owed everything that you most
valued in yourself and your rules of conduct to the sole
perusal of my writings, and is this the man whose acquaintance you disown?" One quotation from Place's letters
will be enough. "I regret my own weakness in having
persuaded myself that trickery would in you, any more
than in other persons who resort to it, produce any but its
usual consequences. I regret still more that I ever lent
myself in any way, for ever so short a time, to assist you
either directly or indirectly in any such practice. Most of
all, I regret that you should have made it necessary for me
to write this to you."

He makes a calculation showing that Godwin muddled
away £1500 a year during the ten years 1804–1814, "notwithstanding he had for the last four or five years paid no
rent for the house he lived in, which was worth £200 a
year." Place's own loss from his connection with this
prince of spongers was something under £400.

Even in the days of the Corresponding Society, Place
had been as keen a student of politics as he was a politician,
and when he became organiser at Westminster, his interest
in the more permanent questions underlying party struggles
became still deeper. By that time political theory in England was in a state of rapid transition. The influence of
the French Revolutionary thinkers was disappearing, and
neither the "classical" political economy nor Bentham's
Utilitarianism had yet established themselves. Such
discussion as went on was largely in the hands of the
"cranks," the persistent men of one idea apiece, who make
popular movements, and thereby often force undesired
criticisms of established opinion upon better-equipped
thinkers. With them Place was always ready to spend
hours of patient discussion, and from them he learnt as
much as from his books.

Thomas Spence, the Land Nationaliser, was a typical specimen of these political Poor Preachers. He had been a schoolmaster in Newcastle, and had conceived of "Spence's glorious plan" of "parochial partnership in land without private landlordism," while engaged in a quarrel between the corporation and freemen of Newcastle about the rents of the Town Moor. In 1792 he was in London, and was imprisoned for selling Paine's "Rights of Man." After his release he published a long series of tracts, of which the best known was the periodical "Pigs' Meat; or, Lessons for the Swinish Multitude" (1793–1795). In 1801 he was again imprisoned for publishing a tract called "The Restorer of Society to its Natural State." Place came to know him in 1792, "when he kept a bookstall at the top of Chancery Lane in Holborn. . . . He was at that time as poor as any man could well be, and with some trifling fluctuations in his affairs he continued in this state to the day of his death. He was a very simple, very honest, single-minded man, querulous in his disposition and odd in his manners. . . . His disposition was strongly marked on his countenance, which marked him as a man soured by adverse circumstances, and at enmity with the world. Still he loved mankind, and firmly believed that the time would come when they would be wise, virtuous, and happy. He was perfectly sincere, and unpractised in the ways of the world to an extent few could imagine in a man who had been pushed about in it as he had been. . . . A man so poor, so high in his notions of independence, so fanatically certain of the unparalleled goodness of his system, and so easily excited, could have no friends amongst the persons with whom he associated. . . . He was unknown to such philosophical men as would have formed a true estimate of his worth, made allowance for his infirmities . . . and led him to a better knowledge of the world. . . . Ordinary men could not be the friends of one whom they could not appreciate ; and he on his part despised such men. . . . He looked upon them as despicable, willing slaves, who deserved no better treatment than they met with, and he frequently told them so." [1] Hone afterwards described "Spence's vehicle, like a baker's close barrow. The pamphlets were exhibited outside, and when he sold one he took it from within, and handed and recommended others, with strong expressions of hate to the powers that were and prophecies of what would happen to the whole race of landlords." [2] He used to distribute copper tokens stamped with the words "Spence's Plan," a phrase which his disciples "chalked on every wall in London." [3] He died in 1814, and handed on his message to Thomas Evans, who in the year of his master's death founded that "Society of Spencean Philanthropists" which so frightened Lord Sidmouth in 1817.

Of Spence Place says, "Almost all the great changes in the religion and government of mankind have either been accomplished, or put in the way to be accomplished, by men whose cast of thought was, like his, concentrated on one object, pursued under all kinds of difficulties, and accomplished at last almost against the consent of the very people on whom they were to operate." [4]

Major Cartwright, the originator of the six points of the Charter,[5] and the founder of Lord Sidmouth's other bugbear, the "Hampden Club," only differed from Spence in the fact that he was a man of some fortune. Place liked the "Old Gentleman," as he was generally called,

[1] 27,808 (152–153).
[2] W. Hone to Place (1830), 27,808 (315). The barrow was also used for selling a mysterious compound called Saloup, 27,808 (310).
[3] 27,808 (230).   [4] 27,808 (151).
[5] See "The Legislative Rights of the Commonalty Vindicated," by John Cartwright (London, 1777, 8vo). This is a second and enlarged edition of a pamphlet published in 1776, and called "Take your Choice." See Address of the Metropolitan Parliamentary Reform Association, 27,810 (5).

and helped him to get up his meetings and petitions,
but found him, apparently, a dreadful bore. "When he
was in town he used frequently to sup with me, eating
some raisins he brought in his pocket, and drinking weak
gin and water. He was cheerful, agreeable, and full of
curious anecdote. He was, however, in political matters
exceedingly troublesome, and sometimes as exceedingly
absurd. He had read but little or to little purpose, and
knew nothing of general principles. He entertained a
vague and absurd notion of the political arrangements
of the Anglo-Saxons, and sincerely believed that these
semi-barbarians were not only a polished people, but that
their 'twofold polity,' arms-bearing and representation,
were universal and perfect." [1]

In 1813 Robert Owen brought to London the manuscript
of that "New View of Society," which may be regarded as
the starting point of modern Socialism. Place writing in
1836 says: "He introduced himself to me, and I found him
a man of kind manners and good intentions, of an imperturbable temper, and an enthusiastic desire to promote the
happiness of mankind. A few interviews made us friends."
. . . "He told me he possessed the means, and was resolved
to produce a great change in the manners and habits of the
whole of the people, from the most exalted to the most
depressed. He found all our institutions at variance with
the welfare and happiness of the people, and had discovered the true means of correcting all those errors
which prevented them having the fullest enjoyment
possible, and, consequently, of being wise and happy.
His project was simple, easy of adoption, and so plainly
efficacious, that it must be embraced by every thinking
man the moment he was made to understand it. He
produced a manuscript, which he requested me to read and
correct for him. I went through it carefully, and it was

[1] 27,850 (108).

afterwards printed. . . . Mr. Owen then was, and is still, persuaded that he was the first who had ever observed that man was the creature of circumstances. On this supposed discovery he founded his system. Never having read a metaphysical book, nor held a metaphysical conversation, nor having even heard of the disputes respecting free-will and necessity, he had no clear conception of his subject, and his views were obscure. Yet he has all along been preaching and publishing and projecting and predicting in the fullest conviction that he could command circumstances or create them, and place men above their control when necessary. He never was able to explain these absurd notions, and therefore always required assent to them, telling those who were not willing to take his words on trust that it was their ignorance which prevented them from at once assenting to these self-evident propositions.

"January 7, 1836, Mr. Owen this day has assured me, in the presence of more than thirty other persons, that within six months the whole state and condition of society in ; Great Britain will be changed, and all his views will be carried fully into effect." [1]

[1] 27,791 (264-268).

CHAPTER III

THE BENTHAMITES

THE history of any definite "school" of philosophic or political opinion will generally show that its foundation was made possible by personal friendship. So few men devote themselves to continuous thought, that if several think on the same lines for many years it is almost always because they have encouraged each other to proceed. And varieties of opinion and temperament are so infinite, that those who accept a new party name, and thereby make themselves responsible for each other's utterances, are generally bound by personal loyalty as well as by intellectual agreement.

The "Benthamite," or, as it became later, the "Utilitarian" school, which adopted Bentham's formula of "the greatest happiness of the greatest number" as its motto, was no exception to this rule. Bentham's writings from the year 1776, when he published the "Fragment on Government," would in any case have had their effect. But the enormous influence which, towards the end of his life, he exerted upon liberal thought in England, was very largely due to the care which he then took to secure that a few able men should always enjoy the most complete intellectual intimacy with himself and each other. Of these men the ablest was James Mill.

Mill was introduced to Bentham in 1808, and from thenceforward dined from time to time at his house in Queen Square.[1] Place about that time came to know

[1] *Cf.* "James Mill: A Biography," by Alexander Bain (London, 1882), page 72.

E

Edward Wakefield,[1] the writer of several good but now forgotten books on social economics. "Soon after we became intimately acquainted Mr. Wakefield introduced Mr. James Mill to me. Mr. Mill at this time resided at Stoke Newington, whence he came occasionally, generally once a week, I believe, to dine with Mr. Bentham, who lived in Queen Square Place, Westminster. Our acquaintance speedily ripened into friendship, and he usually called on me on his way to Mr. Bentham's, when we spent an hour together."[2]

Mill and Place worked hard during 1813 and 1814 on the British and Foreign School Society at the West London Lancastrian Association,[3] and wrote to each other in a tone of warm affection. Thus Place in a letter of October 1814 wrote: "I do not know when I experienced more delight than your letter has this day given me. Somehow or other I have all my life long, and in all circumstances, met with so much of what was excellent, and even exquisite, that I have had a happy life, one enjoyment scarcely passing away before another presented itself. At present they crowd upon me; to be esteemed and confided in by the wise and good was the great end I always pursued, and your letter tells me that I have both deserved and obtained it from one whom everybody considers pre-eminently good and wise. . . . Could I advise or perform anything which tended to promote your comfort, how inexpressibly happy should I be."[4] And again: "You tell me to write soon, and I obey. It is a great pleasure to me to write to you, and were it not that you are too learned in men and things for me to venture any speculation I should indulge in some. I am perfectly contented to be a learner, and am eagerly desirous of instruction. Every one of your letters is to me

---

[1] *e.g.* "An Account of Ireland, Statistical and Political" (London, 1812. 2 vols.).   [2] 27,823 (84).
[3] See Chap. IV. pp. 96, 106–110.   [4] Place to Mill, October 17, 1814.

a lesson. Anxious as I have always been to obtain information, careful as I have likewise been to examine myself and to divest myself of prejudices, yet intensely occupied, as poverty compelled me to be, in a disagreeable and for some years unhealthy business, my opportunities for mental improvement have been comparatively few. It is true I have at all times had the acquaintance of some men of superior intellect, and have, I know, profited by it. But till I became happily acquainted with you I had no person with whom I could compare myself in the beneficial manner I can now do. I am upwards of forty years of age, but mind has little to do with age except in infancy and dotage, and I would fain persuade myself that I am about twenty-two or twenty-three years old, with a good prospect of health and leisure for improvement before me."[1]

Mill himself drops his habit of reserve, and writes with stiff goodwill: "Your place of a friend to me shall not be a sinecure. You had no occasion for this declaration to satisfy you respecting my opinion of you, to which I should have been far from alluding, had it not been for the malignity with which I see your character pursued,[2] and which makes it my duty to declare on all occasions that I have met with few men in my whole life of whom I think so highly."[3]

Mill even writes of his own money affairs, and confesses that "The History of India," on which he had been at work since 1806, had "kept him as poor as a church mouse," that he "practises much economy, a good school for himself and his children," but that he "hopes to be at his ease when the work is finished." He passes from the subject with the words, "so much for these affairs into which few are so far admitted, and as few care whether I have little or

[1] Place to Mill, November 27, 1814.
[2] With reference to the accusation that Place was a Government spy. See pp. 54–56.
[3] James Mill to Place, July 30, 1814 (in the family autograph book).

much."[1]   Place answers : " What you have said of your circumstances does not in the least surprise me.   My wife and I
saw as much long since, and we loved you the more for it."[2]

Place and Wakefield wrote to each other, full of care for
Mill and schemes for his future.   Mill and his family were
now living for a great part of the year at Ford Abbey,[3] the
huge Devonshire mansion which Bentham had rented, and
Wakefield was afraid that he might slip into a permanently
dependent position.   " I am deeply interested about Mill,
for, with all my admiration of Mr. Bentham, he is too good
a man to become a dependant upon any individual; and I
fear that the increasing expenses of his young family must
render him so, unless we can place him at the head of this
new school."[4]   " Mill is hard at work upon his Indian work,
and has wrote it up to the year 1790.   I wish it may ever
repay him for his labour.   He says he is very well, but
looks otherwise—thin in the face; and I misread him if
he be not in a state of anxiety."[5]   " Do you think he is
calculating upon the sale of his work upon India ?   If that
is the case, then I fear he will be disappointed; and as for
maintaining a large family entirely by his pen, the thing is,
I think, impossible, unless he had managed to tumble on
to some popular work, such as Hayley's ' Life of Cowper,'
or something as great."[6]

Place, in answer, asked, " Shall such a man be left to the
chance of sickness to reduce him to absolute want ?   Shall
he be destroyed by anxiety and corroding cares, which the

---

[1] James Mill to Place, October 14, 1814.   [Letter dated afterwards
by F. Place, Jun., and accidentally ascribed to 1817.]

[2] Place to Mill, October 17, 1814.

[3] For a good description of the life at Ford Abbey in 1814, cf.
" Memoirs and Correspondence of Francis Horner " (London, 1843),
vol. ii. p. 178.

[4] Wakefield to Place, August 17, 1814.   The school is the Christo-
mathic School, cf. p. 130 (note).

[5] Wakefield to Place (from Ford Abbey), October 1, 1814.

[6] Wakefield to Place, October 17, 1814.

firmest mind cannot always repel when no prospect of better days presents itself?"[1] He then proposed a scheme for raising £300 among Mill's friends, to be put anonymously to his credit at the bank, a scheme which Wakefield thought might do more harm than good. During Mill's long absences from London, Place managed his business affairs; and Professor Bain says that he has "heard from very good authority that Francis Place . . . made him advances while he was writing the history. These, of course, were all repaid."[2]

Mill, on his part, tried to cure Place of his habit of "raving."[3] In a letter of December 1814 he says: "But I am satisfied you are going on in the right path, and I know now that you can do better than you are doing. Only observe as much as possible of suavity in the manner, while there is anything of asperity in the matter, and you will be sure to succeed."[4] And some months later Place wrote, after describing an outburst, "I suppose you to be looking at me. I see the whole of what you intend, and feel how deficient I often am, but I cannot talk of some things with some people as calmly as I do of two and two being four, but I will endeavour to improve."[5] At the same time, he fears that if he ceases to feel intensely and immoderately, he may ultimately sink into the vegetable Philistinism of the ordinary retired tradesman. "I have always contemplated the probability of being released from business, and I have been afraid of too much caution as tending to produce cold-heartedness. It would be damnable to have little employment and no feeling."[6]

[1] Place to Wakefield, October 7, 1814.
[2] See "James Mill: a Biography," by Alex. Bain (London, 1882), page 163.
[3] Place, in a letter to Ensor, October 13, 1816, quotes Mill's expression, "to rave like Place."
[4] James Mill to Place, December 31, 1814.
[5] Place to Mill, July 20, 1815.
[6] Place to Mill, August 30, 1816.

The two friends exchanged descriptions of their children. Mill recounted the amazing precocity of John Stuart, now eight years old, and his sister Wilhelmina. "My two children, John and Willie, are with me at six A.M., and then we have half a day's work done before any other body is up in the house. John is now an adept in the first six books of Euclid and in Algebra, performing simple questions with great ease, while in Greek he has read since he came here the last half of Thucydides, one play of Euripides and one of Sophocles, two of Aristophanes and the treatise of Plutarch on education. Willie has read along with him several lives in Cornelius Nepos, and has got over the most difficult part of the task of learning Latin, while John wants but little of being able to read Latin with ease. His historical and other reading never stands still, he is at it whenever he has any time to spare. This looks like bragging, but as I tell you the untoward part of my circumstances, it is but right you should hear that which gives me pleasure also. There are few to whom I talk of either." [1]

[1] James Mill to Place (from Ford Abbey), Dec. 7, 1814. A passage in one of Mill's letters throws some light on a disputed point in his early life. "As for Sir John Stuart, he is one of the Barons of the Exchequer in Scotland, and his estate and residence was near my father's. I was at an early age taken notice [of] by him and Lady Jane. When the time came for my going to college, it was my father's intention to send me to Aberdeen, as both nearer and less expensive than Edinburgh. Sir John, however, and Lady Jane insisted that he should let them take me to Edinburgh, which was the more celebrated university ; that they would look after me, and take care that the expense to my father should not be greater than at Aberdeen. I went to Edinburgh, and from that time lived as much in their house as in my father's, and there had many advantages, saw the best company, and had an educated man to direct my education, and who paid for several expensive branches of education, but which for him I must have gone without, and above all, had unlimited access in both town and country to well-chosen libraries. So you see I owe much to Sir John Stuart, who had a daughter, one only child, about the same age as myself, who, besides being a beautiful woman, was in point of intellect and disposition one of the most perfect human beings I have ever known. We grew up together and studied together from children, and were about

Mill and his friends seem often to have discussed the old question as to how far a child's mind is a *tabula rasa* on which education can produce any effect desired. "Wakefield," wrote Place, "is a believer in innate propensities, . . . and so fully is he satisfied of the truth of his theory, that he expects to see your John's innate propensities break out presently and form his character. . . . The position I take against him is, that the generality of children are organised so nearly alike that they may by proper management be made pretty nearly equally wise and virtuous." [1]

Place's own children, though clever enough, were not so remarkable as the little Mills, while his paternal affection expressed itself in a somewhat more human form, and Mrs. Place was apparently not so willing as Mrs. Mill to allow unlimited educational experiments. "Tom," he wrote of one of them, "is a little Bonaparte of a fellow, three years old, with reasoning powers very far beyond his age and beyond his ability to express in words; but his courage, activity in mischief, and his determined manner are the constant causes of as delightful a discord as ever prevailed among as many small brats. I have given all the time I could in any way spare to them, and have no doubt they would be infinitely more to my mind could I bestow a certain portion of time every day on them, notwithstanding the difficulty there is of convincing—I might have said the impossibility of convincing—the grown females that I know at all what I am about." [2] Some of Place's elder children

the best friends that either of us ever had. She married Sir William Forbes, and after producing him six children died a few years ago of a decline. Her poor mother told me with her heart ready to break that she spoke about me with almost her last breath, and enjoined them never to allow the connection which subsisted between us to be broken. So much for the old friendship with Sir J. Stuart, which it is very proper you should know, but which I do not wish to be talked about." (James Mill to Place from Ford Abbey, Oct. 26, 1817.)

[1] Place to Mill, October 30, 1816.
[2] Place to Mill, July 20, 1815.

were now grown up, and to one of them, from her letters evidently a bright and attractive girl, Mill wrote much advice on beginning work at six in the morning, and other points. Mrs. Mill and Mrs. Place enjoyed a separate friendship of their own. In December 1816, Place sent a postscript of kind messages from his wife and daughters to Mrs. Mill: "She is their favourite acquaintance, the more so as she, poor woman, as well as my wife, has 'a grumpy husband who bites her nose off.'"[1]

Mill about this time proposed to settle in France,[2] and there was now a plan that Place, who expected soon to be able to retire from business, should settle there beside him. "You give me abundant pleasure," wrote Mill, "by hinting the probability of your settling yourself down beside me in France. I foresee nothing there which would make it uncomfortable for us to reside as soon as we please. Assure yourself that the French people will soon be very quiet and contented slaves; and the despotism of the Bourbons, a quiet, gentle despotism. There I may live cheap, my children will acquire a familiarity with the language and with the manners and character of a new people. When they have enough of this we shall remove into Germany till the same effects are accomplished, and after that if we please we may go to Italy. We shall then return accomplished people, and men and women of us, I hope, able to do something for the cause of mankind. We shall, at any rate, have plenty of knowledge, the habit of living upon little, and a passion for the improvement of the condition of mankind."[3]

In the course of 1812 Mill introduced Place to Bentham.[4] For three years after this there is no evidence that Place

[1] Place to Mill, December [N.D.] 1816.
[2] For a similar proposal a year earlier, cf. "James Mill: a Biography," p. 139.
[3] James Mill to Place, September 6 [1815].
[4] "Autobiography."

was in any way intimate with the Master. When, in 1814, Bentham and Mill began their yearly residence at Ford Abbey, Place, at Mill's request, sent long letters on "all that goes on in the world, political and domestic."[1] The Bentham MSS. in the British Museum record that on May 21, 1816, Bentham lent Place the Federalist to read.[2] Place's position as a disciple began in August 1817, when he went to stay at Ford Abbey. His letters to Mrs. Place during this visit give a detailed description of the Mill family life.

"I cannot but admire the children here, who give no one any trouble; they have a hard time of it, learning their lessons from six every morning to nine, and saying them, and learning others from eleven to one; and learning again in the afternoon—learning, too, with a precision utterly unknown by others; even little Jim spells words of four syllables well; and Clara reads, as she herself says, 'Natural History.' At present she 'is reading of quadrupeds,' and really knows what she reads in a surprising manner, and explains the meaning of the terms used with ease and correctness. As for crying and bawling, it may be said to have no existence here; some of them cry when scolded or cuffed over their lessons, but it is all but unknown on other occasions. Mrs. Mill is a patient, quiet soul, hating wrangling, and although by no means meanly submissive, manages to avoid quarrelling in a very admirable manner."[3]

A little earlier he had described his own daily life: "I have been pacing the walks from ten to two—four hours' hard work at Latin. I use all the care and diligence I possess or can command at this very, very difficult study; but my master gives me a good character, and says I

[1] James Mill to Place, July 6, 1815.
[2] Brit. Mus. Addl. MSS. 33,564.
[3] Place to Mrs. Place, August 28, 1817.

shall certainly accomplish my purpose. Nouns substan-
tive and adjectives have been gone through, not slightly,
but fully; pronouns as much as they are said to be useful;
the verb *esse-sum* has been subdued; and I am loving
away in all possible moods and tenses with *am-are*. I
shall cease loving in two days, and shall be teaching away
with *doc-eo, doc-ui, doc-tum, doc-ere.* Every day I am
obliged to decline a number of nouns and adjectives
chosen at random by others, and to say all I have gone
through. If I am not at school, no one ever was.[1] Mill
is beyond comparison the most diligent fellow I ever knew
or heard of; almost any other man would tire and give up
teaching, but not so he; three hours every day, frequently
four, are devoted to the children, and there is not a
moment's relaxation. His method is by far the best I
ever witnessed, and is infinitely precise; but he is exces-
sively severe. No fault, however trivial, escapes his notice;
none goes without reprehension or punishment of some
sort. Lessons have not been well said this morning by
Willie and Clara;—there they are now, three o'clock,
plodding over their books, their dinner, which they knew
went up at one, brought down again; and John, who dines
with them, has his book also, for having permitted them
to pass when they could not say, and no dinner will any of
them get till six o'clock. This has happened once before
since I came. The fault to-day is *a mistake in one word.*
Now I could not be so severe; but the learning and
reasoning these children have acquired is not equalled by
any children in the whole world. John is truly a prodigy,
a most wonderful fellow; and when his Logic, his Languages,
his Mathematics, his Philosophy shall be combined with a

---

[1] Any one who went to Ford Abbey seems to have been expected to
work. Place writes to Wakefield (Sept. 3, 1814): "Hume is gone
to Ford Abbey, where he intends staying some time, as he sent his
carriage on, and was, when I saw him, packing up Smith's "Wealth
of Nations" to study there.

general knowledge of mankind and the affairs of the world, he will be a truly astonishing man; but he will probably be morose and selfish. Mill sees this; and I am operating upon him, when the little time I can spare can be so applied, to counteract these propensities, so far as to give him a bias towards the management of his temper, and to produce an extensive consideration of the reasonings and habits of others, when the time shall come for him to observe and practise these things."[1]

"*Wednesday, August* 20.[2]—I have now been here long enough to know all about the family; Mrs. Mill is both good-natured and good-tempered, two capital qualities in a woman; she is, however, not a little vain of her person, and would be thought to be still a girl. Since I have been here there has not been one single instance of *crying* among the children, who certainly give less trouble, and have fewer ridiculous propensities and desires than any I ever knew; notwithstanding they have a plentiful lack of manners, and as much impertinence, sometimes called impudence, as any children need have. You would be surprised to see little Jim trundling a hoop nearly as tall as himself round the Great Hall, going as fast as the others, and turning the corners with admirable dexterity."

"*August* 7, 1817.—All our days are alike, so an account of one may do for all. Mill is up between five and six; he and John compare his proofs, John reading the copy and his father the proof. Willie and Clara are in the saloon before seven, and as soon as the proofs are done with, John goes to the farther end of the room to teach his sisters. When this has been done, and part of the time while it is doing, he learns geometry; this continues to nine o'clock, when breakfast is ready.

"Mr. Bentham rises soon after seven, and about eight

[1] Place to Mrs. Place, August 17, 1817.
[2] Postscript to the foregoing letter.

gets to his employment. I rise at six and go to work; at
nine breakfast in the parlour—present, Mrs. Mill, Mill, I,
John, and Colls.[1]

"Breakfast ended, Mill hears Willie and Clara, and then
John. Lessons are heard under a broad balcony, walking
from end to end, the breakfast parlour on one hand and
pots of flowers rising one above another as high as your
head on the other hand; this place is in the front of the
Abbey. All the lessons and readings are performed aloud,
and occupy full three hours, say till one o'clock.

"From nine to twelve Mr. Bentham continues working; from twelve to one he performs upon an organ in the
saloon.

"From breakfast time to one o'clock I am occupied in
learning Latin; this is also done aloud in the walks, and
already I have conquered the substantives and adjectives.
During this period Colls, who is a good boy, gets a lesson
of Latin from Mill, and of French from me: his is a capital
situation for a boy of genius.

"At one we all three walk in the lanes and fields for
an hour. At two all go to work again till dinner at six,
when Mrs. Mill, Mill, Bentham, I, and Colls, dine together.
We have soup or fish, or both, meat, pudding, generally
fruit, viz., melons, strawberries, gooseberries, currants,
grapes; no wine. The first day I came, wine was put
upon the table; but as I took none, none has since made
its appearance. After dinner, Mill and I take a sharp
walk for two hours, say, till a quarter past eight, then one
of us alternately walks with Mr. Bentham for an hour; then
comes tea, at which we read the periodical publications;
and eleven o'clock comes but too soon, and we all go to
bed.

"Mrs. Mill marches in great style round the green in
front of the house for about half an hour before breakfast

[1] Bentham's amanuensis.

and again after dinner with all the children, till their bed-time." [1]

When Place returned after two months at Ford Abbey he was profoundly influenced by James Mill's philosophy of life, and had caught that "habit of analysis" which John Stuart Mill notices as the result of his father's training.[2] A few days after his return he writes: "I have not been out of the house since Thursday, so off I set to Hyde Park alone, and as I tramped I thought of you and yours, and of the Abbey and Mr. Bentham, and of mine, and of all the world and all its virtues and vices, its pleasures and its pains, upon the misery of some wretch at every hundred yards' distance in this thick, hazy, gloomy day's atmosphere, and I gave away all my money. I prosed on

[1] Place to Mrs. Place, August 7, 1817. The following letter, written on the inner fold of one from Place dated August 4, 1817, reporting his arrival at Ford Abbey, is interesting as a glimpse of John Stuart Mill's mother :—

Mrs. James Mill to Mrs. Place.

"My dear Mrs. Place,—I will take all possible care of your lord and master, and see that his [clothes] return from the wash regularly. I am much pleased to hear that he admires the Abbey. He will pass his time very pleasantly here, I have no doubt. I have recovered my youth now. I was more fatigued than usual, owing to the child not going to the new servant. I think she will answer very well, as there is less to do on account of the washing all being put out. I am very glad, as I brought a great deal of work to do. Give my kind love to Miss Place, and best remembrances to all the rest of the family.—Yours truly and sincerely,   H. Mill."

Sir Samuel Romilly stayed at Ford Abbey during part of the time that Place was there. In a letter to Dumont he describes Place. " He is self-educated, has learnt a great deal, has a very strong natural understanding, and possesses great influence in Westminster, such influence as almost to determine the elections for members of Parliament. I need hardly say that he is a great admirer and disciple of Bentham." ["James Mill : a Biography," by A. Bain (London, 1881), page 78.] Place writes to his wife that Miss Romilly supposed him for some days to be a Member of Parliament. [Place to Mrs. Place, September 29, 1817.]

[2] See J. S. Mill's "Autobiography" (London, 1873), page 137.

happiness and misery, and reviewed my own propensities and conduct, the motives by which I had been governed and the results, and conjectured what the result might have been had different reasons operated."[1]

Mill was now nearly at the end of his twelve years' task, the "History of India." Place took an almost painfully intense interest in the book. Towards the end of 1816 he wrote: "I have been thinking that possibly I might be useful to you in your Indian history, by reading or writing or taking down from dictation, and three or four hours a day are at your service."[2] In the winter of 1817–18, as the work was in the press, Place arranged details with the publisher, helped to revise proofs, and worked at the preparation of the index. When he had read part of the proofs, he writes in terms of enthusiastic praise, but warns Mill that "My opinion must be cautiously taken, because I am not, and cannot be, altogether an impartial evidence. I am too much interested in your prosperity and fame too, that my desire for uncommon success accompanies me in all my reading; and although I endeavour to divest myself of all partiality, and try to read the book as I should read the work of an indifferent person, there can be no doubt that this is never really done."[3]

The history was published at the beginning of January 1818, and was immediately successful. In February there was already a proposal on foot that Mill should be appointed to an assistant examinership in the East India House, with a salary beginning at £800 a year. The appointment was made in May 1819, after a vigorous canvas by Ricardo, Hume, Place, and the rest of his friends. "As soon as I had heard," says Place, "that he had been named as a person fit for the office, . . . I stood

---

[1] Place to Mill, October 20, 1817.
[2] Place to Mill, September 15, 1816.
[3] Place to Mill, October 21, 1817.

on no ceremony with anybody. Mill was to be served; he deserved the best exertions in his favour of every one who knew him, and I, as one who knew his transcendent merits, went to work at once without consulting any one, in a way which I knew no one would advise, no one could think likely to produce any good consequences. It was a chance well worth taking; it was the only one I had, or could have, of serving him effectually."[1]

After his appointment to the India House, Mill had naturally to live in or near London, and Place's long weekly budget of news was no longer needed. But the two remained intimate friends. Place on several occasions stayed with Mill at Marlow and elsewhere, and Mill's letters show that he consulted Place on all important questions. Only once is there any sign of a misunderstanding. In a diary which he kept for 1826, Place writes on May 18: "Walked with James Mill to Cheapside. Home again at eleven A.M. As I am here a recorder of time more than of opinions, I shall not say why it has happened that, such friends as Mill and I are, his name has not before appeared in this diary." Three days later Place went down to stay with the Mills at Dorking, and the diary for the next few months shows them to have been very often together. Yet in spite of Place's constant loyalty, one has the feeling that Mill rather starved the affection of his friends as well as that of his children. " He could help the mass," wrote Place, "but he could not help the individual, not even himself, or his own."[2]

After Mill's appointment Bentham lost his constant companionship, and from 1819 relied more and more on Place. In one of Place's fragments of diary, there is an entry—

" *Tuesday, June* 19, 1827.—From Saturday evening till this morning at nine no one, for a wonder, called upon me

" Autobiography."   [2] *Ibid.*

excepting my old, very dear friend, Jeremy Bentham, who came with a volume of his book now in the press—a volume on Evidence [1]—to request me to read the first 462 pages for the purpose of ascertaining whether (1) the matter was such as would interest the generality of readers who read on matters not quite frivolous; (2) if, as to style, it was such as would not deter them; (3) if *yes* on both these questions, how far it could be aided by notes and references to facts and practice; if *no*, on the second question, how it could be amended, the object being to print so much of the work in a separate volume." This is followed by a note: "Visits from and to Mr. Bentham have not been hitherto mentioned, as each of our houses were as frequently entered by either as his own."

In the diary kept for Bentham by his secretary from 1821 to 1825 [2] there are constant entries of copies of Bentham's works, sent to Place for distribution among his political friends, and of books lent to him for his own reading. From the same diary, it would seem that Place managed most of Bentham's minor business matters. But Bentham by no means thought of Place merely as a useful performer of small commissions. Richard Carlile, who knew both men well, wrote in 1836 that "Jeremy Bentham, twenty years ago, pronounced Mr. Place to be the most fit man living, from extensive knowledge of the state of the country and its parties, the condition and wants of the people, and from his own probity and mental energy, to become a Secretary of State for the Home Department." [3]

---

[1] The reference is to Bentham's "Rationale of Judicial Evidence" (London, 1827. 5 vols.), which was finally put into form and finished by John Stuart Mill. *Cf.* p. 83, and J. S. Mill's "Autobiography" (London, 1873), page 114.

[2] Brit. Mus. Addl. MSS. 33,563.

[3] See the *Old Monthly Magazine*, May 1836, p. 445, article entitled "The Real Nobility of the Human Character," by A. P. [*i.e.* Richard Carlile].

Place in a letter to Hodgskin, in 1817, quotes Bentham as saying, "'Tell Mr. Hodgskin that I am a comical old fellow only for a day or two, until those who do not know me become acquainted with my manner.' And," he adds, "this is strictly the truth, for he is the most affable man in existence, perfectly good-humoured, bearing, and forbearing, deeply read, deeply learned, eminently a reasoner, yet simple as a child; annoyed sometimes by trifles, but never by anything but trifles never worth a contentious observation."[1]

The letters between Place and Bentham[2] are, as would be expected from the fact that they lived within two minutes' walk of each other, and met constantly, mostly short notes sent by hand to ask questions or make appointments. A longer letter than usual, written a year before Bentham's death, is worth quoting :—

J. B. *to* F. P.

"Q. S. P.[3] *April 24, 1831, Sunday.*

"DEAR GOOD BOY,—I have made an appointment for you; and you must absolutely keep it, or make another. It is to see Prentice,[4] and hear him express his regrets for calling you a 'bold bad man.' (Oh, but the appointment it is for Tuesday, one o'clock, commencement of my circumgiration time.)[5] I said you were a *bold* man, but denied your being a *bad* one, judging from near twenty years' intimacy. I asked him why he called you a bad

---

[1] Place to Hodgskin, May 30, 1817.

[2] These are now among the Bentham MSS. in the British Museum ; others are in Place's Letter Books, and among the Bentham MSS. in University College Library.

[3] *i.e.* Queen's Square Place.

[4] Archibald Prentice, author of a "History of the Anti-Corn Law League" (London, 1853. 2 vols.), and several other works. He gives a delightful account of this visit in his "Historical Sketches of Manchester," pp. 379–386.

[5] *i.e.* a trot round his garden for an hour.

F

man; his answer was because of the pains you had taken
to disseminate your anti-over-population (I should have
said your over-population-stopping) expedient. The case
is, he is juggical;[1] Calvinistic; is descended from two
parsonical grandfathers of considerable notoriety. I observed to him that every man is master of his own actions,
but no man of his own opinions; that on the point in
question he was no less far from you than you from him;
and that if every man were to quarrel with every man
whose opinions did not on every point whatsoever coincide
with his, the earth would not be long burdened with the
human race. As to the point in question, I took care not
to let him know how my opinion stood; the fat would
have been all in the fire, unless I succeeded in converting
him, for which there was no time; all I gave him to
understand on the score of religion as to my own senti-
ments was, that I was for universal toleration; and on
one or two occasions I quoted scripture." . . . The rest
of the letter is taken up with a minute description of
Prentice's character.[2]

---

[1] "Jug" (short for Juggernaut) with its derivations, "juggist,"
"anti-jug," &c., were constantly used in the Bentham circle as a
conveniently unintelligible synonym for orthodox Christianity.

[2] A letter of Place's will show his way of addressing Bentham :—

F. P. *to* J. B.

"*December* 24, 1827.

"My dear old Father,—Doone says you desire to have a gossip
with me ; say when and where, and I will write to you.

"The Mechanics' Institution [the present Birkbeck] is about to cele-
brate the anniversary by a dinner, and, instead of having the masses
of ostentatious men who have done nothing to deserve it to be made
stewards, the committee of the Institution are desirous to have for
stewards those benefactors by whose aid it was they became an
organised body, that it may appear clearly that they who were once
its friends are still its friends. Give me leave, then, to put down
your name. You will not be required to attend any meeting, you
will not be liable to expense, nor to be annoyed by any application
whatever.—Yours most sincerely, Francis Place." (Brit. Mus. Addl.
MSS. 33,546, p. 179.)

One service which all Bentham's disciples were allowed
to perform was the writing of Bentham's later books. The
Master used to spend each day his allotted number of
hours in producing those piles of almost illegible manuscript, which are now warehoused at University College.
Their general character may be fairly described by John
Stuart Mill's account of the papers on "Evidence." "Mr.
Bentham had begun this treatise three times, at considerable intervals, each time in a different manner, and
each time without reference to the preceding; two of
the other three times he had gone over nearly the whole
subject."[1] Out of such materials the books through which
Bentham exercised his influence on the thoughts of
Europe were patiently pieced together by his friends.
Dumont spent his whole life in preparing a series of French
editions. John Mill's earliest important literary work consisted in "editing" the "Rationale of Judicial Evidence;"[2]
Bingham, with a great deal of assistance from Place and
Mill, put together the "Book of Fallacies;"[3] Grote, under
the name of Philip Beauchamp, the "Natural Religion;"[4]
and James Mill the "Table of the Springs of Action."[5]
Even Hobhouse was pressed into the service, and writes
early in 1819: "I never was to *translate* Mr. Bentham.
I was to arrange his MSS. and put his words into the
vernacular, which, by the way, you may perhaps call
translating, although I suspect it would be difficult to
find language more to the purpose than Bentham's own."[6]
Place's share in this work consisted, besides his help on the

[1] See J. S. Mill's "Autobiography," pages 114, 115.
[2] *Cf.* J. S. Mill's "Autobiography," page 114.
[3] "The Book of Fallacies," by Jeremy Bentham (London, 1824).
See Place to Hobhouse, August 7, 1819. 27,837 (166, 167).
[4] London, 1822.
[5] "A Table of the Springs of Action," &c., by Jeremy Bentham
(London, 1815).
[6] Hobhouse to Place, April 13, 1819. 27,837 (141, 142).

"Fallacies," in preparing Bentham's "Plan of Parliamentary Reform,"[1] so as to "make the reading more easy to the commonalty," and adding notes to it with the help of Wooller, the Radical editor of the *Black Dwarf*.[2] He also saw "Chrestomathia"[3] through the press, and put together the whole work called "Not Paul, but Jesus," by "Gamaliel Smith."[4]

Place seems at first to have been rash enough to hope that temperate criticism might lead Bentham to improve his way of writing. Bentham's "Codification Papers," he complains in a letter to Mill, "instead of being written in a plain, familiar style, which would allure a common man (and how very few are there who are not common men) to read it, is so written that to comprehend all that is said, each paragraph, nay, each sentence, must be studied, and most men think it trouble enough to study the subject itself, be it what it may, even in the plainest language, without being obliged at the same time to make a study of the phraseology of the author. . . . I can take the necessary pains, for at least two reasons: first, the knowledge I have acquired of Mr. Bentham personally, added to my

[1] Plan of Parliamentary Reform in the form of a Catechism (London, 1818).

[2] Place to Hume, March 1, 1839.

[3] "Chrestomathia," by Jeremy Bentham (London, 1815, 1816, 1817, &c.).

[4] Place does not say this in any of his letters or diaries. The Utilitarian circle for obvious reasons kept that side of their work rather quiet. But Dr. Richard Garnett has a copy of "Not Paul, but Jesus," on the inside leaf of which Place has written, "The matter of this book was put together by me, at Mr. Bentham's request, in the months of August and September 1817, during my residence with him at Ford Abbey, Devonshire." Bentham's rough manuscript of "Not Paul, but Jesus," in University College, is endorsed in Place's hand with the various dates on which he read the sheets, that is to say, mostly during his stay at Ford Abbey. When Bowring published Deontology from Bentham's notes (1834), Place wrote, "It is no work of my very dear and good old master, but of that wild poetical surface man Bowring." (Place to Wheatley, February 21, 1840.)

knowledge of his reputation; second, because I never read anything of his without being both wiser and, as I believe, better in consequence of that reading, or rather studying. . . . I do my duty in thus endeavouring to cause the evil to be removed; for an evil it is, whether the fault be in the writer or in the reader."[1]

Mill replies in a great fright: "Your letter had nearly done mischief. Reading it to him, as he expects your letters, as he sees them come in, should be read, I stumbled on your saying, . . . when observing what followed, I pretended to find a difficulty in reading, and slipped the whole of what you said about the style. He never would have forgiven you, and to excite dislike where no good is to be done by it is evil for both parties. There is no one thing upon which he plumes himself so much as his style, and he would not alter it if all the world were to preach to him till Domesday."[2]

At one time Bentham intended that Place should be his literary executor. On August 9, 1826, Place writes in his diary—"Mr. Bowring—a long conversation respecting Mr. Bentham's will. Mr. B. made his will in 1817, when I was with him at Ford Abbey, making me his executor, and leaving me £1000 for the purpose of arranging and printing from his MSS. Subsequently Mill and I supposed he had made Bowring his executor. This does not appear to be the case; but Bowring has reason to fear that he has altered and complicated his will, and that his MSS. may not be properly attended to."[3]

In the Utilitarian movement there are two distinct periods divided roughly by the year 1824. Up to that time Bentham had been the active leader of the group;

[1] Place to James Mill, October 20, 1817.
[2] James Mill to Place, November 6, 1817.
[3] Bentham's final will made Bowring literary executor, and left Place a mourning ring, which was one of his most valued possessions.

and although Mill and Place were the only two members of the school who were in constant personal intimacy with Bentham himself, Dumont, Brougham, Grote (after 1818), and others would have accepted the name Benthamite.[1] Apart from their writing and thinking, James Mill and Bentham were constantly occupied with practical projects. They used the ordinary methods of committees, subscriptions, and newspaper articles for the direct improvement of schools, and law courts, and political machinery.

In 1823 James Mill's greater son, John Stuart Mill, then seventeen years old, entered the India Office, and began his independent intellectual life. In the spring of 1824 the *Westminster Review* was founded. From 1824 John Stuart Mill, with the younger generation of Utilitarians— Charles Austin, Eyton Tooke, G. J. Graham, and others— formed the real centre of the movement. They wrote books and reviews rather than newspaper articles, and were more really interested in speculative questions than in practical politics or social work.

In the first period Place had taken his full part of the work. He had not only kept Bentham and Mill in contact with the outside world, but himself originated much of their activity. In the second movement he had little or no share. Though he could do effective work in his own way on a newspaper, he could not make himself felt in a contest carried on by the methods of deliberate high literature. If he had been a more skilled writer, or had understood better the conditions of good literary work, his chance would have come in 1824, when the Utilitarians, old and young, found themselves, rather against their will, responsible for the new *Westminster Review.* He was asked to send an article to the first number, but refused, except on condition that no alteration should be made in his work without his consent. "Mine," he said, "must be legitimate children,

---

[1] *Cf.* J. S. Mill's "Autobiography" (London, 1873), page 101.

however ugly and ungraceful they may be." [1] Bentham,
who was superintending the arrangements and providing
the money for the new *Review*, wrote him a long letter
describing and justifying editorial custom, and pointing out
that Mill's articles in the *Edinburgh Review* had been
"cut and slashed without mercy." He enclosed his letter
with a characteristic little note to Bowring, the editor.
" *Ugly or ungraceful* children we cannot adopt, nor can we
traffic in *pigs in a poke.* If you approve of my reply,
perhaps you will send it to the proud man." Three years
later Bowring seems to have accepted Place's terms, and in
July 1826 his first article appeared. Bowring was a most incompetent editor,[2] and the book sent to Place was actually a
"History of Egypt." [3] Place spent a fortnight on his article,
working nine hours a day, and conscientiously examining
such ancient Egyptian history as then existed. Bowring
did not send him a proof, and the article was miserably
misprinted. But however well it had been printed, it would
have remained inexpressibly dull and wooden. Later a
better chance was given him in an article on the " History
of Parliaments," in the form of a review of Major Cartwright's life, which was arranged for and largely written
in 1826, but appeared in October 1827.[4]

The fifty pages occupied by that article simply cannot
be read. Place had been working at Parliamentary history
ever since his visit to Ford Abbey in 1817, and three great
folios in the British Museum [5] contain his notes on the
subject. He had known the old Major well, and an inter-

---

[1] Place to Bowring, September 1823.

[2] *Cf.* J. S. Mill's "Autobiography" (London, 1873), page 97.

[3] See the *Westminster Review*, July 1826, Article VIII., pp. 158-201.
A review of *Histoire de l'Egypt sous le gouvernement de Mohammed-Alij*,
&c., par M. Felix Mengin.

[4] See the *Westminster Review*, October 1827, Article I., pp. 253-303.
A review of "The Life and Correspondence of Major Cartwright,"
edited by his niece, F. D. Cartwright.

[5] 27,853-5.

esting magazine article might be put together from the notices of Cartwright and other reformers actually contained in his papers. But the article gets no further than 1688, and consists of a pointless series of facts from original sources, put together in a style, compared with which that of Stubbs' "Constitutional History" is airy and journalistic.

The promised second instalment of the "History of Parliaments" did not appear, and Place never again succeeded in getting into print anything longer than a pamphlet or a newspaper article. Jeffrey, editor of the *Edinburgh*, wrote to Place in February 1827, that he was willing to take an article from him. "I think your article will be improved by avoiding those asperities of style in which you sometimes indulge, and which are the great blemish of the *Westminster*." [1] But the proposal does not seem to have led to anything. Again when the two Mills seceded from the *Westminster Review* in 1829, Bentham wrote to Bowring, "get Place to set matters right; he is the best man in the world." [2] Perhaps if Place had submitted patiently to the cutting and slashing of a magazine editor, he might have avoided some of those literary faults which henceforward, writing as he was without criticism or direction, steadily increased upon him. He probably could never have acquired certain habits of mind necessary for great literary success. He was absolutely wanting in humour. Writing in 1836 to Mrs. Grote, he mentions Walter Scott, and says, "I never could read even half of any one of his novels. I tasked myself to it; I tried several times at different stories; I never could succeed; I became wearied, and grew angry as often as I made the attempt." [3] And when describing his boyhood, he says, "I read Bunyan's 'Pilgrim's Progress,' and parts of·equally

---

[1] Jeffrey to Place, February 1827 (in the family autograph book).

[2] Bowring to Place, December 7, 1829 (in the family autograph book).

[3] Place to Mrs. Grote, January 8, 1836 ("Autobiography").

absurd books."[1] In the masses of notes on old plays
which he made in 1828 and 1829, he is simply concerned
to prove the increased decency of manners in his own
time, and shows no sign of feeling the poetic value of
what he reads.[2]

But the main source of his defects as a writer was the
fact that he transferred to his literary work the enormously
long hours of an artizan, and the lifeless, mechanical
"stroke" by which such hours are alone made possible.
Most of his deliberate literary work was tired work, and
the result is that his familiar notes are better than his
formal letters, and his letters better than his treatises.

But apart from his literary limitations, there were other
sufficient reasons for Place's falling out of the second stage
of the Utilitarian movement. Bentham and James Mill,
though they broke with the French revolutionary thinkers
and the whole doctrine of Natural Rights, nevertheless
retained many of the characteristic habits of eighteenth-
century thought. They believed themselves to have found
a common-sense philosophy, by which ordinary selfish men
could be convinced that the interests of each invariably
coincided with the interests, if not of all, at any rate, of the
majority. Pleasures, according to this philosophy, are all
of the same kind in so far as they are pleasures, and it
happens that the acts which secure the interests of the
majority are also the most pleasurable. Every man,
therefore, if he were reasonably well educated in his

[1] "Autobiography."
[2] Even in ordinary social intercourse his matter-of-fact seriousness
must have been sometimes rather trying. On April 20, 1826, for
instance, he walked to Rotherhithe "to see Mr. Brunel's tunnel.
Found Lord Darnley, Lady Darnley, and three other women there,
with Sir George Cunningham. They were joined by Lord Paget and
another well-dressed animal whose name I did not hear, who made a
singular discovery. On the steam-engine being named simply as the
engine, he observed that 'it must be very hard work for the engine.'
Got away, not much liking my company." (*Diary*, April 20, 1826.)

youth, would throughout the rest of his life aim at "the
greatest happiness of the greatest number," simply because
he would recognise that that was the way to gain for
himself the greatest amount of "the pleasure of self-
approbation," and because self-approbation, being pure,
contained more units of enjoyment per unit of time than
any other pleasure. This was Place's position. "The
motive to benevolence," he wrote in 1833, "is always
self-approbation. The motive in itself is neither good
nor bad; it is, however, imperative, and I obey it."[1]
"Self-approbation" is a term which can be used as a
meaningless synonym for any kind of human motive, but
if adopted in its ordinary sense as the conscious end of
human action, it is apt to produce the kind of result
which one can trace from time to time all through Place's
letters. When a man is in the mood for that kind of
enjoyment, he is encouraged by such a philosophy to indulge in a good deal of naïve self-glorification; and when
he is out of the mood, he finds it difficult to fix on a
reason for living at all. The life which Place or James
Mill actually lived was too laborious to seem worth much
if tested by the quantity of personal pleasure which they
got from it. Accordingly their prevailing habit of mind
was apt to be that which John Stuart Mill ascribes to his
father. "His standard of morals was Epicurean, inasmuch
as it was Utilitarian, taking as the exclusive test of right
and wrong the tendency of actions to produce pleasure
or pain. But he had . . . scarcely any belief in pleasure.
. . . He thought human life a poor thing at best, after
the freshness of youth and of unsatisfied curiosity had
gone by."[2]

The eighteenth-century quality in the elder Utilitarians
comes out also in their extraordinary positiveness on

---

[1] Place to Harrison, December 14, 1833.
[2] See J. S. Mill's "Autobiography" (London, 1873), page 48.

psychological and metaphysical points. In 1817 James
Mill was beginning to plan the "Analysis of the Human
Mind," which he published in 1829. "If I had time to
write a book," he says, "I would make the human mind
as plain as the road from Charing Cross to St. Paul's."[1]
A year earlier he wrote, "I am reading, at least I have
begun to read, the 'Critique of Pure Reason.' I see clearly
enough what poor Kant is about."[2]

Against this position John Stuart Mill revolted with
all his soul. His "Autobiography" describes his growing
sense of the difficulty of ultimate problems, and his growing dissatisfaction with the mere arithmetical calculation
of pleasure as the end of human existence. "I never indeed wavered," he says, "in the conviction that happiness
is the test of all rules of conduct and the end of life. But
I now thought (in 1830) that this end was only to be
attained by not making it the direct end. Those only are
happy (I thought) who have their minds fixed on some
object other than their own happiness—on the happiness
of others, on the improvement of mankind, even on some
art or pursuit, followed not as a means, but as itself an
ideal end. Aiming thus at something else, they find happiness by the way. . . . Ask yourself whether you are happy,
and you cease to be so."[3]

Place, like Mrs. Grote and the other sectarian Benthamites, was grievously disappointed at this tendency in
John Mill's writings. "I think John Mill," he wrote in 1838,
"has made great progress in becoming a German metaphysical mystic. Eccentricity and absurdity must occasionally be the result."[4]

[1] James Mill to Place, December 6, 1817.
[2] James Mill to Place, October 8, 1816 (autograph).
[3] See J. S. Mill's "Autobiography" (London, 1873), p. 142.
[4] Place to Falconer, September 2, 1838. In 1837 Mrs Grote called
him in a letter to Place, "that wayward intellectual deity" (August
16, 1837).

From Place's diary for 1826 one learns that John Mill, then twenty years old, was a frequent caller at Charing Cross. But the few letters between them which have been preserved are short, and, though friendly enough in manner, confined to business matters.

Bentham died in 1832, and Place, two years later, wrote of him as "my twenty years' friend, my good master from whom I learned I know not how much, as it spread in so many directions. He was my constant, excellent, venerable preceptor, of whom I think every day of my life, whose death I continually lament, whose memory I revere, and whose absence I deplore."[1]

James Mill died on June 23, 1836. Ten days previously Place saw him for the last time. On his return he described his visit in a letter to Mrs. Grote. "Stayed too long with poor Mill, who showed me much more sympathy and affection than ever before in all our long friendship. But he was all the time as much of a bright reasoning man as ever he was, reconciled to his fate, brave and calm to an extent which I never before witnessed, except in another old friend, Thomas Holcroft, the day before and the day of his death."[2]

[1] Place to Harrison, May 2, 1834.
[2] See "James Mill : a Biography," p. 409.

CHAPTER IV

SCHOOLS FOR ALL

" So complete was my father's reliance on the influence of reason over the mind of mankind, whenever it is allowed to reach them, that he felt as if all would be gained if the whole population were taught to read, if all sorts of opinions were allowed to be addressed to them by word and in writing, and if, by the means of the suffrage, they could nominate a legislation to give effect to the opinions they adopted." [1]

The existing system of popular education in England can be traced directly back to the formation of the Royal Lancastrian Association in 1810. In 1798 a young Quaker named Joseph Lancaster had begun to teach a few poor boys in a shed adjoining his father's house in the Borough Road. He was an enthusiastic teacher, with a good deal of personal magnetism, and he soon had more pupils than he could manage himself on the usual method. Dr. Andrew Bell had published in 1797 a pamphlet describing the " Madras System " of setting the children to teach each other.[2] This system Lancaster copied or reinvented, and soon formed vague plans of covering all England with schools, in each of which a thousand children should be taught in squads of ten by a hundred monitors. He believed, and induced others to believe, that this could be done at an annual cost of not more than five shillings per head. But he had more than the

[1] See J. S. Mill, " Autobiography," p. 106.
[2] See " An Experiment in Education, made at the Male Asylum of Madras," &c., by Andrew Bell, D.D., &c. (London, 1797).

usual allowance of the faults of the enthusiastic temperament, and within a few years found himself heavily
in debt and obliged to issue a public appeal for funds.
Place read this appeal in 1804, found time to visit the
school, and "having examined the teacher and seen
the mode of teaching practised," became a subscriber
of half a guinea monthly.[1] Unfortunately Lancaster, after
his success in collecting funds, became still more extravagant, and by 1807 owed £4000, and was in momentary
danger of arrest. From this he was saved by Joseph Fox,
a rich Quaker dentist. Fox paid Lancaster's debts, and
persuaded William Allen, Joseph Forster, and others of the
"Saints" to become trustees. By 1810 they had formed
the Royal Lancastrian Association, on the committee of
which the names of James Mill, Henry Brougham, and
Samuel Rogers appear among a number of Quaker philanthropists and Nonconformist ministers. Lancaster travelled
up and down the country lecturing on his principles; many
Lancastrian schools were founded; and the Church party in
1811 formed the "National Society for the Education of
the Poor in the Principles of the Established Church," with
the avowed object of bringing the growing movement under
safe control.[2] Lancaster, however, soon quarrelled with
the trustees, and, in 1812, set up against their wish a
middle-class boarding school in Tooting. Here he was
more reckless than ever, and when he became bankrupt in
1813, it was found that he had spent £8000 in the previous
four years. Place had a son at the Tooting school, and relates
that Lancaster "sometimes kept one and sometimes two
carriages. He seldom went from home but in a carriage,
and generally had some of his lads in one or two post-
chaises following him; and, as if to waste his time, indulge his love of ostentation and squander the money of
other people, he used to take excursions in the manner

[1] 27,823 (8).   [2] Cf. 27,823 (6).

described to some distance, dine sumptuously, and of course expensively, and return home in the evening. Sometimes these excursions occupied two or three days."[1]

Place gave him much good advice, and for a time vainly attempted to make peace between him and the trustees. After the failure of this attempt, Place took part in the disagreeable arrangements by which Lancaster was pensioned off with the title of Superintendent, and the Royal Lancastrian Association became in 1813 the British and Foreign School Society. Place had already for two years been an intimate friend of James Mill, was "reputed rich," and well known to be an excellent man of business; so that when the Society was reconstructed he was put upon the new committee, and managed to find time for a great deal of work. In January 1814 he writes to his friend Wakefield: "Indeed, I never was so intensely occupied in my life as I have been lately with the two (school) committees, the statute of Elizabeth,[2] closing, balancing, and making out my yearly bills and accounts, and in addition to my usual business fitting out the Dutch officers at Yarmouth to take the field, or rather the mud-banks, of Holland to defend William the First at the expense of their own liberties."[3] His constant fear was that the Lancastrian schools might become instruments of social oppression by being connected with the idea of "charity."[4] For this reason, in drawing up the by-laws for the British and Foreign Society on its formation, he "wholly omitted the words 'poor' and 'labouring poor,'" which had hitherto been employed, "and took special care that" there should be no phrase in "them which could give offence or hurt the feelings of any one."[5] And with the same object he tried to persuade the committee

[1] 27,823 (18, 19).
[2] *i.e.* the Statute of Apprentices, repealed in 1814.
[3] Place to Wakefield, January 2, 1814.
[4] Wakefield to Place, December 7, 1813.   [5] 27,823 (22).

that those parents who were able to do so should be made
to pay a penny a week for the education of each child.

From the first, Wakefield, Place, Mill, and Brougham,
"who," Place says, "is one of the few who see the whole
scope and extent of what it may lead to,"[1] were bent on
nothing less than the organisation of a complete system
of primary and secondary education, at any rate for London.
With regard to primary education, the plan was that the
central institution in the Borough Road should be used
exclusively for the work of training schoolmasters and
mistresses, and that London should be divided into districts, to be controlled by independent school committees.
Place says that with this view "the whole of London
south of the Thames was to be organised somewhat on the
plan of the Bible Society, and a penny a week subscription
was to be pressed in every direction. When the plan was
digested and quite complete, a public general meeting of
the inhabitants was to be called, at which the Royal Dukes,
several noblemen, and a large number of influential inhabitants were to be induced, as could then have been done, to
attend. This meeting was to have been followed by meetings in as many districts as it might be found advisable to
divide this portion of the Metropolis into. I wrote out the
plan carefully, omitting nothing which I thought was at
all likely to be useful. I procured the sheets of Howard's
large plan of London, and having divided the portions
intended to be operated upon according to population into
a number of nearly equal parts, I coloured and hung it up
in the committee room."[2]

In 1813 the West London Lancastrian Association was
formed on Wakefield's suggestion, to arrange for the western
half of London north of the Thames. Districts were allotted
for the inspection of various members, and Wakefield drew

[1] Place to Wakefield, February 20, 1814.
[2] 27,823 (23).

up a valuable report on the educational and social condition of the Drury Lane district, which was afterwards
printed by Brougham's Education Committee in 1816. He
had the idea, of which Mr. Charles Booth has since made
such brilliant use, that if permanent educational visitors
were appointed for all London a thorough collection of
social statistics might be made.[1]

The motto of the West London Lancastrian Association
was the exhilarating phrase, "Schools for All," and every
now and then a note of joyful expectation breaks through
the practical strain of Place's letters. In writing to Allen,
for instance, he speaks of the "health and beauty," the
"mass of intellect" that he had observed in the Lancastrian schools, "which, if properly managed, would
reflect the greatest credit on the country, and all but
infinitely promote the happiness of the rising generation."[2]

[1] Wakefield's proposal was as follows : "The account you give me,"
he says, "is excellent. But let me impress upon you to place each
section under permanent inspection. Many useful queries might be
added to those of the W. L. L. A., particularly to examine whether the
heads of a wretched family can read and write. Do not by any means
allow the books of those sections which I have visited to be considered
as an example—they are not half filled up. A school once established,
and a detailed account of every labouring family shall be furnished to
the Association. The statement of the celebrated Lipsmitch in his
'Divine Ordinances,' that the rate of life in London is of shorter duration than in any great town in Europe, has long been with me an object
of inquiry. Now, if *permanent* visitors can be paid for the whole of
London we shall ascertain the truth of this assertion, and, if possible,
develop the cause, without a knowledge of which a remedy cannot be
proposed, much less applied." (Wakefield to Place, January 6, 1814.)
[2] 27,823 (67). With this letter Place forwarded to Allen three
specimens of illustrated reading lessons, dealing with the commoner
tools, &c., very much on the lines of the illustrated "Readers" now
used in the lower standards of elementary schools. Allen replied
strongly approving, and saying that the lessons were like the Dutch
school-books, and were in "the manner in which Pestalozzi goes to
work." But they were never used, and one of the committee told
Place that "it had been decided privately that no lesson, unless it
was taken from the Scripture, could be laid before the committee."
27,808 (72).

At the same time, Place and his friends were equally
keen in promoting a system of Lancastrian higher schools.
This was Place's own proposal. He had at this time nine
children alive, and it was a matter of serious difficulty for
him to secure for them such education as he desired, at an
expense no greater than he could afford. Writing, in 1833,
of this period, he says: "It was my intention to change,
and had I succeeded in establishing a superior school it
would, I am persuaded, have changed the whole system of
teaching. All the large towns throughout the country
would have set up similar schools, and have produced
incalculable advantages. Some years hence, when the
exertions which have been made, and are still being made,
to increase the desire of men in the middle ranks of life to
have their children properly educated, shall have succeeded, it will scarcely be believed how difficult, not to
say impossible, it was for any man who could not afford
to pay a very large sum of money to procure an adequate
education for his children. I do not mean a merely
classical education, i.e. the rudiments, or very little more
than the rudiments, of Greek and Latin, and some of the
elements of mathematics, which is all that nine in every
ten of those who are classically educated obtain; but I
mean besides these rudiments something more than the
mere elements of mathematics, modern languages, political
economy, politics, and morals, including the broad and
comprehensive doctrine of motives.

"I have never yet been able to find any school, either in
or out of the Metropolis, in which, at an expense within the
amount which an ordinary tradesman is able to pay, he
can have his sons taught as he wishes they should be
taught, or even as persons in inferior stations in Scotland
are taught, defective even as that education is. It was
this knowledge which first induced me to think of the
application of Joseph Lancaster's system to the purpose of

educating the children of those who having comparatively
small means are yet desirous of giving a really useful education to their children."[1] Wakefield took up the idea
eagerly: Mill, "from the first moment the plan was mentioned, heartily concurred in it."[2] He "goes into it most
heartily," says Place elsewhere, "and consents to assist in
procuring money, &c.:"[3] and Wakefield adds that "Mill is
always at work, but never shows himself."[4] Bentham also
"came heartily into the project," . . . and offered his garden
at Queen's Square Place for the site of the school.[5] The
group of friends were immensely cheered by hearing that
the monitorial system had already been applied with success
to secondary education in Scotland. Place's second daughter
Annie had just gone to be governess in a family in Edinburgh. She mentioned her father's plan to Mr. Gray, one
of the masters of the Edinburgh High School, who thereupon wrote to Wakefield to say that he had practised the
Lancastrian method in teaching Latin and Greek for the
last two years, and that it had met with "the most distinguished success. I . . . had no conception of the advantages to be derived from it till I fairly made the experiment. I believe it to be equally applicable whether the
numbers be great or small, and in teaching every branch
of human knowledge. In my own case it has converted a
laborious and often an irksome profession into the most
easy and delightful employment possible. . . . Instead of
that inattention, drowsiness, and even insubordination that
too frequently prevail at the bottom of large classes in the
old way, all is activity, cheerfulness, and prompt obedience:

[1] 27,823 (135).   [2] 27,823 (144).
[3] Place to Wakefield, February 20, 1814.
[4] Wakefield to Place, December 7, 1813. In a letter to Colonel
Jones, written some years later, Place says, "Mr. James Mill . . .
wrote the memorable and admirable essay, 'Schools for All, not
Schools for Churchmen only.'" See 27,824 (349).
[5] 27,823 (144).

. . . no boy becomes incorrigibly idle, because he is kept
in employment, conquers every difficulty, and soon begins
to love his labour."[1] Gray was at once urged to give fuller
details, and in reply wrote a long and enthusiastic description of his experiences, which was copied, circulated, and
finally published. Soon afterwards Place heard that
the plan had also been successfully tried in the academy
at Perth, and Fox received an enthusiastic letter from
Pillans, the Rector of the Edinburgh High School, describing its good effect in his own class. The monitorial
system is now amply discredited, but one can imagine
that it was, at any rate, better than the dreadful old
method, whereby, for hours together, one boy at a time
translated, while two hundred played. It was, indeed, the
first serious attempt in England to think out any system
of class-teaching whatsoever. The master who in those
early years adopted the Lancastrian system, did really try
to provide, in Lancaster's words, "every boy with something to do, and a motive for doing it," and when Gray or
Pillans wrote about the delightfulness of the new system,
they were thinking, not only of the practice by which the
elder boys heard the repetition lessons of the younger, but
of the rapid fire of question and answer between the boys
and the master in the succeeding lesson, the use of the
blackboard in teaching geography, and that general in-
ventiveness in devising expedients and arousing interest,
which the new system seemed to encourage, and the old
had made impossible.[2]

Place and Wakefield recognised the danger as well as
the expense of great boarding-schools, and advocated
higher day-schools, where boys should receive " the advantages which are to be derived from the learning of a
master, and the emulation which results from the society

[1] James Gray to Wakefield, December 17, 1813.
[2] 27,823 (67).

of other boys, together with the affectionate vigilance experienced in the house of their parents." [1] In a letter to
William Allen, [2] Place suggests that these higher schools
should be used to give the young teachers from the Borough
Road some years of secondary education before they began
their professional life, and that evening-classes for adults and
apprentices should be held on the school premises. " I do
not believe," he says elsewhere, " there is at the present
time a single carpenter in this great metropolis who possesses any practical geometry." [3] The actual curriculum
proposed for the higher Lancastrian schools was largely
borrowed from the systematic treatise on Chrestomathia
(*i.e.* Useful Education), at which Bentham was then working; but Place's notes to Bentham's first draft, in June
1814, show that here too he was thinking for himself.
He proposes that mineralogy should be taught by diagrams and specimens, and hints that Bentham might
help William Smith, who is " unable to go to press unless
he can obtain assistance," in bringing out that geological
map which was afterwards to prove the real beginning
of systematic geology in England. He asks very per-
tinently whether more than two cases of English nouns,
except the personal pronouns, should be taught, and urges
the necessity of making boys constantly observe and even
handle geometrical forms in order to enable them to overcome the difficulty in turning their thoughts from number
to dimension, to which he refers in his account of his own
youth. [4] Nor did he overlook the educational value of
games, though he did not realise that a game which is
partly a lesson is neither a good game nor a good lesson.
" It is as necessary," he wrote, "for boys to play together,
as it is that they should be taught together. It is
therefore intended if possible to provide a space large

---

enough for this purpose, in which their games may
be made more attractive and more useful than they
have hitherto been ; where new ones may be introduced :
and thus their very amusements out of school may be
made to conduce to their improvement, and their morals
made much more conducive to their happiness, by
teaching them, as it were, in a little world of their own,
patience, forbearance, and kindness to one another. I see
no reason why their games should not be made the means
of instruction, of calling to remembrance the instruction
they have received. Nothing can be more easy, nothing
more pleasant. The boy who plays at marbles may as well
draw a map as a ring, and by shooting at a marble placed
on Dublin, recollect that by striking it under a certain
angle he will place his ' taw ' in a situation to attack
another marble placed on Cork, or Limerick, or Belfast.
In playing at fives, what should prevent him driving his
ball against the belt of Orion, or the tail of the Bear; and
why may not other games be invented equally entertaining
and instructing ? " [1]

Above all, he dwelt on the social value of a real education. If the leisured classes could be taught to *think*,
Place was convinced that enough social feeling could be
created among them to result in effective action. " I appeal
to your own experience," he wrote in the letter to William
Allen already quoted. " How few are there on whom you
can rely for active co-operation in promoting the happiness
of the people ! Your connection is principally among those
whose rank is at the top of the middle class, who, enjoying
wealth and leisure, might be expected to possess the disposition to do the greatest service to humanity, with the
knowledge necessary to give full effect to their disposition.
But is this so ? Alas, it is not so, and it cannot be expected to exist in any great quantity as we descend ! Why

[1] 27,823 (153).

is this? Plainly because of ignorance; people do not see
how much is in their power; they doubt their own ability
to effect any real and permanent good on a large scale, and
they therefore attribute the evils they have no hope of
removing to the very constitution of society. They would
remove the evils they are constantly obliged to witness,
but unable to contemplate the possibility of accomplishing
their wishes, they endeavour to get rid of uneasy sensations
by trying to forget them, and by continued efforts to free
themselves from them they stifle the best feelings of their
nature, become morose, and disqualify themselves from
the performance of any good whatever; or they relieve
themselves by the performance of what is vulgarly called
charity; they give money, victuals, clothes, &c., and thus
by encouraging idleness and extinguishing enterprise, increase the evils they would remove."[1]

With regard to the monitorial system, Place was no
wiser than his generation. He conceived of it not as a
necessary makeshift in the absence of trained masters
and of money to pay them, but as the best method possible. He quotes with approval Gray's statement that
" boys are better qualified to teach boys than men."[2] In
the "proposals"[3] for a higher Lancastrian school which

---

[1] 27,823 (149, 150). [2] *Cf.* 27,823 (140, 141).

[3] " Proposals for Establishing in the Metropolis a Day School in
which an example may be set of the application of the Methods of Dr.
Bell, Mr. Lancaster, and others, to the higher branches of Education"
(London, 1815), 16 pp. 8vo. Republished 1816 and 1817, with lists of
subscribers, &c., added. Copies of all three editions are preserved in
27,823 (211–235). Place has left the following account of the authorship
of these Proposals : " Mr. Mill returned to town with Mr. Bentham
early in the month of February 1815, Mr. Bentham bringing with him
his ' Chrestomathia' ; and as Mr. Mill and I had reason to believe that
he would attempt to draw up proposals as a prospectus for the intended
school, we set about preparing such proposals as we thought would
sufficiently explain the purpose, and be likely to induce persons to join
us. We were quite certain from what we knew of Mr. Bentham's habit
of endeavouring to exhaust almost everything he took in hand, that the

Place and James Mill drew up in 1815, it is distinctly
declared that "when the boys who are trained in the
school have made sufficient progress to perform the duties
of upper monitors in all the stages of instruction, no ushers,
it is presumed, will be required." [1]

In 1814 the idea that a school building should be specially
constructed for its purpose was valuable, and if not new, at
least newly discovered. But the design of the proposed
Chrestomathic school,[2] as drawn by an architect under
Place's supervision, is such that no good teaching could possibly have been given there. In February 1814 Place had
written to Wakefield, "Mr. Bentham has sent me his books
on the construction of Panopticons and the plates—I shall
read them most carefully." [3] The "books on the construction of Panopticons" [4] were the mass of controversy that
resulted in the creation of Millbank Prison as the one
material memorial of Bentham's genius, and the ground
plan of the new school has a certain resemblance to that
dreary syllogism in brick. It was intended that the building should consist of a single huge polygonal room, with

drawing up of proposals if left to him would terminate in a goodly-
sized pamphlet, if not in a volume. I therefore made notes of what I
considered the principal points necessary to convey a knowledge of our
purpose, and the reasons for each note. From these Mr. Mill and I
composed a paper, which we caused to be printed as 'Proposals,' &c.,
leaving a space in page 13 for the names of the managers when they
should be obtained. This paper was by Mr. Bentham considered as
adequate to the purpose intended, and these Proposals are the papers
commented on by Mr. Bentham in appendix to his 'Chrestomathia,'
printed anonymously in the summer of 1815. . . .

" In 1817 Mr. Bentham republished his 'Chrestomathia' with a new
title-page, on which his name appeared. It was now twice the size in
which it first appeared, having Part II. attached to it, containing what
Mr. Bentham called Appendix V." 27,823 (182, 183).

[1] See the "Proposals" preserved in 27,823 (211-218).
[2] See Bentham's papers on "Chrestomathia" (London, 1815, 1816,
1817, &c.).
[3] Place to Wakefield, February 20, 1814.
[4] See Bentham's "Panopticon, or the Inspection House" (London,
1791), 2 vols., and other papers.

nine concentric rows of desks, divided into blocks by passages leading to the centre; at the centre point the master
was to sit on a revolving chair, "so that he may turn himself round and see every part of the school without rising."
Place even contemplated complacently the fearful din
which would result from monitorial education carried on
under one vast sounding-board. " A boy," he wrote, "who
has been taught to think accurately on one subject only,
amidst discordant noises, without having his attention
drawn off from the subject, has acquired a power of no
ordinary kind." [1]

Even in 1816, when giving evidence before Brougham's
commission, Place seems to have had no more conception
than any one else that Lancaster's method may have helped
to produce that persuasion among parents which he there
laments, that their children in elementary schools "play,
and learn nothing." [2]

But in 1814 a recognition of the limitations of the monitorial system would have been simply one more obstacle
to Place's harmonious working with the other members of
the British and Foreign School Society, and there were
obstacles enough as it was. Most of the rich Quakers
who provided the current funds, and to whom the Society
was heavily in debt, were earnest adherents of evangelical
orthodoxy. Place used to horrify them by using the word
"infidel" as the commonly accepted name for his own
opinions and those of his friends. The British and Foreign
Society had a rule that no reading lesson whatever should
be given except from the Bible. This, by the influence
of Place and Mill, was dropped from the declarations of
principles of the West London Lancastrian Association,
and a statement substituted that "of religious books,

[1] 27,823 (133).
[2] See Place's evidence before the Select Committee of the House of
Commons on Education in the Metropolis, 1816 [June 13].

the Bible alone, without gloss or comment, written or spoken, will be read."[1] At the same time, the rule of the parent society, that all children were to be taken to some place of worship on Sundays, was also omitted. Joseph Fox was the secretary of both societies. Place at first did his best to keep on good terms with him; but by January 1814 he had lost patience, and wrote to Wakefield about Fox: "I would willingly he should take the credit of everything—I care not who has it; but I do not like this accommodation to the dispositions of other men: it is damned hypocrisy. He shall keep all he has obtained of me in this way, but I will practise on him no longer. I have missed many points because I would not gain them by these means, and I will never gain another by them."[2]

In March Fox wrote a long and querulous letter to Place, urging that his drafts should be printed just as he wrote them, and adding that "to write merely to have the very pith and marrow of one's ideas picked out, is what I cannot submit to. Confidence has been placed in Mr. Allen and me in our other quarter, and we have acted as the occasion demanded;"[3] to which Place replied, declining to cease exercising his rights as a member of the committee.[4]

From that time forward Fox steadily ignored the recommendations of committees when he did not agree with them, and pledged the funds of the societies in the most intolerably irresponsible fashion. Everything was justified by a reference to that Inner Light which is the strength and weakness of Quakerism. Place complained indignantly. "The notions he himself formed he succeeded in persuading himself were ordinances of God: and as he thus made his own personal purposes holy, every means

[1] 27,823 (97).   [2] Place to Wakefield, January 2, 1814.
[3] Fox to Place, March 26, 1814.
[4] See Place to Fox, March 27, 1814.

was fair for their accomplishment. . . . His sanctity did
not prevent him being liberal or mean or ostentatious, or
valiant or cowardly, or civil or insolent, for he was one
or the other as suited his purpose, or as he was impelled
by his feelings, or his fears or his hopes." [1]

In March 1814 a small committee was appointed to
investigate an unsavoury scandal about Lancaster. The
evidence against him was conclusive, and he only avoided
certain dismissal by resigning his post of superintendent.
In his letter of resignation he deliberately, and with some
success, set himself to turn the religious members of the
society against Place, whom he calls "a professed adversary
of the sacred writings," "a firebrand of discord," and refers
to as among "those who profess infidel opinions, and boast
of having been leaders and founders of the London Corresponding Society." [2] The intolerant section of the committee, led by Fox, saw an opportunity of attacking Place,
and a special meeting was called at Kensington Palace.
Place attended the meeting, and has left a description of
the concourse of Quakers and dissenting ministers who
always flocked to those meetings which were called at the
Palace, and of Hume, who, every time either of the dukes
spoke to him, kept "bowing his unwieldy, because unmanageable, body as awkwardly as an elephant might be
supposed to do." [3] The Duke of Kent opened the meeting,
and having referred to Lancaster's charges, paused, evidently waiting for a reply. Place, however, being determined not to speak, an embarrassing silence followed. "I
had no desire," says Place, "to embarrass the Duke, who
always behaved in the kindest and best possible manner;
but my course had been taken, and I was resolved not to
depart from it." After a delay, the Duke was about to
proceed further on the subject, when "Mr. Whitbread, in a
hurried manner, and in an undertone, interrupted him by

[1] 27,823 (45).   [2] 27,823 (29-31).   [3] 27,823 (36).

saying, 'Let him alone; let him alone.'" The Duke took
the cue, and said that, as Lancaster had behaved badly
and deserted the Institution, the best way was to dismiss
his letter entirely. " Mr. Whitbread said ' Certainly;' upon
which the Duke of Sussex, who was always good-humoured,
but seldom discreet, called out across the table to me,
' Prosecute him, Place! Prosecute him, Place !' I said
very calmly, 'I never prosecute anybody for what they
say respecting me. I have no personal enmity to Joseph
Lancaster, and he, like every one else, may say what he
pleases of me. What he has said which is true, he is quite
at liberty to say; and for what he has said which is not
true, I care nothing.' Thus terminated this mighty affair." [1]

A more serious incident occurred a few months later,
when, as already described, Sir Francis Burdett denounced
Place as a Government spy,[2] and called for his dismissal from
the West London Lancastrian Association. Against the
advice of Mill and Wakefield, Place now resigned his position
in a society where he believed that he could no longer
be of any use. His formal resignation was conveyed in a
letter in July, but he did not at once cease his work on the
central British and Foreign Committee. Here he had
two main objects—to introduce such a system of accounts
as should give the committee some real control over its
officers, and to put the school in the Borough Road
on a business-like and economical footing. It had now
become a resident training college for the Lancaster
schools throughout the country. But Lancaster's original
idea that it was to be a free school, where the poorest of
poor children should be taught reading and writing and
the printing trade, still affected the management. A ridiculously expensive printing business was carried on in connection with the school. No sufficient attempt was made
to select the children who were taken into the schools, and

[1] 27,823 (36-40).　　　　[2] Cf. p. 56.

the monitors were boarded, lodged, and clothed, though many of them were obviously unfit to become teachers. Place forced Fox to confess that two boys who had just been sent to Edinburgh had cost the institution upwards of £500 each. He then proceeded to argue " that so far from its being necessary for us to take ignorant, ill-bred boys and girls to be trained at an enormous expense, there were plenty of decent, respectable people who would be glad to send their sons and daughters to have them taught the system, on the chance of their being appointed to schools, without any expense to us, and that the boys and girls so sent would come better educated in other respects than any one ever had been educated in the institution, and would, as to manners, be greatly to be preferred."[1] He was anxious as far as possible to avoid a quarrel. Furious as he often was with Fox, yet he pitied his mental sufferings, and had been in spite of the differences of their creeds originally on terms of intimate friendship with him. For William Allen, "good William Allen" as he called him, he always retained a sincere and deep affection, and he admitted that the two men had saved the Lancastrian system. "They had kept it from being extinguished; they had carried it on for six years, certainly expensively and absurdly, yet to some extent with their own money." But the hard fact remained that in the year ending November 10, 1814, £2950 contributed by outside subscribers had been expended, "and yet all that the committee which expended the money did, was furnishing not more than six teachers to other schools (at a cost of £1200) and maintaining two free day-schools, which did not together contain more than 350 boys and girls."[2]

Place failed in this as he failed, for the time, in all his educational schemes. From the beginning he had recog-

---

[1] 27,823 (44–45).
27,823 (47, 48) ; *cf.* also Place to Wakefield, October 7, 1814.

nised how rare was that social enthusiasm which formed
the guiding principle of his own life and those of his
friends, and how weak a force it constituted as compared
with religion or self-interest, or even vanity. In March
1814 he had written to Wakefield: "With what ease you
talk of 3000 shares at £10 each and of two large committees! You will procure neither. There is no political
éclat, no crawling to the great, no ostentation with which
the great may please themselves, no fashion, no reversion
in heaven to be purchased, and wanting all these things,
there remains nothing but an enlarged view of things and
virtue enough to cause activity. Whether there be more
of these than just enough to allow us to crawl on, I very
much doubt. You know how few there are who pursue
the thing from right principles, and how inefficient all
others are."[1] Nevertheless to the end of the year he kept
steadily on with his scheme of reconstruction. Joseph
Hume was on his side; and Mill writes in October to say
that Brougham has told William Allen that he would
"blow up the whole Lancastrian concern if he should find
a tendency for converting it into an instrument of bigotry
and superstition."[2] But Hume despaired of success, and
Brougham never kept his promise of support. There were,
however, other parties on the committee, and Place, in
December 1814, describes in a letter to Mill how he had
walked home arm-in-arm between two dissenting ministers
who hated Fox, and "would be well pleased to get rid of
him in any way, and for what do you think? why, to
make a missionary society of it, to send out preachers all
over the three kingdoms to preach for it. . . . Precious
hypocrites these. Only think of those two lugging hold of
my arms and cramming their nonsense into me that I may
fight Fox for their purpose."[3]

[1] Place to Wakefield, March 25, 1814.
[2] James Mill to Place, October 14, 1814.
[3] Place to James Mill, December 10, 1814.

In the end Place did succeed in converting a majority of the committee to his plan, when Allen and Fox announced that they would resign if the vote of the committee was acted upon. They could of course sell up the whole institution at any moment; Place, therefore, rather than destroy what good was being done, ceased to attend the meetings, and in the summer of 1815 his name was removed by Fox from the committee.

Meanwhile the West London Lancastrian Association was practically dead. The school which the Association had hired from the parent society was given back, and rules insisting on the Bible only being read and on compulsory church-attendance were adopted. Fox, who had killed the scheme, rejoiced over his own zeal in the cause of religion, and called the Association an "abortion." Place, in a letter to Brougham, retorts that "any fool can do mischief, because any fool can by sympathy excite the bad passions in his fellow-fools, and thus Fox has been enabled to triumph." [1]

The further history of the Chrestomathic Higher School project is easily told. Money, in spite of Place's efforts, came in very slowly. The estimated cost of the school building was about £4000, and by 1817 only £2500 had been provided. But the estimate was calculated on the assumption that Bentham would carry out his promise to allow the school to be built in his garden, and already, in October 1817, Mill wrote that although Bentham's "eagerness" to have the school in his garden "was originally very great," and he was still "quite keen," yet it was becoming evident that he would not continue to like the idea, and that "there are a multitude of disagreeables connected with it of which he will not at present allow himself to think, but which will swell into great objections hereafter." [2] This prophecy was exactly fulfilled. Bentham

[1] Place to Brougham, November 23, 1814.   [2] 27,823 (181).

imposed harder and harder conditions, and in 1820, after
an enormous correspondence, his offer of a site was finally
declined, and the project was given up.

Three years later Place saw another chance of educational work in the proposal to found a London Mechanics'
Institute, made by his friend Hodgskin in 1823. He had
now handed over the shop at Charing Cross to his son
and was able for some weeks in the autumn of 1823 to
give "the whole of his time, from morning to night," to
the work of hunting up Trade Union secretaries and
"houses of call," drafting rules and circulars, or collecting
subscriptions from his political acquaintances.[1] By February 1825 he had collected over £1500 out of the £2000
which had then been contributed. There were, of course,
the usual difficulties. The working-men suspected that
the Institute would be controlled by their employers for
their own purposes, and passed a resolution on one occasion
against any request being made for donations to the building fund. On the other hand, possible donors were often
equally suspicious. Place gives, for instance, an account of
an interview with Lord Grosvenor (afterwards Marquis of
Westminster). "He said he had a strong desire to assist
the institution, but he had also some apprehension that
the education the people were getting would make them
discontented with the Government. I said the whole mass
of the people *were* discontented with the Government, and
that although teaching them would not remove their discontent, it would make them less disposed to turbulence."
. . . He said, "True, but *we* must take care of ourselves."[2]
In the result he gave nothing. The London Mechanics' Institute was, however, more successful than the Chrestomathic
school. At the first set of lectures, in March 1824, Place
writes to Burdett, describing his joy at seeing "from 800
to 900 clean, respectable-looking mechanics paying most

[1] 27,823 (244, 245).   [2] 27,823 (278).

marked attention" to a lecture on chemistry.[1]   As years went on the Institute, under Dr. Birkbeck's superintendence, steadily developed; and at this moment, under the name of the "Birkbeck," it is one of the most useful educational agencies in London.[2]

[1] Place to Sir F. Burdett, May 1, 1824. 27,823 (337).

[2] Place states that his own name never appeared in print in connection with the Institute, but in the report of the first anniversary dinner it is mentioned that his health was drunk as one of the founders of the institution, the chairman describing him "as a most useful auxiliary in the formation of the Society." See the Report preserved in 27,824 (55).

CHAPTER V

WESTMINSTER POLITICS, 1815-30

ON July 15, 1815, Napoleon surrendered at Rochefort, and the long war which had covered the whole of Place's political life was at an end. Peace, however, brought with it social conditions even worse than those which had resulted from war prices and war taxation. From the beginning of 1816 England was visited by an unexampled stagnation of trade. " The poor," said Brand in the House of Commons on March 28, 1816, " in many cases have abandoned their own residences. Whole parishes have been deserted, and the crowd of paupers increasing in numbers as they go from parish to parish, spread wider and wider this awful desolation." [1] In May came the agricultural hunger riots at Ely. In July there were " distress meetings " attended by the royal dukes and the magnates of the Church. The trade depression was followed by one of the worst of recorded harvests. " The state of the weather and crops," wrote James Mill to Place on August 26, 1816, " alarms me. There will be no flour in the ear, no work for the people, and scarcity will produce an amount of misery which the heart aches to think of. How many a lovely child and meritorious man and woman will perish in all the miseries of want! A curse—a tenfold curse upon the villains by whom such scenes are prepared." On October 2 Place wrote to Mill: " London is in a sad state ; there are more people unemployed than was ever known at the same time of the year, and many more

[1] Hansard, vol. xxxiii. p. 671.

114

will soon be dismissed. The ensuing winter will be dreadful. Four-fifths of all the tailors are out of work, and the remaining fifth, though they pay a shilling a day out of their wages, cannot save the mass from starving. They are actually starving, and many of them must perish from want of food."

Next year, on June 4, 1817, Place wrote to Thomas Hodgskin in Italy: "What you say of the miseries on the north-eastern side of Italy may be nearly paralleled by some places in England. Take, as an example, that Mr. Wakefield travelling with another person from Worcester towards Wales overtook many groups of distressed people; and upon inquiry where they were going, was told that they had heard of workers being wanted in Wales, and were going thither. They were composed of young and middle-aged men, who were so worn with hunger that many of them could hardly walk. He and his friend gave a shilling to each group, which amounted to eighteen shillings. Hundreds have died, thousands will die of starvation. Comparing the quantity of business done now with the quantity done four years ago, I do not believe that more than one-third of the people can find constant employment."

As long as the war lasted any resistance to the Government had been of necessity local and spasmodic. A Radical member might be elected for Westminster, or a few country labourers might burn ricks or break machines, but any attempt at a national agitation for a political object could always be put down by the cry of treason. With the peace, however, came the first signs of a general democratic movement. In the winter of 1814–15, during the few months between the first Peace of Paris and the Hundred Days, old Major Cartwright formed an association called the Hampden Club, and in April 1815 sent printed petitions all over England for signature, asking for annual parliaments, equal electoral districts, and the suffrage for all direct taxpayers.[1]

In the following year the movement came into the much more capable hands of William Cobbett. In November 1815 Cobbett lowered the price of his *Political Register* from a shilling and a halfpenny to twopence. The " Two-penny Trash," as it came to be called, at once acquired an enormous influence, and through it Cobbett, with his friend " Orator Hunt," began to crystallise the widespread discontent into a definite demand for parliamentary reform.

In the national agitation of 1816–17 Place took little part. He was, till the summer of 1817, still engaged with his business, and his leisure was largely given to that enormous mass of reading which the note-books for those years record. When in 1814 his associates in West-minster countenanced the charge that he was a Govern-ment spy,[2] he had determined to withdraw from open political work, and to this determination he kept as long as he could. Writing of December 1814 he says : " I was now freed from all connection with public politics. In this state I intended to remain, not inactive, not useless. . . . With Mr. Brooks and his coadjutors all co-operation was at an end. . . . I visited nobody. I was, as I have always been, desirous to promote and willing to assist in measures likely to increase the knowledge of the com-monalty, and ready therefore to co-operate with any man or any body of men for this desirable and important object. But I did not intend to mix again in politics beyond writing occasionally in a newspaper, or consulting and advising privately with particular persons."[3] His whole temperament was opposed to the loose-tongued vituperation, the reckless use of second-hand facts, the

[1] 27,809 (8) ; *cf.* also *ante,* p. 62.   [2] See p. 56.
[3] 27,809 (5).

appeals to every form of unthinking prejudice, which were the tools of Cobbett's trade.[1] Indeed, wherever Place mentions Cobbett it is generally with some phrase like " impudent mountebank "[2] or " unprincipled cowardly bully."[3]

The agitation carried on by Cobbett and Hunt from 1816 to 1819 was addressed to the working-classes only, and aimed at separating them entirely from the whole body of well-to-do politicians. Place believed that such a separation must of necessity lead to failure. Cobbett, he says, was " too ignorant to see that the common people must ever be imbecile . . . when not encouraged and supported by others who have money and influence."[4]

In the spring of 1816 Place seems to have thought that the " money and influence " of those Whig Radicals who had drawn their political ideas to some extent from Bentham might be used to help the Reformers in Westminster. Of these, Henry Brougham was by far the ablest, and Place hoped that Brougham might be induced to separate himself from the regular Whig opposition.[5]

---

[1] Place first met Cobbett after the Westminster election of 1807, and the two remained pretty good friends for some years. In January 1810 Cobbett was prosecuted for an article in the *Register* against flogging in the army, and Place helped with the preparation of his defence. He describes how, when they met at the Crown Office to arrange for the picking of the jury, Cobbett "sprung from his chair, threw his hands above his head, and paced the room damning and blasting the Attorney-General." At the trial " he made a long defence, a bad defence, and his delivery of it and his demeanour were even worse than his matter. He was not at all master of himself, and in some parts where he meant to produce great effect he produced laughter. So ludicrous was he in one part that the jury, the judge, and the audience all laughed at him. I was thoroughly ashamed of him, and ashamed of myself for being seen with him. . . . I never saw Cobbett but once after his trial. He called on me in a few days, but I was unable to congratulate him on any part of his conduct. I never spoke to him afterwards." (" Autobiography.")

[2] Article in *Artisan's Newspaper*.

[3] 27,809 (17).   [4] 27,809 (17).

[5] " I wished that Mr. Brougham might be detached from the faction and make common cause with the Reformers," 27,809 (26).

Cochrane's father, Lord Dundonald, was ill, and in the event of his death Cochrane would vacate his seat by becoming a Scotch Peer. No one had been suggested for the seat except Major Cartwright, "who was utterly incompetent, and for whom the electors would not vote."[1] On March 20, 1816, Brougham made a speech in the House on the Salaries of the two Secretaries of the Admiralty, which greatly offended Ministers and as greatly pleased the Reformers. "I was pleased with it,[2] and on the 23rd wrote a letter to him encouraging him to proceed in the course he had at length taken. . . . I was desirous Brougham should if possible be kept up to the mark with a view to his becoming member for Westminster."[3] "Some pains were taken to ascertain if he could be relied upon to maintain the right of the people to annual parliaments, and suffrage as extensive as direct taxation. This having been ascertained, yet not in quite so openly and satisfactory a manner as it was desirable, . . . it became necessary that he should be made known to the electors."[4]

But Brougham was by no means prepared to sacrifice his political future for the sake of the democratic idea.

"Several good opportunities were offered him to mix in a proper way with the electors. He availed himself of none of them. . . . He, a lawyer, mistook the law, and travelled out of his way to justify Ministers for having illegally transported Bonaparte to St Helena. . . . He said that no man dissented from the grant of £60,000 to the Princess Charlotte for an outfit, and £60,000 per annum to her for marrying a German soldier to breed

---

[1] 27,809 (13).
[2] Twelve years later Place wrote : "I have just now read the speech (December 14, 1829). It does by no means appear to deserve the praise I bestowed on it, nor scarcely any praise at all," 27,809 (14).
[3] 27,809 (13).
[4] Place to Bennet, October 12, 1816. See 27,809 (29).

public beggars, while the truth really was, and is, that scarcely a man who was likely to have voted for him thought that a single shilling should either have been given to her or added to her then immense income." [1]

By October 1816 Place had made up his mind. Early in that month he was shown a letter from Brougham asking "what chance there was of his being returned for Westminster in the event of a dissolution." [2]   He answered by describing Brougham's omissions and commissions, and declaring that "the electors . . . say if Brougham is looking to the Court for preferment he has been consistent, but then he ought not to expect to be taken up by the people." [3]

It was just at the time when he determined to abandon the idea of Brougham's candidature that Place had what seems to have been his first interview with Orator Hunt. He wrote to James Mill on September 2, 1816 : "Hunt has been with me.   He is a pretty sample of an ignorant, turbulent, mischief-making fellow, a highly dangerous one in turbulent times.   It was not until he had been two hours with me that I discovered the whole of his reasons for calling upon me.   I should not have known them at all, had he not talked himself into full confidence, and then supposed it was I who reposed it in him. . . . He got warmed and 'as foolish as a waggon-horse,' and told me all he knew in relation to me and Burdett; said it was Wardle who had persuaded Burdett while in the Tower that I was a spy: that he was also persuaded by Wardle; that Burdett had made a mistake; and if he had called me a spy, I had called him a coward and a rascal, and it was time this was put an end to; . . . that an attempt had been made to put the Whigs upon West-

[1] Place to Bennet, October 12, 1816.   See 27,809 (29, 30).
[2] Place to Hodgskin, May 30, 1817.
[3] Place to Bennet, October 12, 1816.   27,809 (30).

minster, and that Brougham had been brought to the Crown and Anchor Tavern by one Mill, a Scotchman, who afterwards turned Westminster up because Brougham had been rejected. *Place.* 'What do you know of Mill?' *Hunt.* 'I never saw the man in my life, but I am told he is one of the Edinburgh Reviewers.' *Place.* 'And what of that?' *Hunt.* 'Why, it is a damned rascally review, and has done a deal of mischief.' *Place.* 'And some good, I hope.' *Hunt.* 'I never see it.' . . . I told Hunt it was miserable to see the avidity with which they (he and his political friends) sought to cut each other's throats, and that it would require nothing more in days of turbulence, whenever they should arise, than for those who hate the people to stimulate them to destroy one another, which would be as easy as putting yeast to the dough to make it rise. . . . Hunt says his mode of acting is to dash at good points, and to care for no one; that he will mix with no committee, or any party; he will act by himself; that he does not intend to affront any one, but cares not who is offended."

On January 28, 1817, Parliament met. By this time Hunt was the most conspicuous figure in the Reform movement. He had presided over a great meeting in the Spa Fields on November 15, 1816, which had been adjourned to December 2, and the second meeting had been followed by an absurd attack on the Tower, organised by a few physical-force revolutionists under the direction of a Government spy. In January 1817 Hunt and Major Cartwright induced Burdett to lend his name to what Place calls the silly plan of collecting some seventy deputies from various towns in England to present petitions on the first day of the Session. Burdett seems to have become alarmed and drove straight to Parliament without taking any notice of Hunt and the deputies.[1]

---

[1] See 27,809 (37).

But enough occurred to give the Government an excuse for repression, and in particular "as the Regent went to open Parliament some groans and hisses were heard, and on his return a pane of glass in the State coach was broken."[1]

On February 3 a message from the Regent on the disturbed state of the country was sent with a sealed bag of papers to the two Houses. The Government and their organs in the press at once set themselves deliberately to excite public terror.[2] "The ministerial newspapers were indefatigable in magnifying every movement into treason and sedition. All the talent, all the acrimony, all the malignity and falsehood which the most venal and corrupt and base amongst the basest of mankind— as some of the fellows connected with the newspapers are—had their full swing against the reformers. Every loyal slave, every one whose situation in corporations was gainful, or who expected to gain, was active in his way."[3]

"The Castlereagh administration . . . in time of peace adopted the means" which Pitt "had used in time of war. They took advantage of the general distress and partial discontent of the people, and employed spies to excite tumults, to form plots, to foment sedition, and to produce treason. . . . Every plot, real or imaginary, every movement of the populace which could be instigated, every paltry penny publication (some of which were their own) which could be made to talk seditiously, as the nonsense they contained was called, were magnified into serious, seditious, outrageous tumults, horrid and widely extended treasons, shaking the very foundations of the Government and threatening its overthrow. And even the poor harmless Spenceans, with their library consisting of an old Bible

[1] 27,809 (49).
[2] See "Sir R. Peel from his Private Correspondence," by C. S. Parker (London, 1891), 8vo, pp. 234-237.   [3] 27,809 (34).

and three or four small publications, a high-priest under
the name of librarian, and some forty or fifty followers,
were held out as a bugbear to all men of landed property,
who were to succumb to these formidable and numerous
speculators, and (be) compelled to resign their lands to
the parishes for the use of the whole community." [1]

"Any administration which is base enough may in times
of severe distress have as many plots and conspiracies as
it pleases.   There are always reckless, desperate men eager
to listen to tales from spies set on to impose upon them.
There are others again so ignorant, that they may be made
to believe almost anything which a cunning fellow may
project under the pretence of bettering their condition.
Such men may be led on imperceptibly to themselves to
lengths they never contemplated going, and to consequences which they could hardly at any time appreciate." [2]

The Whigs in Parliament were more concerned to
prove that they had no dealings with the Radicals than
to oppose coercion.   Some of them voted for the suspension of Habeas Corpus, and for the "Gagging Act" which
followed, and all of them by their abuse of the Reform
leaders helped to encourage the Government.   Place wrote
to his friend Hodgskin on May 30, 1817: "At the opening
of the Session, as no doubt you know, the Regent was
hooted at and pelted, and his Ministers, taking advantage
of this, if they did not themselves cause it, proposed a
suspension of the Habeas Corpus Act."

"At the same moment petitions from all parts for reform
of Parliament were presented, and they ultimately amounted
to as many as would have filled a waggon, and were signed
by at least a million of men. . . . Brougham came to England
just before the Parliament met, and finding himself disappointed for Westminster, knowing, too, that unless he
made a strong party among the Whigs he would not be in

[2] 27,809 (44-46), see pp. 61, 62.   [2] 27,809 (70).

the next Parliament, he at once took a most decided part against the petitioners for reform. Their petition was for annual parliaments, and pretty generally for universal suffrage. Brougham called them all manner of vile names, and imputed to them all manner of vile motives —they were ignorant, deluded, vile, mischievous incendiaries, &c. &c. . . .

"The Ministers found by far the best support for the vile measures they contemplated in the Whigs, who by their abuse of the people gave encouragement to the Ministers to go much further than they themselves contemplated. And these dirty Whigs who had been vigour itself against the claims of the people were perfectly imbecile against the abominable measures of the Ministers, who have all the power and all the law in their own hands to imprison whom they please, for any time they please, at their own will and pleasure, and without any accusation even."[1]

Of the coercive laws of 1817, Place was never able to speak with patience. Ten years later he wrote: "Knowing as I do how much it is in the power of Government to promote the instruction and well-being of the common people, how much the wealth and happiness of the whole community might be increased by proper conduct on the part of the Government, and seeing that instead of performing these important duties it busies itself in matters as mean as they are mischievous and as unjust as they are cruel, I feel quite unable to satisfy myself, and I despair of being able adequately (to express) correct ideas of the singular baseness, the detestable infamy, of their equally mean and murderous conduct."[2]   And again, "They who passed the Gagging Acts in 1817 and the Six Acts in 1819 were such miscreants, that could they have acted thus in a well-ordered community they would all have been hanged, and when I say this, I may add that it

[1] Place to Hodgskin, May 30, 1817.   [2] 27,809 (69).

would have been no more than they deserved. I do not
think that I say anything harshly."[1]

His anger was the greater because he believed at that
time that the suffering of the people was solely due to the
misgovernment of the ruling classes. "By an unvaried
and unqualified support of all the violent measures of
Ministers, both at home and abroad, they have reduced
the mass of the nation to a state of poverty, of dependence,
of starvation; until, alarmed for themselves, they have
established soup-kettles to dole out broth in scanty portions to the industrious people who, but for their conduct,
would have been living as became men—independent men
—on their own earnings."[2]

Place's share in the fight against the Gagging Act was
carried on by means of a little paper called *Hone's Register.*
In January 1817 *Cobbett's Register* was selling 50,000 a
week of its twopenny edition, and Place offered to help
William Hone, a needy bookseller, who was afterwards to
become famous,[3] by writing weekly a similar paper for him.
The second number of the *Register*, published on February
8, 1817, contained Place's reply to Brougham, entitled
"Universal Suffrage and Annual Parliaments against Mr.
Brougham and the Whigs." And in a special fourth
number, entitled the *Register Extraordinary*, on February
17, 1817, he printed, from a copy corrected by Brougham
himself, a report of the speech delivered by Brougham at

[1] Place to Colonel Jones, November 5, 1829.

[2] 27,809 (52). Twelve years later he made a note against this passage,
which shows the effect which his complete acceptance of the Malthusian
economics had then had upon his social views. "Many who are now as
well as myself convinced that the condition of the working people . . .
was almost wholly attributable to the too rapid increase of population,
concurred in the statement" (27,809, 51(b), dated Dec. 26, 1829).

[3] When Hone was three times tried and acquitted for blasphemy in
December 1817 Place gave £5 to a subscription raised on his behalf.
See *The proceedings at the Public Meeting . . . for the purpose of enabling
Wm. Hone to surmount the difficulties in which he has been placed, &c.*
(London, 1818), 8vo. List of Subscribers, p. 21.

the City of London Tavern in June 1814, when he expected to become the Reform candidate for Westminster. " Having determined to print the *Register Extraordinary*," he wrote, " I took care to let Mr. Brougham know not only of my determination, but also the matter it would contain. This perplexed him, so he sent for Mr. Mill and advised him to come to me and if possible prevent the publication. Mr. Mill came, and with his usual honesty told me what had passed. I replied that if Mr. Brougham would assure me that he would desist from attacking the Reformers, and say as many words in the House as should plainly indicate his hostility was at an end, the *Register* should not be printed. I heard no more on the subject. On Monday the *Register* was published, and several thousands were sold in the space of a few hours." [1]

After the appearance of the *Register*, Brougham attacked the Reformers more fiercely than before. Burdett " being out of favour with the Reformers," because of his conduct at the opening of Parliament, Cochrane stood alone in the Commons, and " the speech-making, gabbling Whigs, with Mr. Brougham for leader, anticipated no difficulty in putting him down." [2] To Cochrane, therefore, Place handed a letter, in which Brougham had avowed himself a supporter of many of the doctrines which he was now denouncing, and Cochrane read it in the House.[3]

[1] 27,809 (56). See *Hone's Register*, No. 2, "Universal Suffrage and Annual Parliaments against Mr. Brougham and the Whigs," and the *Register Extraordinary*, No. 4.   [2] 27,809 (50).

[3] Hansard, vol. xxxv. p. 370, February 17, 1817. Place only wrote five numbers of *Hone's Register*. "My other avocations would not permit me to write Weekly Registers, and I was obliged to desist. I was conducting a considerable business at the time, and had with difficulty obtained as much leisure as enabled me to attend to passing events, to listen to people who called on me, and superintend the printing of the *Register*. The crisis was now past, the mischief to the people was certain, the Whigs were scoffed at by Ministers and despised by the people ; I had put *Hone's Register* fairly on its legs ; the profit was considerable, and I was in hopes he would have been able to continue it,

The harvest of 1817 was comparatively successful, and for a few months the distress was relieved. Place consoled himself with the reflection that the campaign against political liberty had failed of its main object. It had not, as the Pitt and Grenville Acts of 1795 had done, crushed out the will to resist. "The people had become too well informed to be deceived."[1]

"Notwithstanding the impediments thrown in the way of the people in their search for knowledge—notwithstanding the Acts passed for the very purpose of strengthening the hands of Ministers—notwithstanding the immense increase of the standing army in time of peace—notwithstanding the excessive number of persons who are more or less dependent on the Government — notwithstanding the monstrous amount of money of which it had the distribution—notwithstanding the increased and increasing influence and patronage it possessed, its actual power was much less than that which Mr. Pitt had."[2]

But the events of 1817 intensified the disgust with which Place regarded the whole body of politicians in Parliament. He wrote of this time: "Nothing but an acquaintance with such men, nothing but hearing from their own mouths the loose notions they entertain on almost all subjects, could convince those who only hear of them in connection with public matters how very little they know, and how very little these idle persons can be prevailed upon to take the trouble necessary to become acquainted with any important matter of politics and legislation. They are proud, conceited, and overbearing. They represent their own money or their patrons. They look towards the Government as the means of providing for themselves or their relations. They are not account-

and by its means have found a maintenance for his family ; to this he was unequal—the sale soon declined. The work lingered on till October 25, and then expired." 27,809 (57).

[1] 27,809 (46).   [2] 27,809 (47, 48).

able to any but their patrons, and are as different from what a set of men elected by the people, and accountable to the people, would be as it is possible to conceive." [1]

At the same time he noticed that the excitement of the time was leading men outside Parliament to do serious intellectual work. In a letter written at the time he said: "The bad conduct of the Whigs produced one effect, it called forth the talents of many men who at once showed the law and customs of Parliament in former times, and the reasonableness of the people's petitions, and, of course, exposed the folly and ignorance of those who in the two Houses had gone out of their way to abuse them. It is surprising that not one man in either House knew enough of the history of his country to do it justice, and thus all the knowledge and all the learning has been exhibited out of the Houses. Several very able treatises have been published, and a great sensation has been produced by a book in favour of universal suffrage and annual Parliaments written by Mr. Bentham. [2] Men have appeared as writers who were never before heard of, and have produced works full of good matter, good style, and good thinking, exhibiting altogether a diffusion of knowledge far surpassing any former period. On this rest our hopes, on this rest the fears of the *legitimates*, who seem to imagine that in proportion as the people grow wiser and more capable of enjoying freedom they should be deprived of it. I have no fears for the result; the corruption will destroy its own means of corrupting, and then we shall start fair again, with full scope for our knowledge and courage." [3]

In the summer of 1817 Place determined to help in this work of political education by gathering the materials for a History of Parliament. "In consequence of the

---

[1] 27,809 (27).   [2] See p. 84.
[3] Place to Hodgskin, May 30, 1817.

agitation of the question of Parliaments and the interest a very large proportion of the people took in the discussion, I set to work to prove from authentic documents the practice and the law of Parliament, and shall, I hope, set the dispute at rest. It is a laborious job, but from being a lazy fellow lying in bed till eight or nine o'clock in the morning, I have risen at six, and work as hard as I can till breakfast-time and from tea-time in the afternoon to ten or eleven at night.

"You will justly remark, what have the usages of antiquity to do with the reasonableness of our present claims? why the customs of a rude age govern us now? What we ought to desire is that we should adopt such an arrangement as may be in accordance with our improved state of knowledge. And this would be conclusive if numbers were not led more by authority than by reason. When Lords Grey and Holland and others in high stations assert roundly that the custom was so-and-so, and, misapplying the word *Right*, tell us that the people have no *right* to certain things they claim to exercise, and no *right* to certain laws, because they did not formerly exist, . . . it becomes necessary for some one to stop the mouths of such preachers by showing them they are teaching false doctrine." [1]

But the mass of materials which resulted from this study [2] was never turned into a book, and Place was forced to devote himself for the next two years to the daily business of political organisation.

Between 1807 and 1818 there was no contested election for Westminster. In the three years 1818–1820 there was one every year. The first of these came at the general election of 1818. Cochrane had accepted the command of the Chilian fleet, and Burdett and the West-

---

[1] Place to Hodgskin, May 30, 1817.
[2] See them in 27,853–27,855.

minster Committee chose Douglas Kinnaird as the second Reform candidate. Place helped in the preliminary discussions, but refused to take any part in the actual business of the election. "I went into it until a public meeting was called at the Crown and Anchor, and then, as I had told those who were acting, I withdrew from all public interference."[1] He had not yet forgiven the committee for the calumnies of 1814, and already felt the inconvenience in politics of a reputation for industry. "I objected," he wrote in 1816, "to become active among men who invariably left me to do all the business, and when I had done it found fault not with the business, but with me, that when they could do without me I was a spy, and when they could not do without me I was a fine fellow."[2]

While Place remained in his tent the committee got into all sorts of difficulties. Cobbett had been carrying on for the last six months a disreputable quarrel with Burdett on money matters. Burdett was lazy and indifferent in the details of his parliamentary work, and Cobbett and Hunt abused the Westminster Committee as a Rump of Burdett's personal followers.[3] Douglas Kinnaird was a young and unknown man.

Under these circumstances an official Whig candidate

[1] Place to Enson (undated), 1819.
[2] Place to Mill, September 2, 1816.
"I cannot consent that anything in which I engage on the part of others should be neglected in any way, or rather that any possible thing should be omitted which could in any way promote the object. Some of my colleagues know this, and whenever, therefore, I am fairly committed they slink away and leave the burden upon me."—Place to Hobhouse, October 29, 1819. 27,839 (188).
[3] "Why were we obliged to fight up Burdett to the popularity he had lost, when, even at the very time he was losing it, he desired to have it increased? How did this happen? Simply by the incessant din Cobbett rang in the ears of the people, and the assistance it received from the old crazy Cartwright and others."—Place to Hobhouse, July 11, 1819. See 27,837 (164).

I

seemed to have a good chance, and Sir Samuel Romilly
was approached. On June 8 he accepted, and wrote in
his diary that he expected an easy victory over Douglas
Kinnaird, "with whose name, till the present moment, the
public was wholly unacquainted, and who is set up by a
little committee of tradesmen, who persuade themselves
that they are all-powerful in Westminster."[1] The Tories
ran Sir Murray Maxwell.

On June 9 Brooks, the chairman of the committee,
wrote to Place, "We are much in want of your assistance
. . . to be put in the way to proceed;"[2] and Percy, the
paid secretary, also wrote, asking him to come down "and
set us a-going, whatever you may do afterwards."[3] On
June 12 Percy wrote again, "I attribute all to your
absence; one word or proposition from you to form the
arrangements would have done it."[4]

On June 15 Place so far gave way as to attend a
meeting on arrangements held in his own house.[5] Meanwhile the poll had begun, and the result of the first few
days gave ground for fear that both the Reform candidates
would be beaten, and that the Whig and Tory would be
elected. The Reform Committee therefore hastily decided
to withdraw Kinnaird, and to concentrate all their resources
on securing Burdett's seat.

This decision was taken on June 17, and on the same
day came an urgent letter from the committee imploring
Place to pay "one more visit" to the committee room.[6]
Place replied raging against the desertion of Kinnaird, and
against a suggested coalition with the Whigs, "which in
my eyes is as base as anything of the sort can possibly be."

Next day, however, he buckled on his armour. Writing
in 1819 he says, "I was obliged to go, so I went, and became

---

[1] Sir S. Romilly's Memoirs, vol. iii. p. 360. See also ante, p. 77, note 1.
[2] 27,841 (153).   [3] 27,841 (154).   [4] 27,841 (178).
[5] 27,841 (212).   [6] 27,841 (253).

at once King, Lords and Commons, Judge, Jury, and Jack Ketch. I found a number of people employed as clerks, a room engaged for me, everything in the utmost confusion, and no person there of any authority or consequence, and, in fact, no one whom I could consult. So I went to work with the tools I found, did just what I pleased, got the matter into form in about three hours, issued books, summoned everybody, set them to work, and in two days had above 200 regular canvassers. I went every morning at six o'clock, and never quitted the room until ten or eleven at night, not even for meals. Generally I had only one each day, and that on a piece of paper at my table. On the last day of the election, at one o'clock, I despatched a canvasser to bring up the last voter who had made a promise, and then I went home; but from the time I went to the time I finally left, I never saw even a single meeting of the committee. The dirty Whigs did all they could to revive the abominable practices of former times, to introduce the old debauchery, but they did not succeed. They gave a public breakfast, set out with profusion; about forty attended. We met this by bills and placards.[1] They offered another at the Hummums; we met this also; and, what must seem incredible, not a dozen people attended it, and only one of these was an elector. This put an end to treating." [2]

Burdett's seat was saved, though he was only second to

[1] "A public breakfast was announced at the Hummums, in Covent Garden. Here all who chose to go might stuff themselves out with the best and most expensive viands, and then like slaves be marched to the poll. This was defeated so completely that no other attempt of the kind has since been made. Men were placed at and near the tavern door with placard poles, on both sides of which was a large posting bill containing these words : 'Esau sold his birthright for a mess of pottage. Electors, sell not yours for a paltry breakfast.'" (Place to Unett and Parkes, January 8, 1828.) But see p. 42. The breakfast, however, of 1819 was not technically "public."

[2] Place to Ensor, 1819 (undated, but apparently written about February 5, 1819).

Romilly. In the country the Whigs gained thirty seats, and increased their numbers from 150 to about 180. Thereupon Brougham wrote a florid article on The State of Parties for the *Edinburgh Review*, in which he declared that "even the more respectable zealots of Reform have failed to estrange them (the people) from their natural leaders. To these leaders they have evinced their willingness to return."[1]

Place set himself steadily to win back both seats for the Reformers, and proposed an elaborate plan for a federal organisation of the various parishes of Westminster on the lines of the ward committees of a modern political association.[2] The fight came sooner than he expected. On November 2, 1818, occurred Romilly's lamentable suicide. "As soon as I heard of Romilly's death—and that was within two hours from the time it happened—I wrote a bill calling upon the electors to support Kinnaird. I printed the bill, and in the course of the next day caused several thousands to be distributed in parcels to the electors who had been the most active during the last election, an alphabetical list having been previously made under my direction as a part of the plan before mentioned.[3]

Kinnaird, however, refused to stand, and Place persuaded the committee to support John Cam Hobhouse. The committee, in their fear of doing anything undemocratic, decided to call a public meeting and to ask for nominations, it being arranged that Hobhouse's name should be proposed. "This," said Place, "was in fact an advertisement for a riot. It should have been to nominate some

---

[1] *Edinburgh Review*, vol. xxx., June 1818, p. 204. For Brougham's authorship of the article, see Hobhouse, "A Defence of the People against Lord Erskine," p. 123.

[2] The original MS. of the plan is preserved, 27,842 (12–21). See the letter to Ensor, 1819, and the account of the working of the plan in the "Authentic Narrative of the Westminster Election of 1819" (in British Museum).   [3] Place to Ensor, 1819.

one person, not to ask the question who ? "[1]   He expressed
this view in a curt note to a leading member of the committee : " Miller, when a man has a set of words ringing in
his ears to which he has attached no specific idea, it is
almost impossible to make that man attend to reason.   He
is not in a state to discriminate. . . . The words that are
doing the mischief are ' Public meeting.' "[2]

The meeting was held on November 17, Place taking no
part in it.[3]   It went off peacefully and successfully.   A
Whig nominated Lord John Russell, and Hunt nominated
Cobbett, who had fled to the United States.   Both were,
however, beaten, and Hobhouse's name carried by an overwhelming majority.

The election would not come on till the meeting of
Parliament in the spring, and there was plenty of time for
careful preparation.   A managing committee met daily,
with Place in the chair.   Hobhouse worked hard at addressing parish meetings, and the organisation grew rapidly.   In
February 1819 Place wrote : " The results are, a large committee in each of the parishes, a general public meeting in
each of the parishes, a complete canvass of the whole city
and liberty by the parish committee, and books in as fine
a state as perhaps it is possible to make them ; a public
dinner also in each of the parishes : and on Monday week
next another public general meeting of the whole body of
the electors, to whom a Report will be made, it then to be
printed and extensively circulated.   You must know that
we never before dared to call a public meeting in the
parishes, never had a proper parish committee, and no

---

[1] Place to Ensor, 1819.

[2] Place to Miller, November 7, 1818.   27,842 (57).

[3] Place wrote at the time : "I shall have no more to do with the
business except at home, and as little as possible there, for I am not disposed when the business has been once made plain and easy to have it
made difficult by others, and then to go to fight through those difficulties."
—Place to Mill, November 5, 1818.   27,842 (51).

system of regular canvassing. The general committee now
consists of upward of 330 persons, and the subscriptions
amount to £1800. This is a New View of Society. All
this has been done very quietly, and at a comparatively
very small expense, and the long period from November 3
to the present moment has been so well occupied that the
enthusiasm of the people, which was roused at the beginning, has never subsided. The Minister has been fairly
driven off the ground, and all the contrivances of the dirty,
sneaking Whigs have ended in nothing. They have done
all they could, but to both the factions the matter has
appeared wholly hopeless. Attempts are now being made
by the high-flying aristocrats to catch a fool who will meet
us at his own expense, but I do not believe they will find
one." [1]

Place's Report to the Westminster electors was presented
to a public meeting on February 9, 1819. It contained a
history of the Westminster Reform movement since the
election of 1809, at which " the electors of Westminster
emancipated themselves from the control of both the
aristocratical factions." It plainly referred to the Whigs
as a "corrupt and profligate faction," and to Lord Grey
as one of those who had been "solemnly pledged" to
the cause of Reform.[2] It added that Westminster
had "become a school of political morality, instead of

[1] Place to Ensor, 1819.
[2] Lord Grey and his son-in-law Lambton (afterwards Lord Durham)
had just before the election denounced the Reformers at a meeting of
the Newcastle Fox Club. Lambton called the " Radical Reformers "
"brawling, ignorant, but mischievous quacks," with whom "the *true*
people of England hold no communication." Lord Grey, with an obvious
reference to the Westminster Committee, reprobated the introduction of
the American "caucus" into English politics. (See unpublished MS. of
the Second Reply to Lord Erskine, and "Narrative," p. 34; also *Morning
Chronicle*, January 6 and 8, 1819.)

This early reference to the Caucus may have been derived from an
article in the *Edinburgh Review* for December 1818 (p. 201).

being, as it formerly was, one common scene of depravity!"[1]

The Report, like most of Place's literary work, was much too long. It would have taken some fifty minutes to read, and the crowded meeting endured about a quarter of an hour of it, but after that cries of " Print it " were heard, and the remainder was taken as read. The Report had not been shown to Hobhouse or Burdett, who perhaps were annoyed at its tone.[2] But Hobhouse in his speech took the same line as the Report. He said that " the country is sick of party,"[3] and that if he were sent to Parliament it would be " as one of those extravagant Reformers "[4] whom the *Edinburgh Review* had been abusing. Finally, he pledged himself to vote for " Parliaments of short duration " and a " full, free, and equal share " for all in the choice of their representatives.[5]

Hitherto the Whigs had sulkily acquiesced in Hobhouse's candidature, but Place's Report and Hobhouse's speech compelled them either to fight or to accept a conspicuous defeat. They first tried to induce Hobhouse to disavow the Report.[6] On his refusal they determined to fight, and at the last moment nominated Lord Melbourne's

[1] " Authentic Narrative," p. 49. The whole Report is there printed, pp. 44-70.
[2] A writer in the *Edinburgh Review* (vol. cxxxiii.), April, p. 300, who had access to the privately printed memoirs of Hobhouse, says : " Citizen Place, who was proud of his pen, wrote a bitter appeal which irritated and divided the party."
[3] " Authentic Narrative," p. 60.   [4] Ibid. p. 63.   [5] Ibid. p. 63.
[6] See Greville, " Memoirs of the Reign of George IV. and William IV.," vol. i. p. 17, February 14, 1819. " George Lamb has been proposed in opposition to Hobhouse. The latter drew this opposition upon himself by his speech, and still more by the reports of his committee, in which they abused the Whigs in unmeasured terms. Lambton went to Hobhouse and asked him if he would disavow the abuse of Lord Grey, which his committee had inserted in the document they printed ; he refused, on which the opposition was determined upon and began. . . . . It is generally supposed that Lamb will win."

brother, George Lamb. The *Morning Chronicle* afterwards
(February 22, 1819) said: " It was not till the evening of
Friday the 12th instant that it was decided on proposing a
Whig candidate the following day, at the nomination of
candidates for Westminster, in opposition to Mr. Hobhouse,
in consequence of his speech on the Tuesday proceeding
out of Mr. Place's report, and it was actually past twelve
on the same night before Mr. Lamb finally decided to
stand."

The election which followed lasted from February 13 to
March 3, 1819, and was fought hard up to the last moment.
The electoral arrangements of those days are open to many
serious objections, but taken in a sporting spirit, they must
have provided glorious fun; and in that spirit high society
in West London went into the battle. Mr. Lamb's canvassers were "composed of the great body of the aristocracy, with the young gentlemen of almost all the Club
Houses;"[2] and Hobhouse described how one of Lamb's
committee was heard to tell his candidate as the best
possible joke, "I have just been shaking hands with these
blackguards for you."[3] Lamb's sister-in-law, Lady Caroline
Lamb (Byron's Lady Caroline Lamb), rushed with her
usual energy into a new form of excitement. She and " a
number of ladies of rank" went round canvassing in the
rain and snow of February 1819. "She was seen galloping
over all parts of Westminster, and where her horse could
not go she walked, leaving few lanes and alleys un-
explored."[4]

Meanwhile all the wit of the West End was directed to

[1] "Authentic Narrative," February 22, 1819, p. 168, quoted from
Morning Chronicle of that day. It was reported that the Whigs had
said amongst them, "If we carry the election, we shall be Ministers
in a fortnight afterwards." ("Narrative," p. 384. See also the unpublished MS. of Place's Second Reply to Lord Erskine.)

[2] "Authentic Narrative," p. 116.

[3] Ibid. p. 159.   [4] Ibid. p. 131.

the task of ridiculing Place. The *Morning Chronicle* published an epigram—

> " ' England,' quoth tailor Place, ' shall quickly see,
> That I have power to make young Hob. M.P.;
> 'Tis strange indeed if I, so devilish clever,
> Can't make the mob roar out, "Hobhouse for ever !" '
> 'Tis stranger still that Snip should not reflect
> The mob may bawl, but others may elect.
> Yet let not Hobhouse feel too much displeasure,
> Poor Snip has only taken a wrong measure." [1]

A pun on Place's name and the " place " which Hob-house's father, Sir Benjamin Hobhouse, received on the occasion of his change of political opinions, appears in several forms, of which perhaps the best is—

> " Old Hobhouse once had got a name,
> But lost *for* Place his better fame,
> So now his son, a louder railer.
> Loses his seat by *Place* the Tailor.
> How fatal to the Hobhouse race
> Is an excessive love of Place !" [2]

The main object of the Whig tactics was to represent the " Rump " as a little knot of " slanderers and levellers," [3] discarded both by gentlemanly politicians and by real Radicals. Orator Hunt was therefore encouraged to come down daily to the hustings in Covent Garden and abuse Hobhouse in support of the bogus candidature of old Major Cartwright. Unfortunately Hunt's work was made extremely easy. Hobhouse after his Radical speech of February 9 had a severe and untimely attack of con-scientiousness, as a result of which he read on the nomination day a laboured and ambiguous statement of his opinions on the franchise question. The statement showed that what he really wanted was not universal suffrage, but the substitution of a uniform and perhaps

---

[1] "Authentic Narrative," p. 300.   [2] 27,842 (523).
[3] *Morning Chronicle*, February 20, 1819.

considerable qualification for the existing anomalies of borough representation; that is to say, the Reform Bill of 1832. Lamb's party offered a thousand pounds for an explanation of the statement, and proved that if it meant anything it implied the disfranchisement of a large section of the Westminster voters. Lamb himself seems to have held just the same views on the franchise as Hobhouse, and represented that he was prepared to go further. Hobhouse having recovered from his conscientiousness outbid Lamb, but the mischief was already done. Lady Caroline persuaded forty incautious voters, living in or near the courts and alleys of Shepherd's Market, May Fair, that "Mr. Hobhouse had abandoned his principles, and that Mr. Lamb was the *Liberty candidate.*" [1]   Sir Charles Wolseley, Thelwall, Wooler, and other honest Radicals, who were more concerned with principles than organisations, appeared on the hustings, repudiated Hobhouse as a "political humbug," and accused Burdett of trying to make Westminster a rotten borough. [2]

It was hardly to be expected that the Whigs would be very scrupulous as to electioneering methods in a contest of this kind. Breakfasts, for instance, were given to ".Mr. Lamb's committee," at one of which twenty-six dozen of wine were drunk. What was more important was that the Whigs hired all the rate collectors of the Westminster parishes as inspectors. The High Bailiff decided that no ratepayer was qualified to vote unless he had actually paid his rates, and left it to the rate-collectors to settle the point in each case. Accordingly if such a voter came up for Lamb no notice was taken; if for Hobhouse, his vote was refused.

[1] "Authentic Narrative," p. 131.
[2] "Well indeed might Mr. Oldfield say in his next edition of his 'History of Boroughs': 'The Borough of Westminster, 14,000 voters; Sir F. Burdett, Patron.'" (Speech by Northmore, in "Authentic Narrative," p. 126.)

Under these conditions it is surprising that the Westminster organisation held together as well as it did.
Lamb was elected with 4465 votes, including those of the
Tories and of the faggot voters attached to the Government Offices. Hobhouse received 3861 votes. He retained throughout the favour of that section of the
population which goes to meetings. Hunt spoke every
day in actual peril of his life. Not a word of Lamb's
speeches reached any one but the reporters. On the last
day a squadron of mounted Whig gentlemen were pelted
out of Covent Garden.

As soon as the election was over, Lord Erskine issued
a pamphlet entitled a "Short Defence of the Whigs against
the Imputations attempted to be cast upon them during
the late Election for Westminster."[1] To this both Place
and Hobhouse replied. Place's "Reply to Lord Erskine"
was finished first, and Hobhouse wrote of it, "The reply is
decisive, a home-thrust."[2] In it Place, with the help of
his new historical reading, drew up a most damaging
account of the Government of England by the Whigs
during the eighteenth century. He defended the Report,
and declared that the contest which was forced upon the
Whigs by its publication has convinced "a large portion
of" the people "that there is no real difference between
the Whig and Tory factions, except the difference which
always existed; namely, that the Tories would exalt the
kingly power that it might trample upon the aristocracy
and the people, while the Whigs would establish an
aristocratical oligarchy to trample on the King and the
people."[3]

In Parliament the Whigs were stronger during the
summer of 1819 than they had been since they left office

[1] See it in the British Museum.
[2] Hobhouse to Place, March 29, 1819. 27,837 (140).
[3] "A Reply to Lord Erskine by an Elector of Westminster," p. 4.

in 1807. The currency question was one of great difficulty, and the ministry suffered from "a want of concert and co-operation.[1]" On May 18, Tierney, as leader of the Opposition, moved for an inquiry into the state of the nation, and received 178 votes to the 357 of the Tories.[2] But when on July 1 Burdett brought forward a studiously moderate resolution in favour of parliamentary reform he found only fifty-eight supporters. The nearer the Whigs thought themselves to office, the more anxious were they to remain unpledged on that point.

Meanwhile, in the manufacturing districts the three years' agitation for radical reform was resulting in a really formidable popular movement, and in Lancashire the long summer evenings were being used for open-air meetings and secret drilling. On July 7, 1819, Lord Sidmouth sent out a circular to the Lord-Lieutenants. On July 30 the Regent issued a proclamation against seditious meetings. On August 16 a huge Reform meeting, with Hunt as chief speaker, took place in St. Peter's Fields, at Manchester. The magistrates determined to arrest Hunt, and with that object instructed a body of yeomanry to force their way through the crowd. The

[1] Wilbraham, Feb. 24, 1819 (in Diary of Lord Colchester, vol. iii. p. 71).

[2] In this debate, Canning, to Place's delight, used the incidents of the Westminster election as a disproof of the claim of the Whigs to be the popular party. "He should have thought they would not so soon have forgot the Westminster election. He had in his time faced popular election, and it was not impossible he might do so again. But he had never been obliged to go home accompanied by a file of grenadiers. His retreat had been effected with somewhat more safety than this *essence of popularity;* this routed cavalcade, this assemblage of ribbons and rubbish, with laurel at their heads and brickbats at their tails, who were rescued from their *overpowering popularity* by his Majesty's Horse-guards." ("Narrative," p. 385. See also Hansard, vol. xl. p. 545, May 18, 1819.) "Party names now go for little. We, at Westminster, killed the Whigs as a party—as Whigs—and Canning shouted their requiem ; 'Ribbons and rubbish. Favours at their heads, and brickbats at their tails.' There ended all respect for that party name." (Place to Burdett, January 7, 1829.)

yeomen were surrounded and used their swords, where-
upon the whole meeting was dispersed by a charge of
Hussars.   Eleven of the spectators were killed, and between four and five hundred wounded.[1]

Place when he heard the news of "Peterloo" wrote to
Hobhouse: "These Manchester yeomen and magistrates
are a greater set of brutes than you form a conception of.
They have always treated the working people in a most
abominable manner.   I know one of these fellows who
swears 'Damn his eyes, seven shillings a week is plenty
for them'; that when he goes round to see how much
work his weavers have in their looms, he takes a well-fed
dog with him, almost, if not entirely for the purpose of,
insulting them by the contrast.   He said some time ago
that 'The sons of bitches had eaten up all the stinging
nettles for ten miles round Manchester, and now they had
no greens to their broth.'   Upon my expressing indignation, he said, 'Damn their eyes, what need you care about
them?   How could I sell you goods so cheap if I cared
anything about them.'   I showed him the door, and never
purchased any of his goods afterwards.   Another of these
fellows, a manufacturer and yeoman, said yesterday, we in
London did not know what a set of damned villains the
fellows at Manchester were.   They must be kept quiet
by the sword.   He was told to take care of himself; he
laughed and said, 'Ah, you know nothing of the weight
of a sabre; that's the argument!'   What but what has
happened could be expected from these fellows when let
loose.   They never for a moment thought of consequences.
They cut down and trampled down the people; and then
it was to end just as cutting and trampling the furze
bushes on a common would end.   You may see what was
thought of the transaction by the conduct of the fellow

[1] See A. Prentice, "Historical Sketches of Manchester" (1851),
p. 167.

who hung the flag he had seized out of his window. The
law will, from the want of proper interference, afford no
redress. Should the people seek it by shooting their
enemies one by one and burning their factories, I should
not be at all surprised, nor much outraged."[1]

Far more menacing even than the Manchester massacre
itself were the signs which showed that the Government
intended henceforth to put down popular agitation by
military force. On August 21 the Regent sent a letter
to the Lord-Lieutenants of Lancashire and Cheshire, requesting them to convey to the magistrates and yeomanry
of those counties "the great satisfaction derived by his
Royal Highness the Prince Regent from their prompt,
decisive, and efficient measures for the preservation of the
public tranquillity."[2]

The Westminster Reformers felt that if the right of
public meeting in England was not to be lost for ever,
it was necessary to assert it now. On August 25, at
9 p.m., Place wrote to Hobhouse: "I have not had a
moment to myself. The people are all in motion, and
I am obliged to put up with being consulted by those
who have brains, and pestered by those who have
none."[3]

As usual his plans were interfered with by the irre-
concilables. "The first movement in London consequent
on the news of the massacre at Manchester was a meeting
precipitately called by Major Cartwright and Wooler. It
was attended in the course of three hours by at least 3000
generally well-dressed persons, but they were disgusted and
driven away by Dr. Watson, Jones, Preston, Thistlewood,
and the meeting came to nothing."[4] After this failure it
was all the more important to secure a really impressive

[1] Place to Hobhouse, August 20, 1819. 27,837 (179).
[2] *Annual Register*, vol. lx, 1819, App. p. 125.
[3] 27,837 (181).
[4] Place to Hodgskin, September 8-12, 1819.

Westminster meeting. In such a meeting Place honestly attempted to induce the Whig leaders to take part.[1]

"As soon as it was known that a Westminster meeting would be certainly held, I had several persons with me who are connected with the Whigs to inquire what was intended to be proposed. The reply was, 'If the Whigs will call the meeting we will join them, if they will not call the meeting we will, and if any of the leading men among them will call upon me I will show them the matters intended to be brought forward; or, if any of them will even request to see them, they shall be called upon.' This was several times repeated, as well to those who called upon me as to some of the people of the *Morning Chronicle*, who were, it was understood, in communication with Mr. Brand, Lord John Russell, and Mr. William Smith, all of whom were in London. But no desire for co-operation was shown. . . . . Not one of them attended the meeting, and the lying *Chronicle* states on the Saturday, only two days after the meeting, that the reason none of the Whigs attended was that the proceedings included propositions for a reform of Parliament. A more deliberate lie was never before told, even by the pre-eminent liar, Perry. But were it true even, what an excuse! The Whigs would not come because parliamentary reform was to be mentioned. Be it so, but then it ought to be clearly understood that the Whigs make no part of the people. Up to this time, Sunday, September 12, there has been no meeting but of Reformers; not a finger has been stirred but by the Reformers; not a shilling has been subscribed but by the Reformers; even the necessary legal assistance would have

[1] Place even decided to suppress a Second Reply to Lord Erskine, which was nearly ready for the press. In a preface to the MS. he says, "The Manchester massacres induced the author to lay it aside. He was resolved that if the Whigs did not do their duty to their country in so trying an occasion, they should have no excuse for not doing it, so far at least as he was concerned."

been wanting but for the aid given by the Reformers; and the open violators of the laws, the murderers of the people, would have had their triumph complete. Add to this that the famous Whig Lord Derby and his son, Lord Stanley, and the other Whig Lord Belgrave, have all applauded the murderers."[1]

The great meeting was held on September 2, and was attended by 100,000 persons, " at the risk of military execution, and under the musquetry and sabres of the household army."[2]

Between September 8 and September 12 Place wrote a long letter to Thomas Hodgskin in Edinburgh, which was to be shown to M'Culloch, the economist and editor of the *Scotsman*. M'Culloch had written a manifesto on Peterloo, in which he lamented the division of classes, vaguely advocated parliamentary reform, and prophesied that "we shall soon see public men and the public, the Whigs and the people, united."

This letter contains, perhaps, the best statement of that strong though moderated optimism with which Place at this period of his career regarded the political outlook. "You say," he wrote, "'the men in ragged coats have proved by their conduct and their resolutions that they understand the business they are about.' This is very true. I know of no paper deserving unqualified praise more than the Smithfield declaration, of which I send you a copy. Mr. M'Culloch says: 'The people possess more singleness of purpose, more honesty, more kind-heartedness and generosity, more principle, moral and religious, than their superiors.' Nothing could be more true or better expressed; and did Mr. M'Culloch mix with the working people as I have done, and obtain their confidence as I have done, even he would be astonished

---

[1] Place to Hodgskin, September 8-12, 1819.
[2] See Hobhouse, " A Trifling Mistake," p. 43.

at finding the qualities he praises existing in an excess, of which by theory he can form but a faint notion. He may well say 'public men have no solid right to those airs of superiority which are commonly expressed by them.' Well may he add that 'it is a mockery to call that law which does not protect the poor as well as uphold the rich.' Mr. M'Culloch says, 'It is quite a mistake to impute the existing discontents to the existing distress; they originate in other causes,' and that 'wise measures will never be adopted without a reform in Parliament.' This is a plain statement of two very important truths, and the conviction of their truth has been steadily and regularly marching and spreading over the face of the country ever since the Constitutional and Corresponding Societies became active in 1792. The effects of this march are no less singular than wonderful. I have watched its progress with some attention, being fully persuaded that it was and is of momentous importance. One of its effects has been almost, if not entirely, overlooked, and when stated will not be believed by those persons who have been so admirably depicted by Mr. M'Culloch. It is that in spite of the demoralising influence of many of our laws, and the operation of the poor-laws, it has impressed the morals and manners, and elevated the character of the working-man. I speak from observation made on thousands of them, and I hold up this fact as enough of itself to satisfy any man not wholly ignorant of human nature as a very portentous circumstance. Look even to Lancashire. Within a few years a stranger walking through their towns was 'touted,' i.e. hooted, and an 'outcomling' was sometimes pelted with stones. 'Lancashire brute' was the common and appropriate appellation. Until very lately it would have been dangerous to have assembled 500 of them on any occasion. Bakers and butchers would at the least have been plundered. Now

K

100,000 people may be collected together and no riot
ensue, and why? Why, but for the fact before stated,
that the people have an object, the pursuit of which
gives them importance in their own eyes, elevates them
in their own opinion, and thus it is that the very
individuals who would have been the leaders of the riot
are the keepers of the peace. In every place as reform
has advanced, drunkenness has retreated, and you may
assume that a cause which can operate so powerfully as
to produce such a change, is capable of producing almost
anything. It must continue to operate still more and
more extensively. It will not be materially retarded, and
cannot by any means be extinguished—as it is the result
of conviction in the minds of the people of their own
importance, and not the ebullitions of enthusiasm—
although that at times has its effects; it will not sub-
side into indifference, notwithstanding its energies will
only be displayed at intervals, and under peculiar circumstances."

On August 27 Hunt was committed for trial, and
released on bail. On September 13 he entered London
in triumph. Place in his description of the day showed
that he was better able than the Whigs to sympathise
with an enemy in times of common danger.

" There was not much waving of handkerchiefs, but
there was a good deal of respect at times paid to the
man. How in a mass of 300,000 people could it be
otherwise? Aye, and he deserved it too, and more than
he got. If the people—I mean the working people—are
to have but one man, they will, as they ought, support
that man at least with their shouts. And there are very
many cases too in which they would fight with him, or
for him. Whose fault is it that no better man goes among
the people? Not theirs; they will cling to the best man
that makes common cause with them. I remember how

I felt when I was a working-man, and know how they
feel, and how far they reason. If none shows himself
but Hunt, Hunt must be their man." [1]

For a moment, however, it looked as if the Whigs might
after all lead the agitation. Hobhouse wrote enthusiasti-
cally to Place to say that Lord Fitzwilliam had been
dismissed from his Lieutenancy for attending an indignation meeting in the West Riding, and that Lord
Tavistock had given £50 to the Defence Fund. Place
answered denying that this meant much. "Tavistock and
his £50! Well, I dare say if I knew him, I should find
him a soft-headed fellow. All his public conduct seems
to say as much for him and no more. Kindness, or at
the least the absence of harshness, and good-nature are
very common characteristics in this sort of animal; and
it is very probable that he is really a good sort of a man.
But we want in public men dogged thinking, clear ideas,
comprehensive views, and pertinacity, i.e. a good share of
obstinacy or hard-headedness." [2]

On November 23, Parliament was specially assembled to
consider the state of the country. For the first fortnight
of the ensuing session Place made a regular analysis of the
proceedings "of the Savage Parliament." His marginal
annotations, "infamous lie," "blundering fool," and "well
done, Wilson," or "good stuff," show the state of mind in
which he read the debates. In the analysis itself, Wilber-
force, who declared that "the great body of the thinking
part of the people were satisfied" with the action of the
Manchester magistrates, is "an ugly epitome of the devil,"
and emphasis is laid on Tierney's approval of the shocking
sentence just passed upon Carlile, and on his declaration
that the Whigs "had ever stood in the front rank against
the deluded Radicals."

[1] Place to Hobhouse, September 19, 1819.   27,837 (192).
[2] 27,837 (192).

The Savage Parliament lasted from November 23 to December 30, and spent that period in passing the celebrated Six Acts,[1] by which writing and speaking on political questions was made nearly as dangerous as under the Pitt and Grenville Acts of 1795. In the debates on the Six Acts the Whigs occasionally made good speeches, but offered no really serious resistance.

The temper of the House of Commons was well shown on December 13 in the discussion on an alleged breach of privilege. Hobhouse in continuation of the controversy with Erskine had published about the beginning of November a pamphlet called "A Trifling Mistake of Lord Erskine corrected." The greater part of this pamphlet consisted of the poorest sort of verbal controversy, but the last few pages are in a different style, and handle with unflinching frankness the situation created by Peterloo. "What prevents the people from walking down to the House and pulling out the members by the ears, locking up their doors, and flinging the key into the Thames? . . . Do we love them? Not at all. . . . Their true practical protectors then, the real efficient anti-Reformers, are to be found at the Horse-guards and the Knightsbridge Barracks. . . . Nothing but brute force, or the pressing fear of it, will reform the Parliament."[2]

Even Burdett declared that he did not defend the language of the pamphlet,[3] and the moral feelings of the House were so outraged that Hobhouse's instant committal to Newgate was carried by 198 to 65, against the moderate proposal that he should first be heard in his defence. Perhaps Burdett's willingness to throw over the language of the pamphlet may have been due to the fact,

---

[1] (1) Against delay of justice; (2) against drilling; (3) against blasphemy and sedition; (4) for disarming; (5) newspaper stamp; (6) against open-air meetings.
[2] "A Trifling Mistake," pp. 49–51.
[3] Hansard, vol. xli., p. 1019, December 13, 1819.

for which there is a good deal of evidence, that the incriminated passages were not written by Hobhouse at all, but by Place.[1]

On January 29, 1820, George III. died, and a general election followed. At Westminster, Burdett and Hobhouse stood against Lamb. The polling lasted from March 9 to March 25. Place inserted in the book in which at that time he recorded his reading: "*March, 1820*—Occupied from seven in the morning every day to midnight in the Westminster election, where my presence seemed so absolutely necessary, that I was unable to take a single meal at home or even so much time as was required to read half a column in a newspaper."

The Westminster Reformers fought under better conditions than in 1819. Hobhouse had been in prison from December 14, 1819, to February 29, 1820, and Burdett was sentenced on March 23 at Leicester to a fine of £2000 and three months' imprisonment for a letter to the Westminster electors, written in the preceding August on the news of Peterloo. Even the most ignorant ratepayer in the Seven Dials could now have no doubt as to who were the "Liberty Candidates." Nor was there any opposition from the extremists. Hunt was in prison, and the conviction of Thistlewood and his companions for the Cato

---

[1] The evidence is shortly as follows :—Carlile in a passage preserved by Place, and not contradicted by him, says : "Even in going to Newgate, by order of the House of Commons, the then Mr. Hobhouse fathered a pamphlet which was not his own, but which was written by Mr. Place " (*Monthly Magazine*, May 1836, p. 455, in an article by A. P.—Richard Carlile).

Place, writing to Hobhouse on October 29, 1819, apologises for his "presumption," apparently in stopping the press while "A Trifling Mistake" was being printed, and says "the alteration in the last page is worth all the expense, and would be worth it were it ten times as much." 27,837 (188). Hobhouse (in " Proceedings as to a Trifling Mistake," pp. 31 and 66) hints that he did not write the last two sheets. The style of the pages is also much more like Place's than Hobhouse's.

Street plot[1] had cowed the small body of real revolutionists in London. The Judges' ruling in an action
against the High Bailiff of Westminster had also made
it impossible for the rate collectors to repeat their wholesale disfranchisement.[2]

Hobhouse and Burdett were elected, with Lamb some
400 votes behind Hobhouse, and Westminster was again
handed over to "the aristocratic borough-mongering control of Messrs. *Brooks, Plaice* & Co."[3]

During the half-year which followed the general election
of 1820 the interest of the whole nation was concentrated
on the attempt of George IV. to divorce his wife. The
new Queen as Princess of Wales had lived abroad since
1813, and the best that could be said of her manner of
life was that it was better than that of her husband.
On the death of George III. the Cabinet opened negotiations with her in the hope that she might be induced to
remain out of England, but on June 5, 1820, she suddenly
landed at Dover, and on June 6 drove into London.
Round her all the discontent of the time instantly
crystallised.

Place's Guard Book of documents relating to the Queen
has been lost, but casual references elsewhere imply that
he helped to direct the agitation. He complains, for
instance, at the Westminster meeting, held on July 4,
to address the Queen, "not a single Whig attended,"[4]
and writes on August 5, 1820: "The Queen has been
here some weeks, and nearly the whole of the people
have repeatedly and vehemently expressed their opinion
on the infamous conduct of the King and his Ministers
towards her. And now when the spirit of the people,

---

[1] The plot to murder all the Ministers at a Cabinet dinner on
February 23, 1820. The plot was betrayed, and in part arranged, by a
Government spy.

[2] See 27,837 (142).   [3] *Morning Post*, March 27, 1820.

[4] Loose sheet in Commonplace Book.

instead of subsiding rises day by day as the Queen becomes more and more determined not to submit to her
powerful and manifold enemies, . . . the dirty sneaking
Whigs, who had held aloof in expectation of the Queen's
submission, and the triumph they in consequence expected
over the people, find themselves in a worse dilemma than
their opponents, and would do almost anything, if anything could be done without the people." [1]

But the evidence of the Queen's guilt was unanswerable,
and Place had to content himself with the hope that the
whole business would go far to destroy any illusions with
respect to royalty which the people might still retain.
" Multitudes of all ranks below the Peerage, even to the
barelegged sailors along shore below London Bridge,
costermongers, and common porters, went in processions
to Brandenburgh House, saw the Queen, and heard her
converse. She was the very woman herself, beyond all
other women, to satisfy the inquisitive people that the
distinction claimed by high rank was merely fictitious.
She was vulgarly familiar and commonplace in her language and deportment, much less genteel in all respects
than many of the well-dressed women who went to her in
the processions. . . . Those of the aristocracy who attended
the Queen had little either in their manners or appearance
to produce any favourable impression on the multitudes
whom, day after day and hour after hour, they had to
introduce to the presence of the Queen. Royalty was.
judged of by the Queen, and aristocracy by the noblemen
and the ladies in her suite, and both fell amazingly in the
estimation of the people." [2]

The Whigs, although they came late into the agitation
on behalf of the Queen, were yet the real gainers by it.
The newspapers which brought thousands of columns of
cheap obscenity into every corner of England, brought

[1] Commonplace Book C, p. 156.   [2] 27,789 (125, 126).

also the speeches in which Brougham and Denman lashed
the King, and the Whigs found that without pledging
themselves to any constitutional change they had become
the leaders of an almost universal popular movement.
On September 12, 1820, Wilbraham wrote from Lathom
House to Lord Colchester: "Radicalism has taken the
shape of affection for the Queen and has deserted its
old form, for we are all as quiet as lambs in this part of
England, and you would not imagine that this could have
been a disturbed country twelve months ago."[1]   And on
November 24, Lord John Russell said to Tom Moore that
"the Queen's business had done a great deal of good in
renewing the old and natural alliance of the Whigs and
the people, and weakening the influence of the Radicals
with the latter."[2]

When the excitement about the Queen died down, Place's
work as a director of Westminster elections, and an organiser
of Westminster meetings, came for a long period to an end.
A rapid improvement of trade put a stop to social exas-
peration and political activity.   At the beginning of 1820
others besides Place thought that the country was on the
verge of civil war.[3]   At its close England had entered into
a period of social peace ; the "truce" had begun "between
Parliament and the people,"[4] which continued until 1831.

In Westminster, Burdett and Hobhouse held their seats
for the next thirteen years without a contest, and the work
of local political organisation took up but a small part of
Place's attention.   The two Reform members for Westminster were after all somewhat of a disappointment.
Burdett was "too rich, too high, and too lazy,"[5] and
Place's letters to him are written in the dryest and most

[1] "Diary and Correspondence of Lord Colchester," vol. iii. p. 164.
[2] "Life of Lord John Russell," by Spencer Walpole, vol. i. p. 122.
[3] Grenville, "Memoirs," vol. i. p. 37.
[4] Article signed "Editor of the *Scotsman*," preserved in 27,809 (268).
[5] 27,791 (116).

formal style. Nor was Hobhouse of the stuff of which
really efficient political workers are made. As early as
August 27, 1819, he writes to Place: "It is, I say, natural
that a politician trudging steadfastly along the thorny,
narrow, and uninviting road should now and then look
about him to see whether the eyes of his countrymen
are upon him. It is natural that he should expect his
perseverance ought to be rewarded by a smile at least." [1]
For two years, and two years only, Hobhouse did "trudge
steadfastly along." In 1826, speaking of the sessions of
1821 and 1822, he said: "We divided on every item of
every estimate—we were glued to these seats. The evening
sun went down upon us in this hostile array, and when
he rose in the morning he shone upon our undiminished
ranks. If an Opposition despised hunger and thirst and
watchfulness for conscience' sake, it was the Opposition
that was led by my friend (Joseph Hume) during those
never-ending sessions." [2]   But on April 18, 1822, he was
already excusing himself. "You are wrong in thinking
me lazy. I can work hard enough when there is anything
to do. But the Den is a damper to industry." [3]

"As it is," Place wrote in 1826, " Burdett and Hobhouse
are little if any better than mere drawling Whigs ; but the
influence of the people in their own affairs was assisted and
maintained in 1820, and the fear of the Reformers still
remains." [4]   In 1827 Place says in his diary (December 7),
that Hobhouse had been writing from his dictation, and
adds, " If this man would learn how to work, he would
make a figure." In 1829 Place wrote to Colonel Jones
of Hobhouse : "When spoken to he says lacrimoniously
enough, ' How hard it is that when a man has done his
best he should give no satisfaction!'" He then describes

---

[1] 27,837 (186).
[2] Hobhouse, Speech on Reform, April 27, 1826.
[3] 27,837 (205).   [4] 27,843 (391).

how Hobhouse shirked all work at that Vestry Bill, by which Place hoped to reform the obscure iniquities of London local government, and proceeds: "He does not suit the electors of Westminster, nor they him, and the probability is that they will not go on much longer together."[1]

But however small might be the direct result of the Westminster contests, they had given Place himself an invaluable political education. He had learned the tactics which suited his own powers. "I know," he wrote to Hobhouse on October 29, 1819, "I have obtained a character for precipitancy, and I know I shall always retain that character. It may be partly deserved, but I know also that it has partly been acquired by acting promptly when action became necessary, it being in my opinion much better and less mischievous to act on those occasions even at the risk of doing wrong, than be, as Bentham calls it, Lord Eldonish."[2]

But above all, he, almost alone among the English politicians of his time, had now an intimate and practical acquaintance with the working of democracy. Universal suffrage in local or national elections meant for him neither a hideous nightmare nor a glorious Utopia, but simply the extension of the system existing in the city of Westminster and the few "open" parishes of the metropolis to the rest of the kingdom. "The people who are the most dreaded are the most confiding. So long as there is no glaring misconduct in their trustees, and no marked oppression upon themselves, they will not interfere; and, spite of all that has been said of demagogues misleading them, if a man cannot show them that they are really oppressed, treated with contumely and plundered, he can produce no effect upon them. Vague generalities will not avail him in parish matters where the people have the power

---

[1] Place to Colonel Jones, November 5, 1829.   [2] 27,837 (188).

to choose their own representatives. To excite them to
any extent sufficient to induce them to act in any way he
must go far beyond supposed grievances, he must have
real grievances to work upon, and even this would not
answer his purpose unless the people had been previously
dissatisfied, were ill used, and saw some chance of a
remedy through the exertions of the demagogue. And
whenever these circumstances existed, a demagogue would
be a very desirable person."

"The truth is, that the vulgarity will not choose men from
among themselves; they never do so when left perfectly
free to choose. In all such cases they invariably choose
men of property, in whom they expect to find the requisite
appropriate talent, honesty, and business-like habits, and
they make fewer mistakes than other men are apt to do.
The reason for this is, they have fewer sinister interests to
induce them to do wrong; their choice is influenced by
the desire to do good to themselves, and it so happens that
their good must always be the public good." [1]

"If they who have the power had the requisite knowledge, they would at once pass an Act giving to every parish
both the right and the power to elect their own Vestries
annually, giving to each Vestry the power to originate and
control all parish matters in every department, compelling
them, however, to proceed in one uniform way all over the
country, doing everything openly, and publishing their
audited accounts every three months. It is objected that
if men are elected for short periods they will have no time
to acquire the necessary experience, but will be continually
displaced by others who will proceed in the same course.
The very reverse is the fact, and always will be so where
the elections are really free, and the periods short, and
accountability as perfect as it can be made. It might be
decided *à priori* that this must be so. Annual election is

[1] Place to Hobhouse, March 22, 1830.

election for life if the representative do his duty in a
becoming manner. If he do otherwise, his removal is a
positive good. . . . I, who have had much to do in
managing and conducting of many associations as well as
of large, very large, bodies of people, and especially of
working people, know that they are the most docile and
most orderly of all classes. . . . The fact really is, not
that they are too clamorous, but that they are too tame
and quiescent. Fear, the child of ignorance, as Hudibras
states, creates bugbears. . . . Our business should be to
dispel fear and put reason in its place." [1]

[1] Place to Hobhouse, March 22, 1830 (?).

CHAPTER VI

THE DISMAL SCIENCE

"THE 'Inquiry into the Wealth of Nations' is not a book much to my taste. It is very proper that such subjects should be discussed, but I own that there is something in the discussion that makes me feel, while engaged in it, a painful contraction of the heart."[1] Place, in criticising this passage, says: "Every man who greatly desires the well-being of his species . . . has no doubt felt the repugnance which Mr. Godwin has mentioned, at finding himself compelled to abandon, as it were, the notions he would fain indulge without alloy, and to descend to calculations and comparisons of losses and gains, of trade, commerce, and manufactures, of the nature of rent, profit, and wages, the accumulation of capital, and the operation of taxes. But he who would essentially serve mankind has no choice; he must submit himself patiently to the pain he cannot avoid without abandoning his duty."[2]

Godwin wrote his complaint in 1820, more than forty years after the publication of the "Wealth of Nations," and both he and Place were probably thinking not so much of Adam Smith, as of the "classical" political economists Malthus, James Mill, Ricardo, and M'Culloch, who first appeared as a force in political thought at the

[1] William Godwin's "Of Population : an Enquiry concerning the Power of Increase in the Numbers of Mankind," &c. (London, 1820), p. 611.

[2] "Illustrations and Proofs of the Principle of Population," by Francis Place (London, 1822), pp. 269, 270.

end of the great war with France. Between 1815 and
1820, everybody in England who thought at all was
forced to form definite opinions on a series of very difficult economic problems. The war had left an enormous
national debt, a depreciated paper currency, a heavy
income tax, a poor law causing more misery than it
relieved, and a system of agriculture depending on a
price of food which only the most rigid protection could
keep up in times of peace. The revolutionary proposals
of Cobbett on the National Debt, and of Thomas Spence
on private ownership of land, were daily becoming better
known and more popular. Journalists, professors, men of
business, and a few statesmen were obliged to take down
Adam Smith from their shelves, and "descend to calculations and comparisons" on Currency, the Law of Rent,
and the causes which regulate International Trade. At
first a rather scattered discussion on particular points was
carried on by letters to newspapers, pamphlets, and magazine articles; but when a general, though incomplete, agreement on principles and methods had shown itself among
the dominant school of writers, systematic treatises were
published, by Ricardo in 1817, by Malthus in 1820, by
James Mill in 1821, and by M'Culloch in 1825.

Place was from the first in the thick of the controversy.
Since 1795 he had read every book or pamphlet of any importance which had appeared on social or economic questions. His correspondence with James Mill, Wakefield,
Ensor, and Hodgskin, from 1813 onwards, is full of economic
disputation. J. B. Say, the most eminent French economist
of the time, when staying for some months in England in
1814, formed a strong personal friendship with Place, and
wrote to him at intervals during the next twelve years.[1]

[1] Place may have been known to other French economists. Blanqui
calls him, "un des hommes les plus judicieux de l'Angleterre." *Dic-
tionnaire de l'Economie Politique*, de MM. Coquelin et Guillaumin
(Paris, 1853), article "Place," vol. ii. p. 369, written by Blanqui.

On economic questions Place's instincts were practical rather than speculative. As soon as he had formed an opinion, he looked round to find the definite persons whom it was important to convince on the particular point. On one matter he long felt himself helpless. When, in 1814, the proposed Corn Law was being discussed, he wrote to James Mill: "It is only for the purpose of diffusing information that it can be at all desirable to interfere with the Corn Laws; for the legislature will certainly do all in its power to keep up the rent of land, and will pass an Act for that purpose next session in spite of everything which can be done to prevent it. The rich landholders will see nothing but the decrease of rents, and having the power they will certainly prevent it, be the consequences whatever they may."[1]

On other points he was more successful. Sergeant Onslow, in 1814, carried through an Act by which the Statute of Apprentices was finally repealed, and English employers were left for a few years absolutely free from legislative interference. Place wrote to Wakefield, "The affair of Sergeant Onslow partly originated with me, but I had no suspicion it would be taken up and pushed as vigorously as it has been, and is likely to be."[2]

A large folio volume in the British Museum[3] contains the record of Place's fight against the Sinking Fund, which Pitt had started in 1786 for the gradual extinction of the National Debt. During the French war the scheme had developed into an incredibly stupid arrangement by which

[1] Place to James Mill, September 9, 1814. His efforts to diffuse information on this subject included the organisation of a riot in Westminster. See p. 57, footnote.
[2] Place to Wakefield, January 2, 1814. See p. 59.
[3] 27,836. This volume contains letters on the question written by Ricardo to Place in 1819, and reprinted in the *Economic Journal*, vol. iii. No. X., June 1893, pp. 289–93.

new stock was created at a loss to the Government in order to buy up old stock. For seventeen years, from 1812 to 1829, Place hammered away at the subject, writing articles for the *Morning Chronicle*, the *Traveller*, and any other paper that would take them, giving away thousands of copies of the same articles in pamphlet form, and towards the end coaching Hume for speeches in the House. In 1829 the whole system was quietly abolished by Act of Parliament, and Place wrote a few days later in his autobiography: "If to exult at the accomplishment of one's wishes be vanity, I plead guilty to that offence. I am as well pleased as I am capable of being at the termination of an affair in which I have no personal interest beyond that which I ought to have for the welfare of the country generally, an affair, however in which I have laboured—as often as circumstances presented the least hope of success—assiduously."

While agitating against the Sinking Fund, Place suffered much inconvenience from the apparently deliberate confusion in which the national accounts were kept. "Mr. Ricardo and Mr. Hume were both very desirous to form accurate conceptions of the Finance Accounts. We had frequent consultations on the subject, to which I gave a very considerable portion of my time, dissecting collating and compiling the Public Finance Accounts and Statements. No balances had ever been stated in any of these accounts. . . . I had for several years past turned my attention to the subject, and understood more of these accounts than perhaps any other person out of office. I was not however able to construct an accurate balance sheet from the accounts and papers printed by order of Parliament. No two papers agreed, and when others were moved for, the disagreement was increased. . . . This at length led to proceedings, which early in the year 1822 terminated in a select committee of the House of Commons "to consider of the best mode of simplifying the accounts annually laid before Parliament."[1]

In 1826 he wrote in a working-men's paper a defence of political economy, and pointed to what the economists had already done. "It was the political economists who developed the baneful effects of the Corn Laws, and it is they, and they alone, who, by their writings, their lectures, their speeches, and their conversations, have so far enlightened the people as at length to produce an almost general demand for the repeal of those mischievous and unjust laws. To the political economists we owe the relaxation of our absurd Navigation Laws. To them we owe the repeal of the manifold laws which constituted the obnoxious laws known by the name of the Combination Laws. To them we owe the knowledge, which is fast pervading the community, respecting a secure currency. Their knowledge has at length made its way into the Houses of Parliament and into the Cabinet, and has produced very important effects. And the good which has resulted from this knowledge has happily been such that ignorance will never more obtain the ascendency. How much more good the principles advocated by the political economists will do this country, it is quite impossible for any one to predict, but that they will be very great, no reasonable man can doubt. The political economists are the great enlighteners of the people. Look at their works from the time of the great man Adam Smith to the 'Essay on Wages,' just published by Mr. M'Culloch, and see if they have not, all along, deprecated everything which was in any way calculated to do injury to the people; see if they have not been pre-eminently the advocates for increasing the knowledge of the working classes in every possible way, and then let any man say, if he can, that they have

[1] "Autobiography."

L

not been as pre-eminently the best friends of those classes." [1]

Place was, however, far from being one of the mere "practical" politicians, of whom he often spoke with unmeasured scorn. He strove by severe and minute study to acquire a consistent intellectual basis for his work. The beautifully written notes which he made when reading Ricardo's "Principles of Political Economy" are nearly as long as the book itself. He was an industrious collector of tables of wages, statistics of population, and any other information by which an old generalisation could be tried or a new one suggested.[2] And he brought to this work an experience of industrial life which saved him from some of the characteristic faults of the Ricardian school. He never consciously or unconsciously looked upon the mass of the people merely as instruments for enriching a "nation" of capitalists and landlords. His anger was always most vehemently excited by the cheap accusations of idleness and vice, which newspapers and members of Parliament were never tired of bringing against the whole working class. In a pamphlet written in 1829, he says: "A labouring man should have no fits of idleness; so says pride, wilfulness, and ignorance. He who of all men, the negro slave excepted, has the fewest inducements to constant, unremitted toil, should be free from idle feelings. This is impossible. Every man has his fits of idleness. No man in any class has always the

---

[1] The *Trades' Newspaper and Mechanics' Weekly Journal*, No. 52, June 18, 1826.

[2] *Cf. e.g.*, the tables of wages from 1777, collected by Place and published in the *Gorgon*, 1818, and a letter from Place to James Mill (September 9, 1814). "Have you seen the Corn Reports of the Lords' Committee? I have been comparing parts of them with the returns to the Population Acts, 1811, [and] the tables of progressive increase of the population in the last century. The table of births, burials, and baptisms when compared with the price of bread and the wages of labour, exhibits some curious and important phenomena."

same desire for exertion or investigation; no, nor even for the pursuit of pleasure, when even pleasure alone is the object of his useless life. No man at all times follows even the most gratifying pursuit or inquiry with the same zeal: relaxation becomes absolutely necessary, and this is sought in change in his pursuits and in change of place, by every one whose means enable him to indulge in what is, in relation to the working-man, called idleness—the word being used in respect to him in its worst and most opprobrious sense. The working-man must have no relaxation; he who drudges constantly against his will, must have no such propensities as are allowed and cherished in his superior; the unintellectual man must exert greater powers of mind than the intellectual man; must show by his conduct that his is the superior understanding, or he is condemned as unworthy; and this is called judging him fairly. The most painstaking, saving, industrious man is not free from the desire of leisure; there are times when he is unable to bring himself to the conclusion that he must continue working. I know not how to describe the sickening aversion which at times steals over the working-man, and utterly disables him, for a longer or shorter period, from following his usual occupation, and compels him to indulge in *idleness*. I have felt it, resisted it to the utmost of my power, but have been so completely subdued by it that, spite of very pressing circumstances, I have been obliged to submit and run away from my work. This is the case with every workman I have ever known; and in proportion as a man's case is hopeless will such fits more frequently occur and be of longer duration. The best informed amongst the workmen will, occasionally, solace themselves at such times with liquor: the uninformed will almost always recur to the same means to procure the excitement which must be procured." [1]

1 " Improvement of the Working People," by Francis Place, Sen. (London, 1834), pp. 13-15. A misprint in the second line is corrected by Place in the copy preserved in 27,825 (217-225).

He had been himself secretary of several trade unions, and refused to denounce as fools or criminals those who would face any suffering rather than accept less than the trade union rate of wages. In 1815 he told the Committee on Mendicity that "When journeymen tradesmen in the Metropolis were unemployed, and however long the period they remained unemployed, they never would work for less than the full wages." Lord Lascelles, the chairman of the committee, called out, "Here is the evil. Do you not think, Mr. Place, that this is very wrong?" "No," he answered, "it is the perfection of wisdom in them. Let us suppose there were 40,000 men unemployed, and 40,000 employed. All the work required is, at the time, done by 40,000 men, and there is no demand for any more. If the 40,000 unemployed men were so unwise as to undersell the others, they might displace them. But these in their turn would be displaced, and they would soon be reduced to the situation to which *you* have reduced the agricultural labourer. They would all be paupers, and being so in this large city, they would lose all the independence and self-respect they now possess; they would no longer dress decently and becomingly; they would lose all the admirable intelligence they possess; they would become vicious and beastly, and full of crimes of all sorts; cruel, vindictive, and miserable beyond all example; and the whole nation would feel the sad consequences. Gentlemen need not be alarmed; there can be no reason for concealment; you, not they, are ignorant of these things. They know them well, understand them thoroughly, and act most wisely. No danger can therefore arise from their seeing in print what they already know." [1]

In the same way, though he defends Malthus' general position, he turns to denounce the crude statement in the

---

[1] Place to James Mill, July 20, 1815. This evidence was omitted from the official report as irrelevant.

"Principles of Population," that no man has a "right" to public support, and that therefore the system of Poor Relief should be entirely abolished. "Mr. Malthus denies to the unemployed poor man the right to eat, but he allows the right to the unemployed rich man. He says, 'Every man may do as he will with his own'; and he expects to be able to satisfy the starving man with bare assertions of abstract rights. Mr. Malthus is not speaking of *legal right*, for, he says, the poor have a *legal right*, which is the very thing he proposes to destroy. It is an abstract right which is denied to the poor man, but allowed to the rich; and this abstract, which has no meaning, although dignified with the title of the 'law of nature, which is the law of God,' is to be explained and taught to the poor, who are to be fully convinced.'" [1]

Again, when, in 1815, all his friends were clamouring for the repeal of the income tax, he opposed them, on the ground that the burden would be "shifted from the rich to the other classes. . . . The rich will be relieved, the middle classes injured, and the labourer distressed." [2] In the same year a Mr. Benett of Warminster, in advocating the Corn Law, "threatened the meeting that, unless the Parliament passed an Act to protect his property, he would remove to a country where his diminished income would support him as it ought to do." Place added, "One thing he omitted to say, which was, to threaten to take the land away." [3] Again and again he denounces the great landlords of his time. "All they cry out against is the high wages of labour, and they exult at every opportunity to reduce them. They (as Paine said some years ago) depend more on breaking the spirit of the people by poverty, than

---

[1] "Illustrations and Proofs of the Principle of Population" (London, 1822), p. 137.

[2] Place to Mill, February 15, 1815.

[3] Place to Mill, January 16, 1815.

they fear goading them into insurrection by oppression.
Thus the whole value of all the improvements in agriculture goes to the landowners, and the price, so far as it is
advanced by the increased rent, is levied by them upon
the people, who are unable to purchase necessaries with
the miserable pittance they receive for their labour."[1]

With all his courage and industry and sympathy,
Place never attained, perhaps never could have attained,
the intellectual force required for original and creative
economic thought. He was to the end a disciple rather
than a maker, and a disciple who accepted without
reserve the one doctrine from which the classical political economy followed as a series of corollaries, Malthus'
celebrated "Principle of Population." Replying, in 1818,
to Ensor, who was just about to publish his essay on
population,[2] and who boasted that it contained, among
other things, "a refutation of Malthus,"[3] Place says:
"As for your answer to Malthus, I shall judge of it
when I see it. I do not know exactly what you mean
when you say, 'I have refuted Malthus.' His propositions,
assumed at random, may be easily refuted: they were
assumed for the purpose of illustration, and are necessarily
incorrect. Much, too, of his reasoning may be refuted.
But I do not expect to see what I call the principle dis-
proved; namely, that in all old settled countries the population presses against starvation, and is kept from increasing
with the rapidity which, but for the want of produce, it
would increase."[4]

It is difficult at the present time to appreciate with
anything like justice the fears of those who studied the
population question at the beginning of this century.

[1] Place to James Mill, October 17, 1814.
[2] "An Inquiry Concerning the Population of Nations," &c., by
George Ensor (London, 1818).
[3] Ensor to Place, January [N.D.] 1818.
[4] Place to Ensor, January 18, 1818.

Food-stuffs can now be brought in time of peace from thinly populated to thickly populated countries with an ease then undreamt of, and whole populations can, as far as transport is concerned, move in search of food with equal ease. The population question has become international rather than national, and its merely numerical urgency has been at least postponed for some centuries. The increase of wealth per head has, during the last half-century, been greatest just in those countries in which population has increased most rapidly. In addition to this, both in Europe and America, the birth-rate during recent years has been steadily falling, while in France population has remained almost stationary. Social distress is still everywhere to be found, but it has no apparent relation either to population per acre, or to excess of births over deaths. Compare with this the facts accessible to those who had to study the results of the first three English censuses of 1801, 1811, and 1821. All statistics went to show that population throughout Europe had been growing at a geometrical ratio, which actually increased during the period of the Napoleonic wars. Emigration hardly existed. There were no railways and no steamships. Each nation had to look to its own fields for its own subsistence, and the law of diminishing returns to agriculture was believed to be already operative in every part of Europe. The English economists saw continually before them the state of Ireland, which had then nearly two million one hundred thousand more inhabitants than at the present time,[1] and where the congestion of population most undoubtedly did keep down the standard of comfort.

In England the increase of population had been accom-

[1] The census of 1821 was the first which was taken in Ireland by the Census Commissioners. Their report returned a population of 6,801,827. The census of 1891 gave a population of only 4,704,750, a decrease of 30.87 per cent.

panied by a rapid improvement of industrial processes; and
yet Place, in 1826, referring to the trade depression of the
preceding winter, could say that "a race has been run between the improvement of machinery and the increase
of population, and population has beaten machinery."[1]
Ricardo, sitting in his study, could quietly prophesy that
this would go on until the "natural" point was reached,
at which, either from the distress consequent on the fall
of wages, or from a decrease of marriages, the death-rate
of the working classes overtook their birth-rate.[2]

But to Place, a merely "scientific" attitude was impossible. When he thought of the "working classes," he
pictured to himself an endless procession of men such as
he had been, with wives and children like his own. The
lowering of wages to their "natural" level meant to him
the repetition, millions of times over, of the starvation
and weariness and despair which he had gone through,
before he had been willing to give up his skilled trade
and apply for work as a parish scavenger. He, like other
political economists, believed that population was in England already redundant, and that no permanent social
improvement could be looked for until its increase had
been checked. But, unlike the others, he was filled with
a burning sense that something had to be *done*, and done
immediately, and done by him, to check it. Malthus had
expressed a hope that late marriages would become the

---

[1] *Diary*, July 19, 1826.
[2] Ricardo, in his "Principles of Political Economy" (London, 1817),
p. 90, says: "The natural price of labour is that price which is necessary to enable the labourers, one with another, to subsist, and to per-
petuate their race, without either increase or diminution." In the
same sense Place writes: "The real wages of the labourer in a redundant population are no more than, according to the habits of the country,
will enable him to subsist and propagate his race, and he must have
the same real wages, and will have no more, while the population is
redundant, whether the taxes remain or are all repealed." (*Diary*,
October 12, 1826.)

rule. But Place was convinced that for the working classes, and, indeed, for all classes, delay of marriage was harmful, even if it were possible.

To go even as far as Malthus and Mill had gone was dangerous. Careful as Malthus had been, his name was already spitten upon by almost every decent and religious-minded man or woman in the country. To doubt that "God sent food for every mouth which He sent into the world" was blasphemous; to inquire further was obscene. With all Place's dogged courage, it must have cost him a struggle before he entered, as he did about 1820, upon a deliberate propaganda of neo-Malthusianism. In a book which he published in 1822, he plainly, though carefully, stated his position, and in the introduction said: "The author is perfectly aware that he has exhibited views and proposed remedies which will with some persons expose him to censure; but he is also aware of the utility of thus exposing himself."[1]

From this time forward Place continually advanced the neo-Malthusian position in argument with every working-man whose confidence or gratitude he could earn, in every working-class newspaper that would admit his letters, and in his correspondence with private friends and public acquaintances. As a consequence his name, for twenty years, was hardly ever mentioned in print without some reference, deprecatory or abusive, to his notorious opinions. Good men refused to be introduced to him, and, in 1834, his help was declined on this ground alone by the strongly liberal "Society for the Promotion of Useful Knowledge."[2]

[1] "Illustrations and Proofs of the Principle of Population," by Francis Place (London, 1822), p. 12.

[2] Cf. the MS. account of matters relating to "Essays for the People," 1834. The rest of the inner circle of the Benthamites seem to have shared Place's opinion, though he alone faced the public scandal. See the letter from Bentham to Place on p. 81, James Mill's article on

Among the leaders of the workmen he met with but little success. "All were opposed," he says, "to the 'Malthusian doctrine,' as they called the 'Principle of Population,' plain and simple as it is, namely, 'The people have the power to increase their number.' All disregarded the fact that the people had increased and were increasing, and over-running the means of subsistence; and that under the hindrances opposed by the landlords to the improvement of husbandry by the application of chemistry and machinery to land, the actual increase of produce was very small, whilst the increase of people was very great, that the disproportion would continually increase, until the time should come when a stop would be put to all increase of capital, and consequently of employment, and the working people be reduced to the mud cabins and potato diet of the Irish cottars, and ruin follow in its train, or that the people should generally revolt, produce a frightful revolution, in which would be sacrificed an incalculable amount of property, and the extirpation of the aristocracy in all its branches." [1]

Place was often accused of invincible prejudice on this point. "On all other subjects but Malthusianism, Mr. Place is a close, a candid, and a most even-tempered reasoner; but doubt the infallibility of his anti-population creed, and he is ready to treat you as the Homoousian Christians did their diphthongal controvertists, the Homoiousians, in the fifth century. The only answers he will condescend to give are, 'You don't understand political economy; your words have no sense in them; they contain no distinct ideas.' " [2]

Colonies in the supplement to the "Encyclopædia Britannica," 1824, vol. iii. p. 257, and the incident recorded of John Mill by Christie. ("John Stuart Mill and Mr. Abraham Hayward, Q.C.," by W. D. Christie, London, 1873, p. 9). For Place's neo-Malthusianism, see letter to Burdett, May 1, 1824, and also 27,823 (337).

[1] 27,819 (74).

[2] The *Northern Liberator*, December 30, 1837, in an article by A. H. Beaumont.

This is not the occasion to enter upon that unwritten chapter of English working-class history which begins with Robert Dale Owen and Francis Place, and ends with Charles Bradlaugh. But without reference to it, it is impossible to understand Place's general position with regard to social reform. His desire was, not that population should be stationary, but that its increase should be slower than the probable improvement in methods of production —in his phrase, that "machinery should be allowed to beat population in the race." He could work for education, democracy, freedom of combination, everything that tended to the general diffusion of knowledge and self-respect, because he believed that knowledge and self-respect were not only good in themselves, but likely to lead to a restraint of population. Once men had become wise on that one point, he was prepared to welcome economic equality, though on an individualistic basis, as readily as political equality. But so long as population continued without restraint, a more equal distribution of wealth would, he thought, simply drag every one down to a common level.[1] "No doubt," he wrote in 1818, "a somewhat better mode of producing, accumulating, and enjoying might be desired, but the time when this will be understood and acted upon is, I fear, very distant. . . . It is not of much consequence whether England contains twelve or fifteen millions of bipeds, or Ireland six or eight millions of similar animals, but of much importance it is that they should be well instructed and well governed, and made comfortable; but these desirable purposes can only be accomplished by restraining their increase."[2]   Or again, when arguing against Ensor in the *Trades' Newspaper*, he says: "In Ireland there are 365 persons to every square mile, while in England there are not more than 200. In England,

---

[1] *Cf.* the same argument in J. S. Mill's "Principles of Political Economy" (London, 1865, 2 vols.), vol. i. pp. 238, 239.

[2] Place to Ensor, January 18, 1818.

with 200 persons to a square mile, there are always a considerable number of poor persons; but in Ireland, with 365 persons to a square mile, a large proportion of the whole population is constantly in a state of such extreme wretchedness that there is no parallel to it in England, except in some few instances, and on some extraordinary occasions. The misery which has some time past prevailed in portions of our manufacturing districts always exists in Ireland. . . . 'But,' says Mr. Ensor, 'there is sufficient food for all the people, if that food was distributed as God intended it should be, for the use, and not the abuse, of the idle and the aristocratic.' This is another fallacy—a misleading, mischievous fallacy. Mr. Ensor's proof that there is food enough is that the people have subsisted. True enough it is that the people who have subsisted have subsisted; and true enough it is that by a better arrangement of society, capital might have increased somewhat faster than it has increased; but if the population had increased as rapidly as capital increased, the people would have been precisely in the same relative situation as they now are; all the difference would have been that the number of sufferers would have been greater than it is. Strange it is that Mr. Ensor should not have seen through his fallacy. That there has been, and that there is, the means of subsistence for the people, is proved by their being alive. But the political economists are not satisfied with this; they want something better for the people; they are not satisfied that those who exist should *barely exist*—that they should have low wages, and no leisure, and no pleasure, no recreation, and no instruction. They are not satisfied that their number should be constantly kept up to the starvation point, and that hunger, disease, and misery should be the only means of keeping down their number." [1] He opposed, on Malthusian grounds, the

---

[1] The *Trades' Newspaper and Mechanics' Weekly Journal*, Jan. 18, 1826.

encouragement of allotments or small holdings;[1] but though he argued against any immediate alteration in the distribution of land, he was for the greater part of his life a land nationaliser. He had been converted in the old days by Thomas Spence, and hoped that when the population difficulty had once been settled, private property in land would come to an end.[2]

On such immediate legislative proposals as could not be judged merely by their effect on the growth of population, Place followed the economists of his time in leaning strongly towards individual freedom. He gave evidence, for instance, before the Committee on Drunkenness in 1834, in favour of absolute free trade in the liquor traffic. But to the end of his life he was too much influenced by the habits of thought which he had learned as a trade union secretary, to be either comfortable or consistent in preaching absolute freedom of industrial contract. He strongly urged, for instance, the trade unions in the factory districts to exclude women and children from the mills,[3] and to lower the hours of labour by general action. He even advocated the exclusion of children and girls under twenty-one by law.[4] On the other hand, the Ten Hours Bill, which proposed to shut the factories outright at the end of the legal day, aroused his strongest opposition, and he wrote

[1] Cf. e.g., Place to Beauclerk, April 7, 1831.
[2] Cf. Place to Whytoch, October 28, 1839. " It is my hope and belief that the time will come when men will be sufficiently wise to agree that all the land shall belong to the people, and that too upon the plan, or some such plan, as Mr. Spence has promulgated, by which the people shall be the sole landlord, and receive all the rent." Cf. also the Northern Liberator, December 30, 1837, and an article in the Traveller for January 1821, which shows that at that time he was against land nationalisation, on account of the great and uncontrolled revenue which it would give to the central Government.
[3] Cf. Place's article, " Handloom Weavers and Factory Workers, a Letter to James Turner, cotton spinner," in J. A. Roebuck's " Pamphlets for the People," September 29, 1835, p. 5.
[4] Ibid, p. 9.

in reference to it, " Every suggestion which does not tend
to the reduction in number of the working people is use·
less, to say the least of it. All legislative interference must
be pernicious. Men must be left to themselves to make
their own bargains : the law must compel the observance of
compacts, the fulfilment of contracts. There it should
end. So long as the supply of labour exceeds the demand
for labour, the labourer will undersell his fellows, and produce poverty, misery, vice, and crime."

" The remedy again is good teaching, which will in time
make men see the evils of redundant population, cause
them to respect themselves, induce them to marry at an
early age, give them a companion in a wife, the only true
companion which a man may ever have for a real and long
continuance, give him a home in which he may improve
himself and enable him to teach the few, very few, children
he may choose to propagate, and enjoy himself as a rational
being ought to do." [1]

It is probable that his intellectual conviction upon
the point of freedom was strengthened by the fact
that his personal acquaintance with industrial life was
confined to a home-working trade. " I have never,"
he wrote in 1835, " seen the inside of a cotton factory.
It is almost certain that I never shall see the inside
of one. I have read all the evidence taken by Committees of Parliament ; I have read books and pamphlets ;
I have conversed with numbers of cottoners, masters as
well as men ; I understand much of the machinery used in
all sorts of mills, and should like to see it in use. But
I cannot voluntarily submit to see the misery of working
it before my eyes. I abhor such scenes of degradation, as
even the best of the cotton-mills cannot be free from.

---

[1] 27,827 (194). See also the "Letter to James Turner," p. 8, and
27,820 (153). Place several times declared that in those trades where
children work the whole family earned no more than a man in trades
open to men only. See, for instance, 27,828 (117).

This will be treated as a ridiculous feeling, as an absurd prejudice; but to me, to whom human beings are valuable as they are intellectual and free, a cotton-mill is more abhorrent than I can find words with which to describe it."[1]

But he seems to hesitate in his individualism when writing of so clear an invasion of individual freedom as a proposed Truck Act. He declares indeed that, "No restrictive laws should exist. Every one should be at liberty to make his own bargain in the best way he can." But he adds, "I cannot, however, but lament that the tendency of this freedom is against the interest of the workman, and in favour of his employer. Whatever any man who employs a large number of work-people proposes as a regulation is sure to be something for his own advantage, and for the disadvantage of the work-people; it can scarcely ever be otherwise." Then he bursts out into a fury against those great employers whom the Truck Acts were intended to check. "I go sick at heart when I think of such men as Yates; I always become a savage when I see them; I would not have such men even for common acquaintances, no, not for 'all the gold which sinews bought and sold have ever earned.'"[2]

[1] See the "Letter to James Turner," p. 9.
[2] Place to Hume, January 7, 1830.

CHAPTER VII

THE CHARING CROSS LIBRARY

" *The writer of this, though by circumstances separated from the immediate acquaintance of Mr. Place for several years past, can, by the experience of eighteen and the well-founded report of forty years, pronounce him a prodigy of useful, resolute, consistent, political exertion, and indefatigable labour, which evidently continues unabated to this day. . . . Francis Place, by his assistant labours and advice given to members of the House of Commons, has produced more effect in that House than any man who was ever a member.*" [1]

There is an old gentleman still alive and active, who can remember being taken as a boy, about the year 1820, up into a big room lined with books at the back of Place's shop, and being told in a reverential voice that this was the headquarters of English Radicalism.[2] Place had been a collector of books ever since his school-days, and continued to collect nearly to the end of his life. From the first the library was especially rich in Parliamentary papers, catalogued by subjects, and in pamphlets and newspaper cuttings, bound and lettered with his own hand. Everything was arranged with that scrupulous "method and tidiness and comfort" to which Place's correspondents often refer.[3]

[1] See article on "The Real Nobility of the Human Character," by A. P. [*i.e.* Richard Carlile], in the *Monthly Magazine*, May 1835, p. 454.
[2] *Cf.* also "Sixty Years of an Agitator's Life," by G. J. Holyoake (London, 1893, 2 vols.), vol. i. p. 215.
[3] *Cf. e.g.*, T. Hodgskin to Place, May 19, 1819.

Francis Place

From the original drawing in South Kensington Museum, by MACLISE,
reproduced in " Fraser's Magazine," April 1836.

To face page 177.

This was the "Civic Palace, Charing Cross," where the "Arch Radical"[1] sat all day long on a high stool at his desk, as before his retirement from business he had sat all day long in the adjoining shop. Every member of Parliament who lived, as most members then did, in Bloomsbury or the City, would pass Charing Cross twice a day. In any case, the House of Commons and Downing Street were both within a few minutes' walk.

"My library," says Place,[2] "was a sort of gossiping shop for such persons as were in any way engaged in public matters having the benefit of the people for their object. . . . No one who knew me would hesitate to consult with me on any subject on which I could either give or procure information." And again, "When I lived at Charing Cross my library was frequented very much in the manner of a common coffee-house room. It was open to a considerable number of persons, many of them members of Parliament."[3] In times of excitement the room became crowded.

A very good description of Place and his daily life about this time, was given in the *Northern Liberator.* "Francis Place . . . is in the sixty-fifth year of his age. He is about five feet seven inches high, with a head which would delight the phrenological taste of our worthy friend Alderman Fife, and is of a stout, stalwart frame. A walk of twenty or thirty miles a day is one of

[1] George Ensor to Place, 1820 [N.D.].

[2] In a loose sheet, dated April 1834. There is a good description of Place and the company at his library in "Lord Melbourne," by Henry Dunckley (1890), pp. 150, 151.

[3] Place to B. Hawes, M.P. [for Lambeth], April 24, 1839. Hawes' reply is interesting, as showing the view taken of Place by his political pupils.

"LAMBETH, *May* 1, 1839.

"My DEAR SIR,—In reply to your note, I only wish you and your library were where it was. The good sentry, well posted as you were, would do us all a world of good. . . . Never mind. I'll fight on and be satisfied with your honest approval—and fight on till you cry hold.

Yours sincerely,   B. HAWES."

M

his favourite amusements; but his time, from six in the morning to eleven at night, is generally spent in his library, where he is surrounded with books, pamphlets, journals, and memoranda of every kind—political, philological, physiological, and every other 'cal' which can be imagined, all arranged in such perfect order that he can put his hand on any book or paper he may want in a moment. The bump of order is in him very prominent indeed."[1]

Among the politicians who attended the "Civic Palace" there were always some who came not merely to gather facts, but to obtain general political guidance from their host. To such Place was rather a hard taskmaster. He never expected them to take his advice, but if they did not he dealt very faithfully with them. "I told Bennet,"[2] he wrote in 1819, "from the first that I should wear him out, and that he would be obliged either to shun me or lead a dog's life with his party. He said, No; I said, Yes. He has done so. But next session he will come again, and as he certainly means well, I shall be pleased to see him. I never suffer the motives which operate in another man's mind to have much influence on my conduct."[3]

A few entries in the private diary for 1826 record Place's experience of a better-known politician, Colonel Torrens.

"*Thursday, October* 12.—A long conversation with Colonel Torrens on the most prominent matters likely to be brought before Parliament in the ensuing session, . . . and the means of keeping himself independent of cabals, which never fail to compromise a man's usefulness."

"*Saturday, October* 28.—Colonel Torrens—is willing to do all he can to get a meeting of such titled and other

---

[1] The *Northern Liberator*, December 30, 1837. Article by the editor, A. H. Beaumont.

[2] The Hon. Grey Bennet, M.P., whom Place coached for some time.

[3] Place to Hobhouse, August 16, 1819.   27,837 (172).

landowners as may be willing to publish a declaration against the Corn Laws."

"*Friday, November* 3.—Colonel Torrens . . . much talk. . . . There is some chance that a nucleus will be formed in the new House of Commons of a few men who are too discreet to join the worn-out, palsied Whigs, and are better informed on the true mode of legislating than men have hitherto been. Cautioned Torrens against joining the club at the Clarendon, in which the miserable Whigs stultify every fresh-catched member."

"*Thursday, November* 16.—Colonel Torrens—who is somewhat puzzled with the annoyance of his pretended Whig friends, who, he says, are advising him not to do anything this session of Parliament, telling him that if he does so he will be called a talking, busy fellow, and will lose himself. . . . I advised him, as I have often done before, not to make speeches, but to say whatever he thought was necessary on subjects which he thoroughly understood."

"*Tuesday, November* 21.—Torrens, it is evident, is playing a game in which he may not, and I hope will not, be a gainer. He admitted that he did not mean to take a manly, decided part . . . but to act cautiously, that is, to feel his way to some place or office."

"*Monday, November* 27.—Colonel Torrens—with whom a long conversation respecting the House of Commons. He, as usual, paltering and shuffling."

"*Tuesday, December* 5.—To Colonel Torrens on the subject of Mr. Hume's motion or notice for to-morrow night relating to the exportation of machinery. Was not a little disappointed at finding Torrens utterly ignorant of the subject, and that, notwithstanding his knowledge of political economy, he talked like a silly old woman of the advantages of impeding the French manufacture of cotton goods. . . . But he is a poor creature, and will make no figure as an opponent of Ministers in what is bad, and will not be worth their purchasing."

"*Wednesday, December* 13.—Colonel Torrens—he is a shuffler, and we do not agree. We shall soon cut."

The entry for a day in 1826, which happens to be in rather shorter form than usual, will give a specimen of Place's average day's work at that time.

"*Monday, April* 10, 1826.—Wrote a long letter to Sir Francis Burdett on the expenses and arrears of the last West. Elections in 1820. The election cost £1600 and £96 still remained unpaid. I have paid £130; and Mr. Henry Brooks, who is liable for the £96, cannot afford to pay it—so I asked Sir F. B. to pay that sum on Henry Brooks's account.

"Heard at the Royal Institution M'Culloch's third Lecture on Political Economy.

"Called on Mr. Hobhouse—had a long conversation, on the case of Dr. Thorpe, and got a promise of an appointment for Dr. Thorpe to see him and Burdett together.

"Walked with my wife, out from half-past ten to half-past two.

"Read at Mr. Hume's request and for the satisfaction of the seamen of the Tyne and Wear who had written to me on the subject, "a Bill to enable commissioners for trying offences upon the sea," &c. &c. Noted it, and wrote to the seamen. The Bill, if passed into a law as it is at present worded, would be an act of injustice towards the seamen.

"Read—six letters sent to me by Mr. Hume—correspondence respecting the absurd Potteries Bill which I noted on the 6th, and about which I conferred with Mr. Mayre the potter.

"*N.B.*—The Bill is bad in every respect, and will not be passed.

"Read proof of Sheet B, vol. ii., 'Travels in Chili and La Plata.'

"Interrupted in the evening by Mr. Tijou and Charles Blake—and afterwards by George White, a clerk in the House of Commons, who came to tell me 'the good news' that ministers had been beaten from their project.

"Read two articles in the *Bolton Chronicle* respecting the miserable state ,of the weavers and others, and containing absurd proposals to fix a minimum of wages and to stop the use of machinery.

"Wrote a short paper composed of questions for the *Bolton Chronicle.*

"Mr. Benn respecting D. Richards, the Vicar, who wants a clause in the Charing X Improvement Bill to compel the parishioners to pay his curate. Refused to see the Dr., but took care to defeat his purpose through Mr. Hobhouse."

It is very curious to note how much Place's businesslike and methodical habits dominated his political as well as his private life. In spite of his constant meetings with politicians and important persons, he seldom made friends with any of them. They were almost invariably treated as persons engaged in business might have been, and just as his customers were invited to come to his shop, so his political associates were expected to come to his library. He consistently declined to call upon them at their own homes under any circumstances. He valued his independence too highly to meet them on any but absolutely equal terms, which he knew by experience it was not always easy for "the tailor" to secure. A year before Colonel Torrens' visits, Place wrote a general account of his relations with all such political catechumens, which explains his attitude admirably. "The various public, political, and parliamentary matters in which I have interfered," said he, " have brought me acquainted

with many great men, and caused me to be most
graciously invited to call upon some of them. This
I have never done, unless something which related to
others made it necessary, and this happened very
seldom. It was a rule with me from the first never to
call on any great man in any other case, and I do not
believe I have seen so many as half-a-dozen lords and
commoners at their own houses, excepting Burdett, Hobhouse, and Hume, and not even either of them unless on
business. To all invitations I have replied, that I was at
home till eleven o'clock in the morning, and after four
o'clock in the afternoon; was always ready to attend to
any suggestion, and to co-operate in any project which
was likely to be useful, and especially if it related to the
working people. With those public men who called I
always communicated freely. Several have expressed a
desire to become better acquainted with me; but this I
always declined, as our circumstances and habits of life
differed greatly, and I could not consent to be patronised,
or to be a 'humble friend'; to come when I was sent for,
and to go when my presence was not quite agreeable, and
to take care not to be in the way when other great men
or women were there. To those who wished to be better
acquainted I said, you can be as much better acquainted
with me as you please by calling here when you have
anything to do for the public good in which I can in
any way assist. But as their notions of what was for the
public good very often differed from my notion of what
was for the public good; as almost the whole of them made
party politics their rule of action; as I disliked both the
great political parties, and as my notions were well known
to be republican, a few interviews were generally sufficient
for their purposes, and our intercourse as generally ceased." [1]

[1] Place to Thomas Campbell, February 10, 1825. [In the "Autobiography," chap. 14.]

Place's greatest and most permanent success as a Parliamentary schoolmaster was with Joseph Hume. Hume's
dogged industry, and the enduring strength of his short
and awkward body, saved him from any accusation of
idleness and frivolity. A certain dulness of feeling was
useful to him, not only in protecting him for thirty
years against the slings and arrows of the House of
Commons, but also in enabling him placidly to receive
and act upon those angry letters and remonstrances which
Place's other pupils must often have found intolerably
overbearing.

Hume was advised by his friend the Duke of Kent
to make Place's acquaintance, and in July 1813 they
were introduced to each other by Fox the Quaker,
with whom Place was then busily engaged in the promotion of the Lancastrian school system.[1] Place, at first,
had no great liking for his new acquaintance, but he was
persuaded by Mill to take Hume up. In a letter to Mrs.
Grote, in 1836, Place described their connection with each
other. "Mill fixed him upon me some twenty-five years
since.[2] I found him devoid of information, dull and
selfish. From the country he came from, India, and the
way in which he commenced his public life here, I had no
reliance on him for good service, and no grounds for placing
confidence in his integrity. Mill said, 'Work on with him
and he will come out; there is much in him that will grow
by good nursing; and even if after a while he turn out ill,
we shall have the advantage of all the good he may have
done.' Our intimacy brought obloquy upon both of us, to
which he was nearly as callous as I was. He was taunted
with 'the tailor his master,' without whom he could do
nothing. I was scoffed at as a fool for spending time

[1] *Cf.* Chap. IV.
[2] James Mill had been at school with Hume at Montrose Academy.
See "James Mill: a Biography," by Alexander Bain (London
1882), p. 7.

uselessly upon 'Old Joe,' upon 'The Apothecary.' He
was treated as no man before him ever was treated, and
worse, too, by the Whigs than by the Tories. Some of the
leading men at Brooks's treated him with feigned respect
to his face, and scoffed at him behind his back, and talked
of him as ' the fellow who dined at three o'clock and knew
nothing of the habits and manners of a gentleman.' The
slightest error in a calculation was imputed to him as
imbecility and ignorance. The mistake of saying ' tear and
wear,' putting the last word first, was matter of exultation
against him, and was held forth by the Whigs as a proof
that he was stupid and good for nothing. Often have I
repeated such things as these to him, and cautioned him
not in anything to rely upon the hollow-hearted, shallow-
headed men who would make friends with him if they saw
therein the prospect of destroying his utility. Mill's pre-
dictions were realised. Hume showed his capabilities and
his imperturbable perseverance, which have beaten down
all opposition; and there he stands, the man of men." [1]

It was easy enough for Place at any time between 1822
and 1827 to justify his furious contempt for ordinary party
politics. George Canning had become Foreign Secretary
and leader of the House of Commons in 1822. For the
next five years he, with Peel as Home Secretary, and
Huskisson as President of the Board of Trade, developed
a policy which was Tory in little but name. Canning did
all that he could do to encourage the reaction against
despotism abroad; while Huskisson and Peel, accepting in
large part the doctrines of the political economists, freed
the internal trade of the country from some of its most
harassing restrictions, and seriously alarmed those whose
rents depended upon protection against foreign imports.
The Whig leaders could only hope to represent themselves
as more advanced than the Tories, by advocating either

[1] Place to Mrs. Grote, May 13, 1836 ("Autobiography").

absolute freedom of trade or a democratic extension of the franchise. But they did not believe in Free Trade, and were nervous about anything except the mildest measures of Parliamentary reform. As long therefore as the Tories allowed the Canningites to lead them the Whigs were a negligible quantity in politics. Writing in 1821, Place declared: "Much has been done by the electors in Westminster since 1806 towards unmasking this faction, and never was it in a more contemptible state than at the present moment. Without power or the hope of power, less popular, and deservedly so, than the party in power, it is of no political importance whatever. Distrusted, if not despised, by a considerable portion of the people, even its name will probably in a few years be lost. Or, if it remain, it will be received as the name of Tories out of place, and will be simply applied to any opposition not composed of Radical reformers, however and of whomsoever constituted." [1]

Under such circumstances the Parliamentary debates became the merest faction fights, and the obvious duty of a reformer in the House of Commons was, not to combine and compromise, but to educate. "Hitherto," complained Place, "the government of the country had been administered on no general principles, but by temporary expedients for the purpose of accomplishing particular objects or to ward off particular inconveniences." [2] He firmly believed that the necessary "general principles" had now been worked out by Bentham and the economists, and that if only they were continually advertised, the steady increase of popular knowledge must ultimately lead to their adoption. It did not matter, therefore, whether the reformers in Parliament numbered six or sixty, provided that they were resolute, consistent, and intelligible. Meanwhile an

---

[1] Article by Place in the *Traveller*, January 4, 1821.
[2] 27,849 (5, 6).

energetic man could carry detailed reforms which should
be not mere "temporary expedients," but logical applications of valid principles. It was "an opinion of" Place's
"that a man must have a good many projects in hand
to accomplish any."[1] The diaries which he kept from
September 1825 till December 1827 show him to have
been toiling and contriving in literally scores of different schemes. Many of them, such as the formation of
mechanics' institutes, the organisation of linen-drapers'
assistants, or the conciliation of a quarrel between the
seamen of London and those of South Shields, were not
directly political. But he was also working at the repeal
of the Wool Laws, the Cutting and Flaying Acts, the laws
prohibiting curriers from becoming tanners, and those
regulating hackney coaches and the system of pressing
seamen. Other schemes of his aimed at improved administration, as, for instance, the appointment of six Finance
Committees of the House of Commons for controlling
supply, the improvement of the law of creditor and debtor,
and the appointment of special commissioners to try
offences committed at sea. And in addition to all this
purely public work, his time was always very much taken
up in helping individual cases of hardship, in negotiating
and settling disputes between employers and workmen,
and in acting as arbitrator in numerous commercial
disputes.

The library at Charing Cross, besides its use as a political
workshop, was also the centre of a very practical system of
publication. "When it was thought advisable to print a
tract for distribution on any subject a notice was put up
over the fireplace, e.g., 'It is proposed to print for distribution an extract from the report of the Select Committee on
Metropolis Police Offices.' This was read by those who

[1] Hodgskin to Place, September 2, 1819 (continuation of letter dated
July 9, 1819).

came in, and they who approved of it put down a sovereign. Some hundreds of pounds were collected in this way, and many tracts were carefully and usefully distributed."[1] The most important of the reprints were Mill's articles from the "Supplement to the Encyclopædia Britannica" (1820–23), including the famous essay on "Government." Among the others, one traces Mill's article on the "Ballot" from the *Westminster Review* of July 1830, a tract by Place himself on the "Law of Libel" (1823), and J. R. M'Culloch's "Essay on Wages" (1826).

By 1826 the proceedings at the Charing Cross Library had evidently at last begun to attract a certain amount of public attention. In that year a writer in the *European Magazine* takes "Francis Place of Westminster, Esq.,"[2] as the fourth of a series of "Characters for Charity's Sake," the preceding three having been Henry Brougham, M.P., John Cam Hobhouse, M.P., and Joseph Hume, M.P.

The article begins with a saying of Archimedes, "Give me *place* for my fulcrum and I'll move the world," and contains six pages of good-humoured and amusing chaff of "this most indefatigable and efficient individual," and the whole company of Benthamite Radicals. "Upon Joseph Hume the country has rained teapots and pepper-castors, and the tide of cyder has emulated the November swell of the Severn; Hobhouse has been plastered with speeches, and pots of beer innumerable have flowed to his glory; and in the matter of Brougham, the very thin-ribbed men of the Modern Athens,[3] forgetting at once their politics and their parsimony, have delved their one arm up to the shoulder in haggis and bathed the other in sheep's-head broth renown. . . . But notwithstanding all this, not even

---

[1] Place to Benjamin Hawes, M.P., April 24, 1839.
[2] The *European Magazine*, New Series, vol. ii. No. 7, March 1826, pp. 227–33.
[3] The reference is to Brougham's celebrated Edinburgh tour, from which he had just then returned.

a ballad singer in *petit* France[1] has trolled the name of
Place, not a bone has been gnawed or a pint of small-beer
emptied to his glory; and that ungrateful country, which
was pouring pots of all denominations, shapes, and sizes
upon the heads of mere puppets of his science, has voted
him nothing, no, not so much as a pointless and eyeless
needle." . . . "Now, speaking candidly and without any
amplification, we scarcely know of a thing that he has not
done—meaning, of course, in the way of promoting civil,
religious, and other kinds of liberty. He is, adopting the
Oriental similitude, the cow's horn upon which stands the
tortoise upon which stand the worlds in all their number
and variety. . . . No one needs to be told that the
whole popular liberties of this country, and, by connection
and consequence, of the world, depend upon the electors of
Westminster; and just as necessarily as the sinking of lead
depends upon its weight, do these electors depend upon
Mr. Place, not only in the choice of the men whom they
entrust as their representatives, but in the very subjects in
which those men deal. When it is said that Sir Francis
Burdett or John Cam Hobhouse made a proposition or a
speech, thus or thus, there is a misnomer in the assertion;
for the proposition or the speech belongs in justice to Mr.
Place, and in all that demonstration of frantic freedom,
that tumultuous tide of popularity which they propel, he
is the influential luminary, the *moon* which stirs up the
waters. . . . Look over the notices of motions, and see
when Joseph [Hume] is to storm sixpence laid out in the
decoration of a public work, or sack the salary of a clerk
in a public office, and when you find that in a day or two
it is to astonish St. Stephen's and delight the land, then
go, if you can find admission, to the library of this indefatigable statesman, and you will discover him schooling
the Nabob like a baby. There upon that three-footed

---

[1] "Petty France," a street in Westminster, since pulled down.

stool, gowned in wholesome grey, with an absolute ava-
lanche of schemes, scraps, and calculations around him,
sits the philosophic sage, delivering his golden rules with
the slowness and the certainty of the choicest alembic;
and yonder, squatted upon a pile of unread pamphlets, sits
the substantial pupil, with his whole countenance perked
into one gigantic ear of astonishment and delight. 'The
wild ass quaffing the spring in the desert,' says the Arabian
proverb, 'is not so lovely as the countenance of him who
drinketh understanding.'

"Nor is it in the senate-house alone that the political
tact and talents of this illustrious man are exerted in
benefiting the world. All those schemes which are now
in progress for rendering Westminster the fountain of
philosophy and civilisation, as well as of liberty, can have
originated with none other than Mr. Place. It is true that
Jeremy Bentham is his senior by a year or two; but still
we see no reason why Jeremy should not be the pupil, and
Mr. Place the instructor; and we are quite sure that of
the other philosophers of Queen's Square [1] he is the manufacturer. Now, the singular part of the business is, that
the others should get all the merit. Those codes, cate-
chisms, and constitutions which, if the world had but
read them, would have done it so much good, all have his
imprint upon them—or rather, perhaps we should say,
his spirit in them. The government of Mill, the political
economy of M'Culloch, the speeches of Dr. Borthwick
Gilchrist, the lectures of Dr. Birkbeck, the poetry of
Bowring, and, as we have sometimes been inclined to
think, the holdings forth of Gast [2] and Gregory—all have a
smack of Place in them. . . .

[1] *i.e.* Bentham's house in Queen's Square Place, Westminster.

[2] Secretary to the Shipwrights' Union and the leading Trade Unionist
at this time in London. He was a friend of Place's. See Webb,
"History of Trade Unionism," p. 76 (*note*).

"We are not sure that he was the absolute inventor of
mechanics' institutions, but we do think that either he or,
which is the same thing, some of his pupils gave to the
London combination bearing that name that unity and
bias which cannot fail to make it a very efficient organ of
civil liberty in Westminster, in the event of a contested
election. . . . Left to mere science and literature, an institution of this kind might have lasted for a while, though
it would soon have gone the way of all institutions; but by
making it political, it is connected with that which is both
inexhaustible and indestructible, and therefore it is made
permanent. Even here, however, Mr. Place is as modest
and as self-denying as he is in his literature, his philosophy,
and his greater politics. He does not always attend, and
when he does, he sits in his corner, 'modest as the maid
that sips alone,' although a knowing person may discover
from the expression of his countenance when the actor
does, and when he does not, give the sense of his author."

In spite, however, of the great influence which Place
had acquired, and of the very real and important reforms
which he had secured, he sometimes lost patience completely. The trickery and dishonesty of the Whig party,
the weakness of the Radicals, and the frequency with
which those whom he had helped allowed themselves to
be cajoled or bought over by Governments opposed to all
progress, disgusted him. Thus, writing to Hume in 1830,
he says: "I am a tolerably patient fellow, but on this one
subject—this rascally House of Commons—I cannot always
command my feelings. This atrocious assembly, whenever I think of it, excites in me indignation, hatred, utter
abhorrence. Whenever I think of them, I involuntarily
run over a long list of their diabolical acts, their abominable conduct, which perhaps has no parallel, and I get ease
only by cursing them most heartily and sincerely. I need
not more particularly point out to you the cause of my

abhorrence. You know these people in their corporate
capacity thoroughly, and can scarcely think better of them
than I do."[1]

The year 1830 seems indeed to have been a particularly
trying one to him. The revival by Scarlett, the Attorney-
General of the Whig Government, of the barbarous press
prosecutions, and the attempt to alter the stamp duty on
newspapers, and to increase the stringency of the law
against their proprietors, had thoroughly aroused him.
He took active steps to combat these proceedings. But
members were dilatory, and all sorts of provoking delays
were put in his way. In the "loose gossiping account"[2]
of his doings during the year 1830, which he wrote late in
that year and in 1831, he reveals the very great chagrin
and disappointment he felt. "These things sometimes vex
me, and almost make me resolve to cut my parliamentary
acquaintance; and this I certainly should do were it not
that the matters I have accomplished encourage me to
hope I shall still be successful. It was only after six years
of continued exertion in a great many ways that I at
length induced Mr. Hume to procure a committee, which
led to the repeal of the laws against combinations of workmen, and the Act which forbade artisans leaving the
country.[3] It was only after long-continued efforts that
the exportation of machinery was brought to the state it
now is. It was in defiance of the opinions of the Speaker
and the Attorney-General that I procured the repeal of
the Cutting and Flaying Act; and it was only after efforts
continued during seven years that I at length was the
means of a committee sitting on the conduct of the Commissioners of Hackney Coaches, which will probably put
an end to the abuses and to the absurd laws which incom-
mode this business and inconvenience the public. If I did

[1] Place to Hume, May 25, 1830.   [2] "Autobiography."
[3] See Chap. VIII.

not console myself with these and similar results, I should
abandon all such efforts, shut out my political friends, and
betake myself to more agreeable pursuits. It is now the
19th November. The Parliament has been sitting for
business only three weeks, and I have been requested to
do as much in the way of research and statement as would
occupy me for three months. I will do no one of these
things, unless I have very good reason to believe that my
time will not be wasted, nor the matters on which I may
employ myself be laid aside. With some I will insist that
old matters be brought forward before I attend to any new
ones, unless these shall be decidedly of as much urgency
as importance." [1] But his despair was always short-lived.
"I am always doing all that can be done," he had once
written, "but I have learned to let that which we cannot
accomplish go without regret." [2]

There is one danger to which those who are in close
contact with the actual facts of political work are peculiarly
liable, but which Place entirely escaped. He did not
become cynical. It often happens that a politician,
having started with the idea that he is following the
rushing current of popular enthusiasm, and having found
that his real work consists in creating, by all sorts of
ingenious shifts, a poor semblance of interest among a
deeply indifferent public, comes to think of himself as a
charlatan, and of his work as a rather disreputable amusement. Place, however, understood the machinery of politics without despising it. "By the word 'people,'" he
once wrote, "when, as in this letter I use the word in a
political sense, I mean those among them who take part
in public affairs, by whom the rest *must* be governed." [3]

From another danger, incident to his position as an ex-

---

[1] "Autobiography," vol. v. chap. 7, under date May 1830.
[2] Place to Wakefield, December 5, 1813.
[3] Place to Sir J. Hobhouse, June 2, 1832.

working-man who had become a powerful politician, he did not perhaps escape so entirely. The facts of his own career were the best demonstration of the validity of his principles, and for a time he was apt to expect his acquaintances to be as interested as he was himself in his wonderful success in gaining education, wealth, and political influence. In February 1825, for instance, Thomas Campbell, the poet, had written a letter in the *Times*, in which he had given an eulogistic description of Place as an argument in favour of establishing a University for London, and putting the highest education within the reach of the commercial classes. Place, therefore, sent Campbell a long private letter describing the exact limits of his knowledge of languages, science, law, political economy, metaphysics, the fine arts, &c., and of the studies by which that knowledge had been acquired. He then proceeds: " The subject on which without pretension I have prided myself most, is the power I have possessed of influencing or governing other men individually and in bodies—I am sure I may say truly by honest means—and for what at the time always appeared to me to be useful purposes. This has always been to me a test of the information I had acquired, and had I not succeeded as I have done, I should have been disappointed, and turned back to inquire why I had failed. I have never interfered in any way, in any one single instance out of my business, for the purpose of any personal advantage whatever, except intellectual advancement. In all public matters in which I have been engaged I have either been the leader or one of the leaders, and I am not aware of any one instance in which I did not obtain as much, and, in some instances, considerably more credit than was due to me." [1]   After his failure, however, as a contributor to the *Westminster Review*, and in other literary work on which he had set his heart, there is little trace in his correspond-

[1] Place to Campbell, February 10, 1825.

N

ence of that self-complacency which is apt to disguise itself as scientific frankness.

But a much heavier blow, and one which left its marks on all he said and did during the remainder of his long and busy life, now befell him. On October 19, 1827, his first wife died of cancer. They had been married for thirty-six years, and she had borne him fourteen children, of whom ten were then alive. She had always been busy in household affairs, and had never attempted to share his intellectual interests, so that he had found it difficult, when his grown-up sons and daughters were at home, to prevent her from feeling herself excluded from their talk. But her death revealed that passionate intensity of feeling which was the real driving force of Place's life. Ten years before, when William Allen became a widower, Place had written that " Allen has no philosophy to enable him to reason rightly, to induce him to see things as they are, none to hold him up against those common calamities which ought to be borne with firmness; and the consequence is that he has been both miserable in mind and ill in body."[1] Now he himself was to learn that no amount of right reasoning can make calamities anything but calamities. His wife was buried in the churchyard of Angmering, the little Sussex village where she died. "On the day of her funeral," Place wrote, " I suffered more than I had ever before done, and more than I believed I could suffer on any occasion, more, I am sure, than I can again suffer. I held up against it all I could, I resisted as much as man could do, but it was useless, and I was utterly subdued, so much so, indeed, that I could willingly have died also. . . . All that was in my power was hiding myself in a barn to indulge my sorrow. Go to the funeral I could not; I had no power left equal to such a purpose, and here, therefore, in the barn I remained . . . a mere child without a par-

[1] Place to J. Mill, October 30, 1816.

ticle of resolution or self-control left in him. . . . Such was the impression on me that for some time after her death I frequently thought I heard her moving along the passages of the house or in the rooms. These noises were made by others, yet I very often looked up expecting to see her." [1]

Of the succeeding months he wrote to his son-in-law at Rio de Janeiro, "No one can imagine how wretched I was. . . . So completely was I thrust out from all which to me was most dear, that I knew not what to do. . . . Much as I love my children, desirous as I am to do them every possible service, it was, and is, quite out of my power to find among them the society which is necessary to my comfort. I cannot, like many other men, go to a tavern; I hate taverns and tavern-company. I cannot drink, I cannot for any considerable time consent to converse with fools. I dislike set, formal dinners, at which a man must either show off or be voted a bore, and show off to very little purpose after all, to come home in the middle of the night discontented. I was utterly uncomfortable. I read and wrote all day, and almost all night. I had some matters of laborious research in hand, and I went on doggedly with them. I thought I might become reconciled to my circumstances. . . . In this, however, I totally failed. . . . I had no one to converse with, no one to talk over, as I had been accustomed to do, the occurrences of the day, no one to sympathise with me in anything I was doing, and my thoughts were therefore turned in upon myself and upon my poor deceased wife. I then went solitarily to my sofa—I could not sleep in the bed, and had discarded it from the day of my poor wife's death—there to endure the thoughts I could not dismiss, there to suffer as I had never before suffered. I assure you, John, that during many nights I never slept at

[1] "Autobiography," chap. 14.

all. I wasted away, and at the end of three months had lost nearly twenty pounds in weight."[1]

Before his wife's death Place had been several times consulted on business matters by Mrs. Chatterley, a clever middle-aged actress at Covent Garden Theatre. She now called to condole with him, and during the year 1828, when absorption in the details of politics had become impossible to him, he formed the habit of spending a few hours each day at her house in Brompton Square. This continued for two years, but though, in 1828 and 1829, he left the library every day at three o'clock, his mornings were occupied as much as ever. On May 4, 1829, for instance, he notes that he has on hand schemes dealing with Corn Laws, Silk Laws, Police, Vestries, Parliamentary Reform, and the employment of children in cotton factories.

In February 1830 he and Mrs. Chatterley were married, and, with some regret, he determined to remain at Charing Cross instead of removing to Brompton Square; to continue to live, that is to say, in the daily work of politics, and not in literature and research. "It was utterly impossible for me to detach myself from the business of others if I resided at Charing Cross. So I at once abandoned the schemes I would willingly have indulged, and especially the attempt I had long since contemplated of writing a history of North America (and for which I have collected upwards of 600 volumes), and at once reconciled myself to my old way of consuming time."[2]

---

[1] Place to J. Miers, March 7, 1828 ("Autobiography," chap. 14).
[2] "Autobiography," vol. v.

CHAPTER VIII

THE COMBINATION LAWS

" The Labour Question may be said to have come into public view simultaneously with the repeal, between sixty and seventy years ago, of the Combination Laws, which had made it an offence for labouring men to unite for the purpose of procuring by joint action, through peaceful means, an augmentation of their wages. From this point progress began." [1]

The repeal of the Combination Laws in 1824–25 was the most striking piece of work that Place ever carried through single-handed. During the eighteenth century there had been passed a series of statutes directed against combinations of journeymen in particular trades. The first of the series was an act of 1721 "for regulating the journeymen tailors within the bills of mortality," and the last the general act of 1799 "to prevent unlawful combinations of workmen." [2] This legislation was not successful in putting a stop to combination ; but, together with the common law as interpreted and developed by the judges, it enabled a master who had a quarrel with his workmen to punish them with the most abominable tyranny.

[1] Extract from an article on "The English Labourer," by the Right Hon. W. E. Gladstone, in the *Weekly Star*, No. 1, vol. i., February 6, 1892.

[2] For the history of the Combination Laws see "The History of Trade Unionism," by Sidney and Beatrice Webb (London, 1894), chap. ii. As to their operation in the case of the London tailors, see "Select Documents Illustrating the History of Trade Unionism in the Tailoring Trade," by F. W. Galton (London, 1896).

A unanimous refusal to work at reduced prices was regarded as sufficient evidence of unlawful combination, and the non-acceptance by an unemployed journeyman of work offered to him by any employer in his trade, meant liability to undergo a long period of imprisonment or to be impressed into his Majesty's sea or land forces. The material which Place collected in eight thick volumes,[1] to illustrate the history of the Combination Laws, includes several cases where the magistrates threatened the men with imprisonment as an alternative to work on the masters' terms, and one case where a summons for combination was used to put a stop to a suit for wages owing.[2] It also shows that, as Place said, the laws "were not so much the consequence of the desire to keep the people in an abject state of subjection to their employers, as of a persuasion that they enabled those employers to get their work done at less expense."[3] "Justice," Place wrote, "was entirely out of the question; the working-men could seldom obtain a hearing before a magistrate—never without impatience and insult; and never could they calculate on even an approximation to a rational conclusion. . . . Could an accurate account be given of proceedings, of hearings before magistrates, trials at sessions and in the Court of King's Bench, the gross injustice, the foul invective and terrible punishments inflicted, would not, after a few years have passed away, be credited on any but the best of evidence."[4]

Many of the statutes against combination nominally applied to the masters equally with the men, but though the masters openly formed agreements to lower wages, with penalties attached to their violation, and circulated black-lists of insubordinate journeymen, not a single case

---

[1] Brit. Mus. Addl. MSS. 27,799–806.

[2] See First Report and Minutes of Evidence of the Select Committee on Artisans and Machinery—Evidence of W. Ablett, March 8, 1824, p. 147. Place's copy, preserved in 27,800 (161).

[3] 27,798 (6).   [4] 27,798 (7, 8).

has been discovered where they were successfully prosecuted for these offences.

Though Place in the year 1799 became an employer, he never forgot what he had suffered as a black-listed and starving journeyman breeches-maker, or while in constant danger of arrest as the underpaid secretary of the carpenters' and plumbers' trade clubs. In a MS. report to the Council of the National Political Union in 1831 he wrote: " When I became a master I did not forget that I had been a journeyman, and I acted accordingly. Never in my life did I call any man who worked for me out of his name. I always paid the highest rate of wages, and whenever the men struck for an increase of wages I never suffered them to leave me, but at all the three strikes which occurred whilst I remained in business I gave the advance as soon as it was asked, though these advances raised the men's wages from a guinea and ninepence a week to six and thirty shillings. Since I left business in 1818 I have constantly employed some portions of my time to promote the welfare of the working people, and at times a very considerable portion of my time, as for instance in procuring, after efforts continued for years, the repeal of the laws against combinations of workmen, and in establishing the mechanics' institutions. This explanation will, I hope, be received as evidence that I really am, what I pretend to be, the ardent and active friend of the working classes." [1]

Place gives the grounds of his hostility to the Combination Laws in a pamphlet written at the time of the debates on the Act of 1825 : "If keeping down wages in some cases, by law, was a national good ; if the degradation of the whole body of the working people by law was desirable ; if perpetuating discord between masters and workmen was useful ; if litigation was a benefit ; if living

[1] MS. Report, preserved in 27,822 (51, 52).

in perpetual violation of law was a proper state for workmen and their employers to be placed in, then the laws
against combinations of workmen were good laws, for to
all these did they tend." [1]

In 1810 the journeymen compositors employed by the
Times were prosecuted for the crime of belonging to a
combination and taking part in a strike. As in 1806 the
scandals of the Westminster election brought Place back
into democratic politics, [2] so now this practical example of
the operation of the Combination Laws started him on the
work of obtaining freedom of association. "The cruel
persecutions of the journeymen printers employed on the
Times newspaper in 1810 were carried to an almost incredible extent. The judge who tried and sentenced some
of them was the then Common Serjeant of London, Sir
John Silvester, commonly known by the cognomen of
"Bloody Black Jack." He was a remarkably large bluff
man, with large, uncouth features, and a somewhat ferocious
aspect. He obtained the cognomen in consequence of his
hasty disposition, the satisfaction he expressed when sen-
tencing criminals, and the heavy sentences he inflicted." [3]
The men were sentenced on December 11, 1810, and the
Times of two days afterwards contains the text of "Bloody
Black Jack's" pronouncement. "Prisoners, you have been
convicted of a most wicked conspiracy to injure the most
vital interests of those very employers who gave you bread,
with intent to impede and injure them in their business;
and, indeed, as far as in you lay, to effect their ruin. The
frequency of such crimes among men of your class of life,
and their mischievous and dangerous tendency to ruin the
fortunes of those employers which a principle of gratitude
and self-interest should induce you to support, demand of

---

[1] "Observations on Huskisson's Speech," by F. P. (Francis Place).
London, 1825, p. 21.
[2] *Cf.* Chap. II.   [3] 27,798 (8).

the law that a severe example should be made of those
persons who shall be convicted of such daring and flagitious
combinations, in defiance of public justice, and in violation
of public order. No symptom of contrition on your part
has appeared—no abatement of the combination in which
you are accomplices has yet resulted from the example
of your convictions."[1] The men were then sentenced to
terms of imprisonment varying from nine months to two
years.

In the same year the master tailors of London made an
effort to obtain such a drastic Act of Parliament as would
enable them to put down the long-established union in the
trade.[2] "I was applied to," says Place, "to subscribe, but I
refused; yet notwithstanding this, I was appointed a member of their committee. I attended once, and explained
to them, very calmly and deliberately, the reasons why I
did not and could not concur with them,—and why I
thought it advisable for them to desist, and make an
attempt to procure the repeal of all the laws against combinations of workmen. I showed them that their present
proceedings could cause nothing but mischief; that they
would not succeed in procuring an Act of Parliament; and
that if they could, it would be evaded, no matter how it
was worded. I showed them how it happened that in
their particular trade, they had never been able to make
use of the law as it stood, and explained to them that, so
long as the men continued to repose confidence in those
they appointed to manage their concerns, no law could
reach them, and that a more severe law would, as they
very well knew, increase that confidence. I gave no offence,

---

[1] The *Times*, December 13, 1810.

[2] Special Acts had been passed in 1721, and again in 1768, fixing the
wages and forbidding combinations in the tailoring trade. The
employers had been attempting for some years to get these laws
strengthened and more stringently administered. See Galton, "The
Tailoring Trade" (*supra*).

but they proceeded; and a Committee (a select committee
of the House of Commons, but an open committee, that is,
a committee which any member who chose might attend)
was appointed to take evidence. When the Committee
had sat two or three days I went down to the House, and
after hearing some witnesses examined, requested that I
might be examined. I had given a sketch of what I wished
to depose, to the parliamentary agent for the journeymen,
who mismanaged the business sadly; but still my evidence
was sufficient to destroy the bill. I was well known by
name in the trade, and pretty well known personally,
though I knew scarcely half-a-dozen of the masters. There
were many in the room, yet in no instance was the person
of any one of them known to me. My evidence produced
a strong ebullition among those who took a different view
of the matter. Mr. Barton was chairman of the Committee; he was a Welsh Judge, and at this time was totally
blind. When my evidence was concluded, some of the
spectators hissed; upon which Mr. Barton, in the name of
the Committee, thanked me for coming forward as I had
done and giving the evidence I had given. Two of the
principal master tailors then told the chairman that they
concurred completely in all I had said, and wished my
evidence should stand as theirs also. It was explained to
the Committee that I was entirely unknown to these
gentlemen, and had had no communication with either of
them. This put an end to the proceedings in Parliament.
Several master tailors called on me afterwards and thanked
me; but not a single journeyman, nor any one for them,
came near me, nor at any subsequent time did they do
anything to promote the repeal of the Combination Laws;
—except a small number at one house of call signing a
petition for that purpose at my request, when I had prepared it for them." [1]

[1] 27,798 (9-11.

The workmen "could not be persuaded to believe that the repeal of the laws was possible. Every one else either thought the laws were useful, or that any attempt to procure their repeal would be loss of time; and some few, as they came gradually into the persuasion that the laws ought to be repealed, refused to have anything to do with so hopeless a case. I was not to be put from my purpose, as I had seen strange things accomplished by perseverance, and I was resolved to persevere.

"In 1814, therefore, I began to work seriously to procure a repeal of the laws against combinations of workmen, but for a long time made no visible progress. As often as any dispute arose between masters and men, or when any law proceedings were had, and reported in the newspapers, I interfered, sometimes with the masters, sometimes with the men, very generally, as far as I could, by means of some one or more of the newspapers, and sometimes by acting as a pacificator, always pushing for the one purpose, the repeal of the laws.

"I wrote a great many letters to trade societies in London, and as often as I heard of any dispute respecting the Combination Laws in the country I wrote to some of the parties, stated my purpose, and requested information. Few condescended to notice my applications, and scarcely any furnished me with the information I wished to have; but many of the country papers inserted the articles I sent to them, and these must have produced some effect, though no signs of any appeared. Working-men had been too often deceived to be willing to trust to any one who was not well known to them. Habitually cunning, and suspicious of all above their own rank in life, and having no expectation of any mitigation, much less of a chance of the laws being repealed, they could not persuade themselves that my communications were of any value to them, and they would not therefore give themselves any trouble about them, much less to give such information as might, they thought, be some day used against them. I understood them thoroughly, and was neither put from my purpose nor offended with them. I was resolved to serve them as much as I could. I knew well enough that if they could be served in this as in many other particulars, it must be done without their concurrence, in spite of them.

"The papers I continued to write for the daily and weekly press were not wholly thrown away; there was, after some time, an evident reluctance in many places to enforce the laws against the workmen; and some who did enforce them no longer met with the general support which had formerly been given to such proceedings.[1]

"In 1818 a Mr. Wade, a wool-comber by trade, as I afterwards learned, commenced a weekly publication called the *Gorgon*,[2] which he sold for three-halfpence. I learned his character and advanced him some money, as did also Mr. Bentham and Mr. Bickersteth. He was an honest man, and although I never saw him, his letters pleased me, and assured me I had done well in procuring him assistance. He repaid all the money which had been lent to him.

"A number of this small publication was distributed among trade societies; copies were sent to some master manufacturers and to some newspapers. The publication was political, but it contained much that related to trade, manufactures, and domestic policy. This paper induced

---

[1] In 1819 Place, in a letter to Hobhouse, wrote : "Only think of it, that I, sitting in my skylight as the sycophant Perry called it, have, by taking advantage of circumstances, induced the *Chronicle*, and even the *Times*, to set the matter on its right footing. The *Star* is a powerful auxiliary, and I expect the *Scotsman*, to whom I have written at much length, will be a useful coadjutor. It has always appeared to me to be good policy to work with the press in any way it may at any time be willing to work for the public good."—Place to Hobhouse, August 16, 1819, 27,837 (173).

[2] Place's own bound volume of the *Gorgon* for 1818-1819 is in the British Museum.

Mr. Hume to come into my project much more than he had hitherto done ; and to observe much more particularly the operations and consequences of the obnoxious laws. I caused several members of Parliament to read the papers on trade as they appeared in the *Gorgon*, and I supplied the editor with much of the matter, which he worked up in his own way into essays.[1] The *Gorgon* was not altogether such a publication as I should have preferred, but is was the only one which could be used with any considerable effect, and this was a sufficient reason why I should assist the proprietor and make the most I could of it. Progress was now made. Many persons began to wish for the repeal of the laws ; almost every member of Parliament whom I knew became convinced that the laws could do no good ; most of them were satisfied they did mischief, and ought to be repealed." [2]

On August 16, 1819, Place wrote in high spirits to Hobhouse : " Next session we shall have a Committee on the wages of labour, and, whether the Act against Combinations of Workmen be or be not repealed, the examination and discussion of the subject will elevate the working-man in his own opinion. If it be repealed, the effect will be much greater than you can have any correct conception of. If it be not repealed, 10,000 petitions will be presented to the two Houses in the following session, signed by from two to three millions of men and women who actually receive wages. I am persuading the workmen in London, Manchester, and some other places openly to commence penny-a-week societies to defray the expenses of sending some of the ablest among them to attend the Committee. The repeal of the Combination

---

[1] See, in particular, an account of the London tailors and their combinations, which appeared in the issues of the *Gorgon* of September 26, October 3 and 10, 1818, and is reprinted by F. W. Galton, " The Tailoring Trade,' pp. 146–160.

[2] 27,798 (12–14).

Laws would make thousands of reformers among the
master tradesmen and manufacturers."[1]   And a few weeks
later he wrote, even more hopefully, to Hodgskin: "When
it was agreed to bring in the bill to repeal so much of the
laws against combinations of workmen as relate to the
rate of wages and hours of working, which is all that is
intended to be done, it was supposed that it would require
several years to get it through the House of Commons.
But, from the decided part the newspapers have taken,
the correspondence which has been going on, and the
number of master tradesmen and manufacturers who not
only desire the repeal, but are willing to petition for it,
and to give evidence also before a Committee of the
House of Commons, hopes are entertained that it may be
got through next session.   Mr. M['Culloch] can do much
service by helping this on, as he is looked to as an
authority on these matters.   It is of vast importance, and
would do more towards destroying the existing animosities
between the working-men and their employers, than any
other circumstance whatsoever."[2]

These high hopes and spirits were not, however, justified
by events, and Place continued to devote his time to the
collection of evidence, and to the personal conversion of
individual members of Parliament, editors and economists.   At last, in 1822, Joseph Hume, encouraged by
several members to bring the matter before the House of
Commons, announced that he intended to bring in a bill
to repeal all the laws against combinations of workmen.

"Parliament," says Place, "was not as yet in a condition
to deal properly with the subject; and I was therefore in
no hurry to urge Mr. Hume to proceed beyond indicating
his purpose.   I supplied him with a considerable quantity
of papers, printed and MS., relating to the subject, advised

[1] Place to Hobhouse, August 16, 1819.
[2] Place to Hodgskin, September 8, 1819.

him to examine them carefully, and promised my assistance to the greatest possible extent for the next session.
These papers were afterwards sent to Mr. M'Culloch at
Edinburgh, who was at this time editor of the *Scotsman*
newspaper, and he made admirable use of them in that
paper. This gave a decided tone to several other country
papers, and caused the subject to be discussed in a way,
and to an extent, which it had never before been. Towards
the end of the session, Mr. Hume informed me that many
of the Opposition members had consented to a repeal of
the laws; and that Mr. Huskisson, Mr. Wallace, Mr.
Copley the Attorney-General, and some others who were
high in office, had promised not to oppose the appointment of a Select Committee to inquire respecting the
efficiency of the laws against combinations of workmen,
and their effects in other particulars. Thus a considerable advance was made." [1]

Of what happened in Parliament during the next two
years, Place has left a detailed chronological account.

"Parliament met on February 4, 1823, and a few days
afterwards Mr. Hume exerted himself to obtain the
concurrence of as many members as he could to his
proposal; he did not, however, make much progress.
But a circumstance soon occurred which induced many
of them to consent to support his proposition for a Committee.

"A Mr. George White, a clerk of committees at the
House of Commons, had formed a partnership with a
Mr. Gravener Henson,[2] a bobbin netmaker at Nottingham;

---

[1] 27,798 (15).
[2] Gravener Henson had long been a leader of the framework
knitters' unions, and is sometimes alleged to have been " King Lud,"
the organiser of the mobs who visited obnoxious manufacturers and
smashed their machinery. He suffered several terms of imprisonment,
and published in 1831 a " History of the Framework Knitters," now a
scarce work.

they, and some half-dozen others, some of them Coventry
men, had concerted a plan with Mr. Peter Moore [1] to bring
in a bill to repeal the laws against combinations of workmen.   White understood the progress Mr. Hume was
making; but he and Mr. Henson had a beautiful scheme
of legislation, as complicated and absurd as two such ill-
instructed men could well contrive.   They meant well,
but did not understand the means necessary to do well.
They were both active, indefatigable men.   White went
to work heartily, and collected from the statutes everything he could find which in any way related to masters
and workmen; this he showed to Peter Moore together
with the draft of a bill; and Mr. Moore at once agreed to
introduce the bill.   This course was taken to prevent Mr.
Hume either from moving for a Committee or bringing in
a bill; and they were very near effecting their purpose.

  " On March 3, 1823, Mr. Moore obtained leave to bring in
his bill. . . . Mr. Moore's bill produced considerable alarm
to many members, and especially to ministers, at whose
request Mr. Moore at length consented that the discussion
on its merits should be postponed to the next session.

  " Parliament met again on February 3, 1824.   Just before
this time appeared the *Edinburgh Review*, No. 78, containing from the pen of Mr. M'Culloch a very excellent
essay on the propriety of repealing the laws against combinations of workmen, and those which forbade the emigration of artisans.   Its effect on many members was
remarkable; several of them told me there was no resisting the conclusive arguments it contained, and one of
them said he was prepared to speak the substance of the
essay in the House.

  " Mr. Hume, however, met with more opposition than he
anticipated.   Mr. Moore's bill was a bug-a-boo.   I advised
him to take no notice of the bill, but to move at once for

_____

[1] Then the member of Parliament for Coventry.

a Select Committee. When the time came for doing so, Mr. Huskisson shrunk back. He advised Mr. Hume to forego his intention of moving for a Committee on the Combination Laws, and to take in only the Emigration of Artisans and the Exportation of Machinery. Mr. Hume was cajoled and gave notice accordingly. This was February 6, and thus was all the labour I had bestowed on the subject, as it had been on other subjects, at once pushed aside; all the letters and all the communications I had made and received were to go for nothing, and the papers for Mr. Hume's guidance were at once rendered useless.

"On his return from the House he came to me with Alderman Wood. Mr. Hume said Mr. Huskisson had consented to the appointment of a Committee on Artisans and Machinery, but he objected to take in the Combination Laws, as Peter Moore would come with his bill, make a schism in the Committee, and cause a deal of trouble. I argued the propriety of taking in the Combination Laws, and Mr. Hume seemed half convinced of the propriety of doing so, but he did not promise to do so. He left with me the motion in the form he proposed to make it, and the names of the members for the Committee, for me to revise. After some very serious consideration, I wrote as follows:—

"'*February* 7, 1824.

"'I am decidedly of opinion that you should take in the Combination Laws, and also that you should at once take Peter Moore into the Committee. Moore is not a man to be put aside, and the only way to put him down is to let him talk his nonsense in the Committee, where being out-voted, he will be less an annoyance in the House. I know Mr. Moore well—know how pig-headed he is, that he will be sure to go in the opposite way to which he is pulled, and I also know that he must be borne with. If you do

not take him into the Committee, he will come with his
book of petty legislation before the House, and compel the
House to negative his mass of absurdities.   The public
will, however, see nothing in this but, as they will conclude,
an evident resolution in the Government not to do justice.
Peter Moore will be looked to by millions, and all sorts of
obloquy will be cast upon every other man in the House.
Moore's Bill might be cut down in the Committee, and if I
were a member of that Committee, I would set my foot to
his on this part of the business, and although I should not
convince him, I would beat him from all his positions.

   " ' The business is really very simple, and it lies in a small
space.   Repeal every troublesome and vexatious enactment,
and enact very little in their place.   Leave workmen and
their employers as much as possible at liberty to make
their own bargains in their own way.   This is the way to
prevent disputes ; but when they do occur, leave them to
settle them amongst themselves, with an appeal to a
Justice of the Peace in cases (and they will be very few)
in which the parties cannot of themselves come to a decision.   Let the magistrate decide on the evidence before
him, and make his decision final.   I have no doubt at all
that you will find this not only by far the pleasantest but
the shortest way of proceeding.—Yours truly,

                                " ' FRANCIS PLACE.'

   " The above was written to be shown to Mr. Huskisson
and others ; it was accompanied by another letter which
was intended to be private.

   " ' 1. It was generally understood last session that you
would move for a repeal of the Combination Laws in this
session.   Nobody seemed to care much about Mr. Moore ;
everybody seemed to rely on Mr. Hume.

   " ' 2. You and I had a similar understanding, and I acted

upon it very extensively. I took every opportunity to prepare people to expect your motion; and many thousands do expect it. I have sent circular letters to a great many houses of call for journeymen, telling them, as I was fully warranted in telling them, that the Committee you would move for was, amongst other matters, to consider of the repeal of the Combination Laws. I have this day been at houses of call for hatters, smiths, carpenters, weavers, boot and shoe makers, and metal workers. To-morrow I am to be at those of the bakers, tailors, plumbers, painters and glaziers, bricklayers, and bookbinders. Now if, after all, you do not go on with the Combination Laws, what will be the consequence? I shall have to say to hundreds of persons that you did agree to go into it; that this was the reason I talked with them on the subject and wrote to them; but that, when the time came, you, without reason, declined doing it. You will at once see that I have no choice. I must say this.

" '3. If you do not go into the Combination Laws by making it one reason for a Committee, Peter Moore will take advantage of the multitude of petitions that *will* be presented to the House; he will introduce *his* bill again. . . .'

" Mr. Hume consulted Mr. Huskisson, and it was agreed that the motion should be made, as I had suggested it. Thus the matter about which so much pains had been taken, so much time, and some money also, had been spent, and which was all but set aside, was again put upon its legs.

On the 12th February, Mr. Hume made his motion, and obtained his Committee. It was with difficulty Mr. Hume could obtain the names of twenty-one members to compose the Committee; but when it had sat three days, and had become both popular and amusing, members contrived to be put upon it, and at length it consisted of forty-eight members.

"When the Committee met for business, Mr. Hume found himself in a very difficult situation; he had been so assiduously employed in various other matters, that it had been impossible for him to give attention to the details of this. He was much annoyed and embarrassed; no one assisted him, and some put obstacles in his way. I offered to attend the Committee as his assistant, but the jealousy of the members prevented this; they ' would not be dictated to '—that is, they would not have the business put in a plain way by the only man who had made himself master of it in all its bearings, because he was neither a member of the honourable House, nor even a gentleman. Thus does pride and ignorance, in all situations, from a Committee of the honourable House to a chandler's shop in an alley, show itself much in the same way, always absurd, always pitiful, very generally mischievous. Happily nothing can subdue Mr. Hume's perseverance, and, like almost every man who perseveres in a right course, he almost always finds himself firm upon his legs at the end of his labour. Mr. Hume wrote a circular letter announcing the appointment of the Committee, and inviting persons to come and give evidence; copies of this were sent to the mayors and other officers of corporate towns, and to many of the principal manufacturers. Some one country paper having obtained a copy, printed it, and it was presently reprinted in all the newspapers, and thus due notice was given to everybody. Meetings were held in many places; and both masters and men sent up deputations to give evidence. The delegates from the working people had reference to me, and I opened my house to them. Thus I had all the town and country delegates under my care. I heard the story which every one of these men had to tell. I examined and cross-examined them; took down the leading particulars of each case, and then arranged the matter as briefs for Mr. Hume : and, as a rule, for the guidance of the witnesses, a copy was given to each. This occupied days and nights, and occasioned great labour ; much of it might have been saved if the Committee would have permitted me to remain in the room and assist the chairman as I had done on former occasions. As it was, I had no choice. Each brief contained the principal questions and answers. That for Mr. Hume was generally accompanied by an appendix of documents, arranged in order with a short account of such proceedings as was necessary to put Mr. Hume in possession of the whole case. Thus he was enabled to go on with considerable ease, and to anticipate or rebut objections.

"Mr. George White was clerk of the Committee. He was at first annoyed by the interference of Mr. Hume, whose conduct had set Peter Moore entirely aside. Mr. Moore never once attended the Committee. Mr. White soon, however, became satisfied that I was pushing the matter in the right way, sought my acquaintance, and gave all the assistance in his power. He told me that some members of the Committee, seeing Mr. Hume's briefs in my handwriting, were much offended, and had hinted at having me called before the Committee, for tampering, as they called it, with the witnesses. It would have well pleased me to have been so called, as I should have been able to have shown up some honourable members in a new light before the public.

"The workmen were not easily managed. It required great care and pains and patience not to shock their prejudices, so as to prevent them doing their duty before the Committee. They were filled with false notions, all attributing their distresses to wrong causes, which I, in this state of the business, dared not attempt to remove. Taxes, machinery, laws against combinations, the will of the

masters, the conduct of magistrates, these were the fundamental causes of all their sorrows and privations. All
expected a great and sudden rise of wages, when the Combination Laws should be repealed; not one of them had
any idea whatever of the connection between wages and
population. I had to discuss everything with them most
carefully, to arrange and prepare everything, and so completely did these things occupy my time, that for more
than three months I had hardly time for rest.

"As the proceedings of the Committee were printed from
day to day for the use of the members, I had a copy sent
to me by Mr. Hume, which I indexed, on paper ruled in
many columns, each column having an appropriate head
or number. I also wrote remarks on the margins of the
printed evidence;[1] this was copied daily by Mr. Hume's
secretary, and then returned to me. This consumed much
time, but enabled Mr. Hume to have the whole mass constantly under his view. And I am very certain that less
pains and care would not have been sufficient to have
carried the business through.

"I had still one fear, namely, of speech-making. I was
quite certain that if the bills came under discussion in the
House they would be lost. Mr. Hume had the good sense
to see this, and wholly to refrain from speaking on them.

"There was another difficulty, not easily to be sur-
mounted, and this was the Report of the Committee.
When evidence before a Select Committee has been taken,
it is usual to discuss the matter of the report, and here it
but too often happens that some sinister interest prevails.
In the present case the report must have been drawn by
me for Mr. Hume, and the consequence would have been
such alterations, omissions, and additions, as would have
made it useless and defeated the purpose intended. It was

---

[1] The volumes of evidence thus prepared and annotated by Place
are now preserved in vols. 27,800-27,801.

therefore agreed to deviate from the usual mode, and draw
up resolutions which, if possible, should be substituted for
a report.   It was quite clear to both me and Mr. Hume
that it would not only be more difficult for members to
cavil at and alter short resolutions, each containing a fact,
than it would be to bedevil a report drawn in the usual
way, but as the means of detecting and exposing sophistry
in this form would be easy and certain, few if any of the
members would make the attempt.   Resolutions were
accordingly drawn, printed, and circulated amongst the
members of the Committee.[1]   They were cavilled at, but
nothing in the way of alteration was proposed.   Time was
thus gained, and at length, when all were pretty well
wearied with attending at the Committee, it was agreed
that Mr. Hume should report the resolutions.   This was
gaining a point of the utmost importance, and ensuring the
progress of the bills through the House.

"There were, however, other difficulties to be encoun-
tered.   Mr. White and I had put the bills into form with
the fewest words possible.   Mr. Hume, however, suffered
the Attorney-General to employ Mr. Anthony Hamond, a
barrister, to draw the bills; he took our MSS., and pretty
specimens of nonsense he made of them !   He had all the
necessary documents, some suggestions in writing, and the
bills themselves as perfectly drawn as we could draw them;
but he knew not how to use them.   This caused considerable perplexity.   We attacked his draft, and afterwards
the printed bills.   He paid but little attention to us, but it
so happened that when the bills were once printed he considered himself as having performed all that he was likely
to be remunerated for, and he gave himself no further
concern about them.   We now got them into our hands,

---

[1] The resolutions as agreed to by the Committee were presented to
Parliament in the Sixth Report of the Select Committee on Artisans
and Machinery, 1824.

altered them as we liked, had MS. copies made and presented to the House. No inquiry was made as to who
drew the bills; they were found to contain all that was
needful, and with some assiduity in seeing members to
induce them not to speak on the several readings, they
passed the House of Commons almost without the notice
of members within or newspapers without.

"When the bill went to the Lords,[1] a new difficulty
occurred. The half-crazy Lord Lauderdale intimated that
he should oppose the bills. He approved, he said, of the
principle of the bills, but it was beneath the dignity of the
House of Lords to pass them, until noble members had
had an opportunity of perusing the evidence taken before
the Commons' Committee, which had not as yet been reprinted by their Lordships' printer. If Lord Lauderdale
had used these words in the Noble House, the bills would
have been put off till the next session, when it is very probable they would have been rejected. With almost incredible pains taken, Lauderdale was induced to hold his
tongue, and three Acts were passed:—

"(i.) An Act to repeal the laws relating to the combinations of workmen, and for other purposes therein mentioned (5 Geo. IV. c. 95).

"(ii.) An Act to consolidate and amend the laws relative
to the arbitration of disputes between masters and workmen (5 Geo. IV. c. 96).

---

[1] A very vigorous canvass of the Lords was made by Hume and
Place. On June 9 Hume wrote to Place: "I send you a letter received from Lord Lansdowne and a copy of my answer to him. I
have also written to Lord Rosslyn to the same purport, and wish you
to press through M'Intosh and Brougham the support of Lords Lauderdale, Ackland, &c. You should send the several deputies now in town
to the several Lords who take a part, and to the Lord Chancellor, Lord
Liverpool, to request their support of the bills. I have written to
Mr. Huskisson to get the support of Lord Liverpool. . . . A canvass
for the bills must be made to ensure success."—Hume to Place,
June 9, 1824, 27,801 (148).

"(iii.) An Act to repeal the laws relative to artisans going abroad (5 Geo. IV. c. 97)."[1]

Place was of opinion that the repeal of the Combination Laws would lead to the disappearance of trade unions. He thought that these were formed chiefly to resist the continuous combination of employers, and to defend the workmen against the tyranny of the law.

In 1811 he had argued, as against the attempt of the London master tailors to impose fresh restrictions upon their workmen, that "the combinations of the men are but defensive measures resorted to for the purpose of counteracting the offensive ones of their masters. . . . When every man knew that he could carry his labour to the highest bidder, there would be less motive for those combinations which now exist, and which exist because such combinations are the *only* means of redress that they have.[2] Again, in 1825, he wrote to Sir Francis Burdett: "Combinations will soon cease to exist. Men have been kept together for long periods only by the oppression of the laws; these being repealed, combinations will lose the matter which cements them into masses, and they will fall to pieces. All will be as orderly as even a Quaker could desire. He knows nothing of the working people who can suppose that, when left at liberty to act for themselves, without being driven into permanent associations by the oppression of the laws, they will continue to contribute money for distant and doubtful experiments, for uncertain and precarious benefits. Even now in a very populous part of the country, and where the people are particularly ill treated, the men have refused to contribute a penny each per week to pay the expense of a delegate to be sent to London. If

---

[1] 27,798 (15–24).

[2] "An Address to the Legislature of Great Britain, from . . . the Master Tailors of London," &c. (London, 1811, 8vo), pp. 3, 4. Brit. Mus. Addl. MSS. 27,799 (16). Reprinted in "The Tailoring Trade," by F. W. Galton (London, 1896), pp. 108–114.

let alone, combinations, excepting now and then, and for particular purposes, under peculiar circumstances, will cease to exist." [1]

These opinions were shown by the event to have been entirely erroneous. The repeal of the Combination Laws, happening to coincide with a time of great commercial prosperity, everywhere produced an outbreak of trade unionism and strikes. From one end of the country to the other masters and men were engaged in industrial conflict.

Nassau Senior a few years later described the removal of the oppressive legislation as having produced "a great moral effect. . . . It confirmed in the minds of the operatives the conviction of the justice of their cause, tardily and reluctantly, but at last fully conceded by the Legislature. That which was morally right in 1824 must have been so, they would reason, for fifty years before." [2] In the winter of 1824–25 the employers petitioned the Government on all sides to re-enact the old laws or to devise some new and even more drastic legislation. Place and Hume did what they could to restrain the men. At Place's instigation Hume wrote letters to the leaders of many of the trades on strike and to many of the provincial newspapers, urging them to desist from their action, and warning them that any violent conduct could only result in the re-enactment of the laws." [3]

Place wrote several similar letters, one of the most interesting of which is that to the Glasgow cotton-weavers.

[1] Place to Sir Francis Burdett, June 20 and 25, 1825, 27,798 (57, 58).
[2] See the MS. Report of Nassau Senior to Lord Melbourne, on Trade Combinations [1831, unpublished, in the Home Office Library], quoted on pp. 92, 93 of the "History of Trade Unionism," by Sidney and Beatrice Webb (London, 1894).
[3] See Hume's letter to the Manchester cotton-spinners, Dec. 27, 1824, to the Glasgow weavers, Sept. 18, 1824, preserved with others and several newspaper cuttings of such letters in 27,801 (241–272).

To Mr. PETER M'DOUGAL *and* Mr. WILLIAM SMITH
at Glasgow.

"LONDON, *Sept.* 1, 1824.

"When you were in London as delegates for the purpose
of being examined by the Select Committee of the House
of Commons on Artisans and Machinery, you had opportunities enough of witnessing the interest I took in the
welfare of the working classes. You then learned that I
had been for several years past employed, as well personally
as by means of the press, in endeavouring to procure the
repeal of the laws against combinations of workmen. I
remind you of this as one proof that, in differing from the
weavers of Glasgow as to the propriety of their present
conduct, I am not very likely to be less disposed towards
their interest than I ever was at any former period. It
seems to me necessary to say this in order to procure the
serious attention of a large body of men, one of whom has
said, and no doubt very justly, 'We have been so often
imposed upon by designing artifice, or led into the ditch
by ignorance, that we can hardly trust anybody.' . . . The
newspapers inform me that the weavers in and near Glasgow
are forming themselves into societies for the purpose of
raising their wages. For attempting by all legal means to
increase the amount of their low wages they deserve com-
mendation. A weaver for his time and talents deserves to
be paid as well as a spinner is paid for his time and talents.
Why a weaver has not been as well paid admits of easy
explanation. The spinners being together in considerable
bodies, were able to a great extent to resist the attempts
made to lower their wages, and by the resistance they made
they saved themselves from the degradation which the
weavers, from being isolated and spread over a large surface, unfortunately experienced. The laws against combinations of workmen, enforced as they were, and the

perversion of the law against conspirators, inflicted many
evils upon workmen. But spite of these laws and their
perversion, those who, from the particular nature of their
employments, were able to evade those laws or oppose themselves in a body to their employers, maintained their ground
and preserved themselves from degradation, whilst those
who were not in such circumstances could not do so, and
this unfortunately was the case of the weavers and some
other journeymen. Those laws which thus degraded and
demoralised the working people having been repealed, and
the weavers for the first time finding themselves at liberty
to act for themselves, might reasonably have been expected
to commit some errors, and this has accordingly happened.
The error I now allude to is the resolution to exclude a
particular factory altogether, to work no more on any terms
for a particular person.   This is equally reprehensible and
absurd.   Reprehensible because the Act repealing the laws
against combinations of workmen should have been accepted by both workmen and employers as an Act of obli-
vion ; and because such a conspiracy as that against Mr.
Hutcheson is equally unreasonable and unjust. Absurd
because it is impracticable. . . . Enough has, I hope, been
said to induce you to abandon the attempt to exclude any
factory, and in future promptly to condemn every such
proposition, let it come from whom it may.—I am, your
well-wisher,   FRANCIS PLACE."[1]

   By this time ministers had become thoroughly alarmed,
and early in the session of 1825 made an effort to undo the
effects of their previous legislation.
   "It unfortunately happened that from the close of the
session in 1824 the price of provisions had been rapidly
rising, and was still rising when the Parliament again
assembled on February 3, 1825. Trade in all its branches

   [1] The letter is preserved in 27,801 (237).

was flourishing, and the workmen were very generally employed. Released from the law which had oppressed them, persuaded that their wages had been kept down lower than they ought to have been, and believing that it was now in their power to obtain an advance, many trades contemplated a strike. Great pains were taken to prevent the men striking, and much effect was produced. Many trades turned their attention solely to the grievances which the operation of the laws had imposed on them, and, having removed these, remained content. Others attempted more: they struck for wages, or to restore their wages to the sum they had some time before been. Some obtained an advance, some were standing out when the Parliament assembled.

" The cotton-spinners of Glasgow were the most reprehensible. They struck at a mill belonging to a Mr. Dunlop, a bad man, at whose factory, it has been observed, ' peace never came.' This led to a strike on the part of the master cottoners against all their workpeople, thousands of whom were deprived of the means of subsistence by their own labour, and reduced to indescribable distress and misery.

" The body of cotton-masters had been merciless oppressors at all times, and on this occasion their conduct towards their workpeople was remarkably cruel. They had, for the fault of some, condemned many thousands to starvation. Still the working people, miserably ill used, and goaded as they were to the act, had done unwisely in attempting to prevent Mr. Hutcheson (whom they considered their particular oppressor) from ever employing his mill again.

" Next to these master cottoners were the shipbuilders, and some of the shipowners, headed by some rich and influential men on the river Thames. The workmen complained of certain obnoxious proceedings of their employers, of breach of contract, and want of regularity in the prices paid for their labour. They did not desire any advance

of wages, but requested a conference for the purposes of
regulation. This was peremptorily refused, and the men
struck. The [ship]builders then came to a resolution not
again to employ any man who belonged to the Shipwrights' Union. Disputes had been going on for some
time amongst the sailors and the shipowners, but the conduct of both the sailors and shipwrights was exemplary;
no disorderly acts could be alleged against them. But as
the shipping interest, as it is called, had the ready ear of
ministers, they most shamefully misrepresented the conduct of the men, and represented the consequences as likely
to lead to the destruction of the commerce and shipping of
the empire. Ministers were so ignorant as to be misled by
these misrepresentations, and were mean and despicable
enough to plot with these people against their workmen.

"The interest of the unprincipled proprietors of the
Times newspaper was intimately connected with the 'shipping interest,' and it lent its best services to their cause.
It stuck at nothing in the way of false assertion and
invective ; it represented the conduct of Mr. Hume as
mischievous in the extreme, and that of the working
people all over the country as perfectly nefarious ; and
it urged ministers to re-enact the old laws, or to enact
new ones, to bring the people into a state of miserable
subjection.

"In this state were matters when the Parliament assembled. Care had been taken to circulate a report that the
laws against combinations would be re-enacted. This spread
alarm all over the manufacturing districts, and had some
effect in keeping the people quiet. I was appealed to from
various places, and by various bodies, many of whom had
been supine while the laws were in existence, but who were
now apprehensive of the recurrence of the evils which had
been removed.

"Nothing indicating any such intention on the part of

ministers had transpired, and on Mr. Hume mentioning
the matter to Mr. Huskisson, he led him to believe that
nothing of the kind was at all contemplated. I therefore
wrote to, and otherwise informed those who had applied to
me, that Mr. Hume's bill would not be repealed, and this,
on my authority, was stated in several of the country
newspapers.

"Just at this time, a fresh deputation of shipbuilders,
men of wealth and influence, waited upon Mr. Huskisson
to complain of the conduct of their men. They endeavoured to persuade him either to repeal Mr. Hume's Act,
or to pass another, the substance of which they laid before
him, and which they said would be much more effectual.
It was a scheme to prevent workmen from subscribing
money for any purpose whatever, unless they first obtained
the consent and approbation of some local magistrate, and
unless that magistrate, or some other such magistrate, also
consented to become their treasurer, and see to the due
application of the money. Either Mr. Huskisson did not
think any interference of the Government was at that time
necessary, or he played the hypocrite to the acme of perfection; for he told Mr. Hume of the visit of the shipbuilders, and said 'he had told them that he did not
understand the matter, and recommended them to see Mr.
Hume, who had paid great attention to it.'

"The shipbuilders called at Mr. Hume's house. Mr.
Hume was, however, unfortunately indisposed, and could
not see them; he, however, wrote a note and requested an
interview, but they took no notice of his request.

"Complaints continued to be made to ministers, and Mr.
Huskisson suggested to Mr. Hume that it would answer all
good purposes if he (Mr. Huskisson) were to notice these
complaints in the House, and threaten the workmen that,
unless their conduct was lawful and their demands reasonable, the old laws should again be restored; and if he (Mr

Hume) were to say something in the same strain. This was done, and it was concluded the matter would rest here. Mr. Hume was therefore much surprised when, in a few days, Mr. Huskisson gave notice that he should on the morrow move for a Committee on the Act of the last session (Mr. Hume's Act). Mr. Hume asked him what it was he intended to propose, when he said he did not intend to restore the old laws, but to introduce some commercial regulations principally relating to the refractory seamen; and that what he intended to say in moving for the Committee would be in favour of the workmen generally. Mr. Hume was thus thrown off his guard. On March 29, Mr. Huskisson made his speech, which he concluded by moving ' for the appointment of a Select Committee to inquire into the effect of the Act 5 Geo. IV. c. 95, in respect to the conduct of workmen and others in different parts of the United Kingdom, and to report their opinion how far it may be necessary to amend or repeal the said Act.'

" Mr. Huskisson commenced his speech by declaring that repealing the Combination Laws seemed likely to be attended with the most inconvenient and dangerous consequences. He admitted that the Act 5 Geo. IV. c. 95 was fair in principle, but not so in practice. He complained that the Committee had made no report, and he made several objections to the resolutions. He excused himself for neither having attended in his place in the Committee, nor to the progress of the bill in Parliament, and having thus cleared his way, he fell furiously to work upon his subject. He pulled the Act to pieces; complained of it as an anomaly. It not only repealed the statute law, but forbade the operation of the common law, which had thus introduced a great public evil. (It had done nothing of the kind, and he did not know the meaning of the words he was using.) The bill had been hurried through the

House without discussion. He then drew a false and exaggerated picture of the state of the country, and predicted the most fatal consequences. Liberty, property, life itself was in danger, and Parliament must speedily interfere. He held the regulations of men in combinations in his hand; some he read, and described their proceedings as very terrible indeed, when in fact there was nothing the least terrible in them. He endeavoured to make his way to the feelings and foolings of the members by the old cant he and his former accomplices had so successfully used against the reformers. Congresses were formed; federal republics were established by these wonderfully wise and hard-working people. He supposed the monstrous absurdity of 'all the different branches of mining, manufacturing, navigating and shipping in the country,' being thus combined into a perpetual confederacy, and drew just such inferences as a three-parts crazy creature might have drawn from his bewildered imagination, with shame be it spoken. It is with shame I write this of a man who should have had more sense and more honesty, but who, at any rate, if he had neither, should have been too proud to have exposed himself thus in the character of a statesman. He described several clauses in the Act as particularly mischievous and utterly repugnant to all good legislation; as, in fact, exciting and encouraging the commission of crimes; and yet, in the end, he was himself compelled to re-enact nearly every one of the clauses he objected to. No fundamental alteration was ultimately made in any one of them, and very few were altered at all. The law is, however, less precise.

"Mr. Hume showed that in those cases where there was anything worth complaining of, the masters were more culpable than the men.

"Mr. Peel[1] related circumstances respecting the ship-

---

[1] Afterwards Sir Robert Peel, at that time Home Secretary.

wrights and sailors which were afterwards shown to be
false. But he relied principally on some outrages which
had been committed in Dublin, reprehensible enough to
be sure, but transient and worthy of little notice.

"The Committee was appointed. When Mr. Huskisson
made his furious speech, Mr. Hume was astonished, and
was very ill prepared to reply to him. He had always
maintained to me that Mr. Huskisson was a man of
honour, incapable of such gross and shameless deception.
I always thought Mr. Hume mistaken; I had observed
Mr. Huskisson much longer than Mr. Hume had, and
entertained no doubt at all that he was courtier enough
to attempt anything likely to answer his purpose. Mr.
Hume was deceived by his too good opinion of Mr.
Huskisson: had he been less credulous he would have
been provided with the means of showing how false and
scandalous and ill-judged the assertions of Mr. Huskisson
were. Many laughed at him for his folly, but any man
may at any time be deceived by any other man to
whom he gives his confidence, if that other man, like Mr.
Huskisson, be mean enough and base enough to lie to
himself, and shameless enough openly to declare that
in public which is in direct contradiction to what he has
pledged himself in private. Mr. Huskisson and Mr. Peel
had concerted the whole matter. They had adopted the
suggestions of the shipbuilders and shipowners, and had
consented to prepare a bill on the basis of their suggestions. They had looked too lightly at the matter, or they
would not have undertaken it; they undervalued the
enemy they had to encounter, and thought to walk over
the field without a battle. It was to be a Committee
more of form than of business, and was to sit but a very
few days. Mr. Huskisson named his Committee from
amongst those whom he knew to be inimical to the
men, and such as were sure to follow his and Mr. Peel's

views. Mr. Hume could not, however, be excluded; there
would have been a demand in the House that he should
be placed on the Committee; and it was therefore advisable to put him on at once. In any other case the old
Committee would have been revived, but that Committee
had acted fairly, had made its purpose generally known,
had examined every one who offered to be examined, with
care and the utmost impartiality. It was not therefore
calculated for a special purpose, and the usual mode was
impudently departed from. Neither Mr. Hume nor I
expected we should be able to beat such a Committee as
we did.

"Mr. Huskisson was unfortunate in wording his motion
'to inquire *respecting the conduct of workmen.*' He might,
had he foreseen the consequence, have so worded his
motion as to have shut us out; as it was he let us in,
spite of every effort which was made to the contrary.
When it was demanded that workmen against whom no
complaint had been made, should be examined for the
purpose of proving the beneficial effects of Mr. Hume's
Act, and the demand was grounded on the words of the
motion, Mr. Huskisson was astounded. He meant no
such thing: it was not intended to have any such inquiries made; and, notwithstanding the words of the
motion, the Committee determined that none of the working people should be examined, excepting only such as
might be personally accused. Even this partial and unjust decision was extended to the exclusion of men
who were accused of heinous crimes which they had not
committed. Another circumstance of moment seems to
have escaped the observation of Mr. Huskisson: this was
the Easter holidays. So near to these holidays was the
appointment of the Committee, that it could not sit for
nearly a fortnight. Mr. Hume and I availed ourselves
of this circumstance, and were indefatigable. I wrote to

many places in the country, and induced them to send up delegates. I went amongst the London trades, persuaded them to meet and appoint delegates to co-operate with those from the country, formed a permanent and large committee of them, induced them to collect moneys, and collected some myself for them. They were thus enabled to pay Parliamentary agents, and other expenses. These men (the deputies) were vigilant and intelligent, especially the shipwrights, some of whom were very clever men, as were some also from Lancashire, Glasgow, Yorkshire, and the sailors from the Tyne. The delay in the meeting of the Committee gave me the opportunity to write the small pamphlet, "Observations on Mr. Huskisson's Speech," &c. Two thousand copies were printed by the Trades Committee, and very carefully distributed, especially amongst members of the two Houses, and considerable effect was produced by it in favour of the men and Mr. Hume's Act. My mind was fully made up. I laid every other matter and thing aside; opened my house to the workmen; did everything I could; and saw everybody who was at all likely either to be made useful, or prevented being mischievous. Nothing that could be done by me, by Mr. Hume, by the Trades Committee, or by others, was omitted to be done; and the effect produced was such as could not have been easily anticipated, nor very easily credited.

"Many of the members who had been on the Committee in the preceding session, requested to be put upon the present Committee, but were refused, Mr. Huskisson telling these gentlemen the Committee would sit no more than three or four days; and yet he contrived to place some half-dozen more of his own partisans upon it.

"When the Committee assembled, the Right Honourable Thomas Wallace [1] was appointed chairman. He was

---

[1] At that time Master of the Mint.

a man singularly well qualified for his office, conversant
with Parliamentary business, not too wise for the purposes
of his masters, but more than sufficiently conceited with
his own wisdom and his own importance. In many
respects he was perhaps the most unmanageable man
that could have been pitched upon. He had a purpose
to accomplish, and would attend to no suggestions from
those who were opposed to him. The Committee were
informed that about half-a-dozen gentlemen would be
examined, and then a bill would be submitted to the
Committee to remedy the evils complained of. Mr. Peel,
who was in a great hurry to come to a conclusion,
proposed a bill on the plan before mentioned, and the
Attorney-General, Copley, was requested to prepare it
forthwith. Both Mr. Hume and I were acquainted with
the intended enactments. We conversed on the subject,
and Mr. Hume undertook to speak to the Attorney-
General. He did so, and put it to Mr. Attorney, how he
could draw a bill on the plan proposed, so as not to make
it the most obnoxious nonsense that ever had been proposed to Parliament? How, if money was not to be subscribed but by permission of a magistrate; and how, if
none but a Justice of the Peace was ever to be a treasurer,
school societies, Bible societies, charitable societies, and
other useful associations, could exist? In fact, how any
association for desirable purposes could be formed in
which contributions were necessary, unless every such
society first obtained an Act of Parliament? Whether,
indeed, in the present state of society, such an Act could
be passed: and whether, if it could be passed, it would
not be calculated to change the character of the whole
body of the people for the worse? Mr. Attorney Copley
saw the force of the objections, shrunk from the task, and
declined drawing the bill. Thus a most material point
was gained. Copley was disliked, and, had he drawn the

bill, would have had to encounter great obloquy. So disgraceful a bill would have caused a great sensation, and would probably have been defeated in consequence of the clamour it would have excited. But that was not the game we had to play. It was our purpose to break down the matter, little by little, in every possible way, and then to encounter what remained as vigorously as we could.

"Notwithstanding the Attorney-General shrunk from the bad work, the shipbuilders of the Thames stuck close to it, and in a bill which they printed as a comment on the report of the Committee, they urged the adoption of the plan they had proposed to ministers; and this bill they caused to be put into the hand of every one of the members as he entered the House on the second reading of the bill.

"The Committee soon found that it was not quite so easy to proceed in the way proposed as they had anticipated. They were not a little surprised at finding the passage to the committee-room blocked up by men demanding to be examined, and still more so at finding that some of them sent in offers to rebut the evidence which had been given on the preceding day. Every accusation was denied almost as regularly as it was made, and evidence to the contrary was offered, not only by notes to the chairman, but by letters to individual members, and this was constantly repeated.

"In the Committee of 1824 every case was made as public as possible. In this Committee great pains were taken that nothing which passed in the Committee should be known, but they were all pains to no purpose. I knew everything that passed, and always had the men ready to reply. Mr. Hume, with unexampled courage and perseverance, supported the claims of the men to be heard. Petitions to be heard were sent to the House and referred to the Committee; they who petitioned attended at the

committee-room and demanded a hearing. The members
could hardly get to their room or from it, so completely
was the passage blocked by the men, and so well had they
been instructed not readily to make way for the members.
This produced considerable effect on the members of the
Committee, and attracted the attention of a great many
members of the House, who in consequence were apprised
of the course the Committee had chosen to adopt.

" Mr. Hume insisted upon it, that his bill had produced
great and extensive good, and he offered the proofs by the
mouths of many witnesses who were anxiously waiting
outside the committee-room to be examined, they having
come from various parts of the United Kingdom for the
very purpose of being examined. The Committee found
themselves in a dilemma, and at length consented to
examine some men. This was a consequence of their
fears. The injustice they contemplated was so very gross
they could not encounter the exposure with which they
were threatened as well in the public papers as in the
House. It was this, and no love of justice, which at length
operated on them. Still they did not give up their intention, but endeavoured to limit the examination to those
only who were accused by name, and to this they adhered
so pertinaciously as to exclude a large number of those
they ought to have examined. They wholly excluded the
deputies from Birmingham, Sheffield, and several other
places, who were in London, and so fully satisfied was I of
the impossibility of inducing them to examine others that
I prevented many places sending deputies.

" The working people of Dublin and Glasgow were
accused of serious crimes. These accusations were recorded by the Committee, and intended to be laid before
the House. Still the Committee would hear none of the
persons whom it was desirable should have been sent from
these places to rebut the accusations. Men's names were

used as having in Glasgow abetted murder; and yet, notwithstanding the very men who had been so named wrote
to Mr. Hume and to the chairman of the Committee
requesting to be examined, the Committee persisted in
refusing to hear them.   The men said, 'We are men of
good character, have done no wrong to any one, are at
work in the same shops and factories in which we have
worked for years, and have nothing objected to us by our
employers; we demand the opportunity to clear ourselves
from the imputation.'   But no, the Committee would not
hear them; it would record the accusation, add the weight
of its authority to it, and leave the accused without a
defence.   Mr. Huskisson was base enough to call the men
thus accused, and thus refused a hearing, 'acquitted
felons'; and yet they were unacquitted, for they had
been accused only before the Committee, who had not
condescended to do either them or themselves the justice
of trying them at the bar of the Committee.

"Notwithstanding this, no one was refused a hearing
who came with a complaint against the workmen; no one
was refused payment for his time and travelling expenses
who gave evidence against the men, while many of the
men who had been weeks in attendance, and were at
length forced on the notice of the Committee and were
examined by them, were refused any remuneration whatsoever.   It was attempted to avoid payment by a mean
shuffle.   It was said the men were not summoned by the
Committee, but it was shown that some of those who had
received the highest rate of pay, and were men of property
who did not need to be reimbursed, were not summoned;
and a direct refusal to give anything to the men was the
consequence.   Some, however, were paid.

"My time was wholly occupied from the day Mr. Huskisson made his speech till some time after the passing of
the Act.   I examined a vast number of persons; made

digests and briefs for Mr. Hume; wrote petitions to the
House and to the Committee; many letters to Mr. Wallace,
the chairman; and many to other persons, all as the agent
of the men, and for their adoption. No one thing that
could be done was omitted, every possible advantage was
taken of even the most minute circumstance, and it was
by these and Mr. Hume's extraordinary exertions that the
intentions of Mr. Huskisson and Mr. Peel were at length
so completely defeated, and the bill called Mr. Wallace's
bill was passed.[1]

"The Committee as it proceeded became exceedingly
indignant. Its anger when it discovered that I obtained
correct accounts of its proceedings was violent and absurd.
It could not bear that I should be thus informed; that
their measures should be anticipated in letters and petitions; and that, spite of all their exertions and the advantages they possessed, they should every day be losing
ground. They threatened to punish me for my temerity.
I was to be sent for, to be questioned, to be reported to the
House, to be committed to Newgate, for daring to interfere
and tampering with their witnesses.

"These were the notions these wise men entertained
of justice. The masters might consult when and where
they pleased; give what instructions they pleased; have
the ears of members of the Committee, and go in and out
of the committee-room while the Committee was sitting as
often as they pleased. But the workmen were to have no
one to assist them; no one was to instruct them, notwithstanding they were the party who most needed instruction.
They, such as the Committee chose, were to go before a
body of their superiors—great squires and members of Parliament—be cross-questioned, bullied, and intimidated, and

---

[1] In a letter to S. Harrison, October 3, 1840, Place says, "The repeal
of the laws against combinations of workmen in 1824 and 1825 cost
me upwards of £250 in money."

no one was either to advise or assist them. So they concluded; so I resolved that it should not be. It happened, however, that every one of the men who entered the committee-room in awe of the great men, came out of it with feelings of contempt for those who had treated them, as they invariably did, with contumely and insult, and while they did so, as invariably exposed their ignorance and their malice to the observation of the men; and this, too, to such an extent as to take away all respect and put the men at perfect ease while under an examination which many had previously looked to with considerable dread.

"Mr. Hume was at first alarmed at the threats of the Committee to send for me. He sent a messenger from the Committee to me with a note expressing his apprehension. I replied by the messenger; and urged him to provoke the Committee thus to commit themselves. He did so; but they could not be prevailed to put their threat into execution. I was very desirous of being examined. I could have contrived to have had questions put to me which would have enabled me to say everything I wished to say, and the newspapers would have given it insertion at length; some because it would have answered their purposes, and others because, as some inserted it, they could not keep it out; most would, however, have done it willingly on my furnishing them with copies. The worst the Committee could have done would have been to report me to the House, and move that I should be called to the bar. In the meantime the examination would have appeared in the newspapers, and a very pretty piece of business they would have made of it. A debate in the House on such a motion would have been a fine exposure of the conduct of the Committee. After all, the House could only have sent me to Newgate for contumacy at their bar; the session was drawing to a close, and I should have been nearly as comfortable in one of the rooms of the gaoler's house as at home.

" I kept on steadily telling the men to inform the Committee that they had been examined and instructed by me. I sent written demands on the chairman for them to be paid as others were paid; and at length some of the men were paid, though only half or one-third the usual sum. There were two shipwrights from Shields named Shippon and Welsh, remarkably sturdy men. They had been examined and were refused any remuneration. They both knew Sir Matthew White Ridley, the member for Newcastle, and on these men I fixed for an experiment. I accordingly wrote a petition to the House against the Committee in their favour. This was an unprecedented step, and it required some nerve on the part of the men to go through with it. It was agreed that a copy of the petition should be sent to the Committee under cover to Sir Matthew White Ridley before it was presented to the House. The Committee was very indignant, and sent for the men. Sir M. W. Ridley was appointed to bully them; and this he did in his own particular style, to the amusement of the men and some two or three members of the Committee. The men were not at all intimidated, but remained unmoved at his threats to send them to prison, as well as their advisers, and the consequence was that Ridley, having uselessly exhausted his stock of abuse, and the Committee finding they could not put the men from their purpose, Ridley tore the petition in pieces, and the men had an order for payment.

" After the report had been printed and the bill came to be discussed, great efforts were made by the shipbuilders and others to introduce coercive clauses, while Mr. Hume was effectually active to modify the bill. There was much vehemence and ill-temper in some of the debates which attended the presentation of petitions, and still more when the bill was in committee of the whole House. Mr. Denman and Mr. John Williams, whose great legal know-

ledge was respected, did good service in showing that the
repeal of the common law was proper. These debates were
considered by the newspaper reporters as matters of small
consequence; and, like many others, might be passed by
so as to save them trouble; and they are very inadequately
reported. Once when the bill was in committee the debate
was singularly acrimonious. I was in the House under
the gallery; was accosted by many members, and assured
by some that there had been no such a stormy debate
during the whole session. The House was thin, and on
the Opposition side not so many as twenty members. Sir
Francis Burdett and Mr. Hobhouse supported Mr. Hume,
but he had to bear the vehement attacks of the whole
Ministerial bench—Huskisson, Peel, Wallace, Canning, the
Attorney-General, &c. &c. No terms either as to truth or
decency of language, to the utmost extent which ingenuity
could use, so as not to be reprehended by the Speaker,
were spared. Wallace gave loose to invective, and was
disgracefully abusive. Huskisson became enraged, and
most grossly insulted Sir Francis Burdett and Mr. Hobhouse. Mr. Peel stuck at nothing; he lied so openly, so
grossly, so repeatedly, and so shamelessly, as even to
astonish me, who always thought, and still do think him,
a pitiful, shuffling fellow. He was repeatedly detected by
Mr. Hume, and as frequently exposed. Still he lied again
without the least embarrassment, and was never in the
smallest degree abashed.[1] This was, upon the whole, a
very disgraceful exhibition.

---

[1] Sir Robert Peel's view of the proceedings may be gathered from
his letter to Mr. Leonard Horner, dated November 29, 1825. "Sufficient precautions," he says, "were not taken in the Act of 1823 (sic),
the first substitute for the old Combination Laws, to prevent that
species of annoyance which numbers can exercise towards individuals,
short of personal violence and actual threat, but nearly as effectual for
its object."—"Sir Robert Peel, from his Private Correspondence,"
edited by C. S. Parker (London, 1891), p. 379.

"Mr. Huskisson accused Mr. Hume of having betrayed the Committee and suffered himself to be led by the opinions of others. He told Mr. Hobhouse he was obliged to talk as he did, in opposition to his better judgment. Mr. Canning and Mr. Peel went over the same ground. Mr. Canning told Sir Francis Burdett he did not understand the matter, but being under surveillance, he was obliged to talk as he did.

"Sir Matthew W. Ridley followed in the same course. I was repeatedly alluded to, and stared at by all the House; but as I caught Mr. Hume's eye several times, and saw that it in no way annoyed him, I remained. When they had all done speaking, Mr. Hume addressed the House, and in about twenty minutes gave an account of his conduct, described the Committee, named me repeatedly as the man to whom he owed much assistance, justified us both, and made, as I thought, a triumphant speech. He challenged any one to show that I had in any way interfered improperly, or had been otherwise than serviceable in all respects. No man on any occasion ever more completely beat his opponents before him. I confess I thought myself a tolerably sturdy fellow; but Mr. Hume's sturdiness had, on this occasion, my most unqualified admiration. I am certain no man but himself could have been found who would have behaved with such unshaken firmness, and so successfully have replied to a host of opponents as he did. It was a very extraordinary instance of intrepidity and tact, and so it has since been acknowledged to have been by men on both sides of the House.

"When the bill was reported I was again in the House, and Mons. J. B. Say[1] was with me. On this occasion the most rancorous hostility was again shown; allusions to me were so particularly personal and graceless, that at

---

[1] See the reference to J. B. Say, the distinguished French economist, at p. 158.

length M. Say proposed that we should leave the House, as
he observed my friends were made uncomfortable, and we
withdrew. Nothing of this was reported in the newspapers.
In matters of this kind little is ever reported; and at all
times as little as can be conveniently of Mr. Hume. He is
generally disliked by the reporters, who, like other men
who follow laborious employments, are disposed to make
the labour as light as they can. They object to Mr. Hume
that his pertinacity prolongs the session, as it very frequently also does the hours the House sits. And on the
two occasions when the House was in committee on the
Combination Laws Bill the reporters not only neglected to
report Mr. Hume as they ought to have done, but they so
reported the debate as to give the appearance of defeat to
him, when, in fact, he was remarkably triumphant.

" Ultimately the Act differed very little from Mr. Hume's
Act. It is substantially the same. The words 'common
law' are omitted, but by the 4th and 5th enacting clauses
it is wholly excluded, both in the commencement and close
of the clauses; and this being the principal purpose of the
Act, the other alterations were of comparatively small
moment. There is a long clause, differently worded in
some particulars from Mr. Hume's Act, respecting intimidation, and the punishments for offences are increased; but
the partial, unjust, and mischievous laws which forbade
combinations of workmen to alter their wages and hours of
working are all swept away, and the new Act 6 Geo. III.
c. 129 has, by the 4th and 5th clauses, declared combinations for these purposes to be legal.

" The principal objection to leaving out the words 'common law' is that the perversity or ingenuity of lawyers
may, in some circumstances, ground vexatious proceedings
on the vagueness of the law; and in other times, men may
be again indicted for conspiracies and horridly punished
when they have committed no crime. This is a state in

which no law should ever be left. Men may combine to
regulate wages and hours of working, but if at any meeting held for either or both of these purposes, the men
should be led to deviate into any other matter, they may
then be, all or any of them, indicted under the common
law for conspiracy; and the mercy they would meet with,
under the operation of this process, may be guessed at by
the terrible punishments many have heretofore endured.
This ground of objection was taken by Lord Rosslyn in the
House of Lords, when the Chancellor Eldon explained that
such proceedings were not contemplated by the Act, and
would not be permitted.[1]

"The laws against combinations were inimical to the
working people in many respects. They induced them to
break and disregard the laws. They made them suspect
the intentions of every man who tendered his services.
They made them hate their employers with a rancour
which nothing else could have produced. And they made
them hate those of their own class who refused to join them,
to such an extent as cordially to seek to do them mischief.
The amendment on the repeal of the laws was immediate,
and has been increasing ever since. The people have come
better together, have now [1829] incomparably more confidence in the good intentions of others to serve them
than they ever had before, and are much better disposed
to serve themselves. None but good results can follow. It
is true the old leaven has not yet worn out. Power-looms
have been broken since the repeal of the Combination Laws,
and now the Spitalfields weavers, in their state of misery,
have destroyed a good deal of silk in the looms. Still the
extent of the mischief has been comparatively small as

[1] Place had considerable success in the House of Lords. In addition
to this declaration from the Chancellor, Lord Rosslyn, at Place's suggestion, proposed several amendments. One of these, which conceded the
right of appeal to Quarter Sessions, was accepted by the Government,
and was afterwards of some value.

compared with former times, and a few years will probably put an end to everything of the kind.

"The tumults caused by combinations of workmen on account of wages have generally ceased. There are now none of those outrageous proceedings which were formerly perpetual; and although it is very probable that there will be occasional ebullitions, it is not at all likely that the conduct so very generally pursued up to the repeal of the Combination Laws will ever again be resumed.[1]

"Soon after the proceedings in 1825 were closed the seamen of the Tyne and Wear sent me a handsome silver vase, paid for by a penny-a-week subscription, and the cutlers of Sheffield sent me an incomparable set of knives and forks in a case. They are not only the finest specimen of workmanship I ever saw, but men well acquainted with cutlery have declared that they excel anything they have ever seen."[2]

[1] 27,798 (25-41).   [2] 27,798 (66).

CHAPTER IX

THE FIRST REFORM CAMPAIGN

ON April 15, 1830, Place after his second marriage returned to Charing Cross, and to his "old way of consuming time." On June 26, George IV. died. His death had been for some time expected, and politicians had been preparing themselves for the consequent general election, and for the accession of a king who was understood to be a reformer. The Whigs were on the look-out for a popular cry, and found it in what was known ten years later as the Condition of the People Question. They therefore moved an amendment to the address declaring that the partial distress mentioned in the king's speech on February 4 was really general. This was a question of fact as to which most members of the House of Commons knew nothing at all; but because it was a question of fact gentlemen could make sonorous declarations of popular sympathy without committing themselves to any definite policy.

Accordingly the "speech-making gabbling Whigs"[1] filled pages of Hansard with vague chatter about their own observations and the testimony of their friends, and in the great Whig club-house at Brooks' men declared that "it would be impossible to go on" beyond June.[2] In the Commons, the Whigs were supported by some dis-affected Tories who had not yet forgiven Wellington for passing Catholic Emancipation in 1829.

---

[1] 27,509 (50).　　[2] 27,789 (142).

Q

But even outside the little circle of the Commons the
Condition of the People Question was being discussed
more widely than it had been since 1817. Prices were
going up, and the newspapers were full of those confused
complaints which any change in the standard of value
always produces. Place looked on with grim disgust.
"Between the landowners on the one side, who wanted
laws to make food dear and commodities cheap, and the
generality of the manufacturing people who wanted high
profits and high wages with cheap produce, there was as
absurd and as unintelligible a state of things as had
perhaps ever existed."[1]

The general impression that times were changing was
heightened by the behaviour of the new king. "George
the Fourth," wrote Place to Hume, "shut himself up from
mere hatred of the people. The present silly man is court-
ing them most absurdly. No sooner was he made king,
than he who had been private became public; he walked
in the streets; he rode among the people; he went about
with his queen in an open carriage; he bowed and waved
his hat, and laughed, and was as merry as the silliest of
the mob. The people, too, took off their hats and hurrahed
and shouted, and were as pleased as so many children with
a new toy. . . . The king goes on making a nonsensical
exhibition of himself and his queen, making speeches as
often as he can find an occasion, speeches which a board-
ing-school girl would be ashamed of. And what is the
consequence of all this? The consequence is that the
seamen of the North have sent a petition to him by a
deputation who are charged to see him, and beg him to
attend to their prayer, which is, that he will redress their
grievances and raise their wages. Others are asking for
and expecting to receive from him similar advantages.
The housekeepers [*i.e.* ratepayers] are much in the same

[1] 27,789 (144).

way; they too expect him to do for them they know not
what."[1]

At the general election in August, as Westminster was
not contested, Place undertook the unpaid "management"
of Middlesex for his friend Hume.[2]   The elections produced
more interest than usual, and at the moment when the
excitement was at its highest, came the Three Days' Revolution in Paris, and the forcible substitution of a constitutional monarchy under Louis Philippe for the reactionary
despotism of Charles X.   Place has described the recep-
tion of the news at Hume's committee-room.

"There had been no arrivals from Paris at London for
three or four days, and great indeed was the anxiety it
caused.   It was said there had been a *coup d'état* which
had succeeded, and this increased the anxiety. . . . When
the news arrived I was in the large room used as a public
room by Mr. Hume's committee.   The anxious state in
which men were had caused a large attendance of highly
respectable people, among whom were many members of
the late Parliament.   The company was in large groups
talking of the probable events at Paris, when a gentleman
came in with a French publication, printed at Paris in the
evening of the 29th [July], announcing the people's victory
after the three days' fighting.   Mr. Hobhouse was near
the door, and was the first to possess himself of the news,
which, having announced, he raised his hat above his head

---

[1] Place to Hume, November 1, 1830.

[2] On this occasion he was made very angry by the eagerness of the
Whig magnates to get as much out of him as possible, and their fear
of demeaning themselves by being grateful.   In his diary he accuses
Hobhouse of contriving " to induce his Whig friends to object, as they
did, to my being placed on the Committee of Middlesex freeholders.
. . . But the most curious circumstance was, that the very same men
who had done so passed a resolution a fortnight before the election
came on, putting the management of the Committee into my hands,
and the uncontrolled disposal of the funds at my discretion !"
("Diary," July 1830.)

and cheered loudly. All present were electrified, and many
cheers were given in as loud voices and as heartily as ever
they were given on board a man-of-war at the moment
of victory. No assembly of men were ever more elated,
or congratulated one another more heartily or more
sincerely."[1]

The easy success of the Revolution of July not only
gave a strong impetus to the movement in favour of Parliamentary Reform in England,[2] but also helped to decide the
particular form which that movement was to take during
the next two years. The first French Revolution had
completely discredited in England any policy of forcible
resistance to Government. Now, however, an organised
rising began to seem not only a reasonable, but a virtuous
and tolerably safe method of solving constitutional difficulties. "This new Revolution produced a very extraordinary effect on the middle classes, and sent a vast number
of persons to me with all sorts of projects and propositions.
Every one was glorified with the courage, the humanity,
and the honesty of the Parisians, and the common people
became eagerly desirous to prove that they too were brave
and humane and honest. All soon seemed desirous to
fight against the Government if it should attempt to
control the French Government."[3]

Place himself came under the influence of this change
of feeling. During the next two years the thought was
always at the back of his mind that, horrible as an armed
revolution must almost necessarily be, and he had no illusions on this point, such a revolution might yet be worth
while. In April 1831 Major Beauclerk wrote: "Most
sincerely do I hope it may not be necessary for us to pass

---

[1] 27,789 (162, 163).

[2] "The 'three days' produced much of our political excitement."—
"The Greville Memoirs, a Journal of the Reigns of King George IV.
and King William IV." (3 vols., London, 1874-1887), vol. ii. p. 219.

[3] "Diary," July 1830.

through the ordeal of a revolution to restore us to a state
of sanity, but much as I dread such a crisis, I must confess
I should prefer it a thousand times to the alternative of
again returning to the same vicious and rotten system."[1]
Place replied: "I hope with you almost against my conviction that we shall be able to avoid a violent revolution
in working out our reformation. A violent revolution in
this country would be dreadful in the extreme. . . . The
horrors perpetrated by the Parisian mobs in the early
stages of their revolution, were the immediate consequences
of supplies not being brought to the city as usual. Contemplate seriously what would be the consequences of the
failure of supplies to this great metropolis. Think of the
mischief which would be produced if neither corn nor
cattle were brought to market for only three days, including one market-day at Smithfield and Mark Lane, and you
will be convinced that the horrors of Paris would be far
exceeded by those of London. . . . Do you think you can
estimate with anything like precision the terrible consequences of a starving and an enraged populace in London
and its example on all parts of the country ? If you do so
you will dread a convulsion as much as I do. Yet I agree
with you that even a convulsion should be risked rather
than have the boroughmongering system continued."[2]

For ten years Place's whole habits of work had been
opposed to "pitched battle" tactics. He had steadily exploited the fact that the most bigoted of Tory Governments
cannot continuously resist the passage of small reforms, or
prevent accumulated small reforms from having their
effect. Now, however, in view of the possibility of an
armed revolution he welcomed the idea that the end of
such concessions was come, and that the Duke of Wellington, like Polignac, would make a final stand against pro-

[1] A. H. Beauclerk to Place, April 7, 1831.
[2] Place to Major Beauclerk, April 7, 1831.

gress. "The Duke thinks this is not the time to meet the wishes of the people. He does not understand them, and has therefore resolved to make no concessions. I hope he will stick to his resolve. If I thought as the Duke thinks, and were in his place, I would permit no change to be made and would be obstinate to the death. It is a question of longer or shorter — change will come. It is a very simple question,—there must be a radical change, not a sham reform, but a radical change from the top to the bottom, and this you may if you please call a revolution.

"The whole scheme of our Government is essentially corrupt, and no corrupt system ever yet reformed itself. Our system could not reform itself if it would. Take away the corruption and nothing remains. His Dukeship and his coadjutors know this as well as I do, but they think they can continue to cajole the people. Catholic emancipation was to appease them. Repeal of taxes on beer and on leather was to satisfy them. . . . He has seen that concession goes for nothing, while anything remains to be conceded, and he will concede no more. Well done, brave Duke! It is a happy circumstance that when the people have obtained the thing they clamoured for, they set very little store by it. This is the security for good government in the end. The Duke is like the school-boy who objected to say A.

'If I say A, I must say B,
And so go on to C and D;
And so no end I see there'll be
If I but once say A B C.'

"But we are told, if all concession be refused the people will become outrageous, and no one can tell what may follow. Yes, I think any one can tell. There will be much grumbling and growling, and meeting and petitioning will follow. They will become more and more dissatisfied;

and in time they will use force, and after a while they will triumph. This is inevitable."[1]

On November 2, King William the Fourth opened his first Parliament. One result of the excitement of the preceding summer was that 129 new members—an unusual proportion in the unreformed House of Commons—had been elected, and though politicians were not so clearly labelled as they are now, the Whigs were known to be hopeful. One sentence in the king's speech produced something like a panic. The Revolution in Paris had been followed by another in Brussels, by which the Belgians had declared themselves independent of the Dutch Crown. " I am endeavouring," the king was made to say, " in concert with my allies, to devise such means of restoring tranquillity as may be compatible with the welfare and good government of the Netherlands, and with the future security of other states." This seemed to point to an attack by Prussia upon Belgium, a new alliance against France, and a repetition of the whole dreary course of the Napoleonic wars.[2]

On that evening Place " dined alone with Mr. Bentham. . . . The printed speech of the king was brought to us soon after dinner, and it greatly disconcerted us. We had no doubt that the Lords had been sounded on the subject, and had warranted the insertion of the hostile paragraphs

[1] Place to Hume, Nov. 1, 1830.

[2] " We expected that arrangements would be made privately for Prussia to assist Holland to recover the Netherlands, that France would then interfere, and there would be a general war. The king's speech was therefore expected with anxiety, and when the time for the Parliament to meet came, the people in the metropolis were unusually agitated. Parliament assembled on the 26th October, and the hopes of the people were dashed to the ground by the passage it contained respecting Belgium. War seemed inevitable, and many were the suggestions to place impediments in its way. Amongst others, a refusal of the housekeepers to pay taxes, and to form themselves into a National Guard. . . . I did not expect any hostile expressions would be put into the king's speech, and I had therefore no expectation of any extraordinary proceedings, nor of any change of ministers." (" Diary," 1830.)

in the speech. Every sort of evil seemed to follow in the train of a general war, and our forebodings were dismal enough."[1]

Wellington had already on that same evening made his celebrated declaration of hostility to any change of the system of representation, and Grey in the Lords, and Brougham in the Commons, had, on behalf of the Whig party, given notice of motions in favour of some undefined measure of Parliamentary reform. In the existing temper of the House of Commons it was generally felt that the Whigs could now come into office as soon as they liked. Next evening Place again saw Mr. Bentham, " when we congratulated ourselves and one another on the occurrence of the preceding evening, being quite convinced that great changes were at hand," but he adds the modest avowal that " we were also a little perplexed at not being able to see exactly how they would be brought about."[2]   On November 7, four days later, Wellington made his defeat inevitable by countermanding, on the ground of his own unpopularity and the danger of a riot, a visit in state by the king to the City, which had been arranged for Lord Mayor's Day.[3]

---

[1] 27,789 (176).   [2] 27,789 (177).

[3] Though Place was perfectly willing to make political use of the possibility of disorder in London, he was at that time doing his best to make the new police (established in 1829) as efficient as possible. His administrative instinct rejoiced over their substitution for the "conceited and interested people who managed the old watch in parishes" [27,789, (182)], and Mr. Thomas, the police-inspector, used to visit him. On one such occasion about this time, " I advised Mr. Thomas not again to wait until his men were attacked, and then, when they had been maltreated and bruised, to take a few vagabonds into custody ; but when he saw a mob prepared to make an attack, to lead his men on and thrash those who composed the mob with their staves as long as any of them remained together, but to take none into custody ; and that if this were done once or twice, there would be no more such mobs. On the 9th November a large mob gathered in the City and sallied through Temple Bar, armed with pieces of wood from a fence in Chancery Lane, for the purpose of beating the police. My advice was

The fall of the Tory ministry and the immediate coming
into office of the Whigs, unchastened and unpledged, was
exactly what Place did not want. "The old Whigs," he
wrote, "thought silence the most prudent course. They
knew that Lord Wellington's administration was drawing to
a close, and they did not like to object to many things which
under other circumstances they would have unsparingly
condemned, and they did not like to propose any of those
reforms which under other circumstances they would have
declared were necessary to save the country from ruin,
lest they should commit themselves and be called upon,
should they be in power, to perform their promises." [1] On
November 8 Place wrote a long letter to Hobhouse, putting
as many of his real reasons for desiring delay as he dared,
and probably a good many more than was wise. "'Miracles
never will cease.' Here am I, 'the furious republican,'
whose opinions have induced many to fear, and more to
hate him, become a *modéré*, writing to you not to accelerate
an instant, but to retard, not a mere reform, but an actual
change.

"The folly of the king and his ministers has precipitated
matters. . . . The king refuses to make a procession along
the streets, and the playhouses are from very fear to be
shut up to-morrow. This is the first time, observe, that
apprehension of violence by the people against an administration has induced them openly to change their plan of
proceeding.

"Put these matters in any way you please. Let men do
all they can to reconcile themselves to the conduct of

followed. The police retreated up Wych Street, and collected to about
sixty men in Catherine Street, from whence they sallied and beat the
mob before them to Temple Bar. This at once put an end to all rioting;
no one was killed, no limb was broken, but many were bruised and
many heads were broken ; but there were no more mobs." ("Diary,"
November 1830.)

[1] 27,789 (181).

ministers. . . . Its nature cannot be changed, neither can
they make it other than the first step in the British
Revolution. You know my opinion of the weakness of the
present Government. You know my opinion that there
never can be a *strong* Government again in England until
there has been a change in its very form, and neither you
nor any one else will argue the contrary against me.

" I, then, want no instant change of ministers. I am as
certain as a man can be who is not desirous to cheat himself or be deceived by others, that a present change of
ministers would do more towards producing or rather
accelerating a revolution than all the other circumstances
of the time taken together; and the time is not yet come
when a radical change can be made, either so effectually as
to prevent other similar changes, or so beneficially as to
answer the purposes of any class of reformers. . . . If they
were to be ousted at once, who are to come in ? Not
another Tory set. There are not Tory materials of sufficient importance to build up an administration which
could continue in office to the end of the session. Not a
Whig administration, for, in spite of the wishes of their
friends, here is hardly anything but imbecility. Who
would be minister ? Earl Grey ? Look at him. Is he
competent to do the duty ? . . . The Marquis of Lansdowne ? Why should the fact be concealed that he is in
no way competent to the duties of the office ? . . . Lord
Holland ? He has gone by, or rather circumstances have
gone by and left him behind. . . .

" Do pray do all you can to prevent the unwise conduct
of your friends in resisting ministers in such a way as to
compel them to resign at once. Abuse their proceedings
as much as you please, but beyond this do nothing to
prevent them sinking gradually as low as possible, and
then leave them to work themselves out of office, which
will happen quite soon enough. . . .

"I have seen a letter from the man whom I consider the most influential man in England, Thomas Attwood of Birmingham,[1] proposing an association to collect the names of persons in London who will pledge themselves to pay no more taxes if ministerial interference should produce the probability of a war with Belgium, and I believe something of the kind will be done. There has long been growing a disposition to refuse paying taxes, but it is only now that rich men who have any influence have countenanced it. Now there are many such willing to take part in it.

"Now mark the consequences. If any considerable portion of the housekeepers were to refuse paying taxes, and especially if this were to happen in London, a revolution would be effected in a week, in spite of the Government and the army. If taxes were refused it would instantly produce a panic, Bank of England notes would no longer circulate, and Government would be powerless. No one would bring a sack of flour, a bullock or a sheep, to the London markets. The moment taxes were really refused the shops would be all closed, decent people would remain at home until the populace and the soldiers had

---

[1] In January 1830, Mr. Thomas Attwood and his friends had founded the formidable "Birmingham Political Union of the Middle and Lower Classes," with a Populist programme, to use the American term, of manhood suffrage and paper money. In regard to the proposal to refuse to pay taxes, Place wrote, "I was induced to put Attwood's proposition into a form which, if not strictly legal, was yet not punishable, as his certainly was, by all who should sign it. I therefore wrote out a declaration in a very few words, thus :—'That in the event of the present ministers so misconducting the affairs of the country as to make it probable we shall be involved in a Continental war, we will consider the propriety of checking so mischievous an event by withholding the means as far as may lay in our power, and will then consider whether or not refusing to pay direct taxes may not be advisable.' This was readily agreed to by a great many of the most prosperous shopkeepers, and by many other persons of property and influence."—27,789 (197).

fought and were reconciled. A provisional government would thus be formed—no man can tell what fortuitous circumstances may produce a revolution. . . . That it will happen before many years have passed away seems to me a reasonable expectation. You know my opinion, that when men ought to act they should act promptly, and go through with the business, be it whatever it may. You know that I have a great dislike to undertake any matter unless circumstances seem to warrant the conclusion that it can be wholly and not partially accomplished. I have always held that when action becomes necessary it is much better to risk doing wrong than doing nothing, and if the Opposition had no choice, I should say, go on, don't hesitate a moment, oust the ministers as soon as possible. But they have a choice, and may do mischief if they refuse or neglect to take that choice." [1]

Events, however, moved much too rapidly for such tactics. On November 15 the Tories were defeated in a division on the Civil List, and Lord Grey took office with a Ministry of Whigs and Canningites, or, as Place describes them, a "motley assembly" of "Whigs, Whig reformers, half-and-half Tories, and others who cared little about anything beyond their emoluments, and knew little beyond what they learned in the drawing-rooms of their associates, the clubs to which they belonged, or the clique with which they congregated. . . . Lord Grey had in 1810 openly abandoned the notions of reform which he had previously promulgated, and quarrelled with those whom he had helped to convince, because they did not apostatise as he did. And they who remembered his conduct placed little reliance on the vague declaration he made on accepting office." [2]

But the Whigs were in, and Place at once took up the

---

[1] Place to Hobhouse, November 8, 1830.
[2] 27,789 (203).

task of worrying them into granting as much reform as possible. "The Reformers," he wrote to Hume on November 22, "will not, however, be again cajoled," and he proceeds to suggest the public cross-examination of ministers on those points on which they were likely to be weak. "A question was put to Lord Althorp on Saturday, thus, 'Will any man in office be permitted to advocate voting by ballot?' The reply was, 'Certainly not.' The question was put by a member of Honourable House, who was prepared to make certain propositions, but on receiving this answer he proceeded no further. The reason for my writing to you now is to tell you these things, and to suggest to you the propriety of asking the same question and another of a like nature in the House." [1]

Lord Melbourne, who was Home Secretary in the new Government, found himself fully occupied by the growth of the more or less revolutionary "Political Unions" in the towns, and the rick-burning by the agricultural labourers in the country.[2] Under these circumstances he sent his brother, Mr. George Lamb, to see Place, and endeavour to induce him "to write two or three papers to the working people, and especially the agricultural labourers, to persuade them to desist from the enormities they were committing. . . . Mr. Lamb said, 'We are of opinion that you can write to them with more effect than any one else.'"[3] But Place declined the task, on the ostensible ground that such pamphlets would be interpreted as a sign of fear and so encourage the labourers to proceed still further. Though he was afterwards persuaded to write a pamphlet to show that rick-burning was of no use as a means of increasing wages, he could not help recognising that "Captain

---

[1] Place to Hume, November 22, 1830.
[2] See "Lord Melbourne's Papers," edited by Lloyd C. Sanders (London, 1889), pp. 120–165.
[3] 27,789 (207–208).

Swing"[1] was helping to bring reform within the range of practical politics.

"Incendiary fires continued to increase, and by the middle of December they had extended over thirteen counties. These fires, and the general discontent of the working people, had caused great alarm, and many were the schemes and projects for putting an end to them, and the Government was compelled to appoint a Special Commission to try such of the incendiaries and rioters as could be caught. This increased the discontent of the working classes, who, though they generally condemned the burning of ricks, found an excuse for the farmers' labourers in their ignorance, their low wages, their pauper allowance, the oppressions they were made to endure, and the want of means and intelligence to meet in societies as mechanics and artisans met, and settle their differences with their employers.

"It seemed certain that no Special Commission nor any other mode of coercion would prevent rick-burning while wages were very low, and were made up by pauper allowances from the parishes; that it was useless either to punish or advise, unless a more just and wiser system were adopted; and a great many persons of property and understanding were of opinion that the fires were calculated to compel attention to the actual state and condition of the labourers, and ultimately to produce such changes as would place them and their immediate employers in a better state than they had for years been, in as good a state, indeed, as it was possible they could be placed by any interference of Government. The measures which it seemed likely would be forced on the Government were thought to be a better administration of the Poor Laws, a repeal of the Corn Laws, of all laws restricting trade and

---

[1] The title given to the leader of the gangs of labourers who went about rick-burning.

commerce, economy in the administration of the public revenue, decrease of taxation, reform of the laws, especially those which related to the administration of justice, and above all, reform of Parliament, which would ensure all the other reforms." [1]

Poor old Richard Carlile [2] put the same idea rather more bluntly in the *Prompter*, [3] and to Place's furious indignation, the Government of Whig rick-owners decided to prosecute him, though the article was one "which would not probably have been noticed by the Wellington Administration." [4] Place stormed at his friends in Parliament, and particularly at Colonel Leslie Grove Jones, [5] who, as Place was careful to point out, had himself used more violent language in letters to the *Times*. [6] The ministry, however, held to their prosecution, and Carlile received the savage sentence of two years' imprisonment and a heavy fine. [7] After this it was not surprising that when Hume proposed to Lord Grey that the Newspaper Stamp Duties should be immediately repealed, he was told that "these matters did not press." [8]

When Parliament met, the Whigs introduced an ill-contrived Budget, including proposals for a heavy tax on steamboat passengers, and an increase of the army by 10,000

[1] 27,789 (206,*207).

[2] Richard Carlile, the well-known martyr of free speech, had lately spent six years (1820–26) in Dorchester gaol.

[3] The *Prompter*, November 27, 1830.

[4] 27,789 (236).

[5] Lieutenant-Colonel Leslie Grove Jones, born 1779, died 1839. He served through the Peninsular War. After leaving the army he took up politics as an advanced Radical and reformer, and gained considerable notoriety by his violent letters in the *Times* signed "Radical," "Justitia," &c.

[6] Place to Jones, January 7, 1831.

[7] At the same time prosecutions were commenced against several other papers [27,789 (238)], which were all abandoned except that against Cobbett, in whose case the jury disagreed.

[8] Place to Hume, January 12, 1831.

men. There seemed now to be no prospect of a Reform
Bill which would make any serious change in the system
of representation. A friend of Place's was, he says, told by
Lord Grey, early in December 1830, "that whatever proposition for reform might be made by ministers, it must be
such an one as the House of Commons would entertain." [1]

Place however hammered on : "The old reformers foresaw that the only chance for the production of a good bill
was, as Lord Grey had said (1797), the resolutions of the
people acting on the prudence of the House." [2] And the
note in his diary for February 1831 is, " Writing petitions
and resolutions for reform of Parliament, and consulting
with persons on this subject."

But the people were now getting thoroughly impatient
for a change to be made. Men outside the House of Commons, Place says, adopted one of Lord John Russell's
phrases, and were everywhere saying, "We must have
reform to save the constitution," by which word, he adds,
"they meant everything and nothing, but it helped them
in the struggle which soon succeeded." [3] "Meetings of
almost every description of persons," wrote Place, "were
held. In cities, towns, and parishes, by journeymen tradesmen in their clubs, and by common workmen who had
no trade clubs or associations of any kind. . . . The systematic way in which the people proceeded, their steady
perseverance, their activity and skill, astounded the enemies
of reform, and produced an effect sometimes observed in
considerable bodies of men, yet scarcely ever in a nation.
The enemies of reform had so strong a feeling of the impossibility of anything like a successful opposition, that
they remained in a state of comparative quiescence quite
at variance with their proceedings on former occasions." [4]

The bill was to be introduced on March 1, and on

[1] 27,789 (209).   [2] 27,789 (263).
[3] 27,789 (273).   [4] 27,789 (252).

February 16, when ministers would be finally making up
their minds on its details, Place sent Hume a message
which he obviously hoped would be passed on : "I think
that as soon as ministers have fairly exposed themselves,
as they will scarcely fail to do on the 1st March, and the
weekly press has got the cue, for the daily press is too
venal and corrupt to be useful in this way; I think I shall
be induced to put aside every man and every thing who or
which now occupies my time, and labour day and night to
expose them in every possible way. And I doubt not I
shall soon find plenty of able coadjutors." [1]

On the evening of March 1, Lord John Russell made
his statement. "I was alone in the evening," says Place,
"anxiously expecting some one to come from the House
to tell me what had occurred. At length, a friend who
had taken a report of about half of Lord John Russell's
speech for the *Morning Chronicle* came in and told me
the particulars of the ministerial plan. It was so very
much beyond anything which I had expected, that, had
it been told to me by a person unused to proceedings in
the House, I should have supposed that he had made a
mistake. Both I and my informant were delighted, and
we at once took measures to cause it to be known in the
coffee-houses in the neighbourhood, whence it spread like
wildfire." [2]

Next day Hobhouse, with whom Place had lately had
"almost daily conversations," [3] called at Charing Cross,
and in his privately printed memoirs has left an account
of the visit. On March 1, after Lord John Russell's
statement, he says: "Burdett and I walked home together, and both agreed that there was very little chance
of the measure being carried. We thought our Westminster friends would oppose the £10 qualification clause;

[1] Place to Hume, February 16, 1831.
[2] 27,789 (265).   [3] 27,789 (264).

R

but we were wrong, for calling the next day on Mr. Place, we found him delighted with the bill, and were told that all our supporters were equally pleased with it."[1]

Place's daily breathings of fire and slaughter had obviously answered their purpose in convincing Hobhouse, and through him the Government, that the reformers would not be easily satisfied. And it is a remarkable proof of the pivotal position of Westminster, that Hobhouse believed that the opposition of that constituency would be fatal to the bill. Place was in fact now offered, with apologies, infinitely more than he had ever dreamt of getting. "The statement," he writes in his diary, "surprised all parties. The reformers, the enemies of reform, and the boroughmongers, were all equally surprised,—and all for the same reason, namely, that the plan of reform had been made so extensive. None believed, none expected any such propositions. But they were plain and easily understood; there was no leaning to party. The fear of a revolution if they were not passed, and the sneaking servility of the ridiculously loyal, who will go with the king, made the propositions acceptable to a much more decided majority of the whole people than any other measure proposed to Parliament had ever before been within the memory of any man living.

"Any general description of the state of feeling would but feebly depict the excitement caused by the proposed reform. But much may be learned from the leading articles of the newspapers, and the accounts they contain of the many meetings held all over the country. It was im-

---

[1] See the *Edinburgh Review*, April 1871, pp. 283–337. The article contains extracts from the memoirs of Sir John Cam Hobhouse, Lord Broughton. The memoirs themselves have not yet been published (1897). Greville says that "Hobhouse told me he had at first been afraid that his constituents would disapprove this measure, as so many of them would be disfranchised, but that they had behaved nobly, and were quite content, and ready to make any sacrifice for such an object." ("The Greville Memoirs, &c.," vol. ii. p. 124.)

possible for me to be an idle spectator."[1]   "I saw that the
time was coming when it would be the duty of every man
to go forward and do his best for the public good.   It
seemed to me that he who neglected this duty was a bad
citizen, and deserved severe reprehension.   True enough
it was that the actual amount of service which each
ordinary man could perform was small, but it was equally
true that unless there was an immense aggregate of such
services, ministers would be unable to carry the bill, which
if carried could not fail greatly to benefit the country,
and tend to the advantage of the whole civilised world.
Undecided in what way I should devote myself to the
public service, I thought my exertions would as yet be
most useful at home, but this notion was soon changed
by the persons who . . . called upon me and induced
me to take the management of a public meeting at the
Crown and Anchor Tavern, on March 4, 1831."[2]

At this meeting Place intended to stiffen the ministers
in giving as much as they had promised by asking for a
great deal more.   He accordingly passed through the
organising committee a series of resolutions in favour
of Triennial Parliaments and the Ballot, "to make the
plan of reform proposed by his Majesty's ministers effectual."[3]   Hobhouse, however, when the meeting began,
jumped on the table, and carried in the name of unanimity
a proposal that no resolution except one of confidence in
ministers should be put, an exhibition of "true Whig
tactics" for which, says Place, the reformers never for-
gave him,[4] and which helped to lose him his seat at
Westminster two years later.

On March 21, the second reading of the bill was carried
by a majority of one.   There was a general illumination
in London, and Place was approached by "a gentleman

<hr>

[1] "Diary," March 1, 1831.   [2] 27,789 (318, 319).
[3] 27,789 (278).   [4] 27,789 (278, 279).

from the Controller of the King's Household," who asked
him to try to arrange that the unilluminated windows of
the Tories should not be broken, as those of protesting
Radicals had been on former occasions. Place refused
to make any such attempt. He recalled the saying of
various London magistrates to "disloyal persons" in the
past, that "a few farthing candles would have saved their
windows." Not much window-breaking was likely to
take place, since no one would now pay money for it, but
if no window were broken, the Tories would argue a reaction of public opinion, and declare that "even the mob
had respected the houses of those who had been falsely
represented as their worst enemies, but whom they knew
were truly their best friends." In the event, as he con-
tentedly remarks, "the windows in a very few houses of
the inveterate Tories were partially broken."[1]

But a majority of one on the second reading meant a
certain defeat in committee. Such a defeat came on
April 19, and was followed by another defeat on the
Estimates on April 21. On April 22 the king was per-
suaded to drive suddenly down to the House and prorogue
Parliament, with a view to its immediate dissolution.

Place was at this time mainly occupied with the work
of the "Parliamentary Candidates' Society," a sub-com-
mittee of which met daily.[2] This society was in intention
a predecessor of the "National Liberal Federation," and
was imitated from "the American Correspondence Societies
and Caucuses,"[3] which are supposed to give the rank
and file of a party some control over its electoral policy.
Its career was, however, a very troubled one. Most of
the well-known men who joined the Committee found
Place's methods too high-handed, and soon left, while
Place himself had as usual the greatest difficulty in

[1] 27,789 (287, 288).   [2] 27,789 (350).
[3] Erskine Perry to Place, April 1, 1831.

keeping his temper among the gentlemen amateurs who tried to combine democratic opinions with fashionable life.

"It is not so with the Tories in public political matters: they persuade themselves that everything they do is genteel. . . . They had no fear of being looked upon as ungenteel, none of being discountenanced by Holland House people and Brooks' Club people, like the poor half-and-half people with whom it was necessary I should associate. . . . Every one of them had the fear of the club before his eyes. Colonel Jones could not as yet bring himself to offend the men with whom he associated at Brooks'. Beauclerk was kept in check by the Travellers'. Perry must not be cut at the Universities'. Hume could not bear the taunts of the House, and nearly all the rest were either similarly circumstanced, or afraid to compromise their gentility by doing what would be condemned as going much too far by their friends—the half dandy, half idiot fashionable people, who sometimes condescended to notice them, or with whom they usually associated, as well as by the fools who would call them vulgar-r-r fellows. . . .

"The working classes, who are of little importance in any useful political proceeding unless countenanced by those called their betters, might have been made useful to the public cause. . . . The shopkeeping race and such as they, who are among the most despicable people in the nation in a public point of view, might have been of much importance, . . . ought on this occasion to have been, and might have been turned to good account, had the men who have leisure and considerable acquirements been in other respects qualified to have proceeded in the right direction. But they were not.

"The curse of gentility is upon them all, and this induces them to attend to minor objects, to neglect major

objects, to trifle with matters the most serious, and when
any considerable difficulty occurs, to shuffle away from it,
and then when reproached with such pitiful conduct, to
make an off-hand lying excuse which an honest boy or
girl would be ashamed to make. These people whenever
they interfere in Liberal political affairs endeavour to
accomplish two incompatible things—first, to go on with
the public matter; secondly, not to lose caste with their
fashionable friends and acquaintances. This being impossible, the first is sacrificed invariably. They shrink
back as it were into their shells. . . . Not one of them
has the courage to cut his drawing-room friends and
become, as he ought to be, a highly useful and important
man." [1]

The particular question on which Place's tactics came
most definitely into contact with the gentlemanly feelings
of his fellow committee-men of the Parliamentary Candidates' Society, was the expediency of collecting and publishing a record for electioneering purposes of the votes
and other public action of Tory members of Parliament.
After the well-known politicians had resigned, the greater
part of the work of the society seems to have consisted
in preparing such records,[2] and shortly after the election
the society, which had been furiously abused by almost
every paper, Whig or Tory, came to a quiet end. Place
wrote its obituary. .

" The Parliamentary Candidates' Society was of short
duration, as such a society ought to be, and as I, at least,
intended it should be. . . . It would, if it had been continued, have degenerated into a cabal for the advantage of
some very few persons, and those by no means the most

[1] 27,789 (336–339).
[2] Place wrote that by April 20 the public characters, in full detail,
of twenty-two members of Parliament had been prepared. They were,
however, never published.—27,789 (369).

respectable."[1] But when all is said, Place probably remembered the society as one of the least fortunate of his
efforts.

The new Parliament met on June 14. It contained a
majority of more than a hundred for "the bill, the whole
bill, and nothing but the bill." "The election of the
members to the new Parliament in 1831 was a very extraordinary circumstance, one which no man could have
anticipated as possible a year before it took place. It
could not have been anticipated that a boroughmongering Parliament would have been called together with an
express recommendation from the king to put an end to
the boroughmongering by which alone it could exist."[2]

He quotes the figures given by the Society of the
Friends of the People in 1793, as to the extent to which
members of the Commons were nominated by individual
owners of property, and proceeds : "This scandalously
corrupt state of the House in 1793 was somewhat increased in 1831, and against this infamous power, and
the infamous manner in which it was used, the people
had to contend. The necessary misgovernment of an
irresponsible king, an irresponsible House of Peers, and
a luxurious, rich, overbearing, benumbing clergy, with a

[1] 27,789 (317). The society was for a time heartily supported by
the Whig newspapers, especially the *Spectator*, which described it as a
society for securing the return of Reform candidates, and for selecting
new candidates to serve the Reform party in Parliament. In a leading
article (Saturday, March 12, 1831, pp. 254, 255), short biographies of a
number of such possible candidates are given, including Grote, Henry
Drummond, Hume, and others, and Place himself, who in a very eulogistic notice is described as "the leader of that organised body which
liberated Westminster and preserved its independence of the Dukes
of Newcastle [mistake for Northumberland] and the Court." Elsewhere Place alludes incidentally to the fact that he was "waited upon
with an offer" to stand for Westminster against Burdett and Hobhouse,
and received "offers from one or two other places of seats, free of
expense," but declined.—27,844 (34).

[2] 27,789 (384).

House of Commons thus chosen or rather appointed—the long war and its multiplied horrors, the waste of human life, the amount of human suffering, the unparalleled waste of the public money . . . were not the greatest evils to the nation which its vicious and vitiating government produced. The bribery, the perjury, the corruption, the immorality and the consequent enormous and widespread criminality and debasing notions it produced, encouraged and maintained all over the country . . . were much more lamentable than all the other evils, enormous as they were." [1]

The bill was, of course, at once reintroduced. Owing to Tory obstruction it proceeded very slowly. "Complaints were made," wrote Place, "but they were useless. The people were angry and were growing sulky when, as the Committee at length approached its termination, they dropped petitioning the House and once more became lively as their attention was turned to the House of Lords." [2] On September 21 it finally passed the House of Commons and was sent to the Lords. There it met with short shrift, and on October 8 the Reform newspapers announced in black-edged editions that, at six o'clock that morning, the Lords had refused the second reading by a majority of forty-one.

---

[1] 27,789 (387, 388).   [2] 27,789 (406, 407).

CHAPTER X

In the general anger and excitement which followed the action of the Lords on October 8, Place kept before him as the one supreme necessity of the situation the continuance of the alliance between the Whig Cabinet and the "People."

The most immediate danger was that the Whigs might abandon part of the Bill, and allow the Lords to save their credit by a compromise. But there was another danger—which Place, better than any one else, was able to estimate—that an agitation for social revolution might develop among the working classes, against which Whigs and Tories would unite as they had united against Cobbett and Hunt in 1817 and 1819. The two possible centres for such a movement were Lancashire and London. In Lancashire the rapid development of the textile industry had divided the whole population into two irreconcilable camps of organised masters and organised men. Preston, like Westminster, was a scot and lot borough, and at a bye-election in 1830 Hunt, standing on a strictly revolutionary platform, had beaten the Whig Irish Secretary, Lord Stanley. At Manchester John Doherty had begun in 1829 that federation of the cotton spinners which was the origin of the socialistic Grand National Trades Union in 1833–34. Doherty called on Place in October 1831. "He maintained that the people ought no longer to be shuffled off with a Bill which could do them no good,

but ought to take the affair into their own hands, and
by force to compel the Government to do what was right."
"I told him," says Place, "it was absurd to expect such a
combination among the working people as would enable
them to defeat the army and others who would not
quietly submit to be plundered. That the working people
unaided by the middle class never had accomplished any
national movement, and that it was insane in him to
suppose that they could effect any change by force. He
acknowledged they never had made a national movement,
but said that they were now resolved to have their *rights*,
and I should soon be convinced I was in error. They were
now organised, were determined to bring the matter to
issue, and if it were possible they could fail, it were better
to be slain in the attempt than to go on as their enemies,
the wealth accumulators, now made them go, in misery
unmitigated, and as they intended, perpetually." [1] But
the working - class leaders in Lancashire received their
ideas from London,[2] and in London Place had for some
years watched the formation of a small group of revolutionary thinkers holding an economic creed much
more definite and coherent than the vague denunciation of social injustice to which Cobbett and Hunt
had trusted. He describes this movement as having
originated in the teachings of Robert Owen and Thomas
Hodgskin.

[1] 27,791 (242).
[2] The "Union" (*i.e.* the London "National Union of the Working Classes") had "great influence over a considerable portion
of the working classes, more especially in the great manufacturing
counties. During the time the Reform Bills were before the Parliament this was particularly the case. The attention of the whole
people was then drawn to the subject, and the working people were
quite as much excited as any class whatever. The consequence of
this excitement was a general persuasion that the whole produce of
the labourers and workmen's hands should remain with them."—
27,791 (242).

Owen since 1817, when his public propaganda began, had kept round him a body of devoted disciples, who believed with him that man was what circumstances made him, and that the existing industrial system made the creation of favourable circumstances impossible. Hodgskin was a man of wider education than Owen, and greater intellectual subtlety. In 1813, being a young naval lieutenant, he had been put upon half-pay for writing a pamphlet against pressing, had then lived in Edinburgh, trying to eke out his pay by writing, and had travelled on the Continent, first as a companion to Place's eldest son, and afterwards by himself on foot.[1]

In Edinburgh he read Ricardo's " Principles of Political Economy," and carried on during 1820 a long argumentative correspondence with Place about the book. In this correspondence Hodgskin developed the "surplus value" theory,[2] that inevitable corollary of Ricardo's "labour value," which, since the publication of Marx's "Capital," has raised in Germany and elsewhere "a Ricardian socialism,

---

[1] For a description of Hodgskin, see 27,791 (263).

[2] For instance, Hodgskin complains, in a letter dated May 28, 1820, of "the want of an accurate distinction between *natural price* and *exchangeable value*. Natural price is measured by the quantity of labour necessary to produce any commodity ; its exchangeable value, or what another will give, or is obliged to give, for this commodity when produced, may or may not be equal to the quantity of labour employed in its production. Mr. R. has, I think, made a mistake by supposing these two things to be equal. They are not, or the wages of labour would always be equal to the produce of labour. It requires, for instance, a certain portion of labour to produce a quarter of corn. This quarter of corn, however, when produced, and in the possession of a man who is at the same time both landlord and farmer, will at present exchange for a prodigious deal greater quantity of labour than it cost to produce it. There is, therefore, a great difference between real natural price and exchangeable value, and by not attending to this Mr. R. has been led into, I think, gross mistakes relative to the decrease of profits in an improving state of society." For Marx's debt to Hodgskin, see "Capital" (English edition, 1887), vol. i. pp. 331, 345, 348 ; vol. ii. pp. 547, 587, 774, 775.

appearing like the ghost of the deceased Ricardian orthodoxy sitting crowned on the grave thereof." [1]

In 1825, just after the struggle against the re-enactment
of the Combination Laws, Hodgskin, then living in London,
published an extremely able pamphlet, entitled "Labour
Defended against the Claims of Capital," by "A Labourer," [2]
in which he attacked the existing system of wealth production and the arguments by which it was defended, and
claimed that all the products of labour should be distributed
among the labourers, manual or mental. Place, though he
had a great personal liking for Hodgskin, steadily fought
against his ideas, and in 1827 unsuccessfully opposed his
appointment to a lectureship on Political Economy at the
Mechanics' Institute. [3]

Hodgskin's own style was too technical to have had
much influence on popular political thought; but William
Thompson brought out "Labour Rewarded" (1827), in
which Hodgskin's doctrine was expanded and put into
rhetorical form. Henceforward the writings and speeches

[1] James Bonar, "Malthus," p. 214.

[2] The greater part of this pamphlet consisted of a temperate and
searching criticism of what are now acknowledged to be two of the
main defects of the "classical" economics, the clumsy assumption that
all commodities were sold exactly a year after the commencement of
their production—and that in consequence all labourers were supported
for each succeeding twelve months by the accumulated capital of their
employers — and the unpardonable *ignoratio elenchi*, by which an
analysis of the differential advantages of land and capital in production
was treated as an ethical and political justification of the landlord and
the capitalist. The constructive proposals amount to little more than a
suggestion that the problem of distribution would be solved if "all
kinds of labour" were "free." A copy is in the British Museum.

[3] 27,823 (369). The lectureship resulted in Hodgskin's longer, but
less outspoken, book, "Popular Political Economy" (1827). In 1820,
Place apparently succeeded in persuading Hodgskin not to write
a large book explaining his position. Hodgskin writes, "I had
the intention, till I received your last letter, to devote all my spare
time first to these subjects, and to put together a book on them," and
then proceeds to sketch a book curiously like Marx's "Capital."
—Hodgskin to Place, June 4th (no year, but apparently 1820).

of the agitators of the time, though mainly consisting of such denunciations of inequality as are to be found in all periods of human history, yet contained ideas and phrases which had obviously come from the more scientific revolutionists. The first number, for instance, of the *Poor Man's Guardian* (1831) contains a poem by "One of the Know Nothings."

> " Wages should form the price of goods ;
> Yes, wages should be all,
> Then we who work to make the goods,
> Should *justly have them all ;*
>
> But if the price be made of rent,
> Tithes, taxes, profits, all ;
> Then we who work to make the goods,
> Shall have—*just none at all."*

Owen was a communist who at this time seems to have believed in aristocratic government, and Hodgskin was politically an anarchist.[1] But in 1831 the Owenite workingmen had come to think of the new criticism of society as the basis of a claim for democracy. Their transition from voluntary communism to social democracy is well illustrated by the successive titles assumed by their organisations in London. In the two years between 1829 and 1831 they successively called themselves "The London Co-operative Trading Association," "The British Association for the Spread of Co-operative Knowledge," "The Metropolitan Trades Union," and finally "The National Union of the Working Classes." William Lovett, the most thoughtful of them, sent Place the following account of the process :[2] "They had read and admired the writings of Robert

---

[1] 27,823 (369) ; *cf.* also 27,791 (263).

[2] Place afterwards knew Lovett well, and liked him. He describes him as follows : "Lovett was a journeyman cabinetmaker, a man of melancholy temperament, soured with the perplexities of the world. He was, however, an honest-hearted man, possessed of great courage, and persevering in his conduct. In his usual demeanour he was mild and kind, and entertained kindly feelings towards every one whom he did

Owen, Peter (*sic*) Thompson, Morgan, Gray, and others, and resolved to be instrumental to the extent of their means and their abilities in spreading a knowledge of these works throughout the country. They intended, however, to avoid the course taken by Robert Owen. He had all along, though in his mild manner, condemned the Radical Reformers, believing, as he did, that reform was to be effected solely on this plan, the Radical Reformers of the working classes believing that his plan could only be carried out when the reforms they sought had been accomplished. Many among them also considered his proceedings inimical to their interests. These notions were at length entertained to so great an extent among his disciples that they opposed him, and carried their own resolutions at the meeting, in direct opposition to those proposed by him. The persons before named, therefore, during Mr. Owen's visit to North America,[1] resolved to take up such parts of his system as they believed would be appreciated by the working classes, and be the means of uniting them for specific purposes, taking care that these purposes should not interfere more than was possible with opinions in the proceedings to be adopted in matters on which great differences of opinion existed. . . .

"The British Association, the central organ of all these societies, some months before its dissolution, was applied

not sincerely believe was the intentional enemy of the working people ; but when either by circumstances or his own morbid associations he felt the sense he was apt to indulge of the evils and wrongs of mankind, he was vehement in the extreme. He was half an Owenite, half an Hodgskinite, a thorough believer that accumulation of property in the hands of individuals was *the* cause of *all* the evils that existed." 27,791 (67). And again, "He is a tall, thin, rather melancholy man, about thirty-two years of age, in ill-health, to which he has long been subject ; at times he is somewhat hypochondriacal ; his is a spirit misplaced."— 27,791 (241). See also Lovett's "Life and Struggles" (an autobiography), London, 1867.

[1] *i.e.* the visit from Nov. 1828 to April 1829.

to by a few carpenters, who held their meetings at a
public-house in Argyle Street, and who, being imbued
with co-operative views, wanted assistance in carrying
into effect some modified plan; this was done by the
advice of Mr. Hetherington, Mr. Warden, and Mr. Foskett.
These persons attended at a meeting in Argyle Street on
Wednesday, April 2, 1831. They first called themselves
'The Metropolitan Trades Union,'[1] and subsequently took
the more extensive name of 'The National Union of the
Working Classes and others.'[2]

"The National Union of the Working Classes sprang
out of another society called 'The British Association for
promoting Co-operative Knowledge.' The Co-operative
Society was a branch of Mr. Robert Owen's plan for
establishing 'a new order of society.' This Association
(*i.e.* the 'British Association, &c.') was formed on May 11,
1829, principally by a number of persons who belonged
to a society in Red Lion Square called 'The London
Co-operative Trading Association.' It was intended to
accumulate a capital for co-operative purposes by dealing
among themselves and acquaintances, and thus saving
the profit of the retail trader. . . .

"The persons who took the lead in this affair were James

---

[1] The published objects of the Metropolitan were in part political.
The first was, "to obtain for all its members the right of electing those
who make the laws which govern them ;" . . . and the second, "to
afford support and protection, individually and collectively, to every
member of the Metropolitan Trades Union, to enhance the value of
labour by diminishing the hours of employment, and to adopt such
measures as may be deemed necessary to increase the domestic comfort
of working-men."—Handbill of the Metropolitan Trades Union, March
23, 1831. 27,791 (247).

[2] 27,791 (244–246). The word "others" caused dissensions, and
"motions were twice made to permit 'None but Wealth Producers' to
be members of the committee, or to hold any office in the Union. In
discussing the proposition it was shown that several of their leaders
were not wealth producers in the meaning of the words, in the re-
stricted sense the words were used, and the motions were not adopted."
—27,891 (281).

Watson,[1] William Lovett, John Cleave,[2] George Foskett, Robert Wigg, Philip and George Skene, William Millard, Thomas Powell, Henry Hetherington,[3] and Benjamin Warden, all working-men. As the affairs of the British Association were now brought to a close, the remainder of its committee, namely, John Cleave, James Watson, William Lovett, Julian Hibbert, and several others joined this new union. These persons conceived it a fit opportunity for blending their own peculiar views of society, especially those of the production and the distribution of wealth, with those of the Radical Reformers."[4]

The National Union of the Working Classes contained in 1831 about 500 regular paying members, as well as about 1000 "who paid only occasionally at times of great excitement, and yet reckoned themselves members."[5] The Union had about a dozen branches in different parts of London, but by far the most important of its activities was the weekly public meeting at the Rotunda in Blackfriars Bridge Road, which, says Place, "would probably contain a thousand persons, and I have seen hundreds outside the doors for whom there was no room within."[6] Their title was too long for general use, and they were usually known as "The Rotundanists."

They had taken no part or interest in the general election of 1831,[7] and were just now exasperated against

See a Memoir of James Watson, by William Linton, and 27,796 (302). When Place died, Watson sent a letter to the *Reasoner*, in which he called him "The English Franklin" (*Reasoner*, 1854, p. 210).

[2] See 27,791 (67).

[3] 1792–1849. Publisher and proprietor of *Poor Man's Guardian*. See Life of, by G. J. Holyoake, 1849.

[4] 27,791 (247, 248).   [5] 27,791 (242).   [6] 27,791 (243).

[7] The new Parliament was now assembled ; there had been a general election, and unusual efforts had been made to procure the return of members likely to promote the passing of the Reform Bills. It will be seen how little this interested the leaders of the "National Union of the Working Classes," since in none of their resolutions is there any expression denoting any particular interest taken by them in the elections. 27,791 (285).

the Whig Government by the fact that several of their members were in prison for selling unstamped publications. Lovett had the additional grievance that his goods had been sold (in September 1831), because he had refused to serve in the Militia, and had given "no vote, no musket" as his reason.[1] The original Co-operative Radicals had been lately joined by Mr. Dios Santos, Mr. William Benbow, the author of a plan for a general strike, and certain other more or less disreputable revolutionists.

Place, who suffered much at their hands, writes of them and of their conduct at the time with undisguised dislike: "There was a strong muster of the men who led the meetings at the Rotunda. Some of these men were remarkably ignorant, but fluent speakers, filled with bitter notions of animosity against everybody who did not concur in the absurd notions they entertained, that everything which was produced belonged to those who, by their labour, produced it, and ought to be shared among them; that there ought to be no accumulation of capital in the hands of any one to enable him to employ others as labourers, and thus by becoming a *master* make slaves of others under the name of workmen; to take from them the produce of their labour, to maintain themselves in idleness and luxury, while their slaves were ground down to the earth or left to starve. They denounced every one who dissented from these notions as a *political economist*, under which appellation was included the notion of a bitter foe to the working classes, enemies who deserved no mercy at their hands. Most of these men were loud and long talkers, vehement, resolute, reckless rascals. Among these men were some who were perfectly atrocious, whose purpose was riot, as providing an opportunity for plundering."[2]

The Rotundanists were often believed to represent the

[1] 27,791 (300).   [2] 27,791 (48).

S

274 WAR ON TWO FRONTS

whole working class in the Metropolis, a belief which they
themselves fully shared. They entertained the "strange
notion," says Place, which has long existed "among small
as well as large bodies of working-men who frequently
meet together, that *they* are *the* working people."[1] And
"it was very generally supposed a vast majority of the
working people in London were members, and that they
were under the control of its managers."[2]

[1] 27,791 (343).

[2] 27,790 (23). On October 25, 1831, James Mill wrote in great
anxiety to Place about a deputation "from the working classes" who
had been preaching communism to Mr. Black, the editor of the *Morning Chronicle*. "Their notions about property look ugly ; they not only
desire that it should have nothing to do with representation, which is
true, though not a truth for the present time, as they ought to see, but
they seem to think that it should not exist, and that the existence of it
is an evil to them. Rascals, I have no doubt, are at work among them.
Black, it is true, is easily imposed upon. But the thing needs looking
into. Nobody has such means of probing the ulcer as you, and nobody
has so much the means of cure. The fools, not to see that what they
madly desire would be such a calamity to them as no hands but their
own could bring upon them."

Place answered :—

"MY DEAR MILL,—As you sometimes take pains to serve the common
people, and as you are an influential man, I send you an essay in reply
to your note. The men who called on Black were not a deputation
from the working people, but two out of half-a-dozen who manage, or
mismanage, the meetings of the Rotunda in Blackfriars Road, and at
the Philadelphian Chapel in Finsbury. The doctrine they are now
preaching is that promulgated by Hodgskin in a tract in 1825, entitled
'Labour Defended against the Claims of Capital,'" . . . and so on
through a long letter. (Place to Mill, October 26, 1831.) A year
later Mill passed on Place's information to Brougham, "The nonsense
to which your Lordship alludes about the rights of the labourer to the
whole produce of the country, wages, profits, and rent, all included,
is the mad nonsense of our friend Hodgskin (*sic*) which he has published as a system, and propagates with the zeal of perfect fanaticism.
Whatever of it appears in the *Chronicle*, steals in through his means, he
being a sort of sub-editor, and Black (the editor) not very sharp in
detecting ; but all Black's opinions on the subject of property are
sound. These opinions, if they were to spread, would be the sub-
version of civilised society ; worse than the overwhelming deluge of
Huns and Tartars." (Mill to Brougham, September 3, 1832, in Bain's
"James Mill," p. 364.)

Such was the position in London—the Ministry anxious
to avoid a contest with the Lords, and the only working-
class political organisation in the hands of a group of
doctrinaire revolutionists, who were convinced that the
Bill would do more harm than good.

For once, however, it was possible to appeal to that rare
but overwhelming force, the political activity of the non-
political man. "There are times and circumstances, and
both were now combined, when quiescent men, who take
the most moderate views of public matters, and are willing
to let political movements take their own course, shake off
their usual apathy, assume a new character, and become
the resolute promoters of the greatest changes. This was
now about to become the case here." [1]

The Bill had been rejected by the Lords on Saturday
morning, October 8, 1831. Next day two young men [2]
came to Place with a proposal for a procession through
London, to present an address to the King on the following Wednesday. This was exactly what Place wanted. A
great procession would be more likely than anything else
to intimidate Ministers, and would raise no difficult questions as to the amount of reform which was to be

[1] 27,791 (24).

[2] Bowyer, "a journeyman bookseller, and a very respectable working-
man," and Powell, "an attorney's clerk," afterwards sub-editor of the
Morning Chronicle. 27,790 (24). Autograph accounts of the procession
by both of them are in the Letter-Book. In his account, Bowyer
describes the situation: "Meetings had been held in the manufacturing districts, at which petitions for universal suffrage had been
agreed to, and delegates had arrived in London from various parts of
the country to enforce the separate claims of the working people. The
language used by these delegates and their associates, and that used by
the unstamped publications, was directed to the object of inducing the
working people to believe that the constituency which the Reform Bill
would create would belong exclusively to the class of tradesmen and
shopkeepers, or, as they were termed, the *middlemen*—a class which
at all times, it was said, had been the worst enemies of the working
people."

demanded, or the economic principles on which the
demand was to be based.[1] He accordingly gave all the
help he could to the proposal, drew up and signed a letter
asking for funds, and gave them a list of probable subscribers, including the name of Tom Young, Lord Melbourne's mysterious factotum,[2] through whose hands a
good deal of the Government's Secret Service Fund seems
to have passed.

On Monday, Place attended four public meetings, ending
up with one at the Rotunda. On Tuesday came bad news.
Parkes wrote from Birmingham to Grote, "I have been
written to by the Government to-day. They are still the
same men, *not* suited to the occasion. I *do* fear their
going out. We have all written up to them, 'PEERS OR
REVOLUTION.' . . . All the cards are ours, and the whole
nation deserves to stand before the world in a pillory if we
are swindled. I only fear a *compromise*."[3] Brougham on
Monday night had said in the Lords: "Careless whether I
give offence in any quarter, I must say that I am so far
moved by some points urged, as to be ready to reconsider
some matters on which I had deemed that my mind was
made up, although in the greater proportion of the objections to the Bill I cannot concur. Nevertheless, I am
uninfluenced as regards the bulk of its principles." And
Lord Althorp had hinted at "modifications" in the
Commons.

Place at once sat down and wrote (9 A.M., Tuesday) a
letter to Hobhouse, which he obviously intended to be
shown to Ministers: "You recommend 'Patience, patience,

---

[1] Place also says that many working-men called on him, whom he
advised to get up "trade meetings and meetings of working-men
indiscriminately," and at these meetings to speak in favour of universal
suffrage, but propose resolutions in support of the Government. 27,790
(23).

[2] 27,790 (25). For Tom Young, see p. 303 and note.

[3] Parkes to Grote, undated, indexed by Place as October 10, 1831.

patience.' The word 'Patience' must mean, if it mean anything, a reasonable expectation that all which is necessary will be done forthwith. Do circumstances warrant such a conclusion? I say no, they do not. If they did, I too should say 'Patience, patience, patience.' I say the people have no sufficient reason to conclude that what ought to be done to ensure the passing of the Reform Bill will be done, and unless they be as 'stupid as waggon horses,' they cannot, ought not to be patient. . . . I have stood up firmly against proceedings which had a tendency to produce a panic. Others of my friends have done the same, and our success was perfect until yesterday afternoon, when at the close of the meeting at the Crown and Anchor Tavern many persons avowed their determination to withdraw their balances from their bankers in gold." [1]

From everywhere came accounts of huge meetings, of occasional riots, and of effusive expressions of confidence in Ministers, founded upon a growing distrust of them.

"So thoroughly were the people at a loss respecting the course which ought to be pursued, that besides attending meetings called by they did not care whom, the people did nothing.[2] "All, however, talked vaguely of 'being firm,' that is, as a man said at one of the public meetings, 'staring at the Government, staring at them firmly.'"[3]

The great London procession (on October 13) was a complete success, though no Rotundanist leader took part in it.[4] But on the same day came leading articles in the *Courier* (the official ministerial paper) and the *Morning*

---

[1] Place to Hobhouse, October 11, 1831.
[2] 27,791 (6).
[3] Place to Parkes, October 13, 1831.
[4] 27,790 (39).

Herald, hinting at a compromise with the Lords and a modified Bill;[1] and Warburton, the Radical member for Bridport, " one of Lord Althorp's most confidential friends,"[2] called on Place with the news that Parliament was to be prorogued for three months.[3]

On that evening Place broke through his habit of working behind the scenes, and took a step which brought his name for a day or two into almost all the newspapers. He went down to a meeting of parochial delegates at the Crown and Anchor Tavern, told them what he had heard of the intentions of Ministers, drew up a strong memorial to the effect that if the Bill were not reintroduced after the shortest possible prorogation, "this country will inevitably be plunged into all the horrors of a violent revolution," and organised a deputation there and then to see Lord Grey at his house in Downing Street. The deputation arrived at a quarter to eleven at night, and were told by Lord Grey that "it would be absurd" for Ministers "to propose a measure which they could not hope to carry through"; that a new Bill would be prepared "not less efficient than the old"; that the preparation of such a Bill would take "much time and consideration"; and finally, and emphatically, that any disturbances would be put down by military force.[4]

The *Courier* and the *Chronicle* during the next few days carried on an angry controversy as to what had been said and intended. Lord Grey gave his account of the interview in the House of Lords on October 17,[5] and Greville writes a month later of "the domiciliary visit of

---

[1] *e.g.* "We have never joined in any cry for 'the whole Bill.'" (*Morning Herald,* October 12, 1831.)
[2] Place to Parkes, October 13, 1831.
[3] 27,790 (54).
[4] 27,790 (61–70).
[5] Hansard, Third Series, vol. viii. 850, 851.

Place and his rabble" as having helped to open the eyes of the moderate members of the Cabinet.[1]

On Saturday, October 15, Grote spoke in favour of confidence in Ministers at a Mansion House meeting, and next day Place wrote to him: "Last Sunday we feared, and had cause to fear, that the working people would not take part with the middle classes. You lamented this; . . . they, however, soon demonstrated their feelings, and proved that they were ready, at any risk, and at any sacrifice, to stand by us. And then what did we do? We abandoned them, deserted, betrayed them, and shall have betrayed them again before three more days have passed over our heads—betrayed them again, for we shall all of us before that time be well acquainted with the new facts, that no Peer will be created, that Parliament will be prorogued for a very long period, that such a Bill as the Lords will please accept will be promised to be brought in a conciliatory Bill. And we, yes we, the dastardly, talking, swaggering dogs, will sneak away with our tails between our legs."[2]

Meanwhile the excitement was sinking, the Tories were announcing a reaction of public opinion, and the only hope of a continued and successful agitation lay in the "political unions of the middle and working classes," which had been formed up and down the country on the Birmingham model. Such a union for London was proposed by Perry on October 15, and initiated by a meeting of fifty persons at the Crown and Anchor on October 19.[3]

Place worked hard at the preliminary organisation, but warned by the fate of the Parliamentary Candidates'

[1] Greville, "Journal of the Reigns of George IV. and William IV.," vol. ii. p. 213 (November 19, 1831).

[2] Place to Grote, October 16, 1831. Mrs. Grote wrote an amusing reply, beginning, "Don't you go for to row my good man." (Mrs. Grote to Place, October 19, 1831.)

[3] 27,791 (8, 9, 31).

Society, took care to leave himself an opening for retreat. "Mr. Perry had acted a capital part, and Major Beauclerk seconded him excellently. But I was unable to place confidence in their steady perseverance. They had faltered in the Parliamentary Candidates' Society. I doubted if they were the men to go through steadily the difficulties and dangers I saw before us. I did not therefore formally become a member of the Union, was not appointed on the committee, nor did I in any way commit myself so as to draw upon me the duty of assisting, as I must otherwise have done, the business of the Union, and be compelled to go on if others abandoned it and it did not progress in the right way. Mr. Perry and Major Beauclerk were willing to take the lead, and they were permitted to do so."[1]

If the Union was to attract any attention, some well-known man must be secured as chairman. Hume refused, and suggested that the very name "Union" should be dropped, "because we have already twenty National Unions in London of the admirers of Mr. Owen and Mr. Hunt, and you will be confounded with them."[2]

At last Burdett accepted the post, on condition that "the Union were made specifically to support Ministers in carrying the Bill."[3] Place at about the same time joined the committee, and his hope that 100,000 members would join seemed likely to be fulfilled.

But the most serious trouble was still to come. If the National Political Union was to claim any authority, it must, according to the political ideas of the time, be formed at a public meeting, and all who presented themselves must be allowed to join. At the preliminary "committee" meetings resolutions moved by the Rotundanists and their sympathisers in favour of universal suffrage and

---

[1] 27,791 (16, 17).
[2] Hume to Major Beauclerk, October 20, 1831. 27,791 (12, 13).
[3] 27,791 (17).

annual parliaments had been with difficulty defeated,[1] and
it seemed likely that amendments in that sense would
be carried at the public meeting advertised for Monday,
October 31, at the Crown and Anchor in the Strand.

Place as usual was waging a war on two fronts. While
he was determined that the Union should assist the Bill
to pass, he was equally determined that it should not be
used to uphold the Bill as a final measure. He therefore
induced the committee to suggest that the object of the
Union, as put to the meeting, should be "to obtain a real
and effectual representation of the middle and working
classes of the people in the Commons' House of Parliament,"[2] and furiously insisted in a letter to Perry that the
resolution should not be confined to a mere support of the
Bill, even though Burdett should threaten to resign.

"The working people would see in the proceeding the
old desire to use them for a purpose and then to abandon
them. The gap between the working and middle classes
would be widened, the rancour that exists would be
increased, and all chance of conciliation put off for years.
. . . I am a member of the Council only because the Union
includes working people. I have some reputation among
them, and can at times exercise a wholesome influence
over more or less of them; this I should lose were my
name to appear to anything which was either ambiguous
or delusive."[3]

October 31 must have been, as Place describes it, a
sufficiently exciting day. The meeting was called for
eleven o'clock, and there was a preliminary meeting to
finally settle the resolutions at half-past ten in a room
"about 25 feet long and 12 broad. "Before eleven o'clock
it was crowded almost to suffocation, and the door was
blocked up with a crowd of persons vainly endeavouring to

[1] 27,791 (39).   [2] 27,791 (39).
[3] Place to Perry, October 28, 1831.

gain admittance.[1] . . . A tumult was expected, and it had therefore been determined to put me in the chair. I am a pretty resolute chairman, and know, I think, how to manage a tumultuous assembly, but it is with extreme difficulty that I was able to manage this." [2]

A resolution in favour of universal suffrage was defeated, but the uproar communicated itself to the crowds in the great Crown and Anchor hall, and it became necessary to adjourn the meeting to Lincoln's Inn Fields. There were twenty thousand persons in the Fields, and "as not more, perhaps, than half of the people assembled could understand what was addressed to them, it was probable that any amendment or new resolutions they (the Rotundanists) proposed would be carried." [3]

Burdett took the chair, lost his temper, and put the crowd against him. After the usual speeches from W. J. Fox [4] and others in denunciation of the Lords, Lovett moved a universal suffrage amendment, and asked the working-men present "what the middle classes wanted except to make them the tools of their purposes." [5] Finally, an amendment of Wakley's,[6] that half the Council of the new Union should consist of working-men, was carried, and the meeting dispersed.

Place concluded that the middle-class politicians would now leave the Union, and that the working classes would not join it. Intending members had been told to enrol themselves at the Crown and Anchor, and "while the vote of thanks, which was not at all merited by the chairman, was being proposed," Place left the meeting and went to the Crown and Anchor. "Here I remained alone till I concluded no one would come, and then I went home." [7]

[1] 27,791 (48).   [2] 27,791 (52).   [3] 27,791 (57).
[4] William Johnson Fox (1786–1864), Unitarian minister, editor of *Monthly Repository;* member of Parliament for Oldham, 1847–1863.
[5] 27,791 (64).
[6] One of the members of Parliament for Finsbury, editor of the *Lancet*, and at this time an ally of the Rotundanists.   [7] 27,791 (70).

This time, however, some of Place's colleagues were more persevering than himself. Erskine Perry came later to the tavern with Roebuck, enrolled names, drew up a cheerful handbill, signed it with Burdett's name, and then "looked in upon Place, who thought the whole thing was crushed in the bud, and that there was very faint possibility of establishing the Union." The two ended the evening by going " down to the Rotunda, where we heard ourselves denounced, and the Union also, as aristocratical, &c., by Cleave and others." [1]

Next morning Place took heart and determined to make the best of the situation. If half the Council was to consist of political working-men, steps must be taken that they should not be Rotundanists; and if, as was very nearly true, there were no effective politicians among the working-men who were not in sympathy with the Rotundanists, such men must be created. Next day, therefore (November 1), Place says: " I and my friends were early at the tavern, and remained there all day and until late at night. Between three and four hundred men entered their names as members. Whenever any respectable working-man took a ticket he was asked questions for the purpose of ascertaining if he were a Rotundanist, and upon finding that he was not, he was invited into the committee room, questioned as to his political notions, and requested to give the name or names and references to the character of any man or men whom he knew in his trade who was a sober, discreet, clever man, and many such men were designated. Almost every man who was invited into the committee room appeared to understand the men who managed at the Rotunda, disliked them much, and were willing to aid us as well as they could to promote the election of such working-men for the Council as were honest, sensible, well-intentioned men,

[1] 27,791 (46, 47). (Perry's notes.)

having the confidence of their fellow-workmen. Many of
our coadjutors came in, and as no time was to be lost,
and no one in our circumstances was to be either idle or to
regard the consumption of his own time, each of them was
despatched to see the workmen who had been named to
us, inquire their characters of their employers and their
neighbours, and then to invite them to join the Union
with a view to their being elected on the Council. The
Bill 'this is not an Union, &c.,' and copies of all our
publications, were given to these men, as they were to
every one who became a member; and in a few days we
had a sufficient number of such men for the Council, and
the certainty that their fellow-workmen would vote for
them. They who were constant attendants at the Rotunda
and other such meetings were much more desirous of
having nonsense talked to them for a penny a week or for
nothing than to work for the good of others and to pay a
shilling to put them in a position to do so, kept away from
the Union, and we saw very clearly that the mischief-
makers had no chance to become members of the Council
in any considerable number. We saw plainly enough that
Wakley's resolution had produced the anticipated consequences, as a comparative few who were not working-men
joined us, and some of those who were not working-men
left us. Still we hoped that if we could succeed in procuring a really respectable Council we should be able to
induce a large number of such persons to join us, and we
were not mistaken." [1]

The Rotundanists had now come to look upon the

---

[1] 27,791 (71, 72). The Government, acting through Mr. Merle, the
editor of the *Courier*, tried exactly the same tactics against the National
Political Union as Place used against the Rotundanists. A "respectable Association" was started, which excluded "persons" (like Place)
"of known Republican opinions." But that sort of tactics requires
skill and perseverance, and the "respectable Association" died in three
weeks. 27,791 (81, 82).

National Political Union as their chief enemy. It was at that time apparently taken for granted by every one that the members of the "Political Unions" were to possess themselves of arms,[1] and this was represented as the creation of an armed force for the prevention of real reform.[2]

Accordingly, the Rotundanists not only advised their members to join the rival Union in such numbers as to capture it, but themselves announced a great meeting on November 7, in the open space by the White Conduit House. Benbow, with a view to this meeting, laid in a stock of heavy constables' staves, which he retailed at a few pence each to such of the members as desired to protect themselves against the police. But he and his friends so overdid their truculence that the Government, alarmed by the riots at Bristol (October 29, 1831), brought up troops to London, and swore in hundreds of special constables.[3] The White Conduit House meeting had to be abandoned, and the National Political Union held the field.

On November the 22nd it was announced that Parliament was to reassemble for the consideration of the Reform Bill on December 6. Lord Grey's plan of a long prorogation and a remodelling of the Bill had therefore been abandoned. How serious the danger had been is shown by Greville's account of the negotiations which went on

---

[1] The *Times* (November 1, 1831) speaks approvingly of it as a system "of voluntary national armament."

[2] "The working people in their meetings deprecated the organising and arming the housekeepers alone as a scheme to depress them." 27,791 (101). The development of the July monarchy in France had shown how effectual a middle-class "National Guard," even of revolutionary origin, might be in keeping the unarmed working classes quiet. The term "National Guard" was already so invidious that, on October 8, 1831, *The Poor Man's Guardian* (the organ of the Rotundanists) proposed a "Popular Guard" against the "National Guard" for England. See it in 27,791 (303).

[3] 27,791 (254).

during November between a section of the Cabinet and the Tory leaders.[1] On November 19, he writes of Ministers as being convinced, "that if existing institutions are to be preserved at all, there is no time to be lost in making such an arrangement as may enable all who have anything to lose to coalesce for their mutual safety and protection."[2] If this had happened the Chartist movement would have begun in 1832 instead of 1837, and the history of the British Empire during the nineteenth century might have been a good deal more like the history of the German Empire after 1871 than most people would now think possible. The negotiations, however, came to nothing, and Parliament was summoned for the reintroduction of the Bill on December 6. Place knew what had been going on both from the gossip of the House of Commons and from Parkes' letters,[3] and he, like the rest, was relieved when the danger, for the moment, was over. After the calling of Parliament for December 6 "the people became calm, and agitation in most places ceased."[4]

Things were still quieter after the new Bill was found to be as good, if not better, than the old one, and it was naturally more difficult to keep the National Political Union

[1] On November 10, 1831, Greville (vol. ii. p. 211) describes the arrangement for a compromise as being carried on by Lord Wharncliffe, Lord Palmerston, and Lord Grey. On November 23, he writes that the Duke of Richmond, Lord Grey, and Lord Palmerston voted in the Cabinet against the calling together of Parliament before Christmas. (Vol. ii. p. 217.)

[2] Greville Memoirs, vol. ii. p. 213.

[3] e.g. "Half the Cabinet stand slyly on tiptoe looking over Lord Grey's shoulders to see if they can discern their successors, and trim to coalesce with them."—Parkes to Grote, October 26, 1831, and November 28, 1831, Parkes to Grote: "I am glad to hear to-day that the silly attempt to compromise is over."

[4] 27,791 (112). The announcement of the short prorogation was accompanied by a proclamation so worded that it might satisfy the King without checking the Unions. Place explained its limitations in a tract for the National Political Union on "The Laws relating to Political Associations." 27,791 (99, 104).

going in quiet than in exciting times. Of the Christmas weeks in 1831 Perry writes: "This fortnight was the most critical period in the existence of the Union. We were without funds. From one to three members per day and no more joined us."[1]

On December 12 Place writes anxiously to Hume: "The cholera will spread all over the country, and by the time the Bill shall have reached the Third Reading, and the country shall have become tired, if not wearied out and disgusted, we shall have quarantine regulations against our shipping in all parts of the world. The consequence may be a great impediment to navigation, diminution of trade and commerce, embarrassment, stagnation, panic, multitudes of people discharged in all our great manufactures. Ministers should look well to this without loss of time; but they are after all but a poor set of creatures, and will probably let the thing take its course. It is plain they have sadly embarrassed themselves by taking in hand a matter too large for them to manage; they hesitated and vacillated about reform like weak men as they are, and then plunged into it rashly. Hardly had they unfolded their scheme than they wished they had not done so, and would have withdrawn it if they could. Insufficient as it is (notwithstanding it is more than any one expected them to propose), it is too much for them, and has made them imbecile for any other good purpose. The people have kept them to it, and they must continue to keep them to it. It seems to be the lot of almost every country that in eventful periods the men who govern shall be especially weak and absurd. Strong-minded, discreet, bold men would have carried the Bill before this time, have had the people with them, and fixed themselves so firmly in power for all good purposes, that Taxes on Knowledge, and Gagging Bills, and Printing Press Registering

[1] 27,791 (121).

Bills would all be repealed, to their honour and glory and the permanent advantage of the country."[1]

After Christmas the apathy in London continued with that startling completeness which only London politicians know. The Council of the National Political Union held weekly meetings, to which the public were admitted. On January 4, 1832, "it was necessary on account of the audience that a show of business should be made. . . . Mr. Wakefield therefore proposed the appointment of a committee to draw up a petition relating to partnerships, more especially banking partnerships. . . . It caused an animated discussion, and interested every one of the auditors."[2]

On February 2 there was friction, and Burdett left the Union. On February 6 there was an election of the Council, with an elaborate object-lesson in voting by ballot. The Rotundanists ran candidates, but they were all beaten by the "ticket" organised by the old committee. And so with debates on the Anatomy Bill[3] and Newspaper Stamps, the winter wore on.

Perhaps after all the trouble that had been taken the National Political Union might not seem a very great thing. But its promoters had secured a vitally important strategic position. They now controlled an organisation which at the critical moment every London reformer must necessarily join.

[1] Place to Hume, December 12, 1831.
[2] 27,791 (126).
[3] The Anatomy Bill (for facilitating the provision of dead bodies for dissection) was a question after Place's own heart, in which unanswerable arguments had to meet almost unconquerable prejudices. He had been working on the point since 1828, when, after arranging for the purchase of an urgently needed "subject" from a resurrection man, he had drawn up a petition to Parliament for a law enabling unclaimed bodies to be dissected. The murders by Burke in 1828, and Bishop in 1831, kept the question alive, and finally in July 1832 the Bill was passed. Place has left a long account of this struggle (27,828, 261–337). He was especially annoyed at the opposition of Wakley, the editor of the Lancet, and himself a surgeon.

CHAPTER XI

THE SECOND REFORM CAMPAIGN

ON March 26, 1832, after another term of obstruction in
the Commons, the Reform Bill was for the second time
introduced into the House of Lords. The most important
change in the situation since the preceding October was
that the King, under the influence of his wife, his sisters,
and his illegitimate children, was now nervous about the
Bill, and disinclined to secure Ministers a majority by
creating Peers. But this change, though known among
the Tory leaders, was unknown elsewhere; and in other
respects, the position of the Lords had been weakened by
the five months' delay. Every man in the country had
been by this time compelled to form an opinion on the
Bill, and most men had come to think with Sydney Smith,
that the Atlantic would beat Mrs. Partington. The Lords
must either enormously increase their power by a victory,
or enormously decrease it by a defeat. The settled doctrines
of the English Constitution—"that nose of wax which
every one twists to his purpose"[1]—against which Bentham
had so often railed, could now be turned against them.
"The theory of 'the Constitution' was against them:
the elucidation by 'constitutional writers' was against
them: the whole doctrine of checks was against them:
that beautiful system so lauded by Whigs and Tories,
and believed by almost everybody, as constituting the
very essence of the best of all possible governments, was

[1] 27,793 (65).

against them. . . . The doctrine of checks had long been a maxim, and so it remained. The answer to all assertions to the contrary was, 'If the king cannot be a check upon the Lords, he is nothing.' "[1]

The danger, on the other hand, that the working classes would break away from the Reform alliance had not grown less. Manchester and London were still the two centres of working-class revolutionary feeling[2] and middle-class intolerance. "The great peculiarity causing a difference between the Political Unions and the Unions of the working classes was, that the first desired the Reform Bill to prevent a revolution, the last desired its destruction as the means of producing a revolution."[3]

One writer sent an article to the *Poor Man's Guardian*, dated Manchester, March 19, in the course of which he said: "The Bill is the most illiberal, the most tyrannical, the most abominable, the most infamous, the most hellish measure that ever could or can be proposed. . . . I therefore conjure you to prepare your coffins, if you have the means. You will be starved to death by thousands if this Bill passes, and thrown on the dunghill or on to the ground naked like dogs."[4]

In Manchester four working-men had been prosecuted by the Whig Attorney-General, and sentenced on March 15 to a year's imprisonment, for a peaceable open-air meeting.[5] In London, Lovett, Watson, and Benbow, the

---

[1] 27,792 (41).

[2] ". . . a revolution in which they might gain, but could not lose. It was this expectation and desire which, to a considerable extent, prevented them (considerable bodies of the working classes) from joining the Political Unions in London, Manchester, Bristol, and other places, and led them to use no efforts to promote the passing of the Bill." 27,792 (15).

[3] 27,793 (76).

[4] See the *Poor Man's Guardian*, April 11, 1832, article entitled, "Last Warning on the Accursed Reform Bill," by One of the Oppressed.

[5] 27,791 (365).

three leaders of the National Union of the Working Classes, were now out on bail for organising a procession on March 21, on which day the Government had ordered a solemn fast as a means of averting the cholera. The Rotundanists had then walked through the streets, carrying a loaf of bread and a round of beef with the inscription, " The True Cure for the Cholera." [1]

Before the debate on the first reading came on, Place drew up for the National Political Union a petition to the House of Lords. This petition was mainly historical, and put Place's views as to the political evolution of English society with a quiet offensiveness that secured its insertion into most of the Reform newspapers : " That your petitioners humbly submit to your noble House that the time has arrived when a great change must be made in the system under which this nation has been long governed.

" That this inevitable change may be gradual and peaceful, or sudden and violent. That it remains with your noble House to determine in which of these two ways the change shall be made. . . .

" That in former times there was little wealth in this country beyond that which was held by the aristocracy in Church and State.

" That there was little learning and knowledge beyond that which the aristocracy possessed, the people being left in a state of profound ignorance. . . .

" That so different, indeed, are the present from former times, that, instead of nearly all the wealth in the nation being possessed by the aristocracy, the whole amount possessed by them is a small fraction. That so different, indeed, are the present from former times, in respect to intellectual acquirements in every branch of knowledge, that it can be no disparagement to the privileged classes to say that the country abounds with men in every depart-

[1] 27,791 (255, 392).

ment of knowledge to whom no superior can be found in
the aristocracy. . . .

"Your petitioners therefore submit to your noble House,
that any endeavour to prevent the proposed reform in the
House of Commons will be an attempt to govern knowledge
by ignorance, than which nothing can be more absurd and
more impossible." [1]

As soon as the Bill was introduced in the Lords it
was seen that it would probably pass a second reading.
Lord Harrowby, on behalf of Lord Wharncliffe and the
"Waverers," who had negotiated with Lord Grey in the
preceding November, announced that he would vote for
the second reading, and "endeavour to alter" the Bill in
Committee. Lord Grey, in reply, said, "He would attend
to suggestions in Committee, and agree to such alterations
as might appear to him reasonable, which did not tend to
destroy the principle of the Bill."

At once suspicions began to be formed, though little was
actually known. One fact, however, reached Place in spite
of "the strictest silence, caution, and secrecy of Ministers." [2] On April 7 he received a letter from Colonel Jones,
stating that there was a "conspiracy" to substitute a
franchise of £20 for the £10 franchise in London. "No
stir," Colonel Jones wrote, "is made by the metropolitan
districts, and this serves as a sufficient excuse to the luke-
warm reformers in the Cabinet. I have worked like a mule
to set them in motion, but in vain. You must try your
hand." [3] He ends by asking for a letter which Lord
Durham could use in speaking against the proposal to
mutilate a Bill "which had been drawn principally by
himself." Place replied: "I am told that Sir Francis Burdett says that withholding the franchise from the metro-

---

[1] A copy of the petition as adopted March 21, 1832, is preserved in
27,792 (18).
[2] 27.792 (37).   [3] 27,792 (44).

politan boroughs is a matter of small importance, that,
notwithstanding they are populous, the people who have
property in them very generally live in other places, where
they will be represented. This, if it be correctly reported
to me, is very absurd language for him to hold. Sir Francis,
on consideration, would not say this any more of Marylebone or Finsbury than he would of Westminster. Let it,
however, be supposed that his words relate only to 'the
dreaded Tower Hamlets.' Of this large and wealthy place
Sir Francis knows nothing. To him, and such as him, it is
an unknown land, and so it is to every one of the Peers.
Very different indeed would be his opinion, or that of any
one else capable of correct observation and reasoning who
should occupy himself for two or three days in walking
about this part of the metropolis and seeing what it contains. He would be surprised at the vast masses of property
there collected, as well as at the people to whom much of
the property belongs, who live there and nowhere else."

" 11 P.M.—Just now, as I was closing this paper, Sir
Francis came in. We have gone over the matter again,
and he concurs in all I have written." [1]

On April 9, after an adjournment over the Easter holidays, the Lords' debate on the second reading began. Things
were still so far quiet that Lord Grey and Lord Melbourne
both referred to the "general silence," and the "silence of
the people," but politicians were already preparing for a
struggle. Cobbett on March 31 had begun to preach in his
Register a "no-rent" campaign among the tenant-farmers,
and the London reformers were gathering facts as to the
military force which would be brought against them in
case of a fight. "The army at this time in Great Britain
consisted of about 11,000 men. This number was never
thought of as having any relation to the number of the
people. It was doubtless thought sufficient for the pur-

---

[1] Place to Colonel Jones, April 9, 1832. 27.792 (50, 51).

poses of intimidation and coercion. Of this 11,000 nearly
7000 were congregated round London, and 4000 alone
remained to coerce all the towns in England, Wales, and
Scotland. It has been seen at the time of the Bristol riots,
how very small a number of troops could be spared when
that large city was being burned by a mere mob, among
whom there was no organisation, and when every other
place, Nottingham alone excepted, was not only quiescent,
but showed no disposition to rioting. And yet a much
larger force than was sent to Bristol would be of no avail
against a more general and well-organised insurrection,
aided and countenanced by other places in the same
state." [1] On the other hand, the aristocratic "club men
were more than ever desirous to provoke the people to
show fight, that they might lick them." [2]

The second reading debate took up four nights, and
was for the most part carried on by both sides in a tone
that caused Place to state in language of studied precision,
"I have had communication with a considerable number"
of Peers "on various occasions, and those communications
have been of kinds and of sufficiently long continuance
to enable me to decide accurately; and true it is that I
never knew one that as a politician was not a mean
shuffler." [3]

On April 14, at seven in the morning, the second reading
was carried by a majority of nine. But the " Waverers,"
who had voted so far with the Government, made no secret
of their intention to transform the Bill in Committee, and
there were many complaints amongst the reformers that
Lord Grey did not make things sure by creating Peers.
Place held it wiser to fight the Lords as they were.
"Several of the best-informed men in the council of the
National Political Union were not desirous that Peers

[1] 27,792 (38, 39).   [2] 27,792 (39).
                    [3] 27,792 (244).

should be made in the gross."[1] On May 7 the Government met their inevitable defeat. Lord Lyndhurst brought forward a procedure resolution, which Lord Grey declared would be fatal to the Bill, and carried it by a majority of thirty-five in a house of 267 Peers.

On the next day (Tuesday, May 8) Lord Grey went down to Windsor and presented to the King a minute signed by the whole Cabinet, with the exception of the Duke of Richmond, asking for the creation of fifty Peers. The King refused, and Lord Grey resigned. Then followed the situation which had been so anxiously hoped and feared. On Wednesday the King, at Lord Lyndhurst's suggestion, sent for the Duke of Wellington, who promised to attempt the formation of a Tory ministry. For six days the attempt went on, but no Tory ministry could maintain any show of defence in the House of Commons to which Peel did not belong, and Peel would not take office. He gave as his reason the fact that the King had required the new ministry to pledge themselves to a Reform Bill as efficient as that introduced by the Whigs. Wellington accepted the condition in order to save the prestige of the Lords : Peel, from whatever motive, refused it.

But of these negotiations nothing was known outside, except the broad facts that the King had refused to create Peers, and that Wellington was forming a government. It was unfortunate for the Tories that Wellington was their only possible Prime Minister. Two years before, his absolute refusal to consent to any degree of reform had brought the Whigs into power. On May 7 he had signed an obstinately worded protest against the second reading. Above all, he was a soldier. In 1830 he had told Charles Greville that his own regiment alone could beat all the populace of London : in October 1831 he had told a Manchester deputation that " the people of England are very

[1] 27.792 (295).

quiet if they are let alone, but if they won't be quiet,
there is a way to make them."[1] His appointment meant
just that open appeal to brute force which infuriates
a nation accustomed to any measure of political liberty.
Men had been in a state of nervous tension even before
the division in the Lords. Place describes the feeling in
London. "On Monday the 7th of May, the excitement
was wound up to the highest pitch it had hitherto attained. It was to a very considerable extent a holiday.
Solicitude was not only visible in the countenances of
men, but in their words and actions also. Anxiety made
them neglectful of business concerns to an extent never
before observed. They seemed to say, ' Let us wait until
to-morrow; let the day pass as it may, we can attend to
nothing correctly until we know the fate of the Reform
Bill, a fate which may determine for us whether we may
pursue our occupations in peace and orderly quietness, or
whether we are to enter into a new and much less pleasant
occupation.'"[2] But as soon as the King's action was
known, London put on the aspect of a city in revolution.
"London was placarded in a manner never before witnessed. The placards called upon the people to support
Ministers, to meet in Unions, parishes, trades, &c., and
demand that the Reform Bill be passed by the Lords."[3]

The Bishop of Lichfield, who was announced to preach
on Sunday at St. Bride's, was mobbed in church, and
with difficulty rescued.[4] The King could hardly venture
abroad. On the day after his sending for the Duke, " a
desperate rush was made at his horses on Constitution
Hill. Execrations, instead of blessings, heretofore be-

---

[1] Quoted by Alderman Potter (afterwards M.P. for Wigan) in a
speech at the meeting of the Union in May 1832. 27,794 (168). Place
says, " I was assured by a general officer who dined with him (the
Duke) at the house of a common friend, that he made no secret of his
wish to carry the threat into execution." 27,794 (22).

[2] 27,792 (203-204).   [3] 22,793 (22).   [4] 27,793 (193, 194).

stowed, were heard, both deep and loud, as his carriage drove off with a military escort. Many such escorts will be necessary should King William take a military ruler to his councils."[1]

But if the King was now unpopular, the Queen, to whom the change in his attitude was ascribed, was simply detested. It has been a not unimportant fact in preserving the balance of the English Constitution, that German court manners are disagreeable to us. Queen Adelaide, the widow, before she married King William, of the Duke of Saxe-Meiningen, had the worst manners of a small German court.[2] The Queen's Theatre announced a change of name, the Adelaide omnibuses plied with paper pasted over the hated letters, and the Reform newspapers printed a paragraph about "German frows" from Cobbett's *Register*, of quite indescribable brutality.

Cards with "No Taxes paid here" were beginning to appear in the windows, and many householders were preparing for a state of siege. "It was somewhat curious to hear, as I heard from several heads of families, the intention which numbers besides themselves entertained of purchasing a quantity of flour, bacon, and potatoes, on which to live during the time the markets might be either wholly deserted or badly supplied."[3] Above all, there were meetings everywhere, and of all sorts and conditions, meetings of trades, of parishes, of the Licensed Appraisers' Western Society (to express their unanimous determination not to distrain for assessed taxes), of the city corporation, all urging the Commons to stop supplies, to appoint Parlia-

[1] 27,793 (20). Extract from the *True Sun*.

[2] Place describes how "the jolly, good-natured, laughing King drove about the streets" at the beginning of his reign, while "the Queen, with her spare form, her sour countenance, and her straight, stiff, German back, sat bolt upright, squeezing out her gracious smiles." 27,789 (152).

[3] 27,793 (143).

mentary Commissioners, to do anything which should make
government by the Duke of Wellington impossible.

Place had now his reward for the work of establishing
the National Political Union during the preceding autumn.
The Union held "general meetings" every evening, at each
of which hundreds of new members joined—"decent,
well-dressed tradesmen," as the *Morning Herald* described
them. Before the general meeting, the Council, now consisting mainly of Place's personal following, regularly held
a preliminary meeting, at which all important resolutions
were taken, and at which Place was always in the chair.

His position in the National Political Union, his reputation for fearlessness,[1] and his personal friendship with
Joseph Parkes, the Birmingham organiser, made him
the chief centre for that preparation for armed resistance to the Duke which had been long considered,
and was now definitely taken in hand. On May 3,
Place, who was already "working like a devil in a mud
wall," wrote to Parkes: "Tell Hadley I am particularly
well pleased at the working of the thing among you and
among the people generally. It is altogether much more
systematic, and in all respects much better than he, and
you, and I, and the Glasgow and Nottingham men, anticipated."[2] In the narration of this time he says: "Communications had been had, as well personally as by
other means, between the leaders of the National Political
Union and many influential men in nearly all the large
towns in England and Scotland and in many other places,
all of which would have followed the example of, or rather
simultaneously with Birmingham, have barricaded their
respective towns, and awaited the result of the proceedings
in London."[3]

---

[1] "I am not conscious to myself of that perfect fearlessness which I
envy so much in you." (Grote to Place, October 20, 1831.)

[2] 27,792 (307).   [3] 27,793 (141).

Before the resignation of Lord Grey the Birmingham Political Union had been heavily in debt,[1] but now the respectable inhabitants were all joining, and the Scots Greys were confined to barracks, sharpening their swords. Even in Manchester the "timid men," the "whole Bill and nothing but the Bill men," and the "Huntites," were now united.[2] Orator Hunt himself declared for the Bill in the House of Commons, and there was in fact no longer any reason for the extremists to stand aside from a contest in which they might hope to come to the front.

On Friday, May 11, a Birmingham deputation came to London, authorised to pledge the Birmingham Union to a rising. "Between eight and nine o'clock on the morning of the 11th I received a note from Mr. Parkes, saying that a spontaneous meeting of 100,000 persons had been held at Birmingham on the preceding afternoon at Newhall Hill; that expresses had been sent to all the London morning newspapers with an account of the proceedings, each of which would have a notice inserted. The people at Birmingham had determined not to pay taxes—to arm themselves. A deputation consisting of himself and others had arrived in London with a petition to the Commons, to be presented in the evening. They would be with me at ten o'clock. They intended being present at the Westminster meeting and at the Common Hall in the City of London, and to call upon the people of London to stand fast by them. All Birmingham had joined the Union. . . . At ten o'clock the Birmingham deputation and several other gentlemen, members of deputations from several important places, assembled in my library. We soon came to a clear understanding on the most material points.

---

[1] Parkes wrote to Place, May 2, 1832, that the Union was £200 in debt, and still had to face the expenses of the great meeting of May 7. He asks Place to collect money in London.   27,792 (305).

[2] See extract from a local paper for May 15, 1832.   27,794 (55).

The state of the Government and the country was as freely as fully discussed. It was clear to us all that it would be impossible for the King to form any administration of which the Duke of Wellington was not placed at the head. It was as clear to us that the public was prepared to resist such an administration, and that if the means they employed should be unsuccessful in preventing its formation, they would at once openly revolt against it. The means of organising the people for effectual resistance were also discussed, and there was a general agreement that Birmingham was the place in which to hoist the standard of revolt, and it was understood that the first hostile defence against the Duke of Wellington's administration should be made there." [1]

Next day (Saturday, 12th) a secret council of deputies was held. "It was agreed to consult during the day in every way with as many influential men as possible, . . . and to meet in a body with as many of the deputies from various parts of the country as could be collected together. Towards noon a meeting was held at a tavern in Covent Garden. Many deputies attended. The business was entered upon at once, and at once every one present was determined to go through with it. There was no reserve on any part of the whole of the case between the people and the Tories. The persons present were all men of substance; some were very rich men. All were persons of influence, and whom circumstances had made of considerable importance. Some were only known to others by name, some not in any way; but it seemed to be concluded that all who were present were good men and true, and there was as much confidence in each other's integrity as there could have been had each been the well-known friend of every one else. . . . It was clearly understood that in the event of Lord Wellington being appointed Premier and

[1] 27,793 (98–1co).

forming an administration, as every one expected would be
at once attempted, that if necessary, as no doubt was entertained that it would be, open resistance should at once be
made, and in the meantime all that could be done should
be done to prevent such an administration being formed." [1]

Place seems to have recognised that all this would probably be reported to the authorities, and to have deliberately
exploited that fact.   There is a good deal to be said for this
combination of conspiracy and advertisement, on the one
condition, that those who engage in it are wholly indifferent
to their personal safety.   "No one who attended the meeting could do harm to any other by reporting what passed.
Were there men among them who came as spies to report
proceedings to the Tories—to the Duke of Wellington and
to Earl Grey, as it is probable there were--still nothing was
to be apprehended.   If the proceedings were reported to
Earl Grey and his colleagues, they could take no step, legal
or illegal, against the parties, even were they disposed to
take any, which it is probable they were not.   Were the
proceedings reported to the Duke of Wellington and the
King, they could use no means of personal annoyance.
They could only proceed by using personal violence, and
to this as yet they dared not resort. . . .   Had they seized
and imprisoned the persons of respectable men on a charge
of a suspicion of high-treason, it would at once have caused
an insurrection, a stoppage of trade and of the circulation
of paper-money, and thus put an end to their power. . . .
The reports which were probably made to the Duke of
Wellington and Earl Grey must have increased their desire
to have the matter settled." [2]

On the military side of the proposed rising Place is somewhat reticent.   Just as in his old tradesman days he had
refused as a breeches-maker to take any share of responsibility for the details of tailoring, so he probably now left all

[1] 27,793 (143, 144).   [2] 27,793 (144, 145).

strictly military details to the professional officers in the movement. Of these he says: "Numbers of military men of all ranks and many naval men, all men of experience, were ready to undertake to organise and conduct the operations of the people,"[1] and added in a note written in his old age: "When in the month of May an insurrection was expected, I had personal communication with no less than thirteen officers, the lowest in rank of whom was a major, all ready to serve the people against the Tories, should the King appoint them to the office of Ministers."[2] His fellow-conspirator, Joseph Parkes, was less cautious, and in a letter to Mrs. Grote (June 1832) says: "I and two friends should have made the revolution, whatever the cost. I had written to General Johnstone,[3] and had got a cover to Colonel Napier, and would have had both in Birmingham, and a Count Chopski, a Pole, by Monday: and I *think* we could have prevented anarchy and set all right in two days."[4] Of these, Count "Chopski" was Count Czapski, a Polish officer, who had been prominently put forward at the great Birmingham meeting on May 7. The "cover to Colonel Napier" introduces a rather complicated story. The officer referred to was Colonel William (afterwards Sir William) Napier, the historian of the Peninsular War. His letters at the time show that he was quite convinced that there would be a fight, and equally convinced that, being a poor man with a large family, it was not his duty to risk anything in it. "I am not disposed to be the leader of the *enfants perdus*," he wrote, six months before, to his wife. "I mean to go with the great stream, and if I can float, it will do for me. No dancing on breakers until I have a good safe lifeboat for

---

[1] 27,793 (142).   [2] 27,790 (244).
[3] This is probably General William Augustus Johnson of the Ceylon regiment, M.P. for Boston, 1820–26, and for Oldham, 1837–47.
[4] 27,794 (164).

you and the babes." [1]   The "cover" to him was a letter
from Tom Young, ex-purser of the Duke of Devonshire's
yacht, whom Lord Melbourne, then Home Secretary, kept
half as private secretary, half as a sort of spy on the
advanced men. [2]   It is not unlikely that Place was thinking
of him when he made his calculation that the proceedings
of the deputies would be reported to the Government.   Perhaps, however, on this occasion Mr. Young did not intend,
until the cat had jumped, to decide whether he was acting
as an *agent provocateur* or as an independent patriot.

His letter was never delivered; but Young afterwards
(June 25, 1832) wrote to Napier, saying that "The display
of energy and a readiness to act on the part of the people,
when the Duke of Wellington was on the eve of coming
in, was greater far than I expected. . . . Are you aware
that, in the event of a fight, you were to be invited to
take the command of Birmingham?"   He then mentions
Parkes and Place, and asks Napier whether he would have
accepted the offer.   Napier answered cautiously, ridiculing
the idea that he would have "co-operated in arms with a
Birmingham attorney and a London tailor against the
Duke of Wellington." [3]

[1] See "Life of General Sir W. Napier" (London, 1864, 2 vols.), vol i.
p. 373.
[2] "Young seldom comes to me but for some purpose connected with
the Home Office, and almost always when they are in a dilemma.   He
is a cleverish sort of fellow, with a vulgar air of frankness which may
at times put people off their guard, but he is not at all the right sort
of man to be private secretary and spy for the Home Secretary. . . .
Any man who would flatter Tom's vanity by leaving him to suppose he
was sucking his brains would assuredly suck Tom's." (Note by Place
in Letter Book, dated August 26, 1832.)   For a description of Tom
Young see "Memoirs of Viscount Melbourne," by W. M. Torrens, 1878,
vol. i. p. 368.   Place seems to have known Melbourne at first as a
customer.   Torrens (*l.c.* p. 188) says that Place was forced on one
occasion to serve him with a writ "instructing his solicitor at the
same time to see what that would do, but, d—n it, nothing further."
[3] The correspondence was published in the *Freeman's Journal*,
October 7 and 10, 1848.   See also "Life of Sir W. Napier" (London,
1864, 2 vols.), vol. ii. pp. 274, 275.

As to the rest of the thirteen officers, any one who reads
the speech of Colonel Leslie Grove Jones at the Marylebone
meeting of May 14 will believe that he was one of them,
and Place implies that Colonel de Lacy Evans, soon to be
Radical member for Westminster, was another. The rank
and file would, of course, have been mainly drawn from the
Political Unions, of whom in the preceding autumn Lord
Grey had written, " Unarmed as a body, they possess arms
as individuals." After the meeting on May 10, a deputation waited on Attwood to offer him a guard of " 1500 men
armed with muskets, &c." The yeomanry in many places
had refused to serve under Tory officers, and some of them
had resigned without returning their weapons. The *Times*
of May 22 says that swords and pike-heads had been
manufactured in Sheffield. Where the ammunition was
collected, Colonel Jones may have known.

What was even more important was that Hobhouse, by
this time become Sir John Cam Hobhouse and Secretary
of War, and Lord Durham, who was Lord Privy Seal and
a member of the Cabinet, seem to have been concerned in
the military preparations. Parkes wrote to Grote on May
14, and, after saying that "soldiers are enrolling themselves in our Union," goes on, " I stopped with Lord
Durham till two this morning alone,"[1] and Colonel Jones
told the huge Marylebone meeting on the same day that,
"at two o'clock this morning I asked the Secretary of War
whether any orders had been given for troops to march
upon London, and he said No."[2] Place gives an interesting, though guarded, account of his conversations with
Hobhouse at this point, from which it incidentally appears
that Place himself believed that the instalment of Reform
offered by the Bill was not only an easier thing to secure
than immediate Universal Suffrage, but under all the
circumstances, a wiser thing to desire. "Hobhouse," he

[1] 27,794 (10).   [2] 27,793 (202).

says, "up to this moment" (Nov. 15) "feared that the Duke would form an administration, and that he might succeed in establishing himself in power by means of the army. . . . We had talked this matter over several times, and as I never doubted the Duke would be at once beaten, I stated my view of the whole case as often as we conversed, and showed what I believed would be the process, step by step, always explaining what to me seemed certain, namely, that the defeat of the Duke, when in power, might be an instant destruction of the Government in Church and State, and the formation of a purely representative government—for which the people were by no means so well fitted as they ought to be, and it was most desirable they should be, before any such change were made. This revolution was therefore undesirable, not only on account of the present mischief in every way in which there could be mischief, but of the future trouble and peril a premature revolution could not fail to produce. This made it the more necessary that anything and everything should be done that could be done to prevent the Duke's accession to power." [1]

Not much in the way of an organised rising was intended or desired in London. The part assigned to Place and his friends was to prevent the seven thousand troops near London being used to crush the movement in the Midlands. "All that seemed necessary to be done was the making such various demonstrations as would cause apprehension to the rulers, and, for the safety of the metropolis and themselves, compel them to keep the soldiers where they were." [2]

Place, with his grimly practical sense of what a revolution meant, did not think that any elaborate preparations would be required for this purpose. "The vast multitude of people who would be deprived of employment, and

---

[1] 27,794 (87).   [2] 27,793 (141).

U

consequently of the means of living, would not, they could not, even if they were so disposed, remain quiescent. Neither would those concerned in trade, and especially the small traders, when forced, as they would instantaneously be, to discontinue their trading. The consequence of this stoppage of trading in the face of a starving multitude of unemployed people would lead to various, and probably extensive, outrages, which all the troops collected in or near London could not prevent. This was now pretty generally understood, and the problem which remained to be solved was how far the army under such circumstances could be depended upon by the Government." [1]

But Place knew how difficult it was to keep a London crowd in hand, and opposed with all the arts of delay a mass meeting on Hampstead Heath, on which the members of the National Political Union had set their hearts. "Had this meeting been called," he says, "more than half a million of persons would have attended. People would have come from considerable distances, trade in London and its environs would have been suspended, and as no arrangement could be made to engage the attention of all present to the same subject at the same time, ample scope would be given to the mischievously-disposed to hold separate meetings on the ground, and propose and carry their own resolutions. This was known to many of us as a matter determined upon by several leaders of workingmen who did not concur in the plan and proceedings of the National Political Union, and to these all the miscreants and vagabonds in the metropolis would have clung." [2]

Instead of the Hampstead gathering, a meeting of the comparatively respectable parishes of Marylebone, St. Pancras, and Paddington was arranged to be held in Regent's Park on May 11. At this meeting Colonel Jones was apparently ordered to be as seditious as possible. If so,

[1] 27,793 (142).   [2] 27,793 (123, 124).

the Colonel carried out his orders thoroughly. "He had been," he said, "at the head of some of the most desperate attacks during the late war, and he now declared that if a necessity arose he would again lead on his countrymen to glory in a cause which he should be more pleased with than any in which he had ever before been engaged."[1]

Meanwhile an attempt was made to organise London by the only existing local areas, the parishes. The first deliberate breach of the law by the National Political Union was the sending of Major Revell, apparently one of the "thirteen officers," as a formally appointed deputy to take the chair at a meeting of the branch Union of Bethnal Green.[2] Other parish meetings are described, for instance, at St. Andrew's, Holborn, in the "inquest room," with the senior churchwarden in the chair.[3] The Lord Mayor and Sheriffs, when at the head of a crowd of 5000 men they drove down to St. Stephen's with their petition on May 8, probably thought that they were leading the whole metropolitan movement. But the reports of the meetings of Common Hall seem to show that Place's old friend Alexander Galloway, who had not forgotten his two years' imprisonment in the Corresponding Society days, was directing the serious work in the City. Mr. Savage at the Marylebone meeting allowed himself a significant reference to the use which might be made of the new City police.

But London, though not for the moment the best centre for an armed rising, was the centre of English credit, and therefore the necessary point for that financial campaign from which Place had always expected most success. On Saturday, May 12, he wrote: "In the afternoon the deputies from Birmingham, other deputies, and several persons who were not deputies, came to my house. They had been in various parts of the metropolis, had conversed with many people—merchants, bankers, traders, and members of

[1] 27,793 (203).   [2] 27,792 (256).   [3] 27,792 (255).

Parliament. All whom they had seen, as well as themselves, were greatly excited at the no longer doubted intelligence that the King had ordered the Duke of Wellington
to form an administration. They observed that such was
the dread of his probable conduct, and so strong the desire
to prevent him doing mischief, that already his protest on
the second reading of the Bill on the 7th May was reprinted,
placarded, and distributed, with a caution to the people
against permitting him to govern them. It was generally
understood that the Duke would endeavour, and would
probably succeed, in forming an administration of desperate
men, and proceed at once to put down the people by force,
cost whatever it might. No one present, however, doubted
that the people would put down the Duke, and each was
ready to do his best for that purpose. It was quite certain
that the bulk of the people would rise *en masse* at the call
of the Unions, and the deputies now in London and other
cities."

"It was now considered necessary that, as soon as it was
ascertained that the Duke had formed an administration,
all the deputies, excepting three sent by the three principal
places, should return home and put the people in open
opposition to the government of the Duke, while the leading reformers in London should themselves remain as quiet
as circumstances would permit, and promote two material
purposes: (1) keeping the people from openly meeting the
troops in battle, supposing the soldiers were willing to fight
them; (2) to take care to have such demonstrations made
as would prevent the soldiers being sent from London, if
it should turn out, as seemed next to impossible, that the
mass of the people did not make these demonstrations
themselves."

"It was very clearly seen that if a much more open
and general run for gold upon the banks, the bankers, and
the Bank of England could be produced, the embarrass-

ment of the Court and the Duke would be increased, and
that if a general panic could be produced, the Duke would
be at once defeated. To this purpose the attention of us
all was turned, and many propositions were made to
increase the demand for gold. Several suggestions were
made, several hints were adopted and agreed to be put in
train ; but some measure which would operate extensively,
and at once, was still desired, and this put us into a perplexity respecting the means of accomplishing this purpose.
Among the persons present were two bankers, and although
they were likely to be inconvenienced greatly, and perhaps
to be considerable losers, they entered very heartily into
the business. There was a general conviction that if the
Duke succeeded in forming an administration, that circumstance alone would produce a general panic, and almost
instantaneously close all the banks, put a stop to the circulation of Bank of England notes, and compel the Bank to
close its doors ; and thus at once produce a revolution. The
question, therefore, among us was, Can we adopt means
to cause such a run upon the banks as may either intimidate the Duke, and induce him to give up the attempt to
form an administration and coerce the people, or prevent
him having the means of aggression if he persists in
his attempt? It was thought we might succeed in one,
and if in the first, prevent the second, and consequently
the revolution, though much deplored, was no longer
feared. While the discussion was going on, some one
said, we ought to have a placard announcing the consequences of permitting the Duke to form an administration and attempting to govern the country, to call upon
the people to take care of themselves by collecting all the
hard money they could, and keeping it, by drawing it from
Savings-Banks, from bankers, and from the Bank of England. This was caught at, and Mr. Parkes set himself to
work to draw up a placard. Among the words he wrote

were these, ' WE MUST STOP THE DUKE.' These words struck me as containing nearly the whole that was necessary to be said. I therefore took a large sheet of paper and wrote thus—

TO STOP THE

DUKE,

GO FOR

GOLD.

" I held up the paper, and all at once said, ' That will do; no more words are necessary.' Money was put upon the table, and in less than four hours bill-stickers were at work posting the bills. The printer undertook to work all night, and to despatch at four o'clock on the next (Sunday) morning six bill-stickers, each attended by a trustworthy person to help him, and see that all the bills were stuck in every part of London. Other persons were engaged to distribute them in public-houses and in shops, wherever the people would engage to put them up, to send them to the environs of London by the carriers' carts, and thus cause as general as possible a display at once.[1] Parcels were sent off by the evening coaches, and by the morning coaches of the next day, to a great many places in England and Scotland, and with some of these parcels a note was also sent, requesting the people to reprint them as posting-bills and as hand-bills." [2]

On Monday (May 14) the *Evening Standard* accused Grote of having originated these placards. He wrote to the papers indignantly denying any approval of the move, and privately to Place, prophesying that it would set all the commercial interest against reform. A few hours afterwards Place replied: " Saturday I was kept in town by

---

[1] See *Morning Post*, May 15, 1832, " A large placard posted about the town yesterday gave the following pithy advice, 'To stop the Duke, call for gold.' "

[2] 27,793 (146–148).

people calling upon me, yesterday the same. This morning my library was thronged like a fair, so many, so much loud talking, so much confused noise, that even *my* head began to ache. So I took an opportunity and started off to the Marylebone meeting to see how it was going on. I took your note with me, thought on what you had written, read it twice over as I went along, reasoned with myself as for you and against you, and satisfied myself, because I could not help it, that I could if I had time show good and sufficient cause against every one of your statements. I only fear lest the demonstration should not go far enough."

So far the preparations had been carried on in daily expectation of the appointment of a Wellington administration. But expressions of anxiety appeared on Monday (May 14) in the Tory papers, and on Tuesday the King again sent for Lord Grey. Place first heard of the event from Hobhouse, and at once wrote again to Grote : " Here is the answer to your note of yesterday. Just at the time when the *Standard* published your letter containing your —what ?—oh ! arguments to prove that ' *Go for Gold* ' was *no go* at all, in came a great man, who seeing the placard on my table pointed to it and exclaimed, ' That is the settler ; that has finished it.' [1] This he said without hesitation before a gentleman whom he had never before seen. When the gentleman was gone, he told me that the placard and some other such matters had worked out the reformation. Earl Grey was gone to the King.[2] That fears of a

---

[1] Note by Place in the Letter Book, "Sir John Hobhouse."

[2] See John Francis, "History of the Bank of England," vol. ii. p. 67. "For a week the Corporation sustained a run upon its specie, which was reduced to £4,919,000. In one day £307,000 were paid. It soon became very questionable whether the run for gold would not drain every banker in the kingdom, and the writing on the wall spoke to those having authority with a power far exceeding the most brilliant oratory. Lord Lyndhurst found it impossible to form a ministry ; and

hitch of a very extraordinary character were entertained.[1] That if it or any other extraordinary matter occurred he would call again in the evening. It is now 11 P.M., and as he has not called I conclude that all is going on well."

In the Lords that evening Grey made a guarded statement that he had "had a communication with his Majesty, which has as yet led to no decided consequences," and moved the adjournment of the House till Thursday (May 17). Baring, in the Commons, announced on behalf of the Tories that "the communications with the Duke of Wellington for the formation of a new ministry are entirely at an end."

Wednesday (May 16) was given up to rejoicing, but in the evening came rumours of another difficulty. On Thursday morning the *Times* announced that the Queen had within the last few hours told her friends "not to despair. The King will do without the Whigs," and in its leading article declared that "Arthur, Duke of Wellington, had better look to consequences. Oppressive and revolting laws *must* be enforced by violence—there is no other method. . . . That is to be our prospect, is it? If so, may the hand of every free Englishman perish from his body, if he do not

Earl Grey was recalled." Francis also says (p. 68) that £1,500,000 was paid in a few days. See also the evidence of Horsley Palmer, Jones Lloyd, Richards, and Ward before the Select Committee on the Charter of the Bank of England, 1831-32.

[1] Note by Place in the Letter Book : "A project of the Queen's which the King countenanced—to depart, he and she clandestinely for Hanover "—Place expands this (27,794 f. 88) : "He [Hobhouse, the name being here erased] very seriously assured me that some steps had been taken with a view to the departure of the King and Queen, when their intention became known and was consequently frustrated. It was not likely such a plot could succeed, but if it had the whole Government would have been dissolved in an instant, and a war with the powers on the Continent would probably have been the consequence. England and France must have made common cause, and they would have had to fight against Austria, Prussia, and Russia, and great indeed would have been the calamities of such a war."

himself and his children and his country right upon the head of the murderer." As a matter of fact, the King was still unwilling to give a specific pledge to make Peers. But he had written, through Sir Herbert Taylor, to each one of the Tory Peers individually, suggesting that "All difficulties in the arrangement in progress will be obviated by a declaration in the House to-night, from a sufficient number of Peers, that in consequence of the present state of affairs they have come to the resolution of dropping their further opposition to the Reform Bill."[1]

Grey accepted office on the understanding that such a declaration would be made. When the Houses reassembled on Thursday, however, Wellington delivered a long and angry speech without making any declaration of the kind. Grey, therefore, would only say that nothing was settled, and add, "Unless I can be assured of the ability of carrying the Bill fully and efficiently through this House, I shall not again return to office."[2] Writing that night, through Sir H. Taylor to the King, Grey says: "As the Peers were leaving the House, Lord Strangford said to somebody near him, 'You see Sir H. Taylor's famous letter did no good.'"[3]

---

[1] "Annual Register," 1832, p. 187.
[2] Hansard, May 17, 1832.
[3] "Correspondence of Earl Grey with King William IV," vol. ii. p. 424. In the "Correspondence of the Princess Lieven and Earl Grey" (London, 1890, 3 vols.), vol. ii. pp. 352, 353, Grey writes on May 18: "When I went to the House, I had, in consequence of communications which I had had from St. James's in the morning, every reason to believe that the Duke of Wellington and others would have *declared* that they abandoned all further opposition to the Bill, . . . and in that case I had the King's authority to declare that I continued in his service. Instead of such a declaration, the Duke of Wellington, in giving what he called an explanation of his conduct, made a most violent attack on me, but said nothing on which I could rely with respect to his future conduct. . . . It was impossible for me, in the circumstances in which I then stood, to make the declaration which I had contemplated, and I could only say that nothing was yet definitely settled. And such is the fact. The Cabinet meets at twelve to consider what step we should now

The Council of the National Political Union met as usual in the evening. Place and others knew what had happened in the Lords, but in accordance with the policy of keeping London in hand as long as possible, it was decided to go on quietly with the routine business of the Union, lest any mention of what had passed in the Lords should produce a riot.[1]

Next day, Friday (May 18), eleven days since the division in the Lords, and nine days since the acceptance of Grey's resignation, came the final crisis. The *Morning Chronicle* announced, "We can only construe the debate of last night into an open declaration of war by the Tory Lords against the people of England. . . . The situation of the country is truly alarming. Lord Grey is only minister *ad interim*. The nation has, in fact, been ten days without any Government. The people are wrought up to the highest point of political excitement; they are only restrained by the personal and moral influence of the men of intelligence and property who lead them, and who, knowing that they may be able to pull down and not to reconstruct, have hitherto restrained any outbreak of popular power. But our accounts from the country confirm us in the opinion that some explosion will speedily take place unless instant means are adopted —we say instant means, because we think that the post of this evening ought to take out *that* decision which can alone restore loyalty, peace, and order. We are otherwise on the eve of the 'barricades.'"

Place received the *Times* and the *Chronicle* at 7 A.M.[2] "Several persons," he says, "came to me before eight o'clock in the morning, each filled with apprehension,

take ; but the matter *must* be settled to-day one way or the other. These men are mad, and I wish they may not be found to have pushed things to an extreme which may produce irreparable mischief."

[1] 27,794 (260).   [2] 27,794 (271).

each having his own version of what had happened. All, however, had come to the same conclusion—resistance to the Duke at any cost, and in every possible way. Others came in, and at about half-past eight a gentleman came with a message from Sir John Hobhouse. He said there was to be a meeting[1] in Downing Street at noon, and Sir John wished me to write a letter to him, telling him all the facts I could, and giving him my opinion of the state of feeling among the people, as far as I could, and my view of prospective results. I therefore, as soon as I could dismiss the persons who were with me, and shut others out for a time, wrote as rapidly as I could the following letter:—'*May* 18, 1832. 9 A.M. Dear Sir John,—The moment it was known that Earl Grey had been sent for, the *demand for gold ceased.* No more placards were posted, and all seemed to be going on well at once. Proof positive this of the cool courage and admirable discipline of the people. We cannot, however, go on thus *beyond to-day.* If doubt remain until to-morrow, alarm will commence again, and panic will follow. No effort to *stop the Duke by going for gold* was made beyond a mere demonstration, and you saw the consequences. What can be done in this way has now been clearly ascertained, and if new efforts must be made, they will not be made in vain.

"'Lists containing the names, addresses, &c., of all persons in every part of the country likely to be useful have been made, the name of every man who has at any public meeting shown himself friendly to reform has been registered. Addresses and proclamations to the people have been sketched, and printed copies will, if need be, be sent to every such person all over the kingdom. Means have been devised to placard towns and villages, to circulate hand-bills, and to assemble the people. So many

[1] Of the Cabinet.   See Lord Grey's letter, p. 313 (*foot-note*).

men of known character, civil and *military*, have entered
heartily into the scheme, that their names when published
will produce great effect in every desirable way. If the
Duke come into power now, we shall be unable longer to
"hold to the laws"; break them we must, be the consequences whatever they may; and we know that all must
join with us to save their property, no matter what may
be their private opinions. Towns will be barricaded, new
municipal arrangements will be made by the inhabitants,
and the first town which is barricaded shuts up all the
banks. "Go for Gold," it is said, will produce dreadful
evils. We know it will, but it will prevent other evils
being added to them. It will *stop the Duke*. Let the Duke
take office as Premier, and we shall have a commotion in
the nature of a civil war, with money at our command. If
we obtain the money, he cannot get it. If it be but once
dispersed, he cannot collect it. If we have money we shall
have the power to feed and lead the people, and in less
than five days we shall have the soldiers with us. . . .' " [1]

It is safe to assert that no such letter was ever before
written by the organiser of a rising to a War Minister, for
the purpose of its being laid before the Executive Government. But Place may have felt, with the instinct born of
long experience in the management of men, that since
everything now turned on the decision of Ministers, the
greatest value of the plot was that it could be used to
influence their minds, and may have calculated that if
Ministers did again resign on that day, it was not likely
that their last act would be to order his arrest.

"At twelve o'clock Mr. Hume came. He said it was apprehended the Duke would be put into office to do as he
pleased, or as he could. That when the House of Commons
adjourned on the preceding evening an arrangement was
made for a meeting at the Treasury on the next morning

[1] 27,794 (278, 279).

(this day) at one o'clock, if nothing was done before ten o'clock in the morning, when Mr. Edward Ellice (Secretary to the Treasury) was to send notices. He had received a notice, and was now going to the meeting. I read the draft of the letter to Sir John Hobhouse, and we talked over arrangements of several kinds. He was, he said, disposed to whatever might be found necessary, either within the House or without it, and so were other members. Several gentlemen, some of them deputies from the country, and some military men, were with me." [1]

At the Cabinet it was decided still to insist on power to create Peers. Grey and Brougham went over to St. James's Palace to communicate that decision. In their absence the Cabinet continued sitting, and sat, indeed, according to Greville, " almost all day."

" At three o'clock Mr. Hume came again. There were then about a dozen gentlemen present, including two military men high in rank. Mr. Hume was greatly agitated. He said all was going wrong, and that the people must look to themselves, as he had no doubt that the House of Commons would look to themselves and to the people, and would do their duty to both. He told me apart that Sir John Hobhouse had requested him to call upon me and tell me what he had told us all. Sir John said he would call himself, if it were possible, in the evening.

" I was confined to the house by the great number of persons who called upon me. They came from various parts of the metropolis, and were persons in various conditions of life. What each related respecting the anxious state of the public and their determination, was in unison, and might therefore be fairly considered the opinion of the people of London. . . . There were numerous meetings in many parts of London, and it was determined that in the event of the Duke's appointment being avowed in the

[1] 27,794 (280, 281).

Houses of Parliament, as it was expected it would be, that all the deputies and others who were up in London on the business of reform should go home by the speediest conveyances, call public meetings, appoint deputies to form a congress to meet at some proper place, to push the demand in every possible way, and to use every other means to embarrass and defeat the Duke.

"Birmingham was to take the lead, which it was prepared to do. The town was to be barricaded at once, and other towns were to follow the example. There was a very complete arrangement for procuring information of what was going on at Weedon Barracks, and there was a probability that the soldiers in these barracks would refuse to act against the people; and it was concluded that in such an event, few or none of the soldiers in other places would obey orders when it was seen that the people were able and willing to protect them. It was intended to seize as many of the families of the Tory Lords as possible, to carry them into the towns, and there to hold them as hostages for the conduct of the Duke towards the reformers. . . . No proceedings beyond those of causing a general demand for gold were to be taken in the first instance. It was to be kept as quiet as possible. It was quite certain that if the Bank closed its doors, and the supply of the markets ceased, a general tumult would immediately take place which no power the Government possessed could put down, nor could it continue in existence many days. Meetings would be called, and the necessary arrangements made to supply the metropolis with food. The army as well as every other department of military force would fall from the hands of the Government.

"An old Guardsman, a general officer, told me that he had seen his friend Lord Melbourne at the Home Office, and had told him the Duke could do nothing with the

army, since he dared not move any part of it away from
the metropolis, and that he could not use it with any
effect in London; and that if he really understood the
situation he would be placed in, he would never for a
moment think of carrying on the Government by force."[1]

"In this fearful state, this unparalleled situation, were
the King and people placed; and the moment had arrived
when the decision of one man, and he one of the silliest,
was compelled to choose between a course which would,
at least for some years, give peace to the nation, though it
might, and probably would, tend to a gradual change of
the whole political institutions of the nation, and that
which even to him it must have become all but certain,
would at once put in jeopardy, if not indeed destroy, not
only those institutions, but the aristocracy with them. Yet
he could not think, as a wiser man would have thought
calmly. He was not one of those men to whom deep
thinking was familiar. Thinking at all on so large a subject must to him have been most painful, and he had those
about him eager enough to save him from any effort of
the kind by their ill-considered suggestions. Decide, however, he must. He dared not let the two Houses of Parliament assemble before his determination was taken, and a
circumstance to be related presently caused him to decide
in the right way. Truly were we in a lamentable situation
when so much for good or evil depended on such a man as
William the Fourth, King of England.

"The crisis was come: both Houses of Parliament were
filled with members, and with as many strangers as could
obtain admission. An immense concourse of people was
assembled outside the Houses, and everybody waited the
expected announcements with the utmost anxiety. It was
fearfully apprehended that the Duke would be appointed;
all confidence in the patriotism of the King had subsided,

[1] 27,794 (281–283).

and the worst consequences were anticipated. The deputies from the towns in various parts of the kingdom had made preparations for their departure, and the evening papers had their forms standing ready to insert the announcements in the Houses of Parliament in second editions, to be forwarded by the mails and coaches to every part of the United Kingdom. In a state of indescribable apprehension and terror, Earl Grey in the Lords, and Lord Althorp in the Commons, announced the exhilarating fact that Ministers, having secured the means to pass the Reform Bills without mutilation, would continue in office.

" At half-past five o'clock, while sitting with some gentlemen waiting to receive the news that they might determine on the course it would be advisable to take, Mr. Howard, a gentleman who had gone to the House of Commons for the purpose of hearing the communication expected to be made, came in in breathless haste, and said he had just heard Lord Althorp make the declaration of his continuance in office, with full powers to carry the Bills. Mr. Howard was scarcely gone when, in a state of high enthusiasm, Sir John Hobhouse came and confirmed the information Mr. Howard had given us. 'An immense load had,' he said, been removed from the minds of all, and pleasant sensations would now take the place of the all but too well grounded apprehensions of most extensive evils, whatever good might ultimately be obtained, and that the people might honestly gratify themselves with their own manly, steady, courageous conduct, which had compelled the unwilling decision in their favour. Sir John stayed but a few minutes. Like every one else, he was eager to spread the good news as far and as wide as he was able.

" On the next morning I was informed that the King determined to appoint Earl Grey in consequence of the following circumstance: At about two o'clock a gentleman came to Earl Grey privately. He was commissioned by the Bank directors to inform him that if nothing was settled in time to be forwarded to the country by the mails, they apprehended that the depositors in Savings-Banks would generally give notice to withdraw their deposits, and convert the amount into cash. That this being known, other persons would also demand gold for paper, and that the run upon all the banks would, in a few days, compel them to close their doors. That Earl Grey requested this gentleman to proceed to the Duke of Wellington and make the communication to him. He did so, and the Duke having immediately made a similar communication to the King, Earl Grey was restored to office with the power he desired. This information was given me by a confidential person of a Cabinet Minister, with an injunction by him that I was not to use his name." [1]

On Sunday morning, May 20, Place sat down and wrote his reflections on the "memorable eleven days." "Here let us hope the turmoil will end. We were within a moment of general rebellion, and had it been possible for the Duke of Wellington to have formed an administration, the King and the people would have been at issue. It would have been soon decided, but the mischief to property, especially to the great landowners and fund-holders, and personally to immense numbers, would have been terrible indeed. Yet upon the coolest calculation it would have been by far less terrible than that which must have resulted from a submission to the Duke of Wellington and the army.

"I always doubted the courage of the people, as well as the judgment to do, at the right time, the thing which might be most requisite to produce the greatest amount of good on any great emergency. There had, however, been no means at any time of judging correctly on this subject,

[1] 27,794 (286–288).

X

the people never in any case having acted for themselves, but always as the tools of some party for party purposes, even when national good was the result of this use which was made of them. This was indeed the first time they ever combined of their own free-will for a really national purpose, and this it is which marks the era as of more importance than any former proceeding—which makes its prospective of still greater importance as the first of an inevitable series, which from time to time will increase the power of the people and lessen that of the Government, until it has either totally destroyed it by a violent ebullition or quietly absorbed it.

"Thanks to the King and his stultified advisers. Thanks to the Duke of Wellington for his blind courage. Thanks to the Tory Lords for their ignorance of the people, since it is to these things we owe the demonstration and communication all over the country of the knowledge and power of the people, and the assurance it has given to all that these important particulars were about equally shared by them in every part of Great Britain, the thorough conviction they have now obtained of the moral power to control the Government, and the confidence that conviction will give to them when the reformed House of Commons at no great distance of time shall, as it must, prove how inadequate will be the Reform Bill to satisfy the expectations of the people. Even a year ago the people as a body may be said to have been essentially loyal, desirous to support the Government of the King, the Bishops, the other Lords, and the Commons. . . . Much of this absurd loyalty has now been destroyed, and can never again exist. The demonstrations made by the King and Lords have shaken those absurd notions, and compelled the people to progress towards entertaining republican opinions to an extent which no one had anticipated.

"So great a change in so short a period, which, from its

THE SECOND REFORM CAMPAIGN 323

very nature, must be permanent, never was so generally and so effectually manifested by any people. Kings and Lords will of themselves, if permitted, in time go quietly out of existence, and as it may be hoped, at least in this country, representative government will be established without tumults or any extensive convulsion.

"The only apprehension which can reasonably be entertained of any considerable disturbance, is want of patience of the people. If they be not too much in a hurry, representative government will be produced exactly at the time when it can best be maintained, and that will be when the people have been prepared to carry it on with the least possible difficulty, and the consequent certainty of reaping all its advantages.

"Had I taken notes of such matters as have come to my knowledge during the last eighteen months, had I noticed the many persons whom the agitation brought me acquainted with, the multitude of things within and without doors in which I have been engaged with other men, the relation would have been at least somewhat curious and extraordinary, but to have made notes would have been unfair towards others. Much of what was said and done was necessarily confidential, and notes might have fallen into [other] hands in the event of ulterior proceedings, and done great mischief. The anticipation of such a probability determined me to make no memorandum, to record no names, to write nothing which could be avoided which might in any way, under any circumstances, be at all likely to commit anybody, and to burn all notes and letters which came to me which were likely to be in the most trifling matter obnoxious, if seized, to the writers— that to Sir John Hobhouse on the 18th of May alone excepted, and this would have been destroyed in the evening but for Lord Grey's restoration to office."[1]

[1] 27,795 (27–30).

CHAPTER XII

THE REFORMED PARLIAMENT

WOULD Lord Grey and his Cabinet follow up their victory?
Place at first thought that some of them might be induced
to try. On June 2, 1832, a fortnight after the collapse of
the opposition to the Reform Bill, Hobhouse called and
asked Place what he thought of "our prospects." Place
replied at length, and Hobhouse urged him to put his
reply in writing. Place begins his long letter by dwelling
on the present opportunity of carrying in peace changes
which, if delayed, might come through civil war, and then
advises that the Radical section of the Cabinet should put
forward an advanced policy, and if it were not accepted,
strengthen their position in the country by resigning.[1] If,
however, he had any real hope that Hobhouse and Durham [2]

---

[1] "What, then, should Ministers do? The answer is short, and, as it
appears to me, clear. Such of them as may be well disposed to do their
duty to the people must, when the Bills are passed, resign. They who
are willing to take upon themselves the responsibility of proposing such
reforms in Church and State as must be proposed by somebody, such as
if not granted will be extorted, must resolve to have their own way, or
not to serve as Ministers. They among them who are able to appreciate
the age, and are disposed to march with its improvements, will refuse to
hold office unless the King submits himself in all matters of State policy
to their guidance." (Place to Hobhouse, June 2, 1832.)

[2] Place seems to have kept up communication with Lord Durham, at
any rate, for some days after the memorable 18th of May. There was a
rumour, for instance, even after Lord Grey's return to office, that the
Government would accept amendments in Committee of the Lords
abolishing some of the new Metropolitan seats. Place hastily got
together the materials for a long statistical speech, which was delivered
by Lord Durham on May 22. The speech was successful, and Lord

would take his advice, it must soon have disappeared. They had been willing to carry a moderate Bill by force, but they were in no hurry to bring on a complete democracy.

Having failed· to induce Ministers to resign, Place attempted the almost equally impossible task of forcing an amendment of the Reform Bill through the weary and demoralised House of Commons. The Bill, when reintroduced in December 1831, contained a new clause, excluding from the register any one who had not paid his rates and annual taxes by July 20 in each year. Place persuaded Warburton in February to oppose this clause in Committee, but neither he nor Warburton could induce any other member to take the point seriously. In an atmosphere so unreal as that of the House of Commons it was easy for men to convince themselves that all their constituents would hasten to avoid disfranchisement by paying their rates as soon as possible. Place, however, after July 20 went round the various parishes in Westminster, and discovered that very few of the ratepayers had actually qualified themselves. The state of things which he discovered was startling. Burdett and Hobhouse refused to attempt to understand the question, but Colonel Evans armed himself with Place's figures, and brought about four debates on the subject in the last week of the session. Meanwhile Place collected facts, interviewed members, wrote letters and newspaper articles, and organised petitions. He was so far successful that Lord Althorp suggested that the strict terms of the Act could be evaded by the registration authorities, and the officials were glad to take the hint. For years afterwards Place

Durham declared, somewhat prematurely, that "the days of flowery oratory were gone for ever," and that the future belonged to him "who would take the trouble to collect facts, and had the capacity to draw correct inferences." 27,795 (116). The speech itself was printed, and is inserted 27,795 (124-134).

complained that the effect had been to enable the over-
seers to put on or keep off almost any one they wished.

His tone was more hopeful when he was urging the
Radicals outside Parliament not to rest after their
victory. In July 1832 he wrote to Lawrence Pitkeithly,
the leader of the Huddersfield working-men: "We wanted
the Reform Bills[1] and a new Parliament under the Bills.
These we shall soon have, and then let whoever may be
Ministers, we must do our duty to ourselves manfully
and continually. We must have petitions in hundreds
for short Parliaments and voting by ballot as means of
procuring reforms in every possible way and to the
greatest possible extent. It is very difficult, and requires
much time to move a nation like this, even when it has
been demonstrated that very small exertions will produce
the greatest good. Even they who are disposed to move
are seldom agreed to work together. If some fundamental
points were selected, and all agreed to push for them,
success would be certain. *The Reform Bills are in
themselves of little value,* but as a commencement of the
breaking up of the old rotten system they are invaluable."[2]

At the general election which followed the passage of
the Bills, Place advised that pledges should be required
from all Reform candidates. He wrote a tract on this
point, which was published by the National Political
Union,[3] in which he said: "Pledges may then be taken

---

[1] *i.e.* the English, Scotch, and Irish Bills.

[2] Place to Lawrence Pitkeithly, July 25, 1832.

[3] "No. 15. National Political Union. On Pledges to be given by
Candidates." (By Francis Place.) "To the electors of the United
Kingdom" (London, July 1832). This action of the National Political
Union gave rise to much discussion among the Reformers. John Mill,
e.g. wrote two very interesting articles against Pledges in the *Examiner*
on 1st July and 15th July 1832, 27,796 (48), and W. J. Fox defended
them in the *Monthly Repository*. The seven points on which Place
suggested the asking for pledges were: (1) Parliamentary Reform

from all. Every elector should recollect that his representative is elected for the unreasonably long period of
seven years, and that he may therefore set his constituents at defiance for that period." In Westminster
Burdett and Hobhouse were requested to pledge themselves to the Ballot, the abolition of the House and Window
Taxes, the Newspaper Stamp Duty, and the repeal of the
Septennial Act. Both declared that "none but fools
demanded pledges, and none but knaves gave them." [1]

Place himself was asked to stand for Westminster, but
refused. When, however, Colonel Evans came forward
against Hobhouse, Place supported him. [2] Evans was
beaten, but defeated Hobhouse at a bye-election a few
months afterwards.

As soon as the general election was over Place wrote to
Joseph Parkes, suggesting that the Birmingham Political
Union should begin a popular agitation for the Ballot
and triennial Parliaments. Parkes replied: "Our glass
here is almost run out, till some circumstances turn it
again. The fact is, that we have all made such heavy
personal and pecuniary sacrifices that we fear that so
recently after the elections, we should not get up a
sufficient public meeting for Birmingham on the Ballot
and Septennial Act. We have the will, but the elections
have taken our last wind; and indeed, a meeting costs
us a great deal of money. . . . Who the devil is to go
on with this public work and his private duty ? I can't;
I am determined to lie fallow as much as I consistently
can; it is impossible to keep up the devotion we have had
here for two years. I had rather go to the Swann River, or

(shorter Parliaments and ballot); (2) Law Reform ; (3) Financial
Reform ; (4) Trade Reform (Free Trade); (5) Church Reform ; (6)
Abolition of Slavery ; (7) Abolition of Taxes on Knowledge.

[1] 27,844 (24).

[2] See "A Letter to the Electors of Westminster," in which Place
defends himself, and refers to Hobhouse's Radical declarations in 1819.

even Botany Bay, than go through the sacrifices and labour of the last eighteen months. I have read no books, I have not slept half enough, I have collected no money, I have neglected my business. Numerous others have done the same. Actually eight leading middlemen of the Union have 'broke.' And as I do not choose so to injure my utility or comfort, I don't mean, Mr. Place, to give so much time to the political plough; I will do my duty nevertheless. We have buried the Tories, and if the Whigs will not do right, the sexton must be called out again. Good-night, old firebrand." [1]

The first reformed Parliament met on January 29, 1833, and was at once occupied with an Irish Coercion Bill. Under any circumstances Place would not have concerned himself very seriously with an Irish question. He had been long convinced that the task of governing Ireland from England was an impossible one, and had perhaps too little sympathy with those who were compelled to attempt it. In his letter to Hobhouse of June 2, 1832, he wrote: "A word or two as to Ireland. There nothing worth doing on a large scale can be done while that country is kept in subjection to this. Stanley's nostrums will only tend to make the bond of union among the Irish the more firm. The Irish must be left to fight it out among themselves before they can arrive at that condition when regeneration can commence, or rather, before any progress can be made towards actual civilisation. I do not consider that to be a state of civilisation in which property is not secure." [2]

<hr/>

[1] Joseph Parkes to Place, January 17, 1833.

[2] Place to Hobhouse, June 2, 1832. 27,795 (228-235). See Place to Ensor, May 27, 1835.

"It is now some fifteen years since you, Mill, and I dined with Richard Taylor, and at his table discussed the matter more fully than we had previously done, of a separation between England and Ireland. Since that time some reading, much conversation, as

But in the spring of 1833 the state of his personal affairs might have prevented him from noticing much more interesting political matter than the dispute between Lord Stanley and Daniel O'Connell.

He had put a large part of his capital into house property, and had left the investment of it to an incompetent or dishonest solicitor. On February 25, 1833, after an examination of his affairs, he found that out of an income of a little more than £1100, some £650 was irrevocably

well with Irishmen of some importance as with Englishmen. and more serious thinking, have confirmed me in my opinion that Ireland *never* can be what it ought to be, what it would have been, if it had been, or if it is to be, an independent country.   I never hesitate in any place, or before any company when Ireland is talked of, to assert that there is but one way permanently to better its people, and that is by a separation, by making Ireland an independent nation, and leaving it to choose a government for itself.   The terms to be these : Ireland to take a reasonable, and consequently a small portion of the public debt, and pay the interest of it ; no customs to be paid on the importation of anything, the produce or manufactures of either country ; and no more tax to be laid on such produce and manufactures than is usually laid thereon when manufactured or produced on the spot.

"I know all the objections which can be made to this project, and some of them are very serious ; but as I am thoroughly persuaded that they will not be removed by the continual dependence of Ireland on England, either with or without an Irish Parliament, I am for putting an end as soon as possible to the present state of things, that a better state of things may commence.   The most important of all the objections is this, that if Ireland were separated from England there would be a terrible civil war among the people.   This is, I think, an inevitable consequence, but it is one that will happen some day ; it is a state the Irish people must pass through, and I am therefore for giving them the earliest possible opportunity to fight it out, and to settle down under a regular government."

Place, like other Radicals of his time, believed in the ultimate solution of most imperial problems by separation.   In his diary for 1830 he says that India should be "independent at as early a period as possible, and that this would be advantageous to both Great Britain and India."   On January 18, 1838, during the Canadian troubles, he sent Lovett Bentham's "Emancipate your Colonies" (1793).   On the other hand, on December 5, 1838, he wrote to Parkes, "The plan of Lord Durham, Federal Colonies, was the only one which could retain the Canadas in peace even for a short time."

lost. Two days afterwards he sat down and wrote out a calculation of his future expenses, ending with: "I am strong, active, healthy, and a better man than most at sixty-one years of age, capable of many things, and willing to undertake some one or more things; and if opportunities should occur, I will embrace them. At present I see nothing likely to be useful in this way, so I must wait. If I would turn sycophant, be a tool and a rascal, I could soon obtain employment under Government; this I will not do."[1]

The house at Charing Cross was now let to his eldest son, who had taken on the business sixteen years before, while Place with his wife and those of the family who were still at home removed to a smaller house (No. 21) in Brompton Square. This, together with the fact that his wife was attacked by cholera and nearly died, kept Place occupied for some months.

Even when he was again at leisure, there were several causes tending to detach him from the daily business of Parliamentary politics. He and his books were no longer easy of access from the House of Commons; he soon ceased to be an elector of Westminster; and he intended to take any useful paid post that might be offered to him.

For a short time in 1834–35 he was Secretary to the Pure Spring Water Company, formed to supply London with water from artesian wells. But it got into the hands of City company promoters and Place resigned, having received £100 for his services. The Company soon afterwards broke up, as the necessary Bill was rejected in the House of Commons.

Nevertheless, Place worked steadily from 1834 to 1836, both in the reconstruction of English local government by the New Poor Law (1834) and the Municipal Reform Bill

[1] "Autobiography."

(1835), and in the long struggle for the abolition of the Newspaper Stamp.

The two Local Government Bills were the result not of the official Whig tradition as represented in the Cabinet, but of "philosophic radicalism" acting through Royal Commissions. Edwin Chadwick, Secretary to the Poor-Law Commission (1832–34), and Place's friend, Joseph Parkes, Secretary to the Muncipal Corporations Commission (1833–1835), were both personal disciples of Jeremy Bentham, and the Bills themselves were the embodiment of principles which the Benthamites had discussed for twenty years.

With the Poor-Law Commissioners Place must have been in touch at least as early as the spring of 1833, for even in the midst of his own misfortunes he found time to help them.

"Early in March 1833," he says, "Lord Althorp wrote to the Commissioners of the Poor-Laws inquiry, and requested them to inform him whether the adoption of the Labour Rate Bill[1] (the renewal) as a temporary and palliative measure would have the tendency to increase the evil of the Poor-Laws. The answer of the Commissioners seemed to me so very likely to do much service if it were put into the proper hands, that I applied for money to enable me to print 10,000 copies, and also for the names of all persons who had either been examined or corresponded with, or were likely to interfere in the matter. The money and the names were furnished. I wrote an appropriate head, printed and sent copies in franks and by coach parcels free of expense to every person indicated. The consequence was that all proceedings were at once dropped, and no more was heard

---

[1] The labour rate was an arrangement by which pauper labourers were forced upon unwilling employers in order to lower the money rate. *Cf.* Report of 1834, p. 108.

of the mischievous Bill, either within or without the House." [1]

He knew Chadwick personally, and a letter which he wrote in July 1833 contains an accurate forecast of the coming Report. [2]

The Commissioners proposed that the administration of the new Act should be superintended by a small body of paid officials, and it occurred to Place that possibly he himself might be appointed.

" I wish," he writes to Harriet Martineau, "the Lord Chancellor would make me one of the Central Commissioners under an Act of Parliament, the leading enactments of which should be the recommendations of the present Poor-Law Commissioners. I would go into the business and help to carry it on with all my heart and soul, would work carefully and promptly and efficiently in the great and good work, would think nothing of obstacles, and be utterly careless of the abuse which will be showered down in all possible forms on the obnoxious Commissioners." [3]

He preserved a letter from Anthony Fonblanque, the editor of the *Examiner*, urging him to put himself forward as a candidate, and his answer, in which he said that "Lord Brougham *knows* that under such a Bill as I have alluded to . . . I should look much more to the elevation of the common people than to the salary; that

---

[1] Place to Parkes, May 11, 1835.

[2] "The remedy, as far as a remedy can be applied, seems short and clear. No assistance either in money, clothes, or food should be given by the parish to any one, in any case whatever, out of the workhouse, some cases of sickness alone excepted, and even then sparingly. The workhouse should be for a district composed of one, two, or more parishes where the inmates might be classed, and good instead of evil produced. The adoption of this plan would for some time cause evil to many, good to multitudes. There could then be no parish payment to make up wages, nor many of the present contrivances to make the people dissolute and reckless." (Place to Wade, July 9, 1833.)

[3] Place to Harriet Martineau, March 4, 1834.

THE REFORMED PARLIAMENT   333

I would diligently, honestly, and, I hope, judiciously execute
the trust for one-half of the salary named." But no man
in power "would willingly have it supposed that he would
have countenanced any proposal to make the Radical
Tailor a King's Commissioner." [1]

Place was, as he expected, passed over, and Brougham
could perhaps have found better reasons for his decision
than that which Place suggested. Chadwick's combination
of dogmatism and industry nearly wrecked the new system
as it was, and Chadwick and Place together would have
gone near to bring about a revolution. Above all, Place
was a known and unflinching partisan on just the point
where the Commissioners were sure to encounter the most
furious vituperation. The word Malthusian punctuates
Times' leaders and Chartist speeches on the new Poor-
Law from 1835 to 1849, and his opinions about the population question were notorious.

The Act as finally passed, though it did not exactly
correspond to Place's sketch of 1833, or to the proposals
of the Commissioners, was yet logical and drastic enough.
Place for the moment abused the Government for having
weakened it, but in August 1834 wrote to Chadwick full of
hopes as to its result, and advising him to print a short
popular analysis for general distribution. From that time
forward he steadily defended the law with tongue and
pen, and kept up even among the extreme democrats a
tiny minority of audible opinion in its favour. The Chartist
Northern Liberator writes in 1837 (December 30) of him
as being "the very head and chief, the life and soul, of the
Poor-Law Amendment Bill."

Place speaks of the removal to Brompton as having
"increased my comfort and diminished my usefulness." [2]
Certainly his correspondence in the summer of 1834 shows

[1] Place to Anthony Fonblanque, March 4, 1834.
[2] Loose sheet, dated April 1834.

that absence from Westminster had brought him an unusual amount of leisure. On May 2 and 3, for instance, he
wrote to his friend Samuel Harrison an enormous letter
of something like seven thousand words, criticising from
the agnostic point of view William Howitt's "Popular History of Priestcraft."

He did not believe that the next step towards a democratic franchise would willingly be taken by any government then possible. But he was convinced that forces
stronger than the will of any government were in operation, and meanwhile he could watch the rise and fall of
ministries with philosophic calm. In July 1834 Lord Grey
resigned, and Lord Melbourne became Premier. Place
supposed that Brougham would now be the real leader of
the Whigs, and knew that in that case the Lords must
either fight or submit to continued humiliation.

"There must be a decisive quarrel with the Lords some
day, and the Lords will in the end be beaten. I think the
Chancellor is the man to carry on a series of useful sub-
ordinate quarrels, which may prepare the way for the
ultimate quarrel, and make it when it comes as little
mischievous and as short as possible. If, for instance,
the Chancellor begins with some measures likely to be
popular, e.g. newspaper stamps, which can and will be
usefully worked out of doors, and the Lords choose to
quarrel with it, and if they should make the quarrel
last for some time, the beating they will get will be of
importance in more ways than one. If the Lords should
swallow the pill without much carping at it, they will
have prepared their noble throats for a bolus, and that
may be the repeal of so much of the 27th clause of the
Reform Act as relates to payments of rates and taxes
as a disqualifying clause. If stamps be removed and
good teaching follows, the machine will work more freely
with little friction, and therefore with very little chance

of breaking any material part of it. Otherwise, it may
go, as the engineers say, 'smash at once.' These are the
general reasons why I wish Brougham to lead." [1]

Melbourne's sudden dismissal by the King on the
appointment of Wellington left him quite unmoved. In
December 1834 he wrote: "With respect to politics as
they now stand, I am quite at ease. Before Wellington
first took office, yet when a change was seen to be at
hand, Hobhouse, being then at the Duke of Bedford's
at Woburn, wrote to me for my opinion respecting
probable public proceedings. I, in reply, said there never
could be what was called a strong or, as to time, a long
administration until very great changes in the whole plan
and system of government had happened. Wellington's
administration cannot continue for two years, and whose
is to follow his? And whose that? &c. &c. In five years
boys now fifteen years of age will be men. In ten years
boys who are ten years old will be men, men of twenty,
thirty, and so on, and time will have quietly sent a large
number of old prejudiced aristocrats to the grave, and
substituted for them young, energetic fellows, brought up
very generally without reverence for authority, and imbued
with notions of representative government. I need not
point out to you the consequences." [2]

Peel on his return from Italy, in December, took over
the premiership from Wellington, and at once dissolved
Parliament. The Whigs came back from the election
seriously weakened in numbers, and dependent for any
possible majority upon Irish and Radical support. A
rough note made by Place at the time states that
Warburton called, on February 9, 1835, ". . . and we
had a very long conversation respecting a plan he had
suggested some time before, and was diligently employed

[1] Place to Parkes, July 17, 1834.
[2] Place to J. Prout, December 21, 1834.

in carrying into effect. It was to induce the reformers, under himself, the Whigs under Lord John Russell, and the Irish under Daniel O'Connell to concur in such matters as were common to all these parties, and agree to sink minor differences and work together for such objects as the three should point out. There were two circumstances on which it seemed essential they should concur, the Speaker and the Address." [1]

A further note says: " 20th February.—The House met last night, and contrary to my expectations elected Mr. Abercrombie, Speaker. This is a good beginning." And on February 25, he writes: "I was much pleased that the amendment to the Address had been carried by a majority of seven."

On April 8, 1835, Peel resigned, and Lord Melbourne took office. But Place's satisfaction at the alliance between the Whigs and the Radicals lasted very few weeks. The Radicals in Parliament felt that they ought to avoid anything which would embarrass the Government, and Place found to his horror that no one, not even Joseph Hume, was willing to continue that resolute assertion of democratic principles in the House, without which the development of democratic opinion in the country could not proceed.

One result of the alliance was that the abolition of the newspaper stamp seemed further off than ever. Since 1819, when the 4d. stamp duty was extended to every periodical costing less than 6d.,[2] Place had fought against " Taxes on Knowledge." As long as the Tories were in power Lord Liverpool, or even Canning, could consistently advocate the restriction of political discussion. But the fact that the Whigs had now held office since 1830, and that the tax remained undiminished, was only to be explained by

---

[1] Loose sheet in Letter Book, 1835.
[2] See p. 148, note.

their rooted disbelief in every principle which they professed to hold.

Year after year Place had brought the question forward.[1] Every year the Chancellor of the Exchequer declared himself in favour of repeal in principle, and every year the Government, for reasons which they dared not avow, continued the tax. Meanwhile the Commissioners of Stamps so used their power of prosecution as to set up a peculiarly odious form of censorship. The *Penny Magazine*, for instance, was allowed to circulate unstamped, while the *Poor Man's Guardian* was prosecuted. Place had suffered personally from the tax. Directly after the general election of 1832, Roebuck and he revived an old plan of starting a penny weekly paper, with the awe-inspiring title of the *Political and Moral Magazine*. Place was to be editor, and offered to give to the work six or seven hours a day.

"If I became editor," he writes to Roebuck, "I should

[1] In January 1831 he had published one of the best and most forcible of his pamphlets, "A letter to a Minister of State respecting Taxes on Knowledge," of which many thousands had been since distributed. On June 15, 1832, Bulwer in the Commons moved for a Committee on the subject. He made a long speech from notes provided by Place, and Lord Althorp congratulated him on the industry which he had shown in his investigation of the subject, and opposed his motion "entirely on a financial ground." This debate was printed by the National Political Union, with notes by Place. In 1833 Althorp mentioned the matter in the Commons, but did nothing. In 1834 Lord Brougham gave evidence before the Committee on Libel Law in favour of complete repeal, which Place reprinted, and circulated 10,000 copies. (Place to Ebenezer Elliott, July 9, 1834. See Repeal of the Stamp Duty, Roebuck's pamphlet for December 1835, p. 8.) He wrote articles on the subject for any paper which would take them, and his letter-books contain a long series of indignant appeals to friends and strangers. The great London dailies were against the abolition of the stamp as likely to injure their monopoly, and on January 19, 1833, the *Times* printed on its leader page an abusive little paragraph against Place (and by implication Lord Althorp) for a supposed plot to destroy its circulation. Grote used to call the repeal of the stamp Place's hobby. (Place to Hume, January 3, 1837.)

Y

make a business of it, and I foresee that it would occupy me six hours a day at the least. To enable me to bestow so much time upon it I must use the mornings for my own affairs, and for such other persons and their affairs as I cannot with justice abandon, to seeing such persons as I may wish to see, or cannot refuse to see, and to taking exercise. I must dine at three, and employ all the rest of the day on the work, rigidly excluding everybody with the exception of some half-a-dozen members of Parliament, whom, for reasons obvious to you, I must admit at all times. . . . If I were willing to let the publication be of the ordinary cast of vulgar politics, I might save half of the time, or even more than half of the time, I have mentioned, but I will not do these things. I think the publication may be made a vehicle to promulgate the true principles of politics, political economy and morals, with such practical applications of these principles in so popular a way as to command the attention and obtain the respect of men who have cultivated understandings, and at the same time please and instruct the working people to an extent which for their own sakes may induce them to purchase it." [1]

James Mill agreed with the project, and he, John Mill, the Grotes, Charles Buller, W. J. Fox, Edwin Chadwick, and others, were to write for it. The necessary funds were provided, and there only remained the question of the newspaper stamp. Warburton, the Vice-President of the proposed company, tried to get Lord Althorp to promise privately that if an assurance were given that no "annoyance of Ministers" were intended by the paper it should not be prosecuted; but Lord Althorp would give no such promise, and on February 5, 1833, refused in answer to a question in the House to pledge himself to a repeal of the tax. The proposal, therefore, was abandoned. "Ministers," wrote Place, "and men in power, with nearly

---

[1] Place to Roebuck, December 27, 1832.

the whole body of those who are rich, dread the consequences of teaching the people more than they dread the effect of their ignorance."[1]

It may be feared that the life of the paper would in any case have been short. The *Political and Moral Magazine* might have been a treasure-house for the future historian, it might have influenced those few working-men and others who can be "induced to purchase papers for their own sakes," that is to say, for the sake of their more serious selves; but the general public would certainly have continued to read publications "of the ordinary cast of vulgar politics." Yet because the Government had prevented the experiment from being tried, the good that the paper might have done grew yearly more important in Place's mind.

A milder man, indeed, than Place might have lost patience when, on May 1, 1835, he received a letter from Hume stating that it was his "wish not to do anything as regards the tax upon newspapers until we know what is to be done by the Ministers," and that meanwhile "any petitions got up or stir made might not do good but harm if Ministers really mean to repeal, of which we can have no knowledge until they all return (from re-election)."[2]

Place replied: "My dear Sir,—Here comes probably the last long political letter you will ever be called upon to read of my writing. . . . I do not in the least comprehend . . . how you would come to the conclusion . . . that no one should 'stir' because 'we can have no knowledge, &c.' If you had said we *must* stir because 'we can have no knowledge, &c.,' it would have been rational. I have lately been congratulating myself that I no longer reside at Charing Cross, and had nearly broken up my connection

---

[1] MS. account of the "Society for the Diffusion of Political and Moral Knowledge."

[2] Hume to Place, April 24, 1835.

with the dawdlers, and that with the exception of two or
three of my parliamentary friends I could now and then,
as I occasionally do, see others, and talk with them on any
subject, barring politics. If it were not that the people do
at times respond to a call made in the right way, I should
have given up all interference in public political matters,
hopeless of any good results. I shall now probably pursue
a course independently of parliamentary men as associated,
and I believe I can do more good without them than with
them.

" When did any Minister, either Whig or Tory, keep his
promise to you ? How often during more than twenty
years have you maintained and acted on the only sound
doctrine, that to accomplish any public purpose steady
perseverance was necessary at all times, and in all seasons,
in good report and in evil report ; and how much good you
have produced, how much evil you have prevented, no one
knows accurately, no, not even yourself."

He then reminds Hume of Lord Althorp's action in
1833: " We were cajoled, as men usually are who rely on
others and refrain from doing their duty to themselves.
Lord Althorp mentioned the subject in the House, but in
such a way as just to enable him to say, as he did say, as
any thorough-going Whig would have said, that he had
proposed the measure, but the House showed no particular
feeling on the subject, so he did not press it. There was
no particular feeling ; no, we had been stultified, and had
neglected the means necessary to produce a feeling. It
shall be no fault of mine if any Minister ever has the
opportunity to repeat Lord Althorp's words. If Ministers
mean us honestly, they will encourage the people to show
themselves, and their desire for the repeal. If they
understood their own position, they would promote the
repeal promptly and vigorously. They would make it
matter of conscience, and not give the Tories a chance to

take the credit of doing it. I am persuaded that there is
as much chance of its being done by a Tory as by a
Whig administration, and I should greatly prefer a Tory
administration which would take off the duty, to a Whig
administration which would not take it off. Scarcely any
man in Parliament besides Lord Brougham appears to know
the actual value of the repeal. In a moral point of view it
is what Archimedes wanted to have in a physical point of
view, a place to stand upon, a fulcrum to move the world.
Do you recollect the fable of the wolves who wished the sheep
to send away the dogs ? If you do not, go and read it." [1]

Hume, though, like Bismarck's emperor, he required
winding up at intervals, still went steadily enough when
he was wound up, and took part in the deputation to
Spring Rice, the Chancellor of the Exchequer, on May 8.
On this occasion " the Exchequer Chancellor told us," writes
Place, " as plainly as any courtier could do who did not use
the words, that we should never have the Stamp Duty
repealed as long as he had the power to prevent it." [2]

On March 30, 1835, the Report of the Municipal Corporations Commission was presented to Parliament. Place's
collection of manuscripts and materials on Municipal Corporations has, unfortunately, been lost, but there is some
evidence that he helped his friend Joseph Parkes with the
preparation of the Report. Parkes, for instance, speaks of
having "inhabited" Place's library in Brompton Square
during May 1834. [3] When the Report was presented the

[1] Place to Hume, May 2, 1835.
[2] Place to Hume, May 12, 1835.
[3] Besides collecting books and papers on municipal corporations,
Place had occasionally concerned himself with the question for some
years past. In 1830, for instance, he had drawn up for Hume a motion
for a return respecting city and borough corporations. In the letter in
which he forwarded a draft of the motion, he wrote of it as a " first
step " in the consideration of the subject, rendered necessary by the fact
that " no man has any knowledge of the municipal laws and customs of
nine out of ten corporations."

Tories were still in office, but even the Whigs, when they came in, showed no eagerness to act upon it.

In his angry letter to Hume of May 2, 1835, Place, after dealing with the newspaper stamp question, proceeds: "Then comes the Corporation Bill. Not a line of this Bill has been penned, nor any plan been brought under consideration. About a week hence it will begin to be taken into consideration, and then come discussions, disputings, writings, printings, revising, and then the matter must be considered by another body. Then will commence the drawing of a Bill to go through the same processes, and by the end of July it may perchance be in Committee in the House of Commons. That any Bill on this subject can pass the House of Commons this session is out of all reasonable expectation."

Against this passage Place writes a marginal note, dated June 4, 1835: "It was found that not to present a Bill as early as could well be done was a risk Ministers could not take, so one was drawn by some of the Commissioners and the Secretary (Parkes), and it is to be presented to-morrow. It is as good as they who drew it dared to make it. It will be altered before presented."

On May 11 Place had written to Parkes saying: "There is now a just complaint that no one interests himself as he ought to do respecting municipal corporations," and enclosing a statement of the "Principles upon which Municipal Government ought to be founded." Parkes replied by proposing that Place should edit a temporary shilling weekly to appear during the remainder of the session, and to be paid for, apparently, out of the party funds.

Place's statement of principles accordingly appeared on June 5 (the day on which Lord John Russell introduced the Bill) as part of the prospectus of the *Municipal Corporation Reformer*, a paper which was to be "a history of a political measure second only in importance to the reformation of Parliament." In the prospectus Place proposes that each town should be governed by a single council of thirteen to thirty-one members, elected annually by household suffrage and the ballot, for single member wards, without property qualification or privileged aldermen. The deliberations of these bodies were to be public, and detailed administration was to be carried out by very small responsible committees, who should be paid for their work, membership of the council, as such, being unpaid. The powers of the councils were to include the control of the magistrates, police, and gaols, of paving, lighting, water, markets, bridges, docks, harbours, sewers, &c., the making of bye-laws, and the administration of all town property and trusts for hospitals, schools, and charities. In his private notes for June 1835 he writes that upwards of 60,000 copies of the prospectus of the *Municipal Reformer* have been printed and distributed;[1] and adds "a goodly mass of republican notions these." On June 13 the *Municipal Corporation Reformer* began to appear. Five numbers only were published, the reason of this comparative failure being, according to Place, that the "expected fierce opposition to the Bill" did not show itself, and that "people relied on the House of Commons and gave themselves little trouble about the proceedings." Perhaps the party contributions to the expense of publishing may have been checked by such incidents as Place's beginning the first number with a detailed and damaging comparison in parallel columns between his own proposals and the Government Bill, and slipping into it a dig at his old enemy, the ratepaying clauses of the Reform Bill.

On July 20 the Bill passed the House of Commons almost unchanged. It soon, however, became clear that

[1] See also an article by Place, entitled "The Peers and the People," in Roebuck's *Pamphlets for the People*, August 29, 1835, where the "principles" are reprinted, and the same statement is made.

Lord Lyndhurst was organising a campaign against it in the Lords. On August 2 Place writes: " Requested to attend a meeting at the house of Mr. Parkes. The Lords are expected to throw out the Corporation Bill. . . . Wrote letter to Mr. Parkes, dated August 3. Copied by Mr. Parkes, original sent to Lord Melbourne."[1]

In this letter he said: " You know that from the first I did not expect that the Lords would pass the Municipal Reform Bill. Now I conclude that every reasonable man is of the same opinion. The Lords reason thus: ' We have already lost more than one of the means we long possessed of influencing the House of Commons. . . . If we lose the advantages which accrue to us from close corporations, if we destroy the affinity between ourselves and these boroughs, the people will be emboldened to proceed to much greater lengths, and will gain power continually at we lose it.' These are arguments which the silliest soul that ever was a lord could understand, and they are acted upon by a majority of the House of Lords.[2] . . . It was fear, not altogether ill-founded, which induced them to agree to the Parliamentary Reform Bill. They see no such pressing necessity now. They are not acted upon by fear to the same extent, and they calculate upon the imbecility of Ministers. It is this imbecility which I too fear. If Ministers had obtained a character for decision and sturdiness, the people would have shown their determination to support them, and this would have operated beneficially on the Lords. They are now rapidly approaching what to them will appear a very great difficulty, but which to more determined men would appear to be no difficulty at all. Their course, if

---

[1] Diary, August 1835.

[2] Lord Lyndhurst, August 3, 1835, said in the House of Lords, " If they (the Corporations) fell, the Church would come next, and the hereditary peerage of the realm afterwards."

they choose to take it, is very simple, and may be described in very few words. They must demand of the
King that he should prorogue the Parliament for, say, five
days, and then hold a short session to pass the Bills. If
the King should refuse, the Ministers should at once
resign, and state in the two Houses the reason why. This
would convince the people that there was a body of
men deserving of public confidence, and to them they
would give it most heartily. . . . No Tory administration
could remain in office." [1]

The second reading in the Lords was carried, but Lord
Lyndhurst and the Tory majority transformed the Bill
beyond all recognition in Committee. Place, who was
confined to his room with sciatica, raged gloriously.
"The Lords," he wrote to Hume, August 30, "have
made a Bill which cannot be amended, a Bill which, however much it may be tinkered at, can never be made
acceptable to the nation, a Bill that will bring disgrace on
all who in the House of Commons may endeavour to make
it passable. . . . The preamble is quite enough. The
alterations made in the preamble are intentional insults,
and should be treated as such. . . . Collision with the
Lords cannot be avoided. They have placed you in
circumstances in which collision or disgrace, little short
of infamy, must be chosen."

"People," he wrote to Parkes on September 5, "silly,
puling people, aye, and those too who ought to know
better, are talking of 'revolutionary measures.' To oppose
Ministers is to promote violent, bloody revolution, plunder,
rape, and the devil knows what besides. . . . The drivellers,
and yet there is not a damned soul among them who does
not say the Lords *must* be reorganised. . . . Reorganise,
indeed; pretty fellows these to be reorganisers, they who
take a kick like dogs, wag their tails, and take another

---

[1] Place to Parkes, August 3, 1835.

kick. . . . Aye, aye, say you, but what if Billy [his Majesty
King William IV.] damned and ——ed his eyes as he
is apt to do, and refused to prorogue? What! why, a
little wholesome agitation like one of those thunder-
storms which purify the air, and do no harm to any one.
. . . Bloody revolution, indeed; no, no, there never can
be such a revolution as long as the people have confidence
in the House of Commons. If we are ever to have a
bloody revolution, it must be from want of confidence in
the House of Commons."

Peel, in the Commons, refused to support the Lords'
amendments; a compromise was arranged, and the Bill was
passed.

On September 30 Parkes wrote: "We have got on a stage,
and you, old postillion, well know it." "Yes," answered
Place on the same day, "and a good one; but recollect
that this was not the question, never was made the
question by me. The question was, Ought Ministers to
have put up with the kicking the Lords bestowed upon
them? I say no; the time was as critical as propitious for
them, and they ought to have turned upon their assailants.
The Lords will not be reformed, not they, but it is good
to make every one see that they must either be reformed
or abolished, that, whenever the time comes, the abolition,
cost what it may, may be perfect."

During the winter of 1835-36 Place worked for two
main objects: the reform of the Corporation of London,
which had been omitted in the Bill of 1835, and 'the
abolition of the Newspaper Stamp. His diary for
December 1835 says, "Occupied in reading and com-
menting on Municipal Corporation Commissioners' inquiry
respecting London, with a view to obtaining further particulars, and framing a Bill for the City of London;" and
for January 1836, "Continue reading, inquiring, and
writing in conjunction with Joseph Fletcher on London

Corporation and the report of the Commissioners (the proofs only)."

There is no sign that Place ever contemplated the present unified government of the Metropolis, but side by side with his work for the reform of the Vestries he had for years past been preparing for an attack on the City. After the passing of the Reform Bill in 1832 he refused to attend the City banquet on the ground that "the whole of the City government" was "a burlesque on the human under-standing more contemptible than the most paltry farce played in a booth at Bartholomew's Fair, and more mis-chievous than any man living is prepared to believe."[1]

When his friend Alexander Galloway, engineer and Common Councillor, protested against his refusal, and ascribed it to his having listened to hearsay reports, Place replied: "You know nothing about the information I have, though you do know I endeavoured to procure a good deal from you, and that you gave me very little. You treat the Corporation property as if it were private property. It is no such thing; it is public property, only applicable to public uses. I will say no more now. If I can get away from Charing Cross I will say what I think should be said in print."[2]

In November 1833, shortly after Parkes' appointment as Secretary of the Municipal Corporation Commission, Place wrote to him about "our corrupt, rotting, robbing, in-famous Corporation of London" and the "Court of Aldermen, old men—no, old women, gossiping, guzzling, drinking, cheating, old chandlers'-shop women, elected for life." He then proceeded to propose his own plan of City Government. He wanted a Common Council, consisting of twenty-one members, elected by ballot for twenty-one City wards. "But, says a member of the Common Council—more than one has said so to me—what would

you do for Committees? Why this, make committees
of threes—make commissioners — pay them reasonably,
but let it be known that they are paid, and how much they
are paid, and report the work they have done for the
money. . . . Give the Mayor £1000 a year at the utmost,
and call him lord if you like it—no shows, no parade, no
feasts, no fooleries. Let there be, say, seven aldermen
at £400 a year each, or a smaller sum to pay them for
their magisterial duties." Never was work more completely wasted than Place's efforts to reform the City.
The mysterious engines of City influences were brought
to bear upon the Government; the Bill which had been
promised for 1836 never appeared, and the proof report
was never even printed.

Meanwhile the question of the Newspaper Stamp was
becoming so urgent that not even Lord Melbourne's
Government could let it alone. Every month the unstamped newspapers increased their sale, and the Government increased its severity. Between 1830 and 1836
there were 728 prosecutions for selling unstamped papers,
219 of which were in 1835, and a still larger proportion
in the first two months of 1836.[1] Hetherington, the proprietor of the *Poor Man's Guardian*, was hiding to avoid
arrest; and Cleave, the editor of the unstamped *Cleave's
Gazette*, was in prison until he could pay £600 penalties,
as well as heavy costs.[2]

In January 1836 Place revived a scheme of the year
before for agitation by correspondence against the stamp.
A ground-floor room in Leicester Square was taken, and
there Place's friend, Dr. Black,[3] and a few working-men
volunteers used to spend their evenings addressing

[1] Hume's speech at the deputation to Lord Melbourne, February 11,
1836.   [2] Ibid.
[3] Dr James Roberts Black of Kentucky, a cadaverous American,
who had come to London in 1834. He cherished a vague project of

circulars, answering letters, and organising petitions. "There were no paid clerks, no messengers, no advertising in newspapers, no public meetings, yet a correspondence was opened with very nearly 3000 respectable persons who were distributed all over the country."[1]

Roebuck was meanwhile evading the law by publishing a weekly undated pamphlet, written by himself, Place, and others, which at one time had a sale of 10,000.[2] On February 11 a deputation saw Lord Melbourne at the Treasury, and Dr. Birkbeck, Hume, Place, and others made long speeches against the tax. Place's great fear was that the Government, with the Whig instinct for slipshod compromise, would lower the stamp instead of abolishing it.

On March 15 Spring Rice, on behalf of the Government, brought forward exactly the scheme which Place had feared. He proposed to deal with stamp duties of all kinds by a long consolidating Act, a clause of which was to lower the newspaper stamp from fourpence to a penny. At the same time the law against unstamped publications was to be made much more stringent, and was to apply to pamphlets as well as newspapers.

Against these proposals Place for the next five months kept up a dogged contest, writing and publishing three pamphlets in March and April, supplying Wakley and Duncombe with notes for their speeches, and trying in vain to stir Hume into vigorous opposition. He was convinced that the Bill would diminish rather than in-

establishing working-men's educational associations. He became Place's constant disciple and follower. Place's grandchildren still remember his visits, and the stern tones in which he used to be reproved for spitting into the fender.

[1] 27,819 (26).

[2] See the pamphlets in British Museum. They contain some of Place's best journalistic work. For the figures as to the circulation, see "James Mill: a Biography," by Alexander Bain, p. 398.

crease the opportunities of obtaining information open to
the working classes. The penny unstamped papers had
succeeded in spite of the law in acquiring a large circulation,
Spring Rice himself stated that one paper which had been
seized before publication was found to be printing forty
thousand copies a week.[1] The new law would put a stop
to all this, and while the rich men's sevenpenny paper
would be reduced to fourpence-halfpenny or fivepence,
the poor man's penny paper would be raised from one
penny to twopence-halfpenny.[2] But the Government,
though they dropped the stamp on pamphlets, kept to
the rest of their proposals, and their Bill was accepted as
a settlement of the question. It was not till 1855 that
the penny stamp was abolished, and only with the repeal
of the advertisement duty in 1853, and the paper duty in
1861, that Taxes on Knowledge ceased, and a penny daily
press became possible in England.

In 1836 nearly the whole Parliamentary session was spent
on an Irish Municipal Bill, which was thrown out by the
Lords and abandoned by the Ministry. Lord Melbourne
remained in office for five more years, and did not retire
until he had finally exhausted any political good-will which
still attached to the name of Whig. His lordship's personal
comfort during those years was possibly increased by the
fact that Place, after 1836, definitely gave up his work
as parliamentary "postillion." "When Fox coalesced with
North," he wrote to Roebuck in October 1836, "it produced
much the same result as the coalition of Whigs and
Radicals is now producing. It made the people distrust
all public men, it put an end to their meetings and their
efforts to procure a reform of the House of Commons,
and this state continued for eight years, when the French
Revolution again roused them and brought them into

[1] Hansard, June 20, 1836.
[2] Letter to Hobhouse, August 10, 1836.

action. . . . Had the House acted properly, had the Reformers acted sensibly and boldly, no one can tell what beneficial changes might have been effected, . . . and why have not these things been done? Why, but because Ministers must be kept in their places; the live lumber, Lord John and Lord Melbourne, and Spring Rice and John Hobhouse, and Glenelg, &c., must not be removed."[1]

He always believed that the Radicals in the House, if they had shown anything like courage, would have crystallised round themselves the growing popular discontent. "Had he at that time (1835) taken the position he ought to have taken," Place wrote of Hume in 1840, "he would soon have been joined by others; but even if he had stood alone for a time, scolded at by Lord John and Lord the Devil and all his imps, . . . he would long ere this have become emphatically the people's man, instead of being as he is now, next to nothing in their estimation."[2]

Or again, "A man in our House of Commons should never compromise. He should always be ready to take whatever he could get, but always under protest, always as a move forwards towards the attainment of the large reform he contemplated, and he should be careful to make the public understand what he intended."

For a moment in 1836 Place even wished that he was in the House. "Vanity apart," he wrote to Roebuck, "or vanity indulged, I care not which, but I do believe that were I in the House, you and I could, aye, and would, do much of what ought to be done, though we should be both bitterly hated—despised we could not be—but the hatred even would not last beyond a session or two."[3]

John Stuart Mill wrote to Place in February 1837, urging him not to "hibernate." Place retorted by declaring, "I

[1] Place to Roebuck, October 3, 1836.
[2] Place to Roebuck, December 23, 1840.
[3] Place to Roebuck, October 3, 1836.

have no present inclination to waste my time with men who are infirm of purpose, and worry myself to no useful purpose." Mill himself was still of an age and inclination to hope for something even of Lord Melbourne; and in writing to Fonblanque, said of this letter, "I shall keep it as a memorial of the spiritless, heartless, imbecility of the English Radicals." [1]

[1] See John Stuart Mill : "Notices of his Life and Works," reprinted from the *Examiner* (London, 1873), p. 8.

CHAPTER XIII

CHARTISM

DURING the Reform agitation Place had noticed that many working-men in London and Lancashire opposed the Bill on the ground that it would strengthen the position of their employers, and that the interest of their employers was necessarily opposed to their own.[1] They believed that, under the conditions of modern industry, the capitalist was enabled in the process of buying labour and selling commodities to retain a huge proportion of the value which labour produced. The clearness of this conception varied, of course, from the definite economic creed of those who had been the personal disciples of Owen or Hodgskin, to the conviction which Bronterre O'Brien inspired in the readers of the *Poor Man's Guardian*, that somehow science was on their side, or the vague feeling of the factory hands that others were growing unjustly rich at their expense.

In the disappointment which followed the passing of the Reform Bill this doctrine spread rapidly, and soon came to form part of the content of the new word "socialism."[2] To its influence were mainly due the two

[1] See p. .
[2] Perhaps the earliest recorded use of this term is in the *Poor Man's Guardian* for August 24, 1833, where a letter appears signed "A Socialist." At first it seems to have meant little more than "Owenite," and the transition to a more general meaning may be seen in a remark of Bronterre O'Brien in the *Northern Star*, June 23, 1838. "If I mis-

most dramatic events of English working-class history—
the Grand National Trades Union of 1833–34, and the
Chartist movement of 1837–39.

John Doherty[1] had been preaching since 1829, that all
the trade unions should be combined in one national
federation, which could be used to secure to the workmen
the whole product of their labour. In 1833 his scheme
was adopted by almost all the existing working-class
organisations. Robert Owen and John Fielden[2] threw
themselves into the movement, which within a few months
enrolled half a million members, and Fielden suggested
that the campaign should be opened by a general strike
for an eight hours' day on March 1, 1834.[3]

Lord Melbourne had been anxiously watching the trade
unions ever since he became Home Secretary, and in August
1833 he issued a solemn warning as to the "criminal
character and evil effects" of the new federation. On
November 4 Joseph Parkes wrote to Place, and offered
on behalf of the Government to print and circulate a
pamphlet if Place would write it, giving "a brief, plain
exposition of the doctrine of wages, an epitome of the
repealed and present law of combination, and advice to
the working classes."[4] Place answered, "If I were sure
that I should not be losing my time I would write such a
paper, but then I should be for doing the workmen the
justice which no one seems to like to have done, and would

take not, all the more intelligent Socialists are becoming Radicals, and
all the more intelligent Radicals are becoming Socialists. . . ." Place,
writing in 1841, says that the people are misled " by notions of equality
in respect to property, and by the doctrines promulgated by Robert
Owen, now known under the name of Socialism." 27,519 (5).

[1] See p. 265.
[2] John Fielden (1784-1849), the Radical M.P. for Oldham, and
supporter of the Ten Hours Bill.
[3] For the whole movement, see Webb, "History of Trade Unionism,"
chapter iii.
[4] Parkes to Place, November 4, 1833.

not assist to promulgate."[1] A month later Place wrote
to Parkes complaining that the factory commissioner
Tufnell had treated the subject in "The Companion to
the Newspaper" purely from the master's point of view,[2]
and Parkes in replying again urged him to write.[3]

Meanwhile the "Grand National Trades Union" was
growing daily, and the Government, Place was told, were
considering a Bill to double the penalties in the Combination Law of 1825. Place wrote instantly to Tom Young,[4]
urging Lord Melbourne to give up this "worse than absurd
proposal," stating that he was "even now carrying on a
correspondence with some members of the committee at
Manchester, to whom I speak as plainly as possible," and
promising to write "one or more addresses to the workmen
when their present foolish project has failed, as it soon will
fail, and when they, in consequence of its failure, will be
disposed to attend to what may he written to them."[5]
His prophecy seemed likely to be fulfilled almost at once.
The funds of the "Grand National" were wasted in a series
of sectional strikes which the executive were powerless to
prevent, and the great eight hours' strike ordered for March 1
was hardly attempted. The movement was already moribund when, on March 17, six agricultural labourers from a
little village near Dorchester were sentenced to the outrageous punishment of seven years' transportation for
"administering illegal oaths" while forming a branch of
the Grand National. Immediately the whole agitation
revived, and a middle-class member of the Manchester
Executive wrote to Place " Ça ira, Ministers have furnished

---

[1] Place to Parkes, November 8, 1833.
[2] Place to Parkes, December 7, 1833.
[3] Parkes said that he had sent Place's letter to Miss Harriet Martineau,
who, as well as Place and Tufnell, seems to have been approached by
the Home Office.
[4] See p. 303.
[5] Place to T. Young, January 8, 1834.

the stimulus. We were very near the condition you predicted we should be in. We are now upon our legs again."[1] Things looked so formidable that Place determined to write at once. He accordingly produced early in April two essays, one the examination of a chairman's speech at the Birmingham meeting held to protest against the Dorchester sentences, and the other entitled "Trades Unions (*i.e.* Federations of Trades) condemned, Trades Clubs justified." These essays, with two others, "Trade Clubs, Strikes, Wages," and "Trades Unions and Trade Clubs of various kinds compared," were too impartial, and perhaps too long, for the purposes of the Government. Parkes did not publish them, and they still remain in manuscript.[2]

On April 21 the London working-men made a huge procession to the Home Office on behalf of the Dorchester labourers, which is the only incident of trade unionism before 1867 that has penetrated into the history books. Place was in constant communication with members of the London committee, explaining the law relating to petitions, and trying to prevent them from breaking it. On the morning of the demonstration he wrote to Parkes, urging the Government to let the processionists alone. "There will be an immense assemblage of people, but of they be let alone and no displays of a provocating nature be made against them, all will go off quietly."[3] "The people," he said a few days before the procession, "would go through the job they had set themselves, and when completely fatigued, as they would be by four or five o'clock in the afternoon, they would go home."[4] At the same time, he gave his own opinion of the conduct

[1] See Place to Parkes, April 21, 1834.
[2] They make up the volume 27,834.
[3] Place to Parkes, April 21, 1834.
[4] Loose MS., dated April 1834.

of the Ministers. "Had the sentence," he wrote, "been passed on the Dorchester labourers and then remitted, had a proclamation been issued [as he had urged immediately after the sentence] declaring the law, and the determination to enforce it, been made, an end would have been put to all the Unions. But the fact is, and it is useless to conceal it, our Ministers have no energy in any case except against the common people." [1] The Government did let the procession alone, and on the next day Lord Melbourne consented to receive a small deputation on behalf of the trades. Tom Young afterwards reported that the Cabinet decided to carry out the sentence, "lest it should be inferred that they had remitted it through fear;" and when Brougham, four years later, was accused by Place of this "narrow-minded cowardice," he admitted that the charge was true.[2]

The law was not changed, but Place had the greatest difficulty in keeping the Government from active administrative interference on the side of the masters in the strikes which occurred in and near London. "The men," he says "working at the gasworks in Westminster struck for an increase of wages, and the chairmen or secretaries of the several companies went to Lord Melbourne, the Home Secretary, and made complaints which the Secretary with singular folly was disposed to entertain; but a gentleman from his office came to me, and I advised him seriously to send away all complainants in such cases with a recommendation to exert themselves in their own concerns. I convinced him that if the Home Secretary was silly enough to interpose in such matters, his time would be wholly occupied with the complaints of, and deputations from.

[1] Place to Parkes, April 21, 1834.
[2] Note in loose MS., dated April 1834. The sentence was remitted in 1836, and the men brought back in 1838. See Webb, "History of Trade Unionism," p. 133.

masters and men."[1] This last argument was likely to
appeal strongly to a man of Lord Melbourne's temperament, and at the same time, as far as his lordship had
any principle, he probably did believe in *laisser faire*.
The gas directors were therefore sent away empty. The
master coopers were at first more fortunate; their men
had struck against a new scale of piece-work by which
wages were seriously reduced, and Sir James Graham,
the First Lord of the Admiralty, " ordered the journeymen
who were employed by Government at the Victualling
Office, Deptford, to make casks for the masters, and permitted the masters to circulate a notice that the trade
might be supplied with casks from his Majesty's Victualling
Office." [2]

Place set up Hume to question the Government. A
long debate ensued on March 13, 1834, in which Sir
James Graham expressed his opinion that the repeal of
the Combination Laws in 1824 had been "questionable
in theory, and in point of practical prudence extremely
doubtful," but promised to discontinue his interference.
On November 14 the London Block Coopers, with an
unusual impulse of gratitude, wrote to Place, stating their
intention of calling the next Sunday morning to present
him with a " Model of a Brewhouse Butt" as a "mark of
respect for . . . the assistance you gave them during their
late strike." [3]

By that time the " Grand National" was broken up, the
" rights of industry men" were defeated, and trade
unionism had received a set back, the effects of which
were felt for the next ten years. Place enforced his view
of the moral upon the sore and beaten Manchester Committee with a plainness of speech which in spite of his

[1] Loose MS., dated April 24.
[2] Ibid.
[3] Family autograph book.

evident sincerity and good-will must have been very hard
to bear. "You will recollect," he writes to James Turner
of Manchester on October 19, 1834, "that when the
scheme was first set on foot to reduce the hours of
working from twelve to eight, retaining the twelve hours'
pay, I told you that the scheme would fail, and I told you
why it would fail, and nothing be done. You know how
it did fail, and nothing was done. Here again I shall be
told that if the working people had held together the
scheme would have been carried into effect. Aye, to be
sure it would; but this was not at all likely, not at all
possible. The working people never did agree on any one
subject, and no man in his senses can expect that even
a twentieth part of them are at all likely to concur in
anything which requires time for its accomplishment.
The working people could, if they chose, establish a purely
representative government on the 1st of March next, and
it is just as likely they will do so as it was that they would
demand eight hours' work and twelve hours' pay on the
1st of March last."

Trade unionism as a means of securing social equality
was now discredited, but the causes which had produced
the "Grand National" were still active, and any proposal which offered a chance of successful revolution was
certain of working-class support. Such a proposal was
drafted in the year 1838 by Place himself, under the
name of the "People's Charter," and issued by the
Working-Men's Association, the leading members of
which were Place's own disciples. In 1835 and 1836
Place and his friend, Dr. J. R. Black, had induced
William Lovett and a few other members of the defunct
National Union of the Working Classes to help in the
agitation against the newspaper stamp.[1] In 1836 the
stamp had been reduced to a penny by a settlement

[1] See p. 348.

which it seemed to be impossible to upset for some time
to come, and Black, whose main idea had always been the
formation of mutual instruction classes, induced Lovett
to start the " Working-Men's Association for benefiting
politically, morally, and socially the useful classes." Place
suggested that the new association should hold conversation meetings on the lines of those which the more
thoughtful members of the London Corresponding Society
had held forty years earlier. His idea was accepted, and
the meetings were held from half-past ten till one o'clock
at Lovett's coffee-house in Gray's Inn Road every Sunday
morning for the first six months of 1837. Of the discussions at these meetings Place always spoke with warm
admiration. After the first he wrote to Colonel Perronet
Thompson, " You should have been with us this morning.
It was remarked by Chapman, and I assent to it, that he
never in his life heard so much sense and so little nonsense among so many people in the same time." [1]

The subject discussed on that day was " Will Free
Trade reduce wages ? " The slips of paper on which Place
made the notes for his own speech, and took down the
points of his opponents, are still preserved.[2] They contain
a singularly compact summary of the three main forms of

[1] Place to Thompson, January 8, 1837.
[2] The notes are as follows :—
"(Place.) No wages if no capital ; certain number of capitalists ;
ditto labourers. Increase of labourers ; none of capital ; wages fall.
Increase of cap(ital) ; none of lab(ourers) ; wages rise. Increase of
both ; wages remain. Inevitable in periods of, say, ten years. Master
cannot reduce wages unless pop(ulation), &c. Cannot prevent increase
of pop(ulation). Masters strike ; men strike ; undersell one another.
Unions, i.e. general unions of all trades, cannot do any good. Trade
societies may ; can only impede, not prevent, fall of wages ; always
weak when trade bad, and vice versa. Produce dividend : (1) Rent,
(2) Wages, (3) Profit ; cannot be otherwise ; no capital, no wages. No
wages, no produce.
"(Owen.) We can support all Europe. Lose our time in discussing
these subjects. Question, is there knowledge enough among the

economic analysis which during the nineteenth century have been presented as political creeds. Place gives the "classical" political economy of mid-century Liberalism, Robert Owen the voluntary communism of Proudhon and Bakounin, and Lovett the "iron law" on which Marx and Lassalle based their social democracy.

The six or seven leading members of the Working-Men's Association formed an able and fairly homogeneous group. Most of them had left the bench, and were living as newsdealers, journalists, small shopkeepers, or paid officials. Eight or nine years of agitation had made them good speakers and organisers. In those years the freshness had worn off their socialist faith, and some of them were near the time when they would be even unduly dominated by the "political economists" whom they had begun by hating.[1] They genuinely liked and respected Place, and years afterwards Lovett wrote of the "clear-headed and warm-hearted old gentleman,"[2] who helped and taught them.

Among these men Place found not only a new opportunity of influence, but consolation for the weariness and disgust which had made him abandon Parliamentary politics. The good of the working-men had always been the first object of his life, but since his return to politics in 1807, his method of action had brought him into perpetual conflict with the impatience and resentment of working-class feeling. He had toiled as the schoolmaster toils for his pupils, without much hope of gratitude, or even of

working people to put an end to all our institutions? Until equality none done. Equality more easy than any other change.

"(*Lovett.*) People would contend for a better state if they had more political power ; . . . Corn Laws ; agricultural labourers would come in competition with manufactures and reduce wages. Reduction would be spent abroad. Living on potatoes, would still be fed upon potatoes."—[27,319 (259–263)].

[1] See p. 273.

[2] "The Life and Struggles of William Lovett" (London, 1876), p. 164.

understanding. Now, however, a changed note shows itself in his correspondence with Lovett, Vincent, Cleave, and the rest. He is as far as ever from sharing their socialist ideas. But it is as men fighting against his own enemies, and discouraged by his own disappointments, that he thinks of them, and not as the impersonal objects of his work. Just at the time when John Stuart Mill wrote of him as an example of "spiritless and heartless imbecility,"[1] Place was sending a letter of comfort to William Lovett. It is a strange sort of comfort, and illustrates well that close-lipped stoicism which the "greatest happiness principle" was apt to develop among its sterner adherents.

"*January* 12, 1837.—There is a tone of melancholy in your note which I have sometimes observed in your manner. I have the greatest possible regard for you, and you can hardly sufficiently appreciate the pleasure I should receive at observing that you were happy. I conclude that your disposition towards despondency arises from two causes—(1) your health not being robust ; (2) that you dwell too much on the misfortunes and miseries of your fellow-men.

"Now, I have seen as many changes as most men, and have [known] the extremes of poverty, but I never have been melancholy, never despaired, never was really unhappy during twelve consecutive hours, and I will tell you why. When I was very young I was persuaded to believe that ' this was the best of all possible worlds.' I found it a very bad one. I did my best to mend it, as we are both now doing. What, then, is the real difference between us ? This—you look on the dark side of the picture, I on the bright one. Your anticipations of the future are gloomy, mine are the reverse. You lament the past, and suffer the recollections it produces to distress you. I take the past and comparing it with the present see an immense change for the better. I see that this and many other countries cannot be used as they were wont to be used in former times, that they are much further removed from the state of mere animals than they were, and that the sum of happiness is much greater than it was ; and hence I infer that it will continue to increase. The process will be slow, very slow, and probably one of fluctuation, but ever advancing. This it is which consoles me. This it was and is that determined me and determines me to be cheerful, and not to permit myself to be depressed, and to annoy myself with matters which I can neither prevent nor mitigate.

"I never go out, however, without seeing poverty and ignorance, and

---

[1] See p. 352.

am constantly obliged to shake off the uneasy feelings these produce, lest I should become a misanthrope. You and I and all such men are apt to value mankind too highly, but not equally so. In proportion as this notion prevails will be our uneasiness. Look at mankind, calmly, rationally, as they are; see the naked savages; see the ferocious Malays, the murderous Ladrones, and ask yourself what is man as Nature made him? Is he so far above a wild beast as that we should be unhappy on his account? Look from these through all gradations and see what he really is, see what a creature of prejudice, bad passions, and ignorance he is. See what a mass of meanness and roguery prevails among all, even among those who are the most cultivated. Look at those who are not compelled to work with their own hands for their maintenance, and see the vile, degrading notions and practices of this class. Look to those who are able to maintain themselves without any kind of employment; look to the rich, the titled, the proud, conceited aristocracy; look at any and all of them as classes, and nowhere will you find mankind such as you and I would wish to see them. Oh no! it is a picture which in its details is so detestable, so utterly repugnant to my notions, that had I not been convinced that 'this is the best of all possible worlds,' bad as it is, I would have left it many years ago. I settled the question with myself thus, and I advise you to follow my example, since it will make you happier, and enable you to increase the happiness of others. I resolved that nothing I saw, nothing I read, nothing I heard, should make me unhappy. I should have added nothing I suffered—that I would be cheerful. I saw that to better the condition of others to any considerable extent was a long uphill piece of work, that my best efforts would produce very little effect. But I saw very distinctly that I could do nothing better, nothing indeed half so good. This made me go on steadily, and kept me as steadily to my resolve not to be unhappy, let whatever might come.

"Now, Lovett, if every one could be persuaded to think thus, and to act thus, the really unhappy would be but few; and this after all is the great lesson to inculcate. Every one who learned it would have his energy and his means to do good greatly increased.—Yours truly,

"FRANCIS PLACE."

As Place's gospel of cheerfulness ends on a note of patient despair, so Lovett's answering apology for his melancholy is really an assertion of optimism. Lovett had at that time in his socialism what Place could not find in his Malthusian economics, a universal remedy for all suffering and all wrong.

"*January* 16, 1837.—DEAR SIR,—I am fully sensible of your kindness towards me, and if more powerful circumstances did not control my desire to avoid looking on the dark side of the picture, I might profit by your kind advice and resolve to be free from cares and apprehensions. But you know, sir, that our feelings depend on our internal structure, influenced by the external world ; and that our philosophy is not always master of the one, nor possesses an absolute command over the other. A highly favourable organisation may have done much for you in this respect ; especially as you had your difficulties to encounter in the midst of youth and vigour, and now, contemplating the difficulties you have braved, in the enjoyment of the rewards of your labour, having no apprehension for the future, possessing your own comfortable home, and surrounded with your friends, you think the course you have pursued may be followed with advantage by others. Youth and vigour of body give us great power to cope with difficulties, and when success attends our exertions a corresponding state of mind gives us still greater energy to master them. But when youth, and strength, and flow of spirits have been wasted in unrequited toil and poverty, and when after years of great physical and mental exertions, after a life of sobriety and industry, you find yourself losing your physical energies (so necessary for those who have to depend on their labour), and getting more and more involved in difficulties inextricable, and having the cares of a family in whose welfare is your highest hope, you need not be surprised if my tone and manner correspond with my situation. Perhaps the scenes I have had to encounter in my journey may have increased my sympathies for my fellow-men ; and while I believe with you that this is the best world of which I have any hope, yet when I feel conscious of how much could be done to make it a comparative paradise of happiness, instead of the hell of toil, of poverty, and crime we find it, I cannot help lamenting that the wise and intelligent few do not carry their views of reformation beyond making comfortable slaves of the many to pamper and support the few.

"True it is that Nature, by casting the savage in the midst of the forest to contend with wolves and tigers for a subsistence has rendered him scarcely superior to the animals of his prey ; yet when we take into account that she has also bestowed faculties on him which have gradually raised him up to subdue all existence to his purposes, and built up that empire of mind which has turned the waste of oaks and acorns into a blooming garden (and still but in the infancy of its culture) ; and when we see that in proportion to the development of intellect, so are the feelings of sympathy, affection, and friendship, and are the passions of love heightened by a thousand enjoyments, who does not sigh for the extension of knowledge unalloyed by the withering blasts of toiling poverty ? You have drawn a faithful picture of the evils attendant on the different classes we find in this country. These evils, I think, may be fairly traced to the circumstances and constitution of society, and not to the organisation of man. What other feelings can you expect than those of slavish and cringing servility, blended with a lust for mere animal enjoyments, from those who are taught to believe themselves born to toil, and to obtain which they must bend cap

CHARTISM 365

in hand to a being who, not a whit better than themselves, must bend
again to the class above him. What can be expected from those whose
sole occupation and attention are engrossed from youth to age in buying
and selling, cheating and swindling, their fellow-men, in order to amass
wealth which their habits and feelings preclude them from enjoying?
Strong indeed must be the mental energy and moral feeling of the few
who brave the contagious influences of such pursuits and escape with
the philosophy of enjoyment.—From your fellow-citizen,

"WILLIAM LOVETT."

But a few months after the formation of the Working-
Men's Association the leaders found themselves too busy
to write long letters on the causes of human happiness,
or to spend their Sunday mornings in academic discussions. The Association had from the beginning professed political as well as educational objects, and in
February 1837 its political programme was defined at a
meeting in the Crown and Anchor Tavern. This consisted
of the famous "six points"—universal[1] suffrage, the ballot,
payment of members, annual parliaments, equal electoral
districts, and abolition of the property qualification for
Parliament—which together had formed Major Cartwright's
plan of Radical reform as early as 1776, and had been ever
since closely connected with the word Radicalism.

The Radicals in Parliament approached the new body,
and on May 31, 1837, a private meeting was held between
thirteen members of Parliament and about sixty members
of the Association. Eleven members signed the six points,
and a committee was appointed to draft a comprehensive
Bill, to be called "The People's Charter."[2] "None of the
members of Parliament," says Place, "gave himself any
further concern respecting the Bill they agreed to draw."[3]

[1] *i.e.* manhood.
[2] 27,819 (57-220).
[3] The working-men on the committee were Henry Hetherington,
John Cleave, James Watson, Richard Moore, William Lovett, Henry
Vincent. See the list of the founders of the National Union of the
Working Classes, p. 272.

This action of the Association coincided with a sudden revival of working-class interest in politics throughout the country. The comparative prosperity which had prevailed since 1832 was succeeded by a depression of trade in 1836–37, and "Working-Men's Associations" with vaguely revolutionary objects appeared spontaneously in many provincial towns.[1] In August, Henry Vincent and John Cleave, their two best speakers, went on a lecturing tour in the north of England, and founded branches. Early in October, Lovett, their best writer, published a singularly eloquent and pathetic Address to the Working Classes.[2] Place made Hume give him three hundred "franks," and by these and other means, sent copies of the Address from one end of the country to the other.

In the early autumn there was a general election on the occasion of the Queen's accession, at which the Radical party in Parliament was almost annihilated; and in November, Lord John Russell made that declaration of contentment with the Reform Bill of 1832, which earned him the nickname of "Finality Jack," and completed the alienation of the Reformers from the Whigs. In the same month Feargus O'Connor, already well known as the most effective mob orator of his time, began to publish the *Northern Star* at Leeds, and to join advocacy of the "five points of Radicalism" to furious abuse of the New Poor-Law. In December, Attwood and the "currency men" of Birmingham revived the Birmingham Political Union[3] on the basis of universal suffrage. By the spring of 1838 a formidable popular movement had already

[1] Place says that the Working-Men's Association had at one time 150 branches. See Place to Hume, December 19, 1839 (in "Autobiography").

[2] 27,819 (221–224). See the Address, preserved also in the volume of Addresses of the London Working-Men's Association, Brit. Mus. 8138, a (1); cf. also Lovett's "Life and Struggles" (London, 1876), pp. 94–97.

[3] See p. 251, *note*.

developed itself in the manufacturing districts, and great open-air meetings were held, at which the New Poor-Law and the Factory system were denounced, and universal suffrage was demanded as a means of immediate social revolution.

On May 8, 1838, the People's Charter, from which the movement was to take its name, at last appeared in pamphlet form. Place writing at the time gives the history of its production. The committee appointed to draft a Bill the year before had, as has been mentioned, neglected to do so. Early in March 1838, however, Lovett asked help from Place, who "undertook the task upon condition that the points and as much of the detail as the Association could easily put together should be prepared, so that in drawing the Bill I might be well aware of their notions. This was done, and I drew the skeleton of a Bill under appropriate heads, and sent it to Mr. Lovett for Mr. Roebuck to complete, as he had again said he would. But his sad state of health did not permit him to keep his promise, and I therefore made the Charter, Lovett assisting me as he could. The Working-Men's Association approved of it, and it was printed. Copies were sent to every Working-Men's Association in Great Britain, to many other Associations and to many persons, with requests that they would suggest such amendments as they might think advisable. . . . Certain propositions in some few details were examined, adopted, and incorporated by desire of the Association by Lovett and me. This amendment has made the Charter more simple. Alterations were also made in the Address, which serves as an introduction; and although that Address is not such an one as I should have drawn, the publication is a very respectable one."[1]

---

[1] Place to Erskine Perry, October 4, 1838; cf. also 27,820 (96-98). For a copy of the Charter, see 27,820 (370-373). There were two

On September 13, 1838, Place wrote to Hume rejoicing in the movement, and (with an obvious desire to improve the occasion) ascribing its success to the inaction of the Radicals in Parliament. "The Tories, under the name of Conservatives in the House of Commons and the Tories in the same House under the name of Whigs, assisted by the misnamed Liberals, had, so they all believed, succeeded in quieting the people, *i.e.* in stultifying them, and had put them into a state of apathy, which at length the *Liberals* began to lament when they found that the apathy was such as had not and could not be paralleled except at the time of the infamous coalition of Fox and North. . . . Then, however, there was no public; now there is a growing public even among the working people and those nearest to them in condition, and the consequence is just that which all well-judging men might, as some did, anticipate. The most active and well-informed among the people, seeing themselves utterly abandoned by those who had promised at the hustings to be their friends, began to stir for themselves, at first with very small numbers, for a reform of Parliament on the broadest possible plan. And their numbers increased with wonderful celerity, and at length they have produced an agitation not at all contemplated or even believed to be possible by those whose condition in life was above them, and have in a very short time been the cause of immense numbers of people in various places coming into active service. This is a *new* feature in society produced by the increased intelligence of the working people. This is the first time that the desire for reform has been moved by them (the working people) and carried upwards. Until now it has always proceeded downwards, and expired when abandoned, as it always has been, by their gentlemen

editions of the Charter, that sent round to the Associations in May 1838, and the amended version published in September 1838.

leaders. It will not again expire, but will go on continu
ally, sometimes with more, sometimes with less, rapidity,
but on it will go."[1]

On September 17 the Working-Men's Association held
an open-air meeting in Palace Yard to inaugurate the
movement in London. They asked Place and Roebuck to
be two of their delegates. Place declined on the ground
that such posts should be taken by younger men, who
"have no objection to be out at night," but suggested that
Roebuck ought to accept, and promised for himself that
"if any circumstance of pressing moment to the people
generally should arise and make it every man's duty to
come out, I would not stay at home, but would put aside
every consideration, come among them, and do my duty to
the best of my ability."[2]

Place's correspondence at the time shows that he
thought Chartism had little chance of immediate success
unless some accident, as had happened in 1832, should
bring politics into a revolutionary position. But he was
sure that a well-managed agitation for the Charter would
create a strong democratic party, led by the new class of
educated working-men, and able to put pressure upon
Parliament.

For instance, in the letter quoted above he wrote: "We
have now, then, obtained to a considerable extent what we
never before had, namely, a very large proportion of the
working people going on with others for the common and
intelligibly declared purpose set forth in the Charter. . . .
They, however, persuade themselves that they shall obtain
the Act in a short time. Disappointment will vex and
perplex them, and numbers will fly off and determine to
adopt violent proceedings. This feeling will not last long.
It will give way to rational feelings again, and then the

[1] Place to Hume, September 13, 1838.
[2] Place to Falconer, September 2, 1838.

2 A

matter will fluctuate, no one can say how long, nor what incidents of a decisive nature will occur, nor how any portion of the whole matter will finally terminate. Good will result, and that too in many ways, but in none more certainly than in preventing the Government from doing many mischievous things."

The kind of agitation for which Place hoped was that which was soon to be illustrated by the Anti-Corn-Law League, an agitation rigidly confined to one proposal, and including every one who could be persuaded by patient and good-natured propaganda to approve of it. Before consenting to draft the Charter, he had made the leaders of the Working-Men's Association promise that they would prevent speeches against the New Poor - Law or for Socialism from being delivered on their platforms.[1] He declared at the time that they were determined "to cease using opprobrious terms and epithets, and to receive every one as a friend who will take the Charter as his guide, and to work on steadily with every such person for the accomplishment of their purpose."[2] "Such Associations," he afterwards wrote, "can only succeed by long-continued, steady, patient, liberal conduct, accepting and using every kind of assistance which may at any time, and in every way, be available, making no absurd pretensions to anything, and especially not to superior wisdom and honesty, but acting with becoming modesty, but with indomitable perseverance."[3]

An agitation on these lines would, he knew, have to overcome the tendency of men engaged in manual labour to confine their desires to their immediate material interests. "Propose," he wrote in 1835, "to a working-man any great measure affecting the whole body, and he

[1] 27,835 (160, b).
[2] Place to Falconer, September 2, 1838.
[3] 27,819 (47).

immediately asks himself the question, What am I to get by it, meaning, what at the *instant* am I to have in my hand, or in my pocket, which I should like to have? To this he replies—nothing. There he sticks; he does nothing; he has not the heart to do anything even for his own advantage if that advantage be remote, and he has no desire to stir himself for the advantage of other persons." [1] But he hoped that this tendency would be cured at least in part by the spread of education, and that if so, "some three or four material things made as simple as possible, and worked at separately, may all be going on at the same time." [2]

Lovett and his friends accepted Place's ideal of agitation, and with occasional lapses tried thenceforth to act on it. But the Chartist movement in its main development belonged to a type of agitation diametrically opposed to that which Place desired. The conception which fired the northern factory hands and pitmen, or the Welsh iron-miners in 1838 and 1839, and again in 1848, was that of a class solidarity depending primarily upon an identity of material interest, and overcoming individual selfishness and inertia by discipline and enthusiasm—a "class-war," to use a modern phrase, which should deliberately antagonise all outside the ranks of the "comrades."

The Working-Men's Association gave Chartism its name and programme, but never had any considerable voice in its direction. It seemed at first as if the movement would be in the hands of Attwood and his "currency" friends in Birmingham. They drew up the form of petition to the Government, which was to be presented by a Convention of delegates from all England in the spring of 1839, and which contained such phrases as: "The good of a party has been advanced to the sacrifice of the good of the nation; the few have governed for the interests of the few; while

[1] Place to William Longson, weaver, Stockport, May 25, 1835.
[2] Ibid.

the interest of the many has been neglected or insolently and tyrannously trampled upon." . . . "We tell your honourable House that the capital of the master must no longer be deprived of its due profit; that the labour of the workmen must no longer be deprived of its due reward; that the laws which make food dear and those which, by making money scarce, make labour cheap, must be abolished. . . ."

At a succession of meetings in the autumn of 1838 the currency men convinced their Socialist audiences of their sincerity by describing the misery of the working classes and denouncing the Government, to whose wickedness that misery was due. They contributed the funds and business ability, without which a big campaign could not be organised, and might well have brought about that alliance between Socialism and proposals of currency change which has become a standing fact in the United States.[1] That they failed was mainly due to the influence of Feargus O'Connor. He never attempted to understand Attwood's "rag-botheration,"[2] and took what economics he had in the earlier years of the movement ready made from the Marxism of Bronterre O'Brien. His idea from the beginning was the formation of what he used to call an "Old Guard" of stalwart Chartists, who should all read the *Northern Star*, and all take him as their unquestioned leader. Both O'Connor and the Birmingham men natu-

---

[1] Place pointed out a danger in this form of agitation which showed itself in Mr. Bryan's campaign of 1896. "The whole of the agitation was made, what the people of Birmingham themselves afterwards called it, 'A Bread and Cheese Question,' probably the worst foundation possible, since a change for the better, however small, would be sure to detach a large proportion of their members from them and cause the whole of them to distrust their leaders, who had taken great pains to make them believe that the distress must not only continue, but must go on increasing until Mr. Attwood's scheme of currency was put into practice." 27,819 (87).

[2] See *Northern Star*, July 20, 1830.

rally opposed the purely political tactics of the London Working-Men's Association. O'Connor denied that they were working-men at all. He appealed against them to the "unshorn chins, blistered hands, and fustian jackets,"[1] and in London set up a Democratic Association in opposition to them. Attwood afterwards said that the "pamphlet called the 'Charter' . . . proceeded from a little clique or junta of men who had little more influence over the workmen of London than over those of Constantinople."[2]

When the Convention met, on February 4, 1839, O'Connor and his party dominated it from the first. Attwood's currency scheme was contemptuously rejected, in spite of the fact that missionaries of the Convention were collecting signatures to a petition, in the wording of which the whole of that scheme was implied. Lovett was made Secretary of the Convention, but the majority of the sixty delegates seem to have been suspicious of him and his Association. "Dr." Taylor, the ablest man among the extreme revolutionists, wrote in the *Northern Star:* "I came to London very much prejudiced against Lovett and all who belonged to the Working-Men's Association, looking upon them as no better than the tools of Place, Grote, Hume, Brougham, and the other leaders of the Malthusian party."[3]

The Convention sat from February till May 1839, in Bolt Court, Fleet Street, imitating the House of Commons for five weary days every week, quarrelling among themselves, and passing resolutions about the state of the People, Ireland, the Poor-Law, the Factory System, and the Rural Police.[4] The movement was now past the point

---

[1] *Northern Star*, February 24, 1838.
[2] 27,819 (241).   [3] 27,821 (144).
[4] "There was little for the Convention to do, besides some matters of detail of small moment, so they made business for themselves . . . made speeches to one another . . ."—Place to Hoare, December 19, 1839 (in "Autobiography").

at which Place could hope to do much by giving advice.
"It is impossible," he wrote on March 6, 1839, "to produce
any effect by reasoning with masses of men when they
are once intent upon any project, be it whatever it may.
Circumstances alone can operate upon them."[1]

On March 11 Lovett wrote to Place (who had been ill
with influenza): "We are beginning to understand each
other better than we did; the unfounded calumnies made
against us in the North are being dissipated, and the blood
and thunder heroes are being done up."[2]

Place replied: "Upon the whole, the proceedings have
been better than I expected. I know well enough how
inexperienced men must act, and I have observed nothing,
except now and then in language, which I have not seen
over and over again in each of our Houses of Parliament.
At first the deputies, as you know I expected they would,
talked as if the whole power of the people was lodged in
their hands, and could be used by them at will. . . . They
are learning a practical lesson of wisdom, and will return
home wiser and better men than they came; but they will
not generally have pleased those who sent them. They
will have seen some part of the great difficulty of moving
a whole people, and will each of them have learnt patience
and forbearance. I hope they will learn perseverance.
They who sent them will not have had the same advantages, and will have learnt nothing; will be disappointed,
and will show their displeasure. It will then become each
of the deputies in his particular district to bear with the
people, and not to give up the cause either for chagrin or
despair. Before the time comes for the deputies to dis-
perse, they will be thoroughly convinced that with a few
exceptions the people instead of being excited will become
torpid. They, the deputies, will also be convinced how

---

[1] Place to Robert Wallace, M.P., March 6, 1839.
[2] Lovett to Place, March 11, 1839.

greatly they miscalculated their own power and influence, and it will behove them, each one as far as his circumstances will permit him, to cheer up the people, and encourage them steadily to pursue their object. Upon the whole much good will be done, good far overbalancing all the trouble and expense which will be occasioned." [1]

Place had never been in the North of England, and could not understand that the Chartist movement had there developed into something very different from the spasmodic revolutionary demonstrations of the London working-men. The manufacturing villages of Lancashire and Yorkshire and South Wales were really in that state of determined unanimity which their delegates described. Pikes were being forged, regular drilling was going on, and nothing but military force could prevent a rising. This fact was gradually brought home to the southern delegates in London, and when on May 13 the Convention moved to Birmingham, Lovett and other " moral force " members had been converted to an intention to use " physical force " if possible.

The rising in the North was prevented by the extraordinary skill with which Sir Charles Napier used his little army of occupation.[2] Ineffectual rioting occurred at Birmingham and elsewhere, and a small body of troops were attacked at Newport. Then the Government hit back, and during the winter of 1839-40 hardly a single Chartist leader escaped imprisonment. As soon as the mischief was done Place set to work to prevent the sentences of death being carried out, to provide for the families of those who were imprisoned, and to organise a protest against the dangerous extension of the law of libel under which Lovett and others had been convicted.[3]

[1] Place to Lovett, March 13, 1839.
[2] See "Life and Opinions of Sir C. J. Napier," by Sir W. F. D. Napier, vol. ii.
[3] "I also am engaged, have for these three months been intensely

Chartism as a means of revolution had failed as completely as Trade Unionism, and the Chartists did not take their beating well. The conception of "solidarity," of a new heaven and a new earth to be achieved by a band of brothers leagued against a world of tyrants and slaves, is the greatest of all revolutionary forces. Perhaps without some measure of it very few men can be induced to fight for their ideas. But it is apt to make those who come under its influence cruel and intolerant in success, and to leave a peculiar kind of nagging bitterness after failure. Chartism in 1840 was little but an organisation for breaking up public meetings. "In London," says Place, "the interruption is made and sustained by from about 120 to 200 men, many of them youths. They go from place to place where Anti-Corn-Law lectures are given; they there make a disgraceful broil, which is reported in the *Northern Star* as 'a glorious victory.' These 150 men call themselves *the people*, and their impudence and tyranny is without example. . . ." "I have a letter before me from the editor of the *Glasgow Argus*, in which he says: 'Nothing is doing here in public. The Chartists have put down public speaking. Nothing could now be done but by tickets of admission.'"[1] "They think," Place says again, "they can effect their purpose by taking pains to make enemies, when they should be seeking to make friends."[2] For one moment.

engaged in every way a man can be engaged in the affairs of others, in doing all I possibly can, first, for William Lovett . . . secondly, in other cases of quite as much importance though not of so much public consequence, and in these cases I have written quires of paper, and been at many places distant from home . . . and I assure you that though I never go out except to take exercise, without which I cannot keep up my health, and though I see no company, waste no time at or after meals, and keep writing on at this time of the year, till eleven o'clock at night, I have wholly neglected matters relating to myself." —Place to Samuel Hoare, December 19, 1839 (in "Autobiography").

[1] Place to Roebuck, December 23, 1840.
[2] Place to Colonel Thompson, January 2, 1841.

indeed, he seemed even to fear that, in any rapid advance towards democracy, it might be such a turbulent minority rather than the steady mass of the people who would come to the front. On March 1, 1841, the Metropolitan Anti-Corn-Law Association held a meeting at the Crown and Anchor Tavern. Next day Place writes to John Collins, the Birmingham "moral force" Chartist, who had been imprisoned with Lovett: "I have seen many uproarious meetings, . . . but I never saw anything which would bear even a distant comparison with what I saw last night. I was very much vexed at, and very much ashamed of, the people before me. There I sat thinking of the terrible evils of the French Revolution in its earlier periods, and sure I am that if the men who composed by far the greater portion of the audience were not restrained by 'their fellow-subjects,' the policemen and the soldiers, all the horrors of the worst scenes in the French Revolution, all its monstrous cruelties and enormous evils of every kind, would be outdone by the men whose heads would readily conceive and whose hands would speedily commit them." [1]

But though he had ceased to hope anything from the existing Chartist organisations, Place still kept up a correspondence with individual Chartists, striving to make them recognise facts and learn patience. "Men are like children," he wrote, "and if you want them to learn a lesson, you must repeat it very many times," [2] and very many times did he explain his conception of democratic tactics to any man who would listen. The Chartists, he declared, "never can have, and consequently never will have, any effective power until the desire for the Charter shall become the strong and fully, and repeatedly, expressed wish over and over again, of a decided majority of the whole of the people.

[1] Place to John Collins, March 2, 1841.
[2] Place to J. G. Symons, September 19, 1840.

Until they shall become convinced of this, and act upon the conviction with good faith and good manners, they will never even approximate towards a conclusion." [1] All through, he was conscious that he was in reality more Chartist than the Chartists themselves. They had taken up the "six points" as a new idea four or five years before, and were not unlikely to take up some other new idea with equal eagerness. Place, "rascally Whig," as they were apt to call him, had worked for the "six points" during half a century. "They would not believe that he who could write this paper was a Chartist and something beyond it, before any beyond a very few of them probably were in existence; that it is within a few months of fifty years since he became persuaded that no government could be really good, nor no people in a sound and wholesome condition, while there was any privileged class or person in the nation." [2]

There is a trace of patient irony in his letters to the Chartist "stalwarts," who, one by one, deserted the monotonous agitation for a distant democracy, and took up some scheme in which they could feel an inventor's delight. Just as Feargus O'Connor himself was to capture the whole Chartist organisation some years later for his joint-stock land scheme, so Lovett came out of prison, in 1840, "almost crazy" with the belief that the Chartists ought to apply all their funds to building great schools, where the children would receive a thorough literary, technical, and sociological education. "I am certain," wrote Place, "you will never have even one school. You will never raise £3000 for such a purpose, and £3000 would not pay for such a school as you have described. I hope to see the time when £20,000,000 will

---

[1] Place to Colonel Thompson, January 2, 1841 (intended for publication ; cf. postscript).

[2] Place to Colonel Thompson, January 2, 1841.

be voted to pay for the building of schools — schools
for all, and not schools for Churchmen, or Chartists,
only—and when a compulsory rate will be levied on all,
in each school district, by a committee of the district, to
pay the expenses of carrying on the schools, in which
the teaching shall be really good and apart from all
religion, and especially from all sectarianism, whether
religious or political." [1]   John Collins, of Birmingham,
set up after his release a "Chartist Church," where, according to Colonel Thompson's enthusiastic description, "On
Sunday they say they preach *Bible politics*, and on week
days any other kind of politics they like. The simple
fact is, they preach what they like throughout." [2]   Henry
Vincent, when released from his eighteen months' imprisonment, found that emotional exhortations to good
living suited his eloquence and his audiences better than
well-worn demonstrations of the Six Points. "In North-
ampton," he wrote, "I publicly administered the teetotal
pledge. I have proposed the formation of public libraries
and lecture-rooms. Every appeal to the intellect and
virtue of the masses is most cordially responded to." [3]

All these things Place answers kindly enough, never
forgetting that his correspondents are men who have
suffered imprisonment in his own cause. He only permits
himself to say in writing to Collins, "Pray, in whatever
you and your colleagues may do, or say, or write, think
less of your own feelings and more of your understandings." [4]   But he lost patience when Vincent, whose
printing business was going badly, and who was heavily
in debt, became dazzled with the idea of an easy candidature for Parliament at Banbury. "You will," wrote

---

[1] Place to Lovett, March 30, 1841.
[2] Colonel T. P. Thompson to Place, April 13, 1841.
[3] Vincent to Place, March 23, 1841.
[4] Place to Collins, January 30, 1842.

Vincent, "perhaps be surprised to hear that I have been called upon to contest Banbury at the ensuing election, *with every prospect of success.* My lectures to the middle and working classes there have produced this state of feeling. Several of the most influential tradespeople are at the head of the move. The constituency is small, and should there be *three* candidates, *my return is certain.* The legal and other incidental expenses will not much exceed £100. Subscriptions are being raised in Banbury. Will you be kind enough to see Mr. Leader and other friends, and solicit a little pecuniary aid for me—a little from those who are favourable to Chartism would treat the House of Commons to a working-man. I shall proceed to Banbury in about a week. This is no childish affair. My friends there are in earnest. . . . I have already more promises than the Tories polled at the last election. Pray help me all you can in the undercurrent. You can do much." [1]

Placed answered the next day : " I must know a good deal more of the circumstances which have captivated you before I can do as you desire. Banbury has not 300 registered voters, and unless you had a requisition signed by a majority of them in their own handwriting, you could not be elected ; and even if you had their signatures, your return would be precarious. . . . You talk like but too many others, as if honesty and patriotism were the rule among the electors, while the fact is that they who are honest go for nothing. They balance one another, and the election is really made by the rascals who ought to be transported for seven years, the lawyers and election-jobbers for fourteen years, and the candidates who pay them for twenty-one years. . . . Your letter is matter of feeling showing great excitation, whereas it ought to have been one of business, statement of facts, calculations, &c.

[1] Vincent to Place, June 3, 1841.

CHARTISM

As it is, it will do more harm than good for me to show it.
[Then] comes a most material question. How are you to
live supposing you were to be elected? How are you to
pay the unavoidable expenses of being a member, no light
matter you may be assured? And when you had sat for a
session, and Parliament was again dissolved and you were
ousted from Banbury, what would you do? . . . To save
time I will give you my advice now instead of doing it, as
I must otherwise do, in a week or a month hence. It is
this, leave off running about the country, your wife with
you, learning nothing which can ever be of any use to
either of you, but much which is likely to tell in the contrary direction.[1] Go to your own business and become a
man of business for the next ten years. You may perhaps
at the end of that time be in a condition to do some public
service. You will be quite in time for enacting the Charter,
or for doing any other great national good. . . . If you
don't like what I have written, put the letter away, and
presently when things have changed with you read it again.
I speak plainly with you because you must believe that I
really mean you well, and because you cannot disguise
the fact to yourself that I know something about the
matter on which I have written." [2]

The Banbury election took place on June 30, 1841, and
Henry Vincent received 51 votes.

The last literary work which Place did was a history of

---

[1] "Long ago William Lovett came to me with Vincent, in consequence of a letter I wrote to him (Vincent), at his own request, on a
speech he made, and on which he prided himself, in which I showed
him that every one of his historical statements, twelve in number, was
erroneous and directly contrary to the facts. Both he and Lovett requested I would put him upon a course of reading, and as he then
said he was going to stick close to business, I gave him advice, undertook to supply him with books and to hold conversations with him
as he went on reading. But he could neither work nor read." (Place
to Gaskell, March 1, 1840.)

[2] Place to Vincent, June 4, 1841.

Chartism, written in the years 1840-43, and left unfinished. In this and in the letters written at the time he tried to reconcile himself to what he believed to be the conditions of working-class progress. He was convinced that rapid and easy advance could only be brought about by patient, tolerant, disillusioned men, and yet he could see no reason to suppose that any but a very few working-men, and those at long intervals, would be patient, or tolerant, or disillusioned.

"A great mass of our unskilled and but little skilled labourers (among whom are the handloom weavers), and a very considerable number of our skilled labourers, are in poverty, if not in actual misery; a large portion of them have been in a state of poverty and great privation all their lives. They are neither ignorant of their condition nor reconciled to it. They live amongst others who are better off than themselves, with whom they compare themselves; and they cannot understand why there should be so great a difference, why others who work no more or fewer hours than themselves at employments not requiring more actual exertion, and in many cases occupying fewer hours in the day, should be better paid than they are, and they come to the conclusion that the difference is solely caused by oppression—oppression of bad laws and avaricious employers. To escape from this state is with them of paramount importance. Among a vast multitude of these people not a day, scarcely an hour, can be said to pass without some circumstance, some matter exciting reflection, occurring to remind them of their condition, which (notwithstanding they have been poor and distressed from their infancy, and however much they may *at times* be cheerful) they scarcely ever cease, and never for a long period cease, to feel and to acknowledge to themselves with deep sensations of anguish their deplorable condition. To men thus circumstanced, any, the most absurd, scheme which promises relief is eagerly seized and earnestly adhered to until long after it has failed, and is even then reluctantly given up, and its failure is always accounted for by something being supposed to have happened which prevented the good the scheme held out from being accomplished; and thus they remain as they were, having learnt nothing, ready to be again deluded by some other scheme, until they hopelessly abandon every effort either to serve themselves or others." [1]

"It should be remembered that every attempt to reform any old institution has necessarily been made by enthusiastic but not well-informed men, who saw but a small portion of the impediments which made their present success impossible. Such men are always, and necessarily, ignorant of the best means of progressing towards the accomplishment of their purpose at a distant time, and can seldom be persuaded that the time for their accomplishment is distant. Few, indeed, such men would interfere at all unless they imagined the change they desired was at hand. They may be considered as pioneers who, by their labours and their sacrifices, smooth the way for those who are to follow them. Never without such persons to move forward, and never but through their errors and misfortunes, would mankind have emerged from barbarism, and gone on as they have done, slow and painful as their progress has been." [2]

. . . .

But in other moods he could hope that the few who had learnt the sad wisdom of political experience might still prove the stronger, and that the working classes might in the end progress, not by successive shortsighted enthusiasms, but by cool and steady perseverance. "As the best men," he wrote elsewhere, "in the working class proceed in their attainment of knowledge they will cease to enforce

[1] 27,819 (8, 9). [2] 27,820 (5).

their mistaken notions, and this will be called abandoning
their caste by those who remain unenlightened; and these
men, and such other men as have power over multitudes
of other men, and have sinister objects to accomplish, will
misinterpret to the many the actions and opinions of those
who may have become more enlightened, and will represent them as enemies of the people whom they would be
the best qualified and best disposed to serve. The people
will continue to be misled, and will look upon their best
friends as their worst enemies, and the more those, their
friends, may attempt to justify themselves and to defend
themselves against absurd and false imputations, the
firmer will be the conviction of the misled, ill-judging
multitude that they are enemies to be shunned. Progress
in the capability of thinking more justly will, however,
increase. Various circumstances will occur tending to
this result. Some of the leaders who have impugned their
fellows will be convinced that they have decided absurdly,
and these will, from time to time, fall into the ranks of
those who have been rejected by the people—will have
become a very considerable number, and will slowly but
surely recover their influence. In the meantime many of
the incorrigible leaders and large numbers of those of
their followers who are unteachable will be wearied out
with continued and rapidly recurring disappointments, and
will draw off, to be replaced by better men; and notwithstanding the times of inactivity and despair which will
occasionally occur, the progress of actual improvement in
right thinking will go on with increased velocity." [1]

[1] 27,819 (7, 8).

CHAPTER XIV

LAST YEARS

In March 1839 Place wrote from Brompton Square,
"Having removed from my well-known residence and,
being quietly settled here, I am gradually dropping out
of notice, and men and things are dropping out of my
notice."[1] He hoped that he would now be able to devote
the rest of his life to the serious historical work for which
he had so long been preparing. Writing of this year he
says, "I had, so I thought, too much neglected other
matters, purposes for which I had long been collecting
materials, and had at length seriously determined to set to
work, arrange my books and papers, and put my matter
together for a Narrative History of the Working People
and their employers, their education, manners, morals,
pastimes, and their improvement since the Revolution of
1688."[2]

Between 1836 and 1839, while working under constant
interruption, he had written his long "History of the
Reform Agitation."[3] Near the beginning of it he says
that he is almost deterred from continuing, "lest I should
waste my time by failing to be, as I earnestly desire to
be, useful to mankind."[4] Most of the many thousand
hours which the work must have taken him were indeed
wasted. By far the greater part of the History consists of

[1] Place to Wallace, March 6, 1839.
[2] Corn-Law Doings, in "Autobiography."
[3] 27,789–27,797.   [4] 27,789 (233).

2 B

laborious précis of speeches delivered each day during the
agitation. These are much too long for the ordinary
student, and the specialist will prefer the full reports in
Hansard or the *Times.* Only at wide intervals there come
a few pages of vigorous narrative or an interesting personal
observation. As a writer of memoirs, Place was indeed
dull on principle. In 1819 he had said, "I hate the
collector and retailer of anecdotes of his friends or of those
he acts with, and I hold him to be a rascal who keeps any
account of his immediate and private intercourse with
other men,"[1] and the History of Reform is most valuable
where he breaks through his own rule. The "History of
the Movements of the Working Classes and Others"[2]
(which forms a continuation of the Reform narrative) is
better, and perhaps the proposed History of the Working
People would have been better still.

But Place, as long as his strength lasted, never enjoyed
complete leisure for literary work. Again and again he
had to give way to that force which requires men to
do that which they have been proved able to do, rather
than that which they desire. The letter, for instance, in
which he declared that he was "dropping out of notice"
was written in answer to one from Robert Wallace, asking
him to influence the working-men on the side of Penny
Postage. Place's letter contains a very long and detailed
scheme for capturing the London Press, followed by an
implied threat that if, as seemed probable, the Government
brought in Twopenny Postage, he would get up an agitation
against it as a "Whig trick." "A man," he says, "must
have been, or must be as I was, a poor journeyman to know
the value of twopence to a respectable working-man. . . .
Without this sort of intercourse no man can . . . comprehend the wide difference between a penny and twopence,

[1] Place to Hobhouse, April 29, 1819.
[2] 27,819–27,822.

how unwilling careful people are of spending twopence, how careless they are of spending a penny." He ends by promising "to do my best in every way."[1]

Place always wondered why the Whig Government, which had so long refused cheap newspapers, granted cheap postage so easily. He could only ascribe it to the skill with which the vague fear of Chartism was brought to bear on the members of Parliament. "If we had not obtained the Act last session," he wrote in 1840, "we should never have obtained it at all. The many months which would have passed before we could again have brought it before the two Houses would have enabled the members to shake off their absurd fear, to become ashamed of themselves for having been at all alarmed, and then they would have rejected the Bill with contempt."

" The way in which the effect was produced and the Act obtained is known to very few, most of whom are members of the House of Commons. The agitation was carried on in a quiet, unostentatious way, which appeared to the generality as no movement at all; but it was a very great and extensive movement, and it was continually being made manifest to our lords and masters every hour and in every possible form."[2] In the tactics, as opposed to the strategy

---

[1] If Place is right, Warburton (see p. 278) deserves more credit than he has received for the introduction of the Penny Post. He was Chairman of the Select Committee, and drew up their Report in 1839. Place says, "To him we are all indebted for the penny postage, since without his excellent report, a work of intense study and great judgment, the penny postage would never have been obtained." (Place to Thompson, March 10, 1840.) Place in 1838 committed himself to a curiously sanguine prophecy as to the effect of postal reform. " If general post letters were charged only one penny, the postage in all cases being paid at the receiving houses, and when the delivery was accelerated by the railways, we should become a wiser and a better people, and by far a more intelligent people, than any which have ever existed, or even (been) contemplated as likely to exist." (Place to Parkes, January 18, 1838.)

[2] (Place to Wheatley, February 21, 1840.) Place says, "I may claim the merit of . . . suggesting the plan for working it out, and by

of politics, Place always held that every effort should be concentrated on influencing the minds of those who have to give the operative vote.

As soon as the prosecutions of 1839–40 had removed the original Chartist leaders, Hume wrote to Place, "I want to know your opinion of the chance of the Chartists now acting more moderately if we were to put ourselves at their head to demand the leading points of the Charter quietly, but by the strongest demonstration of numbers; whether, in fact, the working-men would now join us in our demand for all, but in the understanding that we will be ready to take any part of our demand."[1] Place replied, " There is at present no possibility of doing good to the working people or to anybody else by any proposal for reform in Parliament. The working people are not in a condition to join in any scheme of the sort, neither will they be so for some time to come."[2] And again to Warburton, who made the same proposal, " My advice is wait, have patience, watch events."[3] Meanwhile he tried to coach the middle-class Radicals in the rather difficult art of acting with the working-men of that day. He describes, for instance, in a letter to Peter Taylor an incident at the Radical Club.[4]

assisting the very clever men who were labouring with the full knowledge of all its advantages to effect their invaluable purpose. My efforts in the details were, however, of small value when compared with those of several others." (*Ibid.*) He alludes to a dinner given by Warburton to Rowland Hill, Joseph Parkes, W. A. Ashurst, and himself, who formed themselves into a committee, and determined to prevent the compromise of a twopenny post. At the same time he was helping the cheap circulation of knowledge by working with Warburton to oppose Serjeant Talfourd's Bill extending copyright to sixty years after an author's death. (See Place to Warburton, May 5, 1839, and January 18, 1840.)

[1] Hume to Place, February 9, 1840.
[2] Place to Hume, February 10, 1840.
[3] Place to Warburton, April 7, 1840.
[4] The Radical Club was a monthly dinner club, to which Robert Owen, Mazzini, and others belonged.

"The two great, conspicuous, and constantly pervading faults of the working people are impatience and intolerance. You saw both in Mitchell. At our April dinner, when I was in the chair, I humoured Mitchell and Huggett. They wished the Club to present a petition to the House of Commons in favour of Vincent, and they wished the petition to be such a one as they would have caused to be drawn, which none of the members would have signed. Now these men, like other working-men, have been too ill educated, and have seen too little of the ways of men in associations for business to become either patient or tolerant. The proposal for a petition was to them the whole universe, and excluded anything else. They could not imagine that any other man's notion could deserve attention. Their notion was to them all-important, and hence the petulance, impatience, and intolerance manifested by both. Mitchell spoke thirteen times, Huggett nine times. . . . There was an appearance of difficulty, which I could only get over by allowing them to exhaust themselves, and then to permit me to draw the petition. They were impatient, intolerant, and vehemently suspicious of our sincerity; and the time was consumed in allowing them to talk down their own misconceptions and absurd apprehensions. It was not time lost; the petition effected more than was expected, and they, poor fellows, were entitled to the indulgence."[1]

In 1841 a union between Chartists and Reformers seemed more possible. On January 21 a great meeting was held at Leeds to inaugurate the "New Move,"[2] and

---

[1] Place to Peter A. Taylor, July 14, 1840.
[2] Hamer Stansfield of Leeds wrote to Place on January 13, 1841 : "I cannot help thinking that you have now in your hands the power of doing more good to your country by a single act than any other man in it, of grasping the fruits of your long labours by merely reaching out your hands to take possession. I allude to the opportunity you have at present of bringing about a union between the Chartists and

the *Northern Star* advised the Chartists to swamp it.
Place wrote to those Chartists whom he knew imploring
them to behave reasonably, and was roundly abused for
doing so.[1]

In London the difficulty between the London Chartists
and the Radicals had become in large part one of words.
The Chartists had made the term Universal Suffrage
hateful to the middle-class politicians, while the working-
men believed that Household Suffrage covered a hypo-
critical design for their betrayal.[2] Place inclined to some
new term like "General" Suffrage. "Universal Suffrage,"
he wrote, "General Suffrage, Registration, or Capacity for
Reading Suffrage, any Suffrage with Ballot and Short
Parliaments which would give the mass of the people
the power to elect the members of the House of
Commons, is *Democracy*, and would put an end to every
privileged class and person. The Established Church,
the House of Peers, and the office of King would all be
abolished."[3] But he was convinced that no great change
in the suffrage was immediately possible. In discussing
a proposed Reform society, he said, "The accomplishment
of the ends which the society must propose are far off. . . .
Every one who may expect general results in a short time

our agitation. Last year you thought the attempt premature, and you
were right, but circumstances have somewhat changed since then."
Place began his reply, "If I had any such power as you suppose, it
would have been exerted ere this, for it has long been my custom not to
wait until called upon, but quietly and as effectually as possible to
interfere whenever I see an opening to be useful."

[1] See *Northern Star*, May 22, 1841, where he is accused of a "deep
conspiracy" against Feargus O'Connor ; and November 19, 1742, where
"Franky Place" is accused of giving money to the Working-Men's
Association (which he was then trying to revive).

[2] "It was no more possible for them [the London Chartists] to agree
to the words "Household Suffrage," than it is for your friends to agree
to the words "Universal Suffrage." (Place to Hume, February 10,
1841.)

[3] Place to Hume, February 11, 1841.

will be disappointed."[1] In 1842 a new society was actually
formed, under the name of "The Metropolitan Parliamentary Reform Association," having as its avowed object
the attainment of the Charter, without the use of the name.
It lived exactly twelve months. The Chartist movement
ran its own course till 1848, and that agreement between
the enfranchised and the disfranchised, on which further
extension of the suffrage depended, did not come till 1867.

Place himself from 1840 onwards thought that Parliamentary Reform was less immediately practicable than
the repeal of the Corn Laws. In that year, at the age
of sixty-nine, he came for the first time under the influence of a greater and more persistent organiser than
himself. Richard Cobden had founded the Anti-Corn-
Law League in the winter of 1838–39, and in January
1840 sent a deputation to London to revive the moribund
Anti-Corn-Law Association, which had been founded in
1836. Warburton sent the deputation to Place with a
complimentary letter, saying that he "had been mainly
instrumental in obtaining the Act for the Penny Postage,
and, could set the same machinery at work for the repeal
of the Corn Laws."[2] Place at first refused to interfere "in
any public matter which would require my attendance
away from my own house," but at last C. P. Villiers
(who had been with him on the Postage committee),
Warburton, and others, persuaded him to consent. He
became chairman of the business committee of the
Association, and, as usual, had to do a great part of the
drudgery of organisation.[3] The letters which he received

---

[1] Place to Hume, February, 11, 1841.

[2] Letter quoted by Place to Thompson, March 10, 1840.

[3] A report signed by Place in 1841 produced the last of those
witticisms about Place's name and trade which began in 1818. The
Morning Herald of April 1, 1841, writes: "This report is signed by
that ancient artificer of 'unmentionables,' who used to give gratuitous
instruction to nursling demagogues and aspiring whiglings among the

from Cobden bear an amusing likeness to those which he
had been sending all his life to other people. On February
27, 1840, for instance, Cobden wrote: "My dear Sir,—I
think every possible effort should be made to get your
proceedings into the London papers. The country is now
just ripe to take the cue from the metropolis. Every
movement upon the Corn Law will vibrate through the
length and breadth of the land. A good stirring appeal,
short and pithy, from the Metropolitan Association, calling upon the nation to unite and co-operate against the
bread tax, would be responded to, and such an address
is necessary to put the Association on its proper footing
with the country, and to give it claims upon the community for support. The address ought to appear
immediately in the London papers, and it should recommend petitions to be forwarded immediately for the
abolition of all taxes upon the first necessaries of life.
The *Sun* and *Chronicle* are the two most important
papers for the country. The *Advertiser* is not so much
seen out of London. The object to be kept in view by
your Association, in my humble opinion, ought to be to
influence the country at large more than the metropolis.
London is generally well represented as far as the Corn
question is concerned. But we must change the Parliamentary representation of a great many other boroughs
before we can carry our point with the House of Commons.
I hope you will bear in mind always the great power you
have at command over the country through the London
Press. We in Manchester are looked upon with some
jealousy by the agriculturists (I mean the population
of rural towns, as well as farmers and labourers), but
they will follow the metropolis as their natural leader."

rising hopes of the legislature in their diurnal progresses to and from
the House of Commons. The genius of the old Charing Cross Cabinet
[truly the *genius loci*] still presides, it seems, in all its 'pristine pride of
place.' "

To this Place returned a long answer, in which, after stating that he was working on Corn-Law business from 7 A.M. till midnight, he goes on :—

"The people here differ very widely from you at Manchester. You, some of you, at Manchester resolve that something shall be done, and then *you*, some of you, set to work and see it done, give your money and your time, and need none but mere servants to carry out the details. Our men of property and influence never act in this way. They themselves must be operated upon, and that, too, with care and circumspection, to induce them even to give us their *mites*, and to permit us to put their names on the list of our general committee. Of the committee of eleven appointed at the meeting which you attended, and half-a-dozen whom we put on the next day, we have met no more in committee than three, four, or five, until yesterday, when we met to discuss our constitution, when seven attended. Our subscription does not amount to quite £100.

.   .   .   .   .   .

"London differs very widely from Manchester, and, indeed, from every other place on the face of the earth. It has no local or particular interest as a town, not even as to politics. Its several boroughs in this respect are like so many very populous places at a distance from one another, and the inhabitants of any one of them know nothing, or next to nothing, of the proceedings in any other, and not much indeed of those of their own. London in my time, and that is half a century, has never moved. A few of the people in different parts have moved, and these, whenever they come together, make a considerable number—still, a very small number indeed when compared with the whole number—and when these are judiciously managed, *i.e.* when they are brought to act together, not only make a great noise, which is heard

far and wide, but which has also considerable influence in
many places. But, isolated as men are here, living as they
do at considerable distances, many seven miles apart, and
but seldom meeting together, except in small groups, to
talk either absolute nonsense on miserable party politics,
or to transact business exclusive of everything else, they
will tell you they have no time to give to the Association
to help to repeal the Corn Laws, while the simple fact is
that, with the exception of the men of business (and even
they lose much time), four-fifths of the whole do nothing
but lose their time. With a very remarkable working
population also, each trade divided from every other, and
some of the most numerous even from themselves, and
who, notwithstanding an occasional display of very small
comparative numbers, are a quiescent, inactive race as far
as public matters are concerned. The leaders—those
among them who do pay attention to public matters—are
one and all at enmity with every other class of society.
True it is, as they allege, they have been cajoled and then
abandoned by the middle class as often as they have acted
with them, but their opinions are pushed to extremes, and
are mischievous prejudices. They call the middle class
'shopocrats,' 'usurers' (all profit being usury), 'money-
mongers,' 'tyrants and oppressors of the working people,'
and they link the middle class with the aristocracy
under the dignified appellation of 'murderers of society,'
'murderers of the people.' With such a population so
circumstanced, the well-informed, honest, zealous men few
in number, there is no way of making those who give a
tone to any such project as ours but by such preparatory
measures as I have described, and by unweariedly working
them out."[1]

In September 1840 Cobden wrote to Place a long and
cheery letter, describing all the plans of the League, and

[1] Place to Cobden, March 4, 1840.

asking news of London. Place's reply is gloomy enough. The London public was able to absorb unlimited lectures and circulars without the least trace of an effect. The Association "had not £10 in hand, and did not know how to raise £10 more;" a special summons had been issued for a meeting of the general committee, and one only had attended. Yet if the League would send £250 to London something might be done. Cobden replies :—

"I am sorry to receive your last long letter, which is certainly very much like a dying speech and confession. Is there no hope of sufficient help to keep the thing *nominally* alive? As to Manchester attempting to sustain an unreal show of opinion against the bread tax in London, I think you will agree with me that it would be impossible, and even useless, if it were not so." [1]

In 1841 Place's health began to give way. He went in November to a meeting of the council of the Anti-Corn-Law League in Manchester, caught cold on the journey back, and suffered very severely from bronchitis during the winter. From that time, although he attended committees when he could, his old powers of endurance were gone. He still, however, continued his narrative of the Chartist movement, and began to write regularly as English correspondent of the *Delhi Gazette*, which was owned and edited by one of his sons in India. In 1844 even that came to an end. He was attacked with a sort of paralytic stroke followed by serious brain symptoms. For a year he could neither read nor write, and his recovery was very gradual and incomplete. When he was able to get about again he continued to attend the weekly meetings of the Anti-Corn-Law Committee until the repeal of the law in 1846. In that year he could again for a moment speak of himself as " choke full of public matters "

---

[1] Cobden to Place, October 5, 1840.

when writing to Cobden and urging him not to take office under Lord John Russell. Cobden replied:—

"*July* 1, 1846.—MY DEAR PLACE,—Probably the best answer I can give to your wise and friendly counsels is to tell you briefly what I am going to do. I have obtained leave of absence from Parliament for the rest of the session. I am about to address a letter to my constituents, informing them that I must claim a year's exemption from public life, and shall go abroad to secure it. Thus you see I shall be out of all the danger you have so kindly foreseen. Let me now congratulate you, who have worked so long for the triumph of principles which themselves paved the way for the success of us, the reformers of comparatively yesterday, upon the passing of the repeal measure. I do not forget the merits of those who have gone before me, who broke down the great impediments in our path, and left us only to macadamize the road to victory. It has often been a matter of regret that I have not been able to see you lately, but I have often spoken of you, and inquired after your health. Long may it be preserved. You have lived through by far the most eventful seventy years in the world's history. Nay, the fifty years during which you have been an observer of public events have been more fertile in great and enduring incidents than any five centuries I could select. Bless yourself that you live in times when reform bills, steamboats, railroads, penny postage, and free trade, to say nothing of the ratification of civil and religious liberties, have been possible facts."

Place did not die till 1854, and before he died had much to bear. His second marriage in 1830 turned out fairly well for twelve years. But young Chatterley, the stepson, was a source of constant anxiety and trouble, and Place's home life was embittered by quarrels with his wife about him and about money matters. The remainder of his property was still further diminished, and he was obliged to sell his prints

and many of his books. Yet he was still capable of a
resolute assertion of his old philosophy. There is an entry
in his diary for 1826, "I have limited my desires so as to
bring all that is necessary, and more than is necessary,
within my reach ; and have, I think, brought myself to
this state, that no possible event can make me uncomfortable for twenty-four hours, bodily pain alone excepted."
To this in 1850 he added, in the changed writing and
confused phrases of his extreme old age, "I have since
had more to prove the supposition correct since the above
was written, and most especially during the last five years,
than all that occurred in all my former long life had been
compressed in the same time, even after its amount had
been doubled. Yet thanks to former reasonings, I have
neither lost my cheerfulness, nor even been *unhappy*
during twenty-four consecutive hours."[1]

Twelve months after this was written a separation was
arranged with his wife, and Place went to live with his
married daughter in Hammersmith. His grand-daughter
still remembers his arrival, and the waggon which brought
the remainder of his library to be stacked in a dry stable.
He was now very feeble, but comfortable and happy.
Shortly after his attack in 1844 he had chosen a method
of occupying himself mechanically and yet usefully. "Compelled," he says, "to give up reading, and to be very
cautious as to the time I employ in writing, my life would
have become very monotonous and irksome had I not
discovered a resource in what had at times filled up spaces
and given me occupation when I was compelled to sit and
hear the tales and complaints of various persons. This
occupation consisted of cutting from newspapers notices on
various subjects,and especially of such as related to the working people. I had put away a great quantity of newspapers
and cuttings from newspapers. These I now overhauled,

[1] *Diary*, November 24, 1826. Note added February 22, 1850.

as I did other large quantities which were sent to me.
From these I cut out whatever I thought might be useful
at some future time, in relation to the working-classes most
especially.   I now arranged these papers, pasted them into
books, and put them in form for binding." [1]   Some of these
" guard-books " are in the British Museum, others have been
scattered or destroyed.   On this task he spent two cheerful
and industrious years at his daughter's house.   Joseph
Parkes used to come and talk to him, with Samuel Harrison, the most faithful of his political disciples, who ten
years before had offered to copy letters for him, " well paid
for my trouble in this way by the privilege of reading what
you write." [2]   In 1853 his two clever and hardworking un-
married daughters took a little house with him in Foxley
Terrace, Earl's Court.   Here on January 1, 1854, he was
found to have died suddenly and painlessly in the night.

His death, as has been already said, attracted little attention.   The newspapers during the few weeks preceding the
Crimean War were filled with other matter.   Joseph
Hume, however, himself very old and soon to die, spoke
in his praise at a meeting of the Parliamentary Reform
Association, declaring him to have been " the most dis-
interested reformer he ever knew, valuable in council,
fertile in resource, performing great labours ; but he never
thought of himself.   Honours and advantages he might
often have commanded, but he preferred assiduous and
private services, which he rendered of his own zeal, and
defrayed out of his own wealth." [3]

[1] " Autobiography."   [2] 27,810 (225).
      [3] The *Reasoner*, March 26, 1854.

INDEX

2 c

INDEX 409

Mob dispersed on Lord Mayor's Day, (1830), 248

Monthly Repository, article by W. J. Fox in, 326

Moore, Peter, 208 *seq.*

—— Richard, and People's Charter, 365

Morning Chronicle, the:

—— articles from Place on Sinking Fund, 160

—— connection with Whigs, 143

—— had articles by Hodgskin, 1831, 274

—— on Combination Laws, 204

—— on Westminster election, 1819, 136 *seq.*

—— said to be influential in the country, 392

Morning Herald hints at compromise with Lords, 278

Morning Post, 1832 : account of " Go for Gold," 310

" Municipal Corporation Reform," the, 342 *seq.*

—— Corporation Commission, Report of, 341

—— Government, Place's proposals for, 343

—— Reform Bill, 330 *seq.*, 342 *seq.* ; passed, 346

NAPIER, Sir William, 302, 303

—— Sir Charles, 375

" Narrative History of the Working Classes," planned by Place, 385

National Debt, Cobbett's proposal for, 158

—— Sinking Fund for, 159

" National Society for Education of Poor in Church Principles," 94

" National Union of the Working Classes," 266 *n.*, 269, 291

" Natural Religion," by Bentham, 83

" New Move," the, 339

" New View of Society," a, by Owen, 63

" Newcastle Fox Club," 134

Newspaper cuttings made in Place's old age, 398

Newspaper Stamp Duties, 148, 191, 255, 288, 327, 336–342, 348–350

—— close of agitation, 360

" No-rent " campaign, 293

Northern Liberator references to Place, 170, 177, 333

Northern Star of Leeds, and Chartist agitation, 353, 366, 372, 373, 390

Northumberland, Duke of, and Westminster elections, 41 *seq.*

" Not Paul, but Jesus," by Bentham, 84

Nottingham, disturbances at, 294, 298

O'BRIEN, Bronterre, 353, 372

" Observations on Mr. Hoskisson's Speech," pamphlet by Place, 228

O'Connell, Daniel, 329, 336

O'Connor, Feargus, Chartist, 336, 371 *seq.*

—— Roger, 51, 55

" Offences on the Sea," Bill concerning, 180

Onslow, Sergeant, 159

" O.P." riots, 48

O'Quigley and French Government, 27

Owen, Robert, 63 *seq.*

—— in debate on Free Trade, 361

—— influence on Rotundanists, 266

—— influence on Chartism, 354

PADDINGTON parish meeting on Reform Bill, 306

Paine, Thomas :

—— his " Age of Reason " published by Place and another, 28

—— his " Rights of Man " published, 61

Palmerston, Lord, and Reform Bill, 286

" Panopticons," Bentham's, 104

Parkes, Joseph, of Birmingham :

—— his work in Reform Bill agitation, 276, 298, 299, 302, 303, 309

—— (1832) desired by Place to begin fresh agitation, 327

THE END

Printed by BALLANTYNE, HANSON & Co.
Edinburgh & London

THE WORKING OF DEMOCRACY

By SIDNEY and BEATRICE WEBB

THE HISTORY OF TRADE UNIONISM. 8vo, pp. 574, cloth, with Coloured Map. First Edition published May 1894; Second Edition, 1896. Price 18s.

This work, founded almost entirely upon material previously unpublished, describes the growth and development of the Trade Union Movement in the United Kingdom from 1700 down to 1890, including the political history of the English working-class. The final chapter describes the Trade Union world of to-day in all its varied features, including a realistic sketch of Trade Union life by a Trade Union Secretary, and a classified census founded on the authors' investigations into a thousand separate unions in all parts of the country. A coloured map represents the percentage which the Trade Unionists bear to the population of each county. A bibliography of Trade Union literature is appended.

"To the politician . . . an invaluable guide."—*Observer*, 27th May 1894.

"A masterly piece of work."—*Times*, 5th May 1894.

"This is one of those books, *rari nantes in gurgite vasto* of trash, which every man and woman feeling a human interest in the problem of the age will do well to possess for present study and future reference. . . . The authors have offered the world a book which amounts practically to a history of something far more important than Trade Unionism—that is to say, of the attitude of the State towards Labour in Great Britain at various stages, and of the effect which each attitude produced. . . . The book is really, perhaps unconsciously, a history of the progress of Economical Thought in Britain. . . . To all County Councillors and Members of Parliament who care to look before they leap we would fain say, 'Read this book and inwardly digest it.'"—*National Observer*, 2nd June 1894.

Uniform with the above, by the same Authors.

INDUSTRIAL DEMOCRACY. 8vo, Two Vols., pp. 900, cloth, with Two Diagrams. Published January 1898. Price 25s. net.

The first part of this work contains an analysis of the working of Democracy in the Trade Union world, including its remarkable experience of the Referendum, the Initiative, and Representative Institutions. The second part describes the Trade Union methods and regulations, including Factory Legislation and every form of regulation of labour, in all the various trades of the United Kingdom. The third part supplies a new analysis of the working of industrial competition, and a full exposition of economic theory, leading up to some novel proposals for dealing with the sweated trades. The book contains facts and copious explanations upon every phase of the Labour Question, with an elaborate Index.

LONGMANS, GREEN, AND CO.
LONDON, NEW YORK, AND BOMBAY

2 D

A Classified Catalogue

OF WORKS IN

GENERAL LITERATURE

PUBLISHED BY

LONGMANS, GREEN, & CO.

39 PATERNOSTER ROW, LONDON, E.C.

91 AND 93 FIFTH AVENUE, NEW YORK, AND 32 HORNBY ROAD, BOMBAY.

CONTENTS.

INDEX OF AUTHORS AND EDITORS.

History, Politics, Polity, Political Memoirs, &c.

Abbott.—*A History of Greece* By EVELYN ABBOTT, M.A., LL.D. Part I.—From the Earliest Times to the Ionian Revolt. Crown 8vo., 10s. 6d. Part II.—500-445 B.C. Crown 8vo., 10s. 6d.

Acland and Ransome.—*A Hand-book in Outline of the Political History of England to 1896.* Chronologically Arranged. By A. H. DYKE ACLAND, M.P., and CYRIL RANSOME, M.A. Crown 8vo., 6s.

ANNUAL REGISTER (THE). A Review of Public Events at Home and Abroad, for the year 1896. 8vo., 18s. Volumes of the *ANNUAL REGISTER* for the years 1863-1895 can still be had. 18s. each

Arnold (THOMAS, D.D.), formerly Head Master of Rugby School.

INTRODUCTORY LECTURES ON MODERN HISTORY. 8vo., 7s. 6d.

MISCELLANEOUS WORKS. 8vo., 7s. 6d.

Baden-Powell. — *THE INDIAN VILLAGE COMMUNITY.* Examined with Reference to the Physical, Ethnographic, and Historical Conditions of the Provinces; chiefly on the Basis of the Revenue-Settlement Records and District Manuals. By B. H. BADEN-POWELL, M.A., C.I.E. With Map. 8vo., 16s.

Bagwell.—*IRELAND UNDER THE TUDORS.* By RICHARD BAGWELL, LL.D. (3 vols.) Vols. I. and II. From the first invasion of the Northmen to the year 1578. 8vo., 32s. Vol. III. 1578-1603. 8vo. 18s.

Ball.—*HISTORICAL REVIEW OF THE LEGISLATIVE SYSTEMS OPERATIVE IN IRELAND,* from the Invasion of Henry the Second to the Union (1172-1800). By the Rt. Hon. J. T. BALL. 8vo., 6s.

Besant.—*THE HISTORY OF LONDON.* By Sir WALTER BESANT. With 74 Illustrations. Crown 8vo., 1s. 9d. Or bound as a School Prize Book, 2s. 6d.

Brassey (LORD).—PAPERS AND ADDRESSES.

NAVAL AND MARITIME. 1872-1893. 2 vols. Crown 8vo., 10s.

MERCANTILE MARINE AND NAVIGATION, from 1871-1894. Crown 8vo., 5s.

IMPERIAL FEDERATION AND COLONISATION FROM 1880 to 1894. Cr. 8vo., 5s.

Brassey (LORD) PAPERS AND ADDRESSES—*continued.*

POLITICAL AND MISCELLANEOUS. 1861-1894. Crown 8vo 5s.

Bright.—*A HISTORY OF ENGLAND.* By the Rev. J. FRANCK BRIGHT, D.D. Period I. *MEDIÆVAL MONARCHY:* A.D. 449 to 1485. Crown 8vo., 4s. 6d. Period II. *PERSONAL MONARCHY.* 1485 to 1688. Crown 8vo., 5s. Period III. *CONSTITUTIONAL MONARCHY.* 1689 to 1837. Crown 8vo., 7s. 6d. Period IV. *THE GROWTH OF DEMOCRACY.* 1837 to 1880 Crown 8vo., 6s.

Buckle.—*HISTORY OF CIVILISATION IN ENGLAND AND FRANCE, SPAIN AND SCOTLAND.* By HENRY THOMAS BUCKLE. 3 vols. Crown 8vo., 24s.

Burke.—*A HISTORY OF SPAIN* from the Earliest Times to the Death of Ferdinand the Catholic. By ULICK RALPH BURKE, M.A. 2 vols. 8vo., 32s.

Chesney.—*INDIAN POLITY:* a View of the System of Administration in India. By General Sir GEORGE CHESNEY, K.C.B., With Map showing all the Administrative Divisions of British India. 8vo., 21s.

Corbett.—*DRAKE AND THE TUDOR NAVY,* with a History of the Rise of England as a Maritime Power. By JULIAN CORBETT. With Portraits, Illustrations and Maps. 2 vols. 8vo.

Creighton. — *A HISTORY OF THE PAPACY FROM THE GREAT SCHISM TO THE SACK OF ROME,* 1378-1527. By M. CREIGHTON, D.D., Lord Bishop of London. 6 vols. Crown 8vo., 6s. each.

Cuningham. — *A SCHEME FOR IMPERIAL FEDERATION:* a Senate for the Empire. By GRANVILLE C. CUNINGHAM, of Montreal, Canada. Crown 8vo., 3s. 6d.

Curzon.—*PERSIA AND THE PERSIAN QUESTION.* By the Right Hon. GEORGE N. CURZON, M.P. With 9 Maps, 96 Illustrations, Appendices, and an Index. 2 vols. 8vo., 42s.

De Tocqueville.—*DEMOCRACY IN AMERICA.* By ALEXIS DE TOCQUEVILLE. 2 vols. Crown 8vo., 16s.

History, Politics, Polity, Political Memoirs, &c.—*continued.*

Dickinson.—*THE DEVELOPMENT OF PARLIAMENT DURING THE NINETEENTH CENTURY.* By G. LOWES DICKINSON, M.A. 8vo, 7s. 6d.

Eggleston.—*THE BEGINNERS OF A NATION:* a History of the Source and Rise of the Earliest English Settlements in America, with Special Reference to the Life and Character of the People. By EDWARD EGGLESTON. With 8 Maps. Cr. 8vo.,7s. 6d.

Froude (JAMES A.).

THE HISTORY OF ENGLAND, from the Fall of Wolsey to the Defeat of the Spanish Armada.
  Popular Edition. 12 vols. Crown 8vo. 3s. 6d. each.
  '*Silver Library*' *Edition.* 12 vols. Crown 8vo., 3s. 6d. each.

THE DIVORCE OF CATHERINE OF ARAGON. Crown 8vo., 3s. 6d.

THE SPANISH STORY OF THE AR-MADA, and other Essays. Cr. 8vo., 3s. 6d.

THE ENGLISH IN IRELAND IN THE EIGHTEENTH CENTURY. 3 vols. Cr. 8vo., 10s. 6d.

ENGLISH SEAMEN IN THE SIXTEENTH CENTURY. Cr. 8vo., 6s.

THE COUNCIL OF TRENT. Crown 8vo., 6s.

SHORT STUDIES ON GREAT SUBJECTS. 4 vols. Cr. 8vo., 3s. 6d. each.

CÆSAR : a Sketch. Cr. 8vo, 3s. 6d.

Gardiner (SAMUEL RAWSON, D.C.L., LL.D.).

HISTORY OF ENGLAND, from the Accession of James I. to the Outbreak of the Civil War, 1603-1642. 10 vols. Crown 8vo., 6s. each.

A HISTORY OF THE GREAT CIVIL WAR, 1642-1649. 4 vols. Cr.8vo.,6s.each.

A HISTORY OF THE COMMONWEALTH AND THE PROTECTORATE. 1649-1660. Vol.I. 1649-1651.With 14 Maps. 8vo.,21s. Vol. II. 1651-1654. With 7 Maps. 8vo., 21s.

WHAT GUNPOWDER PLOT WAS. With 8 Illustrations and Plates. Crown 8vo., 7s.

Gardiner (SAMUEL RAWSON, D.C.L., LL.D.)—*continued.*

CROMWELL'S PLACE IN HISTORY. Founded on Six Lectures delivered in the University of Oxford. Cr. 8vo., 3s. 6d.

THE STUDENT'S HISTORY OF ENG-LAND. With 378 Illustrations. Crown 8vo., 12s.
  Also in Three Volumes, price 4s. each.
  Vol. I. B.C. 55—A.D. 1509. 173 Illustrations.
  Vol. II. 1509-1689. 96 Illustrations.
  Vol. III. 1689-1885. 109 Illustrations.

Greville.—*A JOURNAL OF THE REIGNS OF KING GEORGE IV., KING WILLIAM IV., AND QUEEN VICTORIA.* By CHARLES C. F. GREVILLE, formerly Clerk of the Council. 8 vols. Crown 8vo., 3s 6d. each.

HARVARD HISTORICAL STUDIES.

THE SUPPRESSION OF THE AFRICAN SLAVE TRADE TO THE UNITED STATES OF AMERICA, 1638-1870. By W. E. B. DU BOIS, Ph.D. 8vo., 7s. 6d.

THE CONTEST OVER THE RATIFICATON OF THE FEDERAL CONSTITUTION IN MASSA-CHUSETTS. By S. B. HARDING, A.M. 8vo., 6s.

A CRITICAL STUDY OF NULLIFICATION IN SOUTH CAROLINA. By D. F. HOUSTON, A.M. 8vo., 6s.

NOMINATIONS FOR ELECTIVE OFFICE IN THE UNITED STATES. By FREDERICK W. DALLINGER, A.M. Member of the Massachusetts Senate. 8vo., 7s. 6d.
  ** Other Volumes are in preparation.

Hammond.—*A WOMAN'S PART IN A REVOLUTION.* By Mrs. JOHN HAYS HAMMOND. Crown 8vo., 2s. 6d.

Historic Towns.—Edited by E. A. FREEMAN, D.C.L.,and Rev.WILLIAM HUNT, M.A. With Maps and Plans. Crown 8vo., 3s. 6d. each.

Bristol. By Rev. W. Hunt.	Oxford. By Rev. C. W.
Carlisle. By Mandell	Boase.
Creighton, D.D.	Winchester. By G. W.
Cinque Ports. By Mon-	Kitchin, D.D.
tague Burrows.	York. By Rev. James
Colchester. By Rev. E. L.	Raine.
Cutts.	New York. By Theodore
Exeter. By E. A. Freeman.	Roosevelt.
London. By Rev. W. J.	Boston (U.S.) By Henry
Loftie.	Cabot Lodge.

Joyce.—*A SHORT HISTORY OF IRE-LAND,* from the Earliest Times to 1608. By P. W. JOYCE, LL.D. Crown 8vo., 10s. 6d.

History, Politics, Polity, Political Memoirs, &c.—*continued.*

Kaye and Malleson.—*HISTORY OF THE INDIAN MUTINY*, 1857-1858. By Sir JOHN W. KAYE and Colonel G. B. MALLESON. With Analytical Index and Maps and Plans. 6 vols. Crown 8vo., 3s. 6d. each.

Knight.—*MADAGASCAR IN WAR TIME: THE EXPERIENCES OF* 'THE TIMES' *SPECIAL CORRESPONDENT WITH THE HOVAS DURING THE FRENCH INVASION OF* 1895. By E. F. KNIGHT. With 16 Illustrations and a Map. 8vo., 12s. 6d.

Lang (ANDREW).

PICKLE THE SPY: or, The Incognito of Prince Charles. With 6 Portraits. 8vo., 18s.

ST. ANDREWS. With 8 Plates and 24 Illustrations in the Text by T. HODGE. 8vo., 15s. net.

Laurie. — *HISTORICAL SURVEY OF PRE-CHRISTIAN EDUCATION.* By S. S. LAURIE, A.M., LL.D. Crown 8vo., 12s.

Lecky(WILLIAM EDWARD HARTPOLE). *HISTORY OF ENGLAND IN THE EIGHTEENTH CENTURY.*

Library Edition. 8 vols. 8vo., £7 4s.

Cabinet Edition. ENGLAND. 7 vols. Crown 8vo., 6s. each. IRELAND. 5 vols. Crown 8vo., 6s. each.

HISTORY OF EUROPEAN MORALS FROM AUGUSTUS TO CHARLEMAGNE. 2 vols. Crown 8vo., 16s.

HISTORY OF THE RISE AND INFLUENCE OF THE SPIRIT OF RATIONALISM IN EUROPE. 2 vols. Crown 8vo., 16s.

DEMOCRACY AND LIBERTY. 2 vols. 8vo., 36s.

THE EMPIRE: its value and its Growth. An Inaugural Address delivered at the Imperial Institute, November 20, 1893. Cr. 8vo., 1s. 6d.

Lowell. — *GOVERNMENTS AND PARTIES IN CONTINENTAL EUROPE.* By A. LAWRENCE LOWELL. 2 vols. 8vo., 21s.

Macaulay (LORD).

THE LIFE AND WORKS OF LORD MACAULAY. 'Edinburgh' Edition. 10 vols. 8vo., 6s. each.

Vols. I.-IV. *HISTORY OF ENGLAND.*

Vols. V.-VII. *ESSAYS ; BIOGRAPHIES ; INDIAN PENAL CODE ; CONTRIBUTIONS TO KNIGHT'S 'QUARTERLY MAGAZINE'.*

Vol. VIII. *SPEECHES ; LAYS OF ANCIENT ROME ; MISCELLANEOUS POEMS.*

Vols. IX. and X. *THE LIFE AND LETTERS OF LORD MACAULAY.* By the Right Hon. Sir G. O. TREVELYAN, Bart., M.P.

This Edition is a cheaper reprint of the Library Edition of LORD MACAULAY's *Life and Works.*

COMPLETE WORKS.

Cabinet Edition. 16 vols. Post 8vo., £4 16s.

Library Edition. 8 vols. 8vo., £5 5s. 'Edinburgh' *Edition.* 8 vols. 8vo., 6s. each.

HISTORY OF ENGLAND FROM THE ACCESSION OF JAMES THE SECOND.

Popular Edition. 2 vols. Cr. 8vo., 5s.
Student's Edition. 2 vols. Cr. 8vo., 12s.
People's Edition. 4 vols. Cr. 8vo., 16s.
Cabinet Edition. 8 vols. Post 8vo., 48s.
'Edinburgh' *Edition.* 4 vols. 8vo., 6s. each.
Library Edition. 5 vols. 8vo., £4.

CRITICAL AND HISTORICAL ESSAYS, WITH LAYS OF ANCIENT ROME, in 1 volume.

Popular Edition. Crown 8vo., 2s. 6d.
Authorised Edition. Crown 8vo., 2s. 6d., or 3s. 6d., gilt edges.
Silver Library Edition. Cr. 8vo., 3s. 6d.

CRITICAL AND HISTORICAL ESSAYS.

Student's Edition. 1 vol. Cr. 8vo., 6s.
People's Edition. 2 vols. Cr. 8vo., 8s.
'Trevelyan' *Edition.* 2 vols. Cr. 8vo., 9s.
Cabinet Edition. 4 vols. Post 8vo., 24s.
'Edinburgh' *Edition.* 3 vols. 8vo., 6s. each.
Library Edition. 3 vols. 8vo., 36s.

ESSAYS which may be had separately price 6d. each sewed, 1s. each cloth.

Addison and Walpole.	Ranke and Gladstone.
Croker's Boswell's Johnson.	Milton and Machiavelli.
Hallam's Constitutional History.	Lord Byron.
	Lord Clive.
Warren Hastings.	Lord Byron, and The
The Earl of Chatham (Two Essays).	Comic Dramatists of the Restoration.
Frederick the Great.	

MISCELLANEOUS WRITINGS

People's Edition. 1 vol. Cr. 8vo., 4s. 6d.
Library Edition. 2 vols. 8vo., 21s.

History, Politics, Polity, Political Memoirs, &c.—*continued.*

Macaulay (LORD)—*continued.*

MISCELLANEOUS WRITINGS AND SPEECHES.
Popular Edition. Crown 8vo., 2s. 6d.
Cabinet Edition. Including Indian Penal Code, Lays of Ancient Rome, and Miscellaneous Poems. 4 vols. Post 8vo., 24s.

SELECTIONS FROM THE WRITINGS OF LORD MACAULAY. Edited, with Occasional Notes, by the Right Hon. Sir G. O. Trevelyan, Bart. Crown 8vo., 6s.

MacColl.—*THE SULTAN AND THE POWERS.* By the Rev. MALCOLM MACCOLL, M.A., Canon of Ripon. 8vo., 10s. 6d.

Mackinnon.—*THE UNION OF ENGLAND AND SCOTLAND: A STUDY OF INTERNATIONAL HISTORY.* By JAMES MACKINNON, Ph.D. Examiner in History to the University of Edinburgh. 8vo., 16s.

May.—*THE CONSTITUTIONAL HISTORY OF ENGLAND* since the Accession of George III. 1760-1870. By Sir THOMAS ERSKINE MAY, K.C.B. (Lord Farnborough). 3 vols. Cr. 8vo., 18s.

Merivale (THE LATE DEAN).
HISTORY OF THE ROMANS UNDER THE EMPIRE. 8 vols. Crown 8vo., 3s. 6d. each
THE FALL OF THE ROMAN REPUBLIC: a Short History of the Last Century of the Commonwealth. 12mo., 7s. 6d.

Montague. — *THE ELEMENTS OF ENGLISH CONSTITUTIONAL HISTORY.* By F. C. MONTAGUE, M.A. Crown 8vo., 3s. 6d.

Richman.—*APPENZELL: PURE DEMOCRACY AND PASTORAL LIFE IN INNER-RHODEN.* A Swiss Study. By IRVING B. RICHMAN, Consul-General of the United States to Switzerland. With Maps. Crown 8vo., 5s.

Seebohm (FREDERIC).
THE ENGLISH VILLAGE COMMUNITY Examined in its Relations to the Manorial and Tribal Systems, &c. With 13 Maps and Plates. 8vo., 16s.
THE TRIBAL SYSTEM IN WALES: Being Part of an Inquiry into the Structure and Methods of Tribal Society. With 3 Maps. 8vo., 12s.

Sharpe.—*LONDON AND THE KINGDOM:* a History derived mainly from the Archives at Guildhall in the custody of the Corporation of the City of London. By REGINALD R. SHARPE, D.C.L., Records Clerk in the Office of the Town Clerk of the City of London. 3 vols. 8vo. 10s. 6d. each.

Smith.—*CARTHAGE AND THE CARTHAGINIANS.* By R. BOSWORTH SMITH, M.A., With Maps, Plans, &c. Cr. 8vo., 3s. 6d.

Stephens.—*A HISTORY OF THE FRENCH REVOLUTION.* By H. MORSE STEPHENS. 3 vols. 8vo. Vols. I. and II. 18s. each.

Stubbs.—*HISTORY OF THE UNIVERSITY OF DUBLIN,* from its Foundation to the End of the Eighteenth Century. By J. W. STUBBS. 8vo., 12s. 6d.

Sutherland.—*THE HISTORY OF AUSTRALIA AND NEW ZEALAND,* from 1606 to 1890. By ALEXANDER SUTHERLAND, M.A., and GEORGE SUTHERLAND, M.A. Crown 8vo., 2s. 6d.

Taylor.—*A STUDENT'S MANUAL OF THE HISTORY OF INDIA.* By Colonel MEADOWS TAYLOR, C.S.I., &c. Cr. 8vo., 7s. 6d.

Todd. — *PARLIAMENTARY GOVERNMENT IN THE BRITISH COLONIES.* By ALPHEUS TODD, LL.D. 8vo., 30s. net.

Wakeman and Hassall.—*ESSAYS INTRODUCTORY TO THE STUDY OF ENGLISH CONSTITUTIONAL HISTORY.* By Resident Members of the University of Oxford. Edited by HENRY OFFLEY WAKEMAN, M.A., and ARTHUR HASSALL, M.A. Crown 8vo., 6s.

Walpole.—*HISTORY OF ENGLAND FROM THE CONCLUSION OF THE GREAT WAR IN 1815 TO 1858.* By SPENCER WALPOLE. 6 vols. Crown 8vo., 6s. each.

Wood-Martin.—*PAGAN IRELAND: AN ARCHÆOLOGICAL SKETCH.* A Handbook of Irish Pre-Christian Antiquities. By W. G. WOOD-MARTIN, M.R.I.A. With 512 Illustrations. Crown 8vo., 15s.

Wylie. — *HISTORY OF ENGLAND UNDER HENRY IV.* By JAMES HAMILTON WYLIE, M.A., one of H. M. Inspectors of Schools. 3 vols. Crown 8vo. Vol. I., 1399-1404, 10s. 6d. Vol. II., 15s. Vol. III., 15s. [Vol. IV. *In the press.*

Biography, Personal Memoirs, &c.

Armstrong.—*THE LIFE AND LETTERS OF EDMUND J. ARMSTRONG.* Edited by G. F. SAVAGE ARMSTRONG. Fcp. 8vo., 7s.6d.

Bacon.—*THE LETTERS AND LIFE OF FRANCIS BACON, INCLUDING ALL HIS OCCASIONAL WORKS.* Edited by JAMES SPEDDING. 7 vols. 8vo., £4 4s.

Bagehot.—*BIOGRAPHICAL STUDIES.* By WALTER BAGEHOT. Crown 8vo., 3s. 6d.

Blackwell. — *PIONEER WORK IN OPENING THE MEDICAL PROFESSION TO WOMEN:* Autobiographical Sketches. By Dr. ELIZABETH BLACKWELL. Cr. 8vo., 6s.

Boyd (A. K. H.) ('A.K.H.B.').

TWENTY-FIVE YEARS OF ST. ANDREWS. 1865-1890. 2 vols. 8vo. Vol. I. 12s. Vol. II. 15s.

ST. ANDREWS AND ELSEWHERE: Glimpses of Some Gone and of Things Left. 8vo., 15s.

THE LAST YEARS OF ST. ANDREWS: SEPTEMBER 1890 TO SEPTEMBER 1895. 8vo., 15s.

Brown.—*FORD MADOX BROWN:* A Record of his Life and Works. By FORD M. HUEFFER. With 45 Full-page Plates (22 Autotypes) and 7 Illustrations in the Text. 8vo., 42s.

Buss.—*FRANCES MARY BUSS AND HER WORK FOR EDUCATION.* By ANNIE E. RIDLEY. With 5 Portraits and 4 Illustrations. Crown 8vo, 7s. 6d.

Carlyle.—*THOMAS CARLYLE:* A History of his Life. By JAMES ANTHONY FROUDE.

1795-1835. 2 vols. Crown 8vo., 7s.
1834-1881. 2 vols. Crown 8vo., 7s.

Digby.—*THE LIFE OF SIR KENELM DIGBY, by one of his Descendants,* the Author of 'The Life of a Conspirator,' 'A Life of Archbishop Laud,' etc. With 7 Illustrations. 8vo., 16s.

Erasmus.—*LIFE AND LETTERS OF ERASMUS.* By JAMES ANTHONY FROUDE. Crown 8vo., 6s.

FALKLANDS. By the Author of 'The Life of Sir Kenelm Digby,' 'The Life of a Prig,' etc. With Portraits and other Illustrations. 8vo.

Fox. — *THE EARLY HISTORY OF CHARLES JAMES FOX.* By the Right Hon. Sir G. O. TREVELYAN, Bart.

Library Edition. 8vo., 18s.
Cabinet Edition. Crown 8vo., 6s.

Halifax.—*THE LIFE AND LETTERS OF SIR GEORGE SAVILE, BARONET, FIRST MARQUIS OF HALIFAX.* With a New Edition of his Works, now for the first time collected and revised. By H. C. FOXCROFT. 2 vols. 8vo.

Halford.—*THE LIFE OF SIR HENRY HALFORD, BART., G.C.H., M.D., F.R.S.,* By WILLIAM MUNK, M.D., F.S.A. 8vo., 12s. 6d.

Hamilton.—*LIFE OF SIR WILLIAM HAMILTON.* By R. P. GRAVES. 8vo. 3 vols. 15s. each. ADDENDUM. 8vo., 6d. sewed.

Harper.—*A MEMOIR OF HUGO DANIEL HARPER, D.D.,* late Principal of Jesus College, Oxford, and for many years Head Master of Sherborne School. By L. V. LESTER, M.A. Crown 8vo., 5s.

Havelock.—*MEMOIRS OF SIR HENRY HAVELOCK,* K.C.B. By JOHN CLARK MARSHMAN. Crown 8vo., 3s. 6d.

Haweis.—*MY MUSICAL LIFE.* By the Rev. H. R. HAWEIS. With Portrait of Richard Wagner and 3 Illustrations. Crown 8vo., 7s. 6d.

Holroyd.—*THE GIRLHOOD OF MARIA JOSEPHA HOLROYD (Lady Stanley of Alderley).* Recorded in Letters of a Hundred Years Ago, from 1776 to 1796. Edited by J. H. ADEANE. With 6 Portraits. 8vo., 18s.

Jackson.—*THE LIFE OF STONEWALL JACKSON.* By Lieut.-Col. G. F. HENDERSON, York and Lancaster Regiment. With Portrait, Maps and Plans. 2 vols. 8vo.

Lejeune.—*MEMOIRS OF BARON LEJEUNE,* Aide-de-Camp to Marshals Berthier, Davout, and Oudinot. Translated and Edited from the Original French by Mrs. ARTHUR BELL (N. D'ANVERS). With a Preface by Major-General MAURICE, C.B. 2 vols. 8vo., 24s.

Luther. — *LIFE OF LUTHER.* By JULIUS KÖSTLIN. With Illustrations from Authentic Sources. Translated from the German. Crown 8vo., 7s. 6d.

Macaulay.—*THE LIFE AND LETTERS OF LORD MACAULAY.* By the Right Hon. Sir G. O. TREVELYAN, Bart., M.P.
Popular Edition. 1 vol. Cr. 8vo., 2s. 6d.
Student's Edition. 1 vol. Cr. 8vo., 6s.
Cabinet Edition. 2 vols. Post 8vo., 12s.
Library Edition. 2 vols. 8vo., 36s.
'*Edinburgh' Edition.* 2 vols. 8vo., 6s. each.

Biography, Personal Memoirs, &c.—*continued.*

Marbot.— THE MEMOIRS OF THE BARON DE MARBOT. Translated from the French. 2 vols. Crown 8vo., 7s.

Nansen.—FRIDTIOF NANSEN, 1861-1893. By W. C. BRÖGGER and NORDAHL ROLFSEN. Translated by WILLIAM ARCHER. With 8 Plates, 48 Illustrations in the Text, and 3 Maps. 8vo., 12s. 6d.

Place.— THE LIFE OF FRANCIS PLACE. By GRAHAM WALLAS.

Rawlinson.— A MEMOIR OF THE LATE SIR HENRY RAWLINSON, BART., K.C.B., F.R.S., D.C.L., ETC. Written chiefly by his brother, the Rev. GEORGE RAWLINSON, Canon of Canterbury. With Contributions by the late Sir Henry's eldest son, and by Field-Marshal LORD ROBERTS.

Reeve.—THE LIFE AND LETTERS OF HENRY REEVE, C.B., late Editor of the 'Edinburgh Review,' and Registrar of the Privy Council. By J. K. LAUGHTON, M.A.

Romanes.—THE LIFE AND LETTERS OF GEORGE JOHN ROMANES, M.A., LL.D., F.R.S. Written and Edited by his WIFE. With Portrait and 2 Illustrations. Crown 8vo., 6s.

Seebohm.—THE OXFORD REFORMERS —JOHN COLET, ERASMUS AND THOMAS MORE : a History of their Fellow-Work. By FREDERIC SEEBOHM. 8vo., 14s.

Shakespeare. — OUTLINES OF THE LIFE OF SHAKESPEARE. By J. O. HALLI-WELL-PHILLIPPS. With Illustrations and Fac-similes. 2 vols. Royal 8vo., £1 1s.

Shakespeare's TRUE LIFE. By JAMES WALTER. With 500 Illustrations by GERALD E. MOIRA. Imp. 8vo., 21s.

Verney. —MEMOIRS OF THE VERNEY FAMILY.
Vols. I. & II., DURING THE CIVIL WAR. By FRANCES PARTHENOPE VERNEY. With 38 Portraits, Woodcuts and Fac-simile. Royal 8vo., 42s.
Vol. III., DURING THE COMMONWEALTH. 1650-1660. By MARGARET M. VERNEY. With 10 Portraits, &c. Royal 8vo., 21s.

Wakley.—THE LIFE AND TIMES OF THOMAS WAKLEY, Founder and First Editor of the 'Lancet,' Member of Parliament for Finsbury, and Coroner for West Middlesex. By S. SQUIRE SPRIGGE, M.B. Cantab. With 2 Portraits. 8vo., 18s.

Wellington.—LIFE OF THE DUKE OF WELLINGTON. By the Rev. G. R. GLEIG, M.A. Crown 8vo., 3s. 6d.

Travel and Adventure, the Colonies, &c.

Arnold.—SEAS AND LANDS. By Sir EDWIN ARNOLD. With 71 Illustrations. Crown 8vo., 3s. 6d.

Baker (SIR S. W.).
EIGHT YEARS IN CEYLON. With 6 Illustrations. Crown 8vo., 3s. 6d.
THE RIFLE AND THE HOUND IN CEYLON. With 6 Illustrations. Crown 8vo., 3s. 6d.

Bent.—THE RUINED CITIES OF MASHONALAND : being a Record of Excavation and Exploration in 1891. By J. THEODORE BENT. With 117 Illustrations. Crown 8vo., 3s. 6d.

Bicknell.—TRAVEL AND ADVENTURE IN NORTHERN QUEENSLAND. BY ARTHUR C. BICKNELL. With 24 Plates and 22 Illustrations in the Text. 8vo., 15s.

Brassey.—VOYAGES AND TRAVELS OF LORD BRASSEY, K.C.B., D.C.L., 1862-1894. Arranged and Edited by Captain S. EARDLEY-WILMOT. 2 vols. Cr. 8vo., 10s.

Brassey (THE LATE LADY).
A VOYAGE IN THE 'SUNBEAM;' OUR HOME ON THE OCEAN FOR ELEVEN MONTHS.
Cabinet Edition. With Map and 66 Illustrations. Crown 8vo., 7s. 6d.
Silver Library Edition. With 66 Illustrations. Crown 8vo., 3s. 6d.
Popular Edition. With 60 Illustrations. 4to., 6d. sewed, 1s. cloth.
School Edition. With 37 Illustrations. Fcp., 2s. cloth, or 3s. white parchment.

Travel and Adventure, the Colonies, &c.—*continued.*

Brassey (THE LATE LADY)—*continued.*

SUNSHINE AND STORM IN THE EAST.
Cabinet Edition. With 2 Maps and 114 Illustrations. Crown 8vo., 7s. 6d.
Popular Edition. With 103 Illustrations. 4to., 6d. sewed, 1s. cloth.

IN THE TRADES, THE TROPICS, AND THE 'ROARING FORTIES.'
Cabinet Edition. With Map and 220 Illustrations. Crown 8vo., 7s. 6d.
Popular Edition. With 183 Illustrations. 4to., 6d. sewed, 1s. cloth.

THREE VOYAGES IN THE 'SUNBEAM'.
Popular Ed. With 346 Illust. 4to., 2s. 6d.

Browning.—*A GIRL'S WANDERINGS IN HUNGARY.* By H. ELLEN BROWNING. With Map and 20 Illustrations. Crown 8vo., 3s. 6d.

Froude (JAMES A.).

OCEANA: or England and her Colonies. With 9 Illustrations. Crown 8vo., 2s. boards, 2s. 6d. cloth.

THE ENGLISH IN THE WEST INDIES: or, the Bow of Ulysses. With 9 Illustrations. Crown 8vo., 2s. boards, 2s. 6d. cloth.

Howitt.—*VISITS TO REMARKABLE PLACES.* Old Halls, Battle-Fields, Scenes, illustrative of Striking Passages in English History and Poetry. By WILLIAM HOWITT. With 80 Illustrations. Crown 8vo., 3s. 6d.

Jones. — *ROCK CLIMBING IN THE ENGLISH LAKE DISTRICT.* By OWEN G. JONES. With numerous Plates.

Knight (E. F.).

THE CRUISE OF THE 'ALERTE': the Narrative of a Search for Treasure on the Desert Island of Trinidad. With 2 Maps and 23 Illustrations. Crown 8vo., 3s. 6d.

WHERE THREE EMPIRES MEET: a Narrative of Recent Travel in Kashmir, Western Tibet, Baltistan, Ladak, Gilgit, and the adjoining Countries. With a Map and 54 Illustrations. Cr. 8vo., 3s. 6d.

THE 'FALCON' ON THE BALTIC: a Voyage from London to Copenhagen in a Three-Tonner. With 10 Full-page Illustrations. Crown 8vo., 3s. 6d.

Lees and Clutterbuck.—B.C. 1887 : *A RAMBLE IN BRITISH COLUMBIA.* By J. A. LEES and W. J. CLUTTERBUCK. With Map and 75 Illustrations. Crown 8vo., 3s. 6d.

Max Müller.—*LETTERS FROM CONSTANTINOPLE.* By Mrs. MAX MÜLLER. With 12 Views of Constantinople and the neighbourhood. Crown 8vo., 6s.

Nansen (FRIDTJOF).

THE FIRST CROSSING OF GREENLAND. With numerous Illustrations and a Map. Crown 8vo., 3s. 6d.

ESKIMO LIFE. With 31 Illustrations. 8vo., 16s.

Oliver.—*CRAGS AND CRATERS:* Rambles in the Island of Réunion. By WILLIAM DUDLEY OLIVER, M.A. With 27 Illustrations and a Map. Cr. 8vo., 6s.

Quillinan.—*JOURNAL OF A FEW MONTHS' RESIDENCE IN PORTUGAL,* and Glimpses of the South of Spain. By Mrs. QUILLINAN (Dora Wordsworth). New Edition. Edited, with Memoir, by EDMUND LEE, Author of 'Dorothy Wordsworth,' &c. Crown 8vo., 6s.

Smith.—*CLIMBING IN THE BRITISH ISLES.* By W. P. HASKETT SMITH. With Illustrations by ELLIS CARR, and Numerous Plans.

Part I. ENGLAND. 16mo., 3s. 6d.

Part II. WALES AND IRELAND. 16mo., 3s. 6d.

Part III. SCOTLAND. [*In preparation.*

Stephen. — *THE PLAY-GROUND OF EUROPE.* By LESLIE STEPHEN. New Edition, with Additions and 4 Illustrations. Crown 8vo., 6s. net.

THREE IN NORWAY. By Two of Them. With a Map and 59 Illustrations. Crown 8vo., 2s. boards, 2s. 6d. cloth.

Tyndall.—*THE GLACIERS OF THE ALPS:* being a Narrative of Excursions and Ascents. An Account of the Origin and Phenomena of Glaciers, and an Exposition of the Physical Principles to which they are related. By JOHN TYNDALL, F.R.S. With numerous Illustrations. Crown 8vo., 6s. 6d. net.

Vivian.—*SERVIA:* the Poor Man's Paradise. By HERBERT VIVIAN, M.A. 8vo.

Veterinary Medicine, &c.

Steel (JOHN HENRY).

A TREATISE ON THE DISEASES OF THE DOG. With 88 Illustrations. 8vo., 10s. 6d.

A TREATISE ON THE DISEASES OF THE OX. With 119 Illustrations. 8vo., 15s.

A TREATISE ON THE DISEASES OF THE SHEEP. With 100 Illustrations. 8vo., 12s.

OUTLINES OF EQUINE ANATOMY: a Manual for the use of Veterinary Students in the Dissecting Room. Cr. 8vo., 7s. 6d.

Fitzwygram. — HORSES AND STABLES. By Major-General Sir F. FITZ-WYGRAM, Bart. With 56 pages of Illustrations. 8vo., 2s. 6d. net.

Schreiner. — THE ANGORA GOAT (published under the auspices of the South African Angora Goat Breeders' Association), and a Paper on the Ostrich (reprinted from the Zoologist for March, 1897). By S. C. CRONWRIGHT SCHREINER. 8vo.

'Stonehenge.' — THE DOG IN HEALTH AND DISEASE. By 'STONE-HENGE'. With 78 Wood Engravings. 8vo., 7s. 6d.

Youatt (WILLIAM).

THE HORSE. Revised and Enlarged by W. WATSON, M.R.C.V.S. With 52 Wood Engravings. 8vo., 7s. 6d.

THE DOG. Revised and Enlarged. With 33 Wood Engravings. 8vo., 6s.

Sport and Pastime.

THE BADMINTON LIBRARY.

Edited by HIS GRACE THE DUKE OF BEAUFORT, K.G., and A. E. T. WATSON.

Complete in 28 Volumes.   Crown 8vo., Price 10s. 6d. each Volume, Cloth.

** The Volumes are also issued half-bound in Leather, with gilt top. The price can be had from all Booksellers.

ARCHERY. By C. J. LONGMAN and Col. H. WALROND. With Contributions by Miss LEGH, Viscount DILLON, &c. With 2 Maps, 23 Plates and 172 Illustrations in the Text. Crown 8vo., 10s. 6d.

ATHLETICS AND FOOTBALL. By MONTAGUE SHEARMAN. With 6 Plates and 52 Illust. in the Text. Cr. 8vo., 10s. 6d.

BIG GAME SHOOTING. By CLIVE PHILLIPPS-WOLLEY.

Vol. I. AFRICA AND AMERICA. With Contributions by Sir SAMUEL W. BAKER, W. C. OSWELL, F. C. SELOUS, &c. With 20 Plates and 57 Illustrations in the Text. Crown 8vo., 10s. 6d.

Vol. II. EUROPE, ASIA, AND THE ARCTIC REGIONS. With Contributions by Lieut.-Colonel R. HEBER PERCY, Major ALGERNON C. HEBER PERCY, &c. With 17 Plates and 56 Illustrations in the Text. Cr. 8vo., 10s. 6d.

BILLIARDS. By Major W. BROAD-FOOT, R.E. With Contributions by A. H. BOYD, SYDENHAM DIXON, W. J. FORD, &c. With 11 Plates, 19 Illustrations in the Text, and numerous Diagrams. Cr. 8vo., 10s. 6d.

BOATING. By W. B. WOODGATE. With 10 Plates, 39 Illustrations in the Text, and 4 Maps of Rowing Courses. Cr. 8vo., 10s. 6d.

COURSING AND FALCONRY. By HARDING COX and the Hon. GERALD LASCELLES. With 20 Plates and 56 Illustrations in the Text. Crown 8vo., 10s. 6d.

CRICKET. By A. G. STEEL and the Hon. R. H. LYTTELTON. With Contributions by ANDREW LANG, W. G. GRACE, F. GALE, &c. With 12 Plates and 52 Illustrations in the Text. Crown 8vo., 10s. 6d.

CYCLING. By the EARL OF ALBE-MARLE and G. LACY HILLIER. With 19 Plates and 44 Illustrations in the Text. Crown 8vo., 10s. 6d.

DANCING. By Mrs. LILLY GROVE, F.R.G.S. With Contributions by Miss MIDDLETON, The Hon. Mrs. ARMYTAGE, &c. With Musical Examples, and 38 Full-page Plates and 93 Illustrations in the Text. Crown 8vo., 10s. 6d.

DRIVING. By His Grace the DUKE of BEAUFORT, K.G. With Contributions by other Authorities. With 12 Plates and 54 Illustrations in the Text. Cr. 8vo., 10s. 6d.

Sport and Pastime—*continued.*
THE BADMINTON LIBRARY—*continued.*

FENCING, BOXING, AND WRESTLING. By WALTER H. POLLOCK, F. C. GROVE, C. PREVOST, E. B. MITCHELL, and WALTER ARMSTRONG. With 18 Plates and 24 Illust. in the Text. Cr. 8vo., 10s. 6d.

FISHING. By H. CHOLMONDELEY-PENNELL.

Vol. I. SALMON AND TROUT. With Contributions by H. R. FRANCIS, Major JOHN P. TRAHERNE, &c. With 9 Plates and numerous Illustrations of Tackle, &c. Crown 8vo., 10s. 6d.

Vol. II. PIKE AND OTHER COARSE FISH. With Contributions by the MARQUIS OF EXETER, WILLIAM SENIOR, G. CHRISTOPHER DAVIS, &c. With 7 Plates and numerous Illustrations of Tackle, &c. Crown 8vo., 10s. 6d.

GOLF. By HORACE G. HUTCHINSON. With Contributions by the Rt. Hon. A. J. BALFOUR, M.P., Sir WALTER SIMPSON, Bart., ANDREW LANG, &c. With 25 Plates and 65 Illustrations in the Text. Cr. 8vo., 10s. 6d.

HUNTING. By His Grace the DUKE OF BEAUFORT, K.G., and MOWBRAY MORRIS. With Contributions by the EARL OF SUFFOLK AND BERKSHIRE, Rev. E. W. L. DAVIES, G. H. LONGMAN, &c. With 5 Plates and 54 Illustrations in the Text. Cr. 8vo., 10s. 6d.

MOUNTAINEERING. By C. T. DENT. With Contributions by Sir W. M. CONWAY, D. W. FRESHFIELD, C. E. MATTHEWS, &c. With 13 Plates and 95 Illustrations in the Text. Cr. 8vo., 10s. 6d.

POETRY OF SPORT (THE).— Selected by HEDLEY PEEK. With a Chapter on Classical Allusions to Sport by ANDREW LANG, and a Special Preface to the BADMINTON LIBRARY by A. E. T. WATSON. With 32 Plates and 74 Illustrations in the Text. Crown 8vo., 10s. 6d.

RACING AND STEEPLE-CHASING. By the EARL OF SUFFOLK AND BERKSHIRE, W. G. CRAVEN, the Hon. F. LAWLEY, ARTHUR COVENTRY, and ALFRED E. T. WATSON. With Frontispiece and 56 Illustrations in the Text. Cr. 8vo., 10s. 6d.

RIDING AND POLO.

RIDING. By Captain ROBERT WEIR, the DUKE OF BEAUFORT, the EARL OF SUFFOLK AND BERKSHIRE, the EARL OF ONSLOW, &c. With 18 Plates and 41 Illustrations in the Text. Cr. 8vo., 10s. 6d.

SEA FISHING. By JOHN BICKERDYKE, Sir H. W. GORE-BOOTH, ALFRED C. HARMSWORTH, and W. SENIOR. With 22 Full-page Plates and 175 Illustrations in the Text. Crown 8vo., 10s. 6d.

SHOOTING.

Vol. I. FIELD AND COVERT. By LORD WALSINGHAM and Sir RALPH PAYNE-GALLWEY, Bart. With Contributions by the Hon. GERALD LASCELLES and A. J. STUART-WORTLEY. With 11 Plates and 94 Illusts. in the Text. Cr. 8vo., 10s. 6d.

Vol. II. MOOR AND MARSH. By LORD WALSINGHAM and Sir RALPH PAYNE-GALLWEY, Bart. With Contributions by LORD LOVAT and Lord CHARLES LENNOX KERR. With 8 Plates and 57 Illustrations in the Text. Crown 8vo., 10s. 6d.

SKATING, CURLING, TOBOGANING. By J. M. HEATHCOTE, C. G. TEBBUTT, T. MAXWELL WITHAM, Rev. JOHN KERR, ORMOND HAKE, HENRY A. BUCK, &c. With 12 Plates and 272 Illustrations in the Text. Crown 8vo., 10s. 6d.

SWIMMING. By ARCHIBALD SINCLAIR and WILLIAM HENRY, Hon. Secs. of the Life-Saving Society. With 13 Plates and 106 Illustrations in the Text. Crown 8vo., 10s. 6d.

TENNIS, LAWN TENNIS, RACKETS AND FIVES. By J. M. and C. G. HEATHCOTE, E. O. PLEYDELL-BOUVERIE, and A.C. AINGER. With Contributions by the Hon. A. LYTTELTON, W. C. MARSHALL, Miss L. DOD, &c. With 12 Plates and 67 Illustrations in the Text. Crown 8vo., 10s. 6d.

YACHTING.

Vol. I. CRUISING, CONSTRUCTION OF YACHTS, YACHT RACING RULES, FITTING-OUT,&c. By Sir EDWARD SULLIVAN, Bart., THE EARL OF PEMBROKE, LORD BRASSEY, K.C.B., C. E. SETH-SMITH, C.B., G. L. WATSON, R. T. PRITCHETT, E. F. KNIGHT, &c. With 21 Plates and 93 Illustrations in the Text, and from Photographs. Crown 8vo., 10s. 6d.

Vol. II. YACHT CLUBS, YACHTING IN AMERICA AND THE COLONIES, YACHT RACING, &c. By R. T. PRITCHETT, THE MARQUIS OF DUFFERIN AND AVA, K.P., THE EARL OF ONSLOW, JAMES McFERRAN, &c. With 35 Plates and 160 Illustrations in the Text. Crown 8vo., 10s. 6d.

Sport and Pastime—*continued.*

FUR, FEATHER, AND FIN SERIES.

Edited by A. E. T. WATSON.

Crown 8vo., price 5s. each Volume, cloth.

* *The Volumes are also issued half-bound in Leather, with gilt top. The price can be had from all Booksellers.*

THE PARTRIDGE. Natural History by the Rev. H. A. MACPHERSON; Shooting, by A. J. STUART-WORTLEY; Cookery, by GEORGE SAINTSBURY. With 11 Illustrations and various Diagrams in the Text. Crown 8vo., 5s.

THE GROUSE. Natural History by the Rev. H. A. MACPHERSON; Shooting, by A. J. STUART-WORTLEY; Cookery, by GEORGE SAINTSBURY. With 13 Illustrations and various Diagrams in the Text. Crown 8vo., 5s.

THE PHEASANT. Natural History by the Rev. H. A. MACPHERSON; Shooting, by A. J. STUART-WORTLEY; Cookery, by ALEXANDER INNES SHAND. With 10 Illustrations and various Diagrams. Crown 8vo., 5s.

THE HARE. Natural History by the Rev. H. A. MACPHERSON; Shooting, by the Hon. GERALD LASCELLES; Coursing, by CHARLES RICHARDSON; Hunting, by J. S. GIBBONS and G. H. LONGMAN; Cookery, by Col. KENNEY HERBERT. With 9 Illustrations. Crown 8vo., 5s.

RED DEER.—Natural History. By the Rev. H. A. MACPHERSON. Deer Stalking. By CAMERON OF LOCHIEL.—Stag Hunting. By Viscount EBRINGTON.—Cookery. By ALEXANDER INNES SHAND. With 10 Illustrations by J. CHARLTON and A. THORBURN. Crown 8vo., 5s.

THE RABBIT. By J. E. HARTING, etc. With Illustrations. [*In preparation.*

WILDFOWL. By the Hon. JOHN SCOTT MONTAGU. With Illustrations. [*In preparation.*

THE SALMON. By the Hon. A. E. GATHORNE-HARDY. With Illustrations. [*In preparation.*

THE TROUT. By the MARQUIS OF GRANBY, etc. With Illustrations. [*In prep.*

André.—*COLONEL BOGEY'S SKETCH-BOOK.* Comprising an Eccentric Collection of Scribbles and Scratches found in disused Lockers and swept up in the Pavilion, together with sundry After-Dinner Sayings of the Colonel. By R. ANDRÉ, West Herts Golf Club. Oblong 4to., 2s. 6d.

BADMINTON MAGAZINE (THE) OF SPORTS AND PASTIMES. Edited by ALFRED E. T. WATSON ("Rapier"). With numerous Illustrations. Price 1s. monthly.

Vols. I.-IV. 6s. each.

DEAD SHOT (THE): or, Sportsman's Complete Guide. Being a Treatise on the Use of the Gun, with Rudimentary and Finishing Lessons in the Art of Shooting Game of all kinds. Also Game-driving, Wildfowl and Pigeon-shooting, Dog-breaking, etc. By MARKSMAN. With numerous Illustrations. Crown 8vo., 10s. 6d.

Ellis.—*CHESS SPARKS;* or, Short and Bright Games of Chess. Collected and Arranged by J. H. ELLIS, M.A. 8vo., 4s. 6d.

Folkard.—*THE WILD-FOWLER:* A Treatise on Fowling, Ancient and Modern, descriptive also of Decoys and Flight-ponds, Wild-fowl Shooting, Gunning-punts, Shooting-yachts, &c. Also Fowling in the Fens and in Foreign Countries, Rock-fowling, &c., &c., by H. C. FOLKARD. With 13 Engravings on Steel, and several Woodcuts. 8vo., 12s. 6d.

Ford.—*THE THEORY AND PRACTICE OF ARCHERY.* By HORACE FORD. New Edition, thoroughly Revised and Re-written by W. BUTT, M.A. With a Preface by C. J. LONGMAN, M.A. 8vo., 14s.

Francis.—*A BOOK ON ANGLING:* or, Treatise on the Art of Fishing in every Branch; including full Illustrated List of Salmon Flies. By FRANCIS FRANCIS. With Portrait and Coloured Plates. Crown 8vo., 15s.

Sport and Pastime—*continued.*

Gibson.—*TOBOGGANING ON CROOKED RUNS.* By the Hon. HARRY GIBSON. With Contributions by F. DE B. STRICKLAND and 'LADY-TOBOGANNER'. With 40 Illustrations. Crown 8vo., 6s.

Graham.—*COUNTRY PASTIMES FOR BOYS.* By P. ANDERSON GRAHAM. With 252 Illustrations from Drawings and Photographs. Crown 8vo., 3s. 6d.

Lang.—*ANGLING SKETCHES.* By ANDREW LANG. With 20 Illustrations. Crown 8vo., 3s. 6d.

Lillie.—*CROQUET:* its History, Rules and Secrets. By ARTHUR LILLIE, Champion, Grand National Croquet Club, 1872; Winner of the 'All-Comers' Championship,' Maidstone, 1896. With 4 Full-page Illustrations by LUCIEN DAVIS, 15 Illustrations in the Text, and 27 Diagrams. Crown 8vo., 6s.

Longman.—*CHESS OPENINGS.* By FREDERICK W. LONGMAN. Fcp. 8vo., 2s. 6d.

Madden.—*THE DIARY OF MASTER WILLIAM SILENCE:* a Study of Shakespeare and of Elizabethan Sport. By the Right Hon. D. H. MADDEN, Vice-Chancellor of the University of Dublin. 8vo., 16s.

Maskelyne.—*SHARPS AND FLATS:* a Complete Revelation of the Secrets of Cheating at Games of Chance and Skill. By JOHN NEVIL MASKELYNE, of the Egyptian Hall. With 62 Illustrations. Crown 8vo., 6s.

Park.—*THE GAME OF GOLF.* By WILLIAM PARK, Jun., Champion Golfer, 1887-89. With 17 Plates and 26 Illustrations in the Text. Crown 8vo., 7s. 6d.

Payne-Gallwey (SIR RALPH, Bart.).

LETTERS TO YOUNG SHOOTERS (First Series). On the Choice and use of a Gun. With 41 Illustrations. Crown 8vo., 7s. 6d.

LETTERS TO YOUNG SHOOTERS (Second Series). On the Production, Preservation, and Killing of Game. With Directions in Shooting Wood-Pigeons and Breaking-in Retrievers. With Portrait and 103 Illustrations. Crown 8vo., 12s. 6d.

Payne-Gallwey (SIR RALPH, Bart.) —*continued.*

LETTERS TO YOUNG SHOOTERS. (Third Series.) Comprising a Short Natural History of the Wildfowl that are Rare or Common to the British Islands, with complete directions in Shooting Wildfowl on the Coast and Inland. With 200 Illustrations. Crown 8vo., 18s.

Pole (WILLIAM).

THE THEORY OF THE MODERN SCIENTIFIC GAME OF WHIST. Fcp. 8vo., 2s. 6d.

THE EVOLUTION OF WHIST: a Study of the Progressive Changes which the Game has undergone. Cr. 8vo., 2s. 6d.

Proctor.—*HOW TO PLAY WHIST: WITH THE LAWS AND ETIQUETTE OF WHIST.* By RICHARD A. PROCTOR. Crown 8vo., 3s. 6d.

Ribblesdale.—*THE QUEEN'S HOUNDS AND STAG-HUNTING RECOLLECTIONS.* By LORD RIBBLESDALE, Master of the Buckhounds, 1892-95. With Introductory Chapter on the Hereditary Mastership by E. BURROWS. With 24 Plates and 35 Illustrations in the Text, including reproductions from Oil Paintings in the possession of Her Majesty the Queen at Windsor Castle and Cumberland Lodge, Original Drawings by G. D. GILES, and from Prints and Photographs. 8vo., 25s.

Ronalds.—*THE FLY-FISHER'S ENTOMOLOGY.* By ALFRED RONALDS. With 20 coloured Plates. 8vo., 14s.

Thompson and Cannan. *HAND-IN-HAND FIGURE SKATING.* By NORCLIFFE G. THOMPSON and F. LAURA CANNAN, Members of the Skating Club. With an Introduction by Captain J. H. THOMSON, R.A. With Illustrations. 16mo., 6s.

Wilcocks.—*THE SEA FISHERMAN:* Comprising the Chief Methods of Hook and Line Fishing in the British and other Seas, and Remarks on Nets, Boats, and Boating. By J. C. WILCOCKS. Illustrated. Cr. 8vo., 6s.

Mental, Moral, and Political Philosophy.

LOGIC, RHETORIC, PSYCHOLOGY, &C.

Abbott.—*THE ELEMENTS OF LOGIC.* By T. K. ABBOTT, B.D. 12mo., 3s.

Aristotle.

THE ETHICS: Greek Text, Illustrated with Essay and Notes. By Sir ALEXANDER GRANT, Bart. 2 vols. 8vo., 32s.

AN INTRODUCTION TO ARISTOTLE'S ETHICS. Books I.-IV. (Book X. c. vi.-ix. in an Appendix). With a continuous Analysis and Notes. By the Rev. EDWARD MOORE, D.D., Cr. 8vo. 10s. 6d.

Bacon (FRANCIS).

COMPLETE WORKS. Edited by R. L. ELLIS, JAMES SPEDDING and D. D. HEATH. 7 vols. 8vo., £3 13s. 6d.

LETTERS AND LIFE, including all his occasional Works. Edited by JAMES SPEDDING. 7 vols. 8vo., £4 4s.

THE ESSAYS: with Annotations. By RICHARD WHATELY, D.D. 8vo., 10s. 6d.

THE ESSAYS. Edited, with Notes, by F. STORR and C. H. GIBSON. Crown 8vo, 3s. 6d.

THE ESSAYS: with Introduction, Notes, and Index. By E. A. ABBOTT, D.D. 2 Vols. Fcp. 8vo., 6s. The Text and Index only, without Introduction and Notes, in One Volume. Fcp. 8vo., 2s. 6d.

Bain (ALEXANDER).

MENTAL SCIENCE. Cr. 8vo., 6s. 6d.

MORAL SCIENCE. Cr. 8vo., 4s. 6d.

The two works as above can be had in one volume, price 10s. 6d.

SENSES AND THE INTELLECT. 8vo., 15s.

EMOTIONS AND THE WILL. 8vo., 15s.

LOGIC, DEDUCTIVE AND INDUCTIVE. Part I. 4s. Part II. 6s. 6d.

PRACTICAL ESSAYS. Cr. 8vo., 2s.

Baldwin.—*THE ELEMENTS OF EXPOSITORY CONSTRUCTION.* By Dr. CHARLES SEARS BALDWIN, Instructor in Rhetoric in Yale University.

Bray (CHARLES).

THE PHILOSOPHY OF NECESSITY: or, Law in Mind as in Matter. Cr. 8vo., 5s.

THE EDUCATION OF THE FEELINGS: a Moral System for Schools. Cr. 8vo., 2s. 6d.

Bray.—*ELEMENTS OF MORALITY,* in Easy Lessons for Home and School Teaching. By Mrs. CHARLES BRAY. Crown 8vo., 1s. 6d.

Crozier.—*HISTORY OF INTELLECTUAL DEVELOPMENT:* on the Lines of Modern Evolution. By JOHN BEATTIE CROZIER. Vol. I. Greek and Hindoo Thought; Græco-Roman Paganism; Judaism; and Christianity down to the Closing of the Schools of Athens under Justinian, 529 A.D. 8vo., 14s.

Davidson.—*THE LOGIC OF DEFINITION,* Explained and Applied. By WILLIAM L. DAVIDSON, M.A. Crown 8vo., 6s.

Green (THOMAS HILL).—*THE WORKS OF.* Edited by R. L. NETTLESHIP.

Vols. I. and II. Philosophical Works. 8vo., 16s. each.

Vol. III. Miscellanies. With Index to the three Volumes, and Memoir. 8vo., 21s.

LECTURES ON THE PRINCIPLES OF POLITICAL OBLIGATION. With Preface by BERNARD BOSANQUET. 8vo., 5s.

Hodgson (SHADWORTH H.).

TIME AND SPACE: A Metaphysical Essay. 8vo., 16s.

THE THEORY OF PRACTICE: an Ethical Inquiry. 2 vols. 8vo., 24s.

THE PHILOSOPHY OF REFLECTION. 2 vols. 8vo., 21s.

Hume.—*THE PHILOSOPHICAL WORKS OF DAVID HUME.* Edited by T. H. GREEN and T. H. GROSE. 4 vols. 8vo., 56s. Or separately, Essays. 2 vols. 28s. Treatise of Human Nature. 2 vols. 28s.

James.—*THE WILL TO BELIEVE,* and Other Essays in Popular Philosophy. By WILLIAM JAMES, M.D., LL.D., etc. Crown 8vo., 7s. 6d.

Justinian.—*THE INSTITUTES OF JUSTINIAN:* Latin Text, chiefly that of Huschke, with English Introduction, Translation, Notes, and Summary. By THOMAS C. SANDARS, M.A. 8vo., 18s.

Kant (IMMANUEL).

CRITIQUE OF PRACTICAL REASON, AND OTHER WORKS ON THE THEORY OF ETHICS. Translated by T. K. ABBOTT, B.D. With Memoir. 8vo., 12s. 6d.

FUNDAMENTAL PRINCIPLES OF THE METAPHYSIC OF ETHICS. Translated by T. K. ABBOTT, B.D. (Extracted from 'Kant's Critique of Practical Reason and other Works on the Theory of Ethics.') Crown 8vo, 3s.

INTRODUCTION TO LOGIC, AND HIS ESSAY ON THE MISTAKEN SUBTILTY OF THE FOUR FIGURES.. Translated by T. K. ABBOTT. 8vo., 6s.

Mental, Moral and Political Philosophy—*continued.*

Killick.—*HANDBOOK TO MILL'S SYSTEM OF LOGIC.* By Rev. A. H. KILLICK, M.A. Crown 8vo., 3s. 6d.

Ladd (GEORGE TRUMBULL).

PHILOSOPHY OF KNOWLEDGE: an Inquiry into the Nature, Limits and Validity of Human Cognitive Faculty. 8vo., 18s.

PHILOSOPHY OF MIND : An Essay on the Metaphysics of Psychology. 8vo., 16s.

ELEMENTS OF PHYSIOLOGICAL PSYCHOLOGY. 8vo., 21s.

OUTLINES OF PHYSIOLOGICAL PSYCHOLOGY. A Text-book of Mental Science for Academies and Colleges. 8vo., 12s.

PSYCHOLOGY, DESCRIPTIVE AND EXPLANATORY: a Treatise of the Phenomena, Laws, and Development of Human Mental Life. 8vo., 21s.

PRIMER OF PSYCHOLOGY. Cr. 8vo., 5s. 6d.

Lewes.—*THE HISTORY OF PHILOSOPHY,* from Thales to Comte. By GEORGE HENRY LEWES. 2 vols. 8vo., 32s.

Lutoslawski.—*THE ORIGIN AND GROWTH OF PLATO'S LOGIC.* By W. LUTOSLAWSKI. 8vo.

Max Müller (F.).

THE SCIENCE OF THOUGHT. 8vo., 21s.

THREE INTRODUCTORY LECTURES ON THE SCIENCE OF THOUGHT. 8vo., 2s. 6d. net.

Mill.—*ANALYSIS OF THE PHENOMENA OF THE HUMAN MIND.* By JAMES MILL. 2 vols. 8vo., 28s.

Mill (JOHN STUART).

A SYSTEM OF LOGIC. Cr. 8vo., 3s. 6d.

ON LIBERTY. Crown 8vo., 1s. 4d.

CONSIDERATIONS ON REPRESENTATIVE GOVERNMENT. Crown 8vo., 2s.

UTILITARIANISM. 8vo., 2s. 6d.

EXAMINATION OF SIR WILLIAM HAMILTON'S PHILOSOPHY. 8vo., 16s.

NATURE, THE UTILITY OF RELIGION, AND THEISM. Three Essays. 8vo., 5s.

Romanes.—*MIND AND MOTION AND MONISM.* By GEORGE JOHN ROMANES, LL.D., F.R.S. Cr. 8vo., 4s. 6d.

Stock (ST. GEORGE).

DEDUCTIVE LOGIC. Fcp. 8vo., 3s. 6d.

LECTURES IN THE LYCEUM ; or, Aristotle's Ethics for English Readers. Edited by ST. GEORGE STOCK. Crown 8vo., 7s. 6d.

Sully (JAMES).

THE HUMAN MIND : a Text-book of Psychology. 2 vols. 8vo., 21s.

OUTLINES OF PSYCHOLOGY. 8vo., 9s.

THE TEACHER'S HANDBOOK OF PSYCHOLOGY. Crown 8vo., 6s. 6d.

STUDIES OF CHILDHOOD. 8vo, 10s. 6d.

CHILDREN'S WAYS: being Selections from the Author's 'Studies of Childhood,' with some Additional Matter. With 25 Figures in the Text. Crown 8vo., 4s. 6d.

Sutherland. — *THE ORIGIN AND GROWTH OF THE MORAL INSTINCT.* By ALEXANDER SUTHERLAND, M.A.

Swinburne. — *PICTURE LOGIC :* an Attempt to Popularise the Science of Reasoning. By ALFRED JAMES SWINBURNE, M.A. With 23 Woodcuts. Crown 8vo., 5s.

Weber.—*HISTORY OF PHILOSOPHY.* By ALFRED WEBER, Professor in the University of Strasburg. Translated by FRANK THILLY, Ph.D. 8vo., 16s.

Whately (ARCHBISHOP).

BACON'S ESSAYS. With Annotations. 8vo., 10s. 6d.

ELEMENTS OF LOGIC. Cr. 8vo., 4s. 6d.

ELEMENTS OF RHETORIC. Cr. 8vo., 4s. 6d.

LESSONS ON REASONING. Fcp. 8vo., 1s. 6d.

Zeller (Dr. EDWARD, Professor in the University of Berlin).

THE STOICS, EPICUREANS, AND SCEPTICS. Translated by the Rev. O. J. REICHEL, M.A. Crown 8vo., 15s.

OUTLINES OF THE HISTORY OF GREEK PHILOSOPHY. Translated by SARAH F. ALLEYNE and EVELYN ABBOTT. Crown 8vo., 10s. 6d.

PLATO AND THE OLDER ACADEMY. Translated by SARAH F. ALLEYNE and ALFRED GOODWIN, B.A. Crown 8vo., 18s.

SOCRATES AND THE SOCRATIC SCHOOLS. Translated by the Rev. O. J. REICHEL, M.A. Crown 8vo., 10s.

ARISTOTLE AND THE EARLIER PERIPATETICS. Translated by B. F. C. Costelloe, M.A., and J. H. MUIRHEAD, M.A. 2 vols. Crown 8vo., 24s.

Mental, Moral, and Political Philosophy—*continued*.

MANUALS OF CATHOLIC PHILOSOPHY.
(Stonyhurst Series).

A MANUAL OF POLITICAL ECONOMY. By C. S. DEVAS, M.A.   Crown 8vo., 6s. 6d.

FIRST PRINCIPLES OF KNOWLEDGE. By JOHN RICKABY, S.J.   Crown 8vo., 5s.

GENERAL METAPHYSICS.   By JOHN RICKABY, S.J.   Crown 8vo., 5s.

LOGIC.   By RICHARD F. CLARKE, S.J. Crown 8vo., 5s.

MORAL PHILOSOPHY (ETHICS AND NATURAL LAW).   By JOSEPH RICKABY, S.J. Crown 8vo., 5s.

NATURAL THEOLOGY.   By BERNARD BOEDDER, S.J.   Crown 8vo., 6s. 6d.

PSYCHOLOGY.   By MICHAEL MAHER, S.J.   Crown 8vo., 6s. 6d.

History and Science of Language, &c.

Davidson.—*LEADING AND IMPORTANT ENGLISH WORDS:* Explained and Exemplified.   By WILLIAM L. DAVIDSON, M.A. Fcp. 8vo., 3s. 6d.

Farrar.—*LANGUAGE AND LANGUAGES:* By F. W. FARRAR, D.D., F.R.S.   Crown 8vo., 6s.

Graham. — *ENGLISH SYNONYMS*, Classified and Explained : with Practical Exercises. By G. F. GRAHAM. Fcp. 8vo., 6s.

Max Müller (F.).

THE SCIENCE OF LANGUAGE.—Founded on Lectures delivered at the Royal Institution in 1861 and 1863. 2 vols. Crown 8vo., 21s.

Max Müller (F.)—*continued*.

BIOGRAPHIES OF WORDS, AND THE HOME OF THE ARYAS. Crown 8vo., 7s. 6d.

THREE LECTURES ON THE SCIENCE OF LANGUAGE, AND ITS PLACE IN GENERAL EDUCATION, delivered at Oxford, 1889.   Crown 8vo., 3s. net.

Roget.—*THESAURUS OF ENGLISH WORDS AND PHRASES.*   Classified and Arranged so as to Facilitate the Expression of Ideas and assist in Literary Composition. By PETER MARK ROGET, M.D., F.R.S. Recomposed throughout, enlarged and improved, partly from the Author's Notes, and with a full Index, by the Author's Son, JOHN LEWIS ROGET.   Crown 8vo. 10s. 6d.

Whately.—*ENGLISH SYNONYMS.*   By E. JANE WHATELY.   Fcp. 8vo., 3s.

Political Economy and Economics.

Ashley.—*ENGLISH ECONOMIC HISTORY AND THEORY.* By W. J. ASHLEY, M.A.   Crown 8vo., Part I., 5s.   Part II. 10s. 6d.

Bagehot.—*ECONOMIC STUDIES.* By WALTER BAGEHOT.   Crown 8vo., 3s. 6d.

Barnett.—*PRACTICABLE SOCIALISM.* Essays on Social Reform.   By the Rev. S. A. and Mrs. BARNETT.   Crown 8vo., 6s.

Brassey.—*PAPERS AND ADDRESSES ON WORK AND WAGES.* By Lord BRASSEY. Edited by J. POTTER, and with Introduction by GEORGE HOWELL, M.P. Crown 8vo., 5s.

Devas.—*A MANUAL OF POLITICAL ECONOMY.* By C. S. DEVAS, M.A.   Cr. 8vo., 6s. 6d. *(Manuals of Catholic Philosophy.)*

Dowell.—*A HISTORY OF TAXATION AND TAXES IN ENGLAND,* from the Earliest Times to the Year 1885.   By STEPHEN DOWELL, (4 vols. 8vo).   Vols. I. and II. The History of Taxation, 21s.   Vols. III. and IV. The History of Taxes, 21s.

Jordan.—*THE STANDARD OF VALUE.* By WILLIAM LEIGHTON JORDAN, Fellow of the Royal Statistical Society, &c.   Crown 8vo., 6s.

Macleod (HENRY DUNNING).

BIMETALISM.   8vo., 5s. net.

THE ELEMENTS OF BANKING.   Cr. 8vo., 3s. 6d.

THE THEORY AND PRACTICE OF BANKING. Vol. I. 8vo., 12s. Vol. II. 14s.

THE THEORY OF CREDIT.   8vo. Vol. I., 10s. net. Vol. II., Part I., 10s. net. Vol. II., Part II., 10s. net.

A DIGEST OF THE LAW OF BILLS OF EXCHANGE, BANK-NOTES, &c.
[In the press.

Mill.—*POLITICAL ECONOMY.*   By JOHN STUART MILL.
Popular Edition.   Crown 8vo., 3s. 6d.
Library Edition.   2 vols.   8vo., 30s.

Political Economy and Economics—*continued.*

Mulhall.—*INDUSTRIES AND WEALTH OF NATIONS.* By MICHAEL G. MULHALL, F.S.S. With 32 full-page Diagrams. Crown 8vo., 8s. 6d.

Soderini.—*SOCIALISM AND CATHOLICISM.* From the Italian of Count EDWARD SODERINI. By RICHARD JENERY-SHEE. With a Preface by Cardinal VAUGHAN. Crown 8vo., 6s.

Symes.—*POLITICAL ECONOMY:* a Short Text-book of Political Economy. With Problems for Solution, and Hints for Supplementary Reading; also a Supplementary Chapter on Socialism. By Professor J. E. SYMES, M.A., of University College, Nottingham. Crown 8vo., 2s. 6d.

Toynbee.—*LECTURES ON THE INDUSTRIAL REVOLUTION OF THE 18TH CENTURY IN ENGLAND:* Popular Addresses, Notes and other Fragments. By ARNOLD TOYNBEE. With a Memoir of the Author by BENJAMIN JOWETT, D.D. 8vo., 10s. 6d.

Vincent.—*THE LAND QUESTION IN NORTH WALES:* being a Brief Survey of the History, Origin, and Character of the Agrarian Agitation, and of the Nature and Effect of the Proceedings of the Welsh Land Commission. By J. E. VINCENT. 8vo., 5s.

Webb (SIDNEY and BEATRICE).
THE HISTORY OF TRADE UNIONISM. With Map and full Bibliography of the Subject. 8vo., 18s.
INDUSTRIAL DEMOCRACY: a Study in Trade Unionism. 2 vols. 8vo.

STUDIES IN ECONOMICS AND POLITICAL SCIENCE.
Issued under the auspices of the London School of Economics and Political Science.

THE HISTORY OF LOCAL RATES IN ENGLAND: Five Lectures. By EDWIN CANNAN, M.A. Crown 8vo., 2s. 6d.

GERMAN SOCIAL DEMOCRACY. By BERTRAND RUSSELL, B.A. With an Appendix on Social Democracy and the Woman Question in Germany by ALYS RUSSELL, B.A. Crown 8vo., 3s. 6d.

SELECT DOCUMENTS ILLUSTRATING THE HISTORY OF TRADE UNIONISM.
 1. The Tailoring Trade. Edited by W. F. GALTON. With a Preface by SIDNEY WEBB, LL.B. Crown 8vo., 5s.

DEPLOIGE'S REFERENDUM EN SUISSE. Translated, with Introduction and Notes, by C. P. TREVELYAN, M.A. [In preparation.

SELECT DOCUMENTS ILLUSTRATING THE STATE REGULATION OF WAGES. Edited, with Introduction and Notes, by W. A. S. HEWINS, M.A. [In preparation.

HUNGARIAN GILD RECORDS. Edited by Dr. JULIUS MANDELLO, of Budapest. [In preparation.

THE RELATIONS BETWEEN ENGLAND AND THE HANSEATIC LEAGUE. By Miss E. A. MACARTHUR. [In preparation.

Evolution, Anthropology, &c.

Clodd (EDWARD).

THE STORY OF CREATION: a Plain Account of Evolution. With 77 Illustrations. Crown 8vo., 3s. 6d.

A PRIMER OF EVOLUTION: being a Popular Abridged Edition of 'The Story of Creation'. With Illustrations. Fcp. 8vo., 1s. 6d.

Lang.—*CUSTOM AND MYTH:* Studies of Early Usage and Belief. By ANDREW LANG. With 15 Illustrations. Crown 8vo., 3s. 6d.

Lubbock.—*THE ORIGIN OF CIVILISATION,* and the Primitive Condition of Man. By Sir J. LUBBOCK, Bart., M.P. With 5 Plates and 20 Illustrations in the Text. 8vo., 18s.

Romanes (GEORGE JOHN).

DARWIN, AND AFTER DARWIN: an Exposition of the Darwinian Theory, and a Discussion on Post-Darwinian Questions.
Part I. THE DARWINIAN THEORY. With Portrait of Darwin and 125 Illustrations. Crown 8vo., 10s. 6d.
Part II. POST-DARWINIAN QUESTIONS: Heredity and Utility. With Portrait of the Author and 5 Illustrations. Cr. 8vo., 10s. 6d.
Part III. Post-Darwinian Questions: Isolation and Physiological Selection. Crown 8vo., 5s.

AN EXAMINATION OF WEISMANNISM. Crown 8vo., 6s.

ESSAYS. Edited by C. LLOYD MORGAN, Principal of University College, Bristol. Crown 8vo., 6s.

Classical Literature, Translations, &c.

Abbott.—*HELLENICA.* A Collection of Essays on Greek Poetry, Philosophy, History, and Religion. Edited by EVELYN ABBOTT, M.A., LL.D. 8vo., 16s.

Æschylus.—*EUMENIDES OF ÆSCHYLUS.* With Metrical English Translation. By J. F. DAVIES. 8vo., 7s.

Aristophanes. — *THE ACHARNIANS OF ARISTOPHANES,* translated into English Verse. By R. Y. TYRRELL. Crown 8vo., 1s.

Aristotle.—*YOUTH AND OLD AGE, LIFE AND DEATH, AND RESPIRATION.* Translated, with Introduction and Notes, by W. OGLE, M.A., M.D., F.R.C.P., sometime Fellow of Corpus Christi College, Oxford. 8vo., 7s. 6d.

Becker (PROFESSOR).

GALLUS : or, Roman Scenes in the Time of Augustus. Illustrated. Post 8vo., 3s. 6d.

CHARICLES : or, Illustrations of the Private Life of the Ancient Greeks. Illustrated. Post 8vo., 3s. 6d.

Butler.—*THE AUTHORESS OF THE ODYSSEY, WHERE AND WHEN SHE WROTE, WHO SHE WAS, THE USE SHE MADE OF THE ILIAD, AND HOW THE POEM GREW UNDER HER HANDS.* By SAMUEL BUTLER, Author of 'Erewhon,' etc. With Illustrations. 8vo.

Cicero.—*CICERO'S CORRESPONDENCE.* By R. Y. TYRRELL. Vols. I., II., III., 8vo., each 12s. Vol. IV., 15s. Vol. V., 14s.

Egbert.—*INTRODUCTION TO THE STUDY OF LATIN INSCRIPTIONS.* By JAMES C. EGBERT, Junr., Ph.D. With numerous Illustrations and Facsimiles. Square crown 8vo., 16s.

Lang.—*HOMER AND THE EPIC.* By ANDREW LANG. Crown 8vo., 9s. net.

Lucan.—*THE PHARSALIA OF LUCAN.* Translated into Blank Verse. By Sir EDWARD RIDLEY. 8vo., 14s.

Mackail.—*SELECT EPIGRAMS FROM THE GREEK ANTHOLOGY.* By J. W. MACKAIL. Edited with a Revised Text, Introduction, Translation, and Notes. 8vo., 16s.

Rich.—*A DICTIONARY OF ROMAN AND GREEK ANTIQUITIES.* By A. RICH, B.A. With 2000 Woodcuts. Crown 8vo., 7s. 6d.

Sophocles.—Translated into English Verse. By ROBERT WHITELAW, M.A., Assistant Master in Rugby School. Cr. 8vo., 8s. 6d.

Tacitus. — *THE HISTORY OF P. CORNELIUS TACITUS.* Translated into English, with an Introduction and Notes, Critical and Explanatory, by ALBERT WILLIAM QUILL, M.A., T.C.D. 2 vols. Vol. I. 8vo., 7s. 6d. Vol. II. 8vo., 12s. 6d.

Tyrrell.—*TRANSLATIONS INTO GREEK AND LATIN VERSE.* Edited by R. Y. TYRRELL. 8vo., 6s.

Virgil.

THE ÆNEID OF VIRGIL. Translated into English Verse by JOHN CONINGTON. Crown 8vo., 6s.

THE POEMS OF VIRGIL. Translated into English Prose by JOHN CONINGTON. Crown 8vo., 6s.

THE ÆNEID OF VIRGIL, freely translated into English Blank Verse. By W. J. THORNHILL. Crown 8vo., 7s. 6d.

THE ÆNEID OF VIRGIL. Translated into English Verse by JAMES RHOADES. Books I.-VI. Crown 8vo., 5s. Books VII.-XII. Crown 8vo., 5s.

Poetry and the Drama.

Allingham (WILLIAM).

IRISH SONGS AND POEMS. With Frontispiece of the Waterfall of Asaroe. Fcp. 8vo., 6s.

LAURENCE BLOOMFIELD. With Portrait of the Author. Fcp. 8vo., 3s. 6d.

FLOWER PIECES ; DAY AND NIGHT SONGS ; BALLADS. With 2 Designs by D. G. ROSSETTI. Fcp. 8vo., 6s. large paper edition, 12s.

Allingham (WILLIAM)—*continued.*

LIFE AND PHANTASY : with Frontispiece by Sir J. E. MILLAIS, Bart., and Design by ARTHUR HUGHES. Fcp. 8vo., 6s. ; large paper edition, 12s.

THOUGHT AND WORD, AND ASHBY MANOR : a Play. Fcp. 8vo., 6s.; large paper edition, 12s.

BLACKBERRIES. Imperial 16mo., 6s.

Sets of the above 6 vols. may be had in uniform Half-parchment binding, price 30s.

Poetry and the Drama—*continued.*

Armstrong (G. F. SAVAGE).

POEMS : Lyrical and Dramatic. Fcp. 8vo., 6s.

KING SAUL. (The Tragedy of Israel, Part I.) Fcp. 8vo., 5s.

KING DAVID. (The Tragedy of Israel, Part II.) Fcp. 8vo., 6s.

KING SOLOMON. (The Tragedy of Israel, Part III.) Fcp. 8vo., 6s.

UGONE : a Tragedy. Fcp. 8vo., 6s.

A GARLAND FROM GREECE : Poems. Fcp. 8vo., 7s. 6d.

STORIES OF WICKLOW : Poems. Fcp. 8vo., 7s. 6d.

MEPHISTOPHELES IN BROADCLOTH : a Satire. Fcp. 8vo., 4s.

ONE IN THE INFINITE : a Poem. Crown 8vo., 7s. 6d.

Armstrong.—*THE POETICAL WORKS OF EDMUND J. ARMSTRONG.* Fcp. 8vo., 5s.

Arnold.—*THE LIGHT OF THE WORLD:* or, The Great Consummation. By Sir EDWIN ARNOLD. With 14 Illustrations after HOLMAN HUNT. Crown 8vo., 6s.

Beesly (A. H.).

BALLADS AND OTHER VERSE. Fcp. 8vo., 5s.

DANTON, AND OTHER VERSE. Fcp. 8vo., 4s. 6d.

Bell (MRS. HUGH).

CHAMBER COMEDIES : a Collection of Plays and Monologues for the Drawing Room. Crown 8vo., 6s.

FAIRY TALE PLAYS, AND HOW TO ACT THEM. With 91 Diagrams and 52 Illustrations. Crown 8vo., 6s.

Cochrane (ALFRED).

THE KESTREL'S NEST, and other Verses. Fcp. 8vo., 3s. 6d.

LEVIORE PLECTRO : Occasional Verses. Fcap. 8vo., 3s. 6d.

Goethe.

FAUST, Part I., the German Text, with Introduction and Notes. By ALBERT M. SELSS, Ph.D., M.A. Crown 8vo., 5s.

FAUST. Translated, with Notes. By T. E. WEBB. 8vo., 12s. 6d.

Gurney.—*DAY-DREAMS :* Poems. By Rev. ALFRED GURNEY, M.A. Crown 8vo., 3s. 6d.

Ingelow (JEAN).

POETICAL WORKS. 2 vols. Fcp. 8vo., 12s.

LYRICAL AND OTHER POEMS. Selected from the Writings of JEAN INGELOW. Fcp. 8vo., 2s. 6d. cloth plain, 3s. cloth gilt.

Lang (ANDREW).

GRASS OF PARNASSUS. Fcp. 8vo., 2s. 6d. net.

THE BLUE POETRY BOOK. Edited by ANDREW LANG. With 100 Illustrations. Crown 8vo., 6s.

Layard.—*SONGS IN MANY MOODS.* By NINA F. LAYARD. And *THE WANDERING ALBATROSS,* &c. By Annie Corder. In one volume. Crown 8vo., 5s.

Lecky.—*POEMS.* By W. E. H. LECKY. Fcp. 8vo., 5s.

Lytton (THE EARL OF), (OWEN MEREDITH).

MARAH. Fcp. 8vo., 6s. 6d.

KING POPPY : a Fantasia. With 1 Plate and Design on Title-Page by ED. BURNE-JONES, A.R.A. Cr. 8vo., 10s. 6d.

THE WANDERER. Cr. 8vo., 10s. 6d.

LUCILE. Crown 8vo., 10s. 6d.

SELECTED POEMS. Cr. 8vo., 10s. 6d.

Poetry and the Drama—*continued.*

Macaulay.—*LAYS OF ANCIENT ROME,* *&c.* By Lord MACAULAY.
Illustrated by G. SCHARF. Fcp. 4to., 10s. 6d.
————————— Bijou Edition. 18mo., 2s. 6d. gilt top.
————————— Popular Edition. Fcp. 4to., 6d. sewed, 1s. cloth.
Illustrated by J. R. WEGUELIN. Crown 8vo., 3s. 6d.
Annotated Edition. Fcp. 8vo., 1s. sewed, 1s. 6d. cloth.

Macdonald (GEORGE, LL.D.).

A BOOK OF STRIFE, IN THE FORM OF THE DIARY OF AN OLD SOUL: Poems. 18mo., 6s.

RAMPOLLI: GROWTHS FROM A LONG-PLANTED ROOT: being Translations, New and Old (mainly in verse), chiefly from the German; along with 'A Year's Diary of an Old Soul'. Crown 8vo., 6s.

Morris (WILLIAM).
POETICAL WORKS—LIBRARY EDITION.
Complete in Ten Volumes. Crown 8vo., price 6s. each.

THE EARTHLY PARADISE. 4 vols. 6s. each.

THE LIFE AND DEATH OF JASON. 6s.

THE DEFENCE OF GUENEVERE, and other Poems. 6s.

THE STORY OF SIGURD THE VOLSUNG, AND THE FALL OF THE NIBLUNGS. 6s.

LOVE IS ENOUGH; or, the Freeing of Pharamond: A Morality; and *POEMS BY THE WAY.* 6s.

THE ODYSSEY OF HOMER. Done into English Verse. 6s.

THE ÆNEIDS OF VIRGIL. Done into English Verse. 6s.

Certain of the POETICAL WORKS may also be had in the following Editions:—

THE EARTHLY PARADISE.
Popular Edition. 5 vols. 12mo., 25s.; or 5s. each, sold separately.
The same in Ten Parts, 25s.; or 2s. 6d. each, sold separately.
Cheap Edition, in 1 vol. Crown 8vo., 7s. 6d.

Morris (WILLIAM)—*continued.*

LOVE IS ENOUGH; or, the Freeing of Pharamond: A Morality. Square crown 8vo., 7s. 6d.

POEMS BY THE WAY. Square crown 8vo., 6s.

*** For Mr. William Morris's Prose Works, see pp. 22 and 31.

Nesbit.—*LAYS AND LEGENDS.* By E. NESBIT (Mrs. HUBERT BLAND). First Series. Crown 8vo., 3s. 6d. Second Series. With Portrait. Crown 8vo., 5s.

Riley (JAMES WHITCOMB).

OLD FASHIONED ROSES: Poems. 12mo., 5s.

A CHILD-WORLD: POEMS. Fcp. 8vo., 5s.

Romanes.—*A SELECTION FROM THE POEMS OF GEORGE JOHN ROMANES, M.A., LL.D., F.R.S.* With an Introduction by T. HERBERT WARREN, President of Magdalen College, Oxford. Crown 8vo., 4s. 6d.

Shakespeare.—*BOWDLER'S FAMILY SHAKESPEARE.* With 36 Woodcuts. 1 vol. 8vo., 14s. Or in 6 vols. Fcp. 8vo., 21s.

THE SHAKESPEARE BIRTHDAY BOOK. By MARY F. DUNBAR. 32mo., 1s. 6d.

Tupper.—*POEMS.* By JOHN LUCAS TUPPER. Selected and Edited by WILLIAM MICHAEL ROSSETTI. Crown 8vo., 5s.

*** *The author of these Poems was a Sculptor, and afterwards Art Instructor in Rugby School. He died in 1879, having been a very close associate of the Pre-Raphaelite Brotherhood, and contributing in verse and prose to their magazine, the ' Germ,' in 1850.*

Wordsworth. — *SELECTED POEMS.* By ANDREW LANG. With Photogravure Frontispiece of Rydal Mount. With 16 Illustrations and numerous Initial Letters. By ALFRED PARSONS, A.R.A. Crown 8vo., gilt edges, 6s.

Wordsworth and Coleridge.—*A DESCRIPTION OF THE WORDSWORTH AND COLERIDGE MANUSCRIPTS IN THE POSSESSION OF Mr. T. NORTON LONGMAN.* Edited, with Notes, by W. HALE WHITE. With 3 Facsimile Reproductions. 4to., 10s. 6d.

Fiction, Humour, &c.

Allingham.—*CROOKED PATHS.* By FRANCIS ALLINGHAM. Crown 8vo., 6s.

Anstey (F., Author of 'Vice Versâ'). *VOCES POPULI.* Reprinted from 'Punch'. First Series. With 20 Illustrations by J. BERNARD PARTRIDGE. Crown 8vo., 3s. 6d.

THE MAN FROM BLANKLEY'S: a Story in Scenes, and other Sketches. With 24 Illustrations by J. BERNARD PARTRIDGE. Post 4to., 6s.

Astor.—*A JOURNEY IN OTHER WORLDS:* a Romance of the Future. By JOHN JACOB ASTOR. With 10 Illustrations. Cr. 8vo., 6s.

Beaconsfield (THE EARL OF). *NOVELS AND TALES.* Complete in 11 vols. Crown 8vo., 1s. 6d. each.

Vivian Grey.	Sybil.
The Young Duke, &c.	Henrietta Temple.
Alroy, Ixion, &c.	Venetia.
Contarini Fleming, &c.	Coningsby.
	Lothair.
Tancred.	Endymion.

NOVELS AND TALES. The Hughenden Edition. With 2 Portraits and 11 Vignettes. 11 vols. Crown 8vo., 42s.

Black.—*THE PRINCESS DÉSIRÉE.* By CLEMENTINA BLACK. With 8 Illustrations by JOHN WILLIAMSON. Cr. 8vo., 6s.

Crump.—*WIDE ASUNDER AS THE POLES.* By ARTHUR CRUMP. Cr. 8vo., 6s.

Deland.—*PHILIP AND HIS WIFE.* Crown 8vo., 2s. 6d.

Diderot. — *RAMEAU'S NEPHEW:* a Translation from Diderot's Autographic Text. By SYLVIA MARGARET HILL. Crown 8vo., 3s. 6d.

Dougall.—*BEGGARS ALL.* By L. DOUGALL. Crown 8vo., 3s. 6d.

Doyle (A. CONAN).

MICAH CLARKE: A Tale of Monmouth's Rebellion. With 10 Illustrations. Cr. 8vo., 3s. 6d.

THE CAPTAIN OF THE POLESTAR, and other Tales. Cr. 8vo., 3s. 6d.

THE REFUGEES: A Tale of the Huguenots. With 25 Illustrations. Cr. 8vo., 3s. 6d.

THE STARK MUNRO LETTERS. Cr. 8vo, 6s.

Farrar (F. W., DEAN OF CANTERBURY).

DARKNESS AND DAWN: or, Scenes in the Days of Nero. An Historic Tale. Cr. 8vo., 7s. 6d.

GATHERING CLOUDS: a Tale of the Days of St. Chrysostom. Cr. 8vo., 7s. 6d.

Fowler (EDITH H.).

THE YOUNG PRETENDERS. A Story of Child Life. With 12 Illustrations by PHILIP BURNE-JONES. Crown 8vo., 6s.

THE PROFESSOR'S CHILDREN. With 24 Illustrations by ETHEL KATE BURGESS. Crown 8vo., 6s.

Froude.—*THE TWO CHIEFS OF DUNBOY:* an Irish Romance of the Last Century. By JAMES A. FROUDE. Cr. 8vo., 3s. 6d.

Gilkes.—*KALLISTRATUS:* an Autobiography. A Story of Hannibal and the Second Punic War. By A. H. GILKES, M.A., Master of Dulwich College. With 3 Illustrations by MAURICE GREIFFENHAGEN. Crown 8vo., 6s.

Graham.—*THE RED SCAUR:* A Novel of Manners. By P. ANDERSON GRAHAM. Crown 8vo., 6s.

Gurdon.—*MEMORIES AND FANCIES:* Suffolk Tales and other Stories; Fairy Legends; Poems; Miscellaneous Articles. By the late LADY CAMILLA GURDON, Author of 'Suffolk Folk-Lore'. Crown 8vo., 5s.

Haggard (H. RIDER).

HEART OF THE WORLD. With 15 Illustrations. Crown 8vo., 6s.

JOAN HASTE. With 20 Illustrations. Crown 8vo., 3s. 6d.

THE PEOPLE OF THE MIST. With 16 Illustrations. Crown 8vo., 3s. 6d.

MONTEZUMA'S DAUGHTER. With 24 Illustrations. Crown 8vo., 3s. 6d.

SHE. With 32 Illustrations. Crown 8vo., 3s. 6d.

ALLAN QUATERMAIN. With 31 Illustrations. Crown 8vo., 3s. 6d.

MAIWA'S REVENGE: Cr. 8vo., 1s. 6d.

COLONEL QUARITCH, V.C. Cr. 8vo. 3s. 6d.

CLEOPATRA. With 29 Illustrations. Crown 8vo., 3s. 6d.

Fiction, Humour, &c.—*continued.*

Haggard (H. Rider)—*continued.*

BEATRICE. Cr. 8vo., 3s. 6d.

ERIC BRIGHTEYES. With 51 Illustrations. Crown 8vo., 3s. 6d.

NADA THE LILY. With 23 Illustrations. Crown 8vo., 3s. 6d.

ALLAN'S WIFE. With 34 Illustrations. Crown 8vo., 3s. 6d.

THE WITCH'S HEAD. With 16 Illustrations. Crown 8vo., 3s. 6d.

MR. MEESON'S WILL. With 16 Illustrations. Crown 8vo., 3s. 6d.

DAWN. With 16 Illustrations. Cr. 8vo., 3s. 6d.

Haggard and Lang.—*THE WORLD'S DESIRE.* By H. Rider Haggard and Andrew Lang. With 27 Illustrations. Crown 8vo., 3s. 6d.

Harte.—*IN THE CARQUINEZ WOODS* and other stories. By Bret Harte. Cr. 8vo., 3s. 6d.

Hope.—*THE HEART OF PRINCESS OSRA.* By Anthony Hope. With 9 Illustrations by John Williamson. Crown 8vo., 6s.

Hornung.—*THE UNBIDDEN GUEST.* By E. W. Hornung. Crown 8vo., 3s. 6d.

Jerome.—*SKETCHES IN LAVENDER: BLUE AND GREEN.* By Jerome K. Jerome, Author of 'Three Men in a Boat,' etc. Crown 8vo., 6s.

Lang.—*A MONK OF FIFE;* being the Chronicle written by Norman Leslie of Pitcullo, concerning Marvellous Deeds that befel in the Realm of France, 1429-31. By Andrew Lang. With 13 Illustrations by Selwyn Image. Cr. 8vo., 6s.

Lyall (Edna).

THE AUTOBIOGRAPHY OF A SLANDER. Fcp. 8vo., 1s., sewed.
Presentation Edition. With 20 Illustrations by Lancelot Speed. Crown 8vo., 2s. 6d. net.

THE AUTOBIOGRAPHY OF A TRUTH. Fcp. 8vo., 1s., sewed; 1s. 6d., cloth.

DOREEN. The Story of a Singer. Crown 8vo., 6s.

WAYFARING MEN. Crown 8vo., 6s.

Levett-Yeats (S.).

THE CHEVALIER D'AURIAC. Crown 8vo., 6s.

A GALAHAD OF THE CREEKS, and other Stories. Crown 8vo., 6s.

Melville (G. J. Whyte).

The Gladiators. | Holmby House.
The Interpreter. | Kate Coventry.
Good for Nothing. | Digby Grand.
The Queen's Maries. | General Bounce.
Crown 8vo., 1s. 6d. each.

Merriman.—*FLOTSAM:* The Study of a Life. By Henry Seton Merriman, With Frontispiece and Vignette by H. G. Massey, A.R.E. Crown 8vo., 6s.

Morris (William).

THE WATER OF THE WONDROUS ISLES. Crown 8vo., 7s. 6d.

THE WELL AT THE WORLD'S END. 2 vols. 8vo., 28s.

THE STORY OF THE GLITTERING PLAIN, which has been also called The Land of the Living Men, or The Acre of the Undying. Square post 8vo., 5s. net.

THE ROOTS OF THE MOUNTAINS, wherein is told somewhat of the Lives of the Men of Burgdale, their Friends, their Neighbours, their Foemen, and their Fellows-in-Arms. Written in Prose and Verse. Square crown 8vo., 8s.

A TALE OF THE HOUSE OF THE WOLFINGS, and all the Kindreds of the Mark. Written in Prose and Verse. Second Edition. Square crown 8vo., 6s.

A DREAM OF JOHN BALL, AND A KING'S LESSON. 12mo., 1s. 6d.

NEWS FROM NOWHERE; or, An Epoch of Rest. Being some Chapters from an Utopian Romance. Post 8vo., 1s. 6d.

*** For Mr. William Morris's Poetical Works, see p. 20.

Newman (Cardinal).

LOSS AND GAIN: The Story of a Convert. Crown 8vo. Cabinet Edition, 6s.; Popular Edition, 3s. 6d.

CALLISTA: A Tale of the Third Century. Crown 8vo. Cabinet Edition, 6s.; Popular Edition, 3s. 6d.

Oliphant.—*OLD MR. TREDGOLD.* By Mrs. Oliphant. Crown 8vo., 6s.

Phillipps-Wolley.—*SNAP:* a Legend of the Lone Mountain. By C. Phillipps-Wolley. With 13 Illustrations. Crown 8vo., 3s. 6d.

Quintana.—*THE CID CAMPEADOR:* an Historical Romance. By D. Antonio de Trueba y la Quintana. Translated from the Spanish by Henry J. Gill, M.A., T.C.D. Crown 8vo., 6s.

Fiction, Humour, &c.—*continued.*

Rhoscomyl (OWEN).

THE JEWEL OF YNYS GALON: being a hitherto unprinted Chapter in the History of the Sea Rovers. With 12 Illustrations by LANCELOT SPEED. Cr. 8vo., 3s. 6d.

BATTLEMENT AND TOWER: a Romance. With Frontispiece by R. CATON WOODVILLE. Crown 8vo., 6s.

FOR THE WHITE ROSE OF ARNO: a Story of the Jacobite Rising of 1745. Crown 8vo., 6s.

Sewell (ELIZABETH M.).

A Glimpse of the World.	Amy Herbert.
Laneton Parsonage.	Cleve Hall.
Margaret Percival.	Gertrude.
Katharine Ashton.	Home Life.
The Earl's Daughter.	After Life.
The Experience of Life.	Ursula. Ivors.

Cr. 8vo., 1s. 6d. each cloth plain. 2s. 6d each cloth extra, gilt edges.

Stevenson (ROBERT LOUIS).

THE STRANGE CASE OF DR. JEKYLL AND MR. HYDE. Fcp. 8vo., 1s. sewed. 1s. 6d. cloth.

THE STRANGE CASE OF DR. JEKYLL AND MR. HYDE; WITH OTHER FABLES. Crown 8vo., 3s. 6d.

MORE NEW ARABIAN NIGHTS—THE DYNAMITER. By ROBERT LOUIS STEVENSON and FANNY VAN DE GRIFT STEVENSON. Crown 8vo., 3s. 6d.

THE WRONG BOX. By ROBERT LOUIS STEVENSON and LLOYD OSBOURNE. Crown 8vo., 3s. 6d.

Suttner.—*LAY DOWN YOUR ARMS* (Die Waffen Nieder): The Autobiography of Martha Tilling. By BERTHA VON SUTTNER. Translated by T. HOLMES. Cr. 8vo., 1s. 6d.

Taylor. — *EARLY ITALIAN LOVE-STORIES.* Edited and Retold by UNA TAYLOR. With 12 Illustrations by H. J. FORD.

Trollope (ANTHONY).

THE WARDEN. Cr. 8vo., 1s. 6d.

BARCHESTER TOWERS. Cr. 8vo., 1s. 6d.

Walford (L. B.).

IVA KILDARE: a Matrimonial Problem. Crown 8vo., 6s.

MR. SMITH: a Part of his Life. Crown 8vo., 2s. 6d.

THE BABY'S GRANDMOTHER. Cr. 8vo., 2s. 6d.

COUSINS. Crown 8vo., 2s. 6d.

TROUBLESOME DAUGHTERS. Cr. 8vo., 2s. 6d.

PAULINE. Crown. 8vo., 2s. 6d.

DICK NETHERBY. Cr. 8vo., 2s. 6d.

THE HISTORY OF A WEEK. Cr. 8vo. 2s. 6d.

A STIFF-NECKED GENERATION. Cr. 8vo. 2s. 6d.

NAN, and other Stories. Cr. 8vo., 2s. 6d.

THE MISCHIEF OF MONICA. Cr. 8vo., 2s. 6d.

THE ONE GOOD GUEST. Cr. 8vo. 2s. 6d.

'PLOUGHED,' and other Stories. Crown 8vo., 2s. 6d.

THE MATCHMAKER. Cr. 8vo., 2s. 6d.

Weyman (STANLEY).

THE HOUSE OF THE WOLF. Cr. 8vo., 3s. 6d.

A GENTLEMAN OF FRANCE. Cr. 8vo., 6s.

THE RED COCKADE. Cr. 8vo., 6s.

Watson.—*RACING AND CHASING:* a Volume of Sporting Stories and Sketches. By ALFRED E. T. WATSON, Editor of the 'Badminton Magazine'. With numerous Illustrations.

Whishaw (FRED.).

A BOYAR OF THE TERRIBLE: a Romance of the Court of Ivan the Cruel, First Tzar of Russia. With 12 Illustrations by H. G. MASSEY, A.R.E. Crown 8vo., 6s.

A TSAR'S GRATITUDE. Cr. 8vo., 6s.

Woods.—*WEEPING FERRY,* and other Stories. By MARGARET L. WOODS, Author of 'A Village Tragedy'. Crown 8vo., 6s.

Popular Science (Natural History, &c.).

Butler.—*OUR HOUSEHOLD INSECTS.* An Account of the Insect-Pests found in Dwelling-Houses. By EDWARD A. BUTLER, B.A., B.Sc. (Lond.). With 113 Illustrations. Crown 8vo., 3s. 6d.

Furneaux (W.).

THE OUTDOOR WORLD; or The Young Collector's Handbook. With 18 Plates 16 of which are coloured, and 549 Illustrations in the Text. Crown 8vo., 7s. 6d.

BUTTERFLIES AND MOTHS (British). With 12 coloured Plates and 241 Illustrations in the Text. Crown 8vo., 7s. 6d.

LIFE IN PONDS AND STREAMS. With 8 coloured Plates and 331 Illustrations in the Text. Crown 8vo., 7s. 6d.

Hartwig (DR. GEORGE).

THE SEA AND ITS LIVING WONDERS. With 12 Plates and 303 Woodcuts. 8vo., 7s. net.

THE TROPICAL WORLD. With 8 Plates and 172 Woodcuts. 8vo., 7s. net.

THE POLAR WORLD. With 3 Maps, 8 Plates and 85 Woodcuts. 8vo., 7s. net.

THE SUBTERRANEAN WORLD. With 3 Maps and 80 Woodcuts. 8vo., 7s. net.

THE AERIAL WORLD. With Map, 8 Plates and 60 Woodcuts. 8vo., 7s. net.

HEROES OF THE POLAR WORLD. 19 Illustrations. Cr. 8vo., 2s.

WONDERS OF THE TROPICAL FORESTS. 40 Illustrations. Cr. 8vo., 2s.

WORKERS UNDER THE GROUND. 29 Illustrations. Cr. 8vo., 2s.

MARVELS OVER OUR HEADS. 29 Illustrations. Cr. 8vo., 2s.

SEA MONSTERS AND SEA BIRDS. 75 Illustrations. Cr. 8vo., 2s. 6d.

DENIZENS OF THE DEEP. 117 Illustrations. Cr. 8vo., 2s. 6d.

Hartwig (DR. GEORGE)—*continued.*

VOLCANOES AND EARTHQUAKES. 30 Illustrations. Cr. 8vo., 2s. 6d.

WILD ANIMALS OF THE TROPICS. 66 Illustrations. Cr. 8vo., 3s. 6d.

Helmholtz.—*POPULAR LECTURES ON SCIENTIFIC SUBJECTS.* By HERMANN VON HELMHOLTZ. With 68 Woodcuts. 2 vols. Cr. 8vo., 3s. 6d. each.

Hudson (W. H.).

BRITISH BIRDS. With a Chapter on Structure and Classification by FRANK E. BEDDARD, F.R.S. With 16 Plates (8 of which are Coloured), and over 100 Illustrations in the Text. Cr. 8vo., 7s. 6d.

BIRDS IN LONDON. With numerous Illustrations from Drawings and Photographs.

Proctor (RICHARD A.).

LIGHT SCIENCE FOR LEISURE HOURS. Familiar Essays on Scientific Subjects. 3 vols. Cr. 8vo., 5s. each.

ROUGH WAYS MADE SMOOTH. Familiar Essays on Scientific Subjects. Crown 8vo., 3s. 6d.

PLEASANT WAYS IN SCIENCE. Crown 8vo., 3s. 6d.

NATURE STUDIES. By R. A. PROCTOR, GRANT ALLEN, A. WILSON, T. FOSTER and E. CLODD. Crown 8vo., 3s. 6d.

LEISURE READINGS. By R. A. PROCTOR, E. CLODD, A. WILSON, T. FOSTER and A. C. RANYARD. Cr. 8vo., 3s. 6d.

. *For Mr. Proctor's other books see Messrs. Longmans & Co.'s Catalogue of Scientific Works.*

Stanley.—*A FAMILIAR HISTORY OF BIRDS.* By E. STANLEY, D.D., formerly Bishop of Norwich. With Illustrations. Cr. 8vo., 3s. 6d.

Popular Science (Natural History, &c.)—*continued.*

Wood (Rev. J. G.).

Homes without Hands: A Description of the Habitation of Animals, classed according to the Principle of Construction. With 140 Illustrations. 8vo., 7s., net.

Insects at Home : A Popular Account of British Insects, their Structure, Habits and Transformations. With 700 Illustrations. 8vo., 7s. net.

Insects Abroad: a Popular Account of Foreign Insects, their Structure, Habits and Transformations. With 600 Illustrations. 8vo., 7s. net.

Bible Animals: a Description of every Living Creature mentioned in the Scriptures. With 112 Illustrations. 8vo., 7s. net.

Petland Revisited. With 33 Illustrations. Cr. 8vo., 3s. 6d.

Out of Doors; a Selection of Original Articles on Practical Natural History. With 11 Illustrations. Cr. 8vo., 3s.·6d.

Wood (Rev. J. G.)—*continued.*

Strange Dwellings: a Description of the Habitations of Animals, abridged from ' Homes without Hands '. With 60 Illustrations. Cr. 8vo., 3s. 6d.

Bird Life of the Bible. 32 Illustrations. Cr. 8vo., 3s. 6d.

Wonderful Nests. 30 Illustrations. Cr. 8vo., 3s. 6d.

Homes under the Ground. 28 Illustrations. Cr. 8vo., 3s. 6d.

Wild Animals of the Bible. 29 Illustrations. Cr. 8vo., 3s. 6d.

Domestic Animals of the Bible. 23 Illustrations. Cr. 8vo., 3s. 6d.

The Branch Builders. 28 Illustrations. Cr. 8vo., 2s. 6d.

Social Habitations and Parasitic Nests. 18 Illustrations. Cr. 8vo., 2s.

Works of Reference.

Longmans' *Gazetteer of the World.* Edited by George G. Chisholm, M.A., B.Sc. Imp. 8vo., £2 2s. cloth, £2 12s. 6d. half-morocco.

Maunder (Samuel).

Biographical Treasury. With Supplement brought down to 1889. By Rev. James Wood. Fcp. 8vo., 6s.

Treasury of Geography, Physical, Historical, Descriptive, and Political. With 7 Maps and 16 Plates. Fcp. 8vo., 6s.

The Treasury of Bible Knowledge. By the Rev. J. Ayre, M.A. With 5 Maps, 15 Plates, and 300 Woodcuts. Fcp. 8vo., 6s.

Treasury of Knowledge and Library of Reference. Fcp. 8vo., 6s.

Historical Treasury. Fcp. 8vo., 6s.

Maunder (Samuel)—*continued.*

Scientific and Literary Treasury. Fcp. 8vo., 6s.

The Treasury of Botany. Edited by J. Lindley, F.R.S., and T. Moore, F.L.S. With 274 Woodcuts and 20 Steel Plates. 2 vols. Fcp. 8vo., 12s.

Roget. — *Thesaurus of English Words and Phrases.* Classified and Arranged so as to Facilitate the Expression of Ideas and assist in Literary Composition. By Peter Mark Roget, M.D., F.R.S. Recomposed throughout, enlarged and improved, partly from the Author's Notes, and with a full Index, by the Author's Son, John Lewis Roget. Crown 8vo., 10s. 6d.

Willich.--*Popular Tables* for giving information for ascertaining the value of Lifehold, Leasehold, and Church Property, the Public Funds, &c. By Charles M. Willich. Edited by H. Bence Jones. Crown 8vo., 10s. 6d.

Children's Books.

Crake (REV. A. D.).

EDWY THE FAIR; or, The First Chronicle of Æscendune. Cr. 8vo., 2s. 6d.

ALFGAR THE DANE; or, The Second Chronicle of Æscendune. Cr. 8vo. 2s. 6d.

THE RIVAL HEIRS: being the Third and Last Chronicle of Æscendune. Cr. 8vo., 2s. 6d.

THE HOUSE OF WALDERNE. A Tale of the Cloister and the Forest in the Days of the Barons' Wars. Crown 8vo., 2s. 6d.

BRIAN FITZ-COUNT. A Story of Wallingford Castle and Dorchester Abbey. Cr. 8vo., 2s. 6d.

Lang (ANDREW).—EDITED BY.

THE BLUE FAIRY BOOK. With 138 Illustrations. Crown 8vo., 6s.

THE RED FAIRY BOOK. With 100 Illustrations. Crown 8vo., 6s.

THE GREEN FAIRY BOOK. With 99 Illustrations. Crown 8vo., 6s.

THE YELLOW FAIRY BOOK. With 104 Illustrations. Crown 8vo., 6s.

THE PINK FAIRY BOOK. With 67 Illustrations. Crown 8vo., 6s.

THE BLUE POETRY BOOK. With 100 Illustrations. Crown 8vo., 6s.

THE BLUE POETRY BOOK. School Edition, without Illustrations. Fcp. 8vo., 2s. 6d.

THE TRUE STORY BOOK. With 66 Illustrations. Crown 8vo., 6s.

THE RED TRUE STORY BOOK. With 100 Illustrations. Crown 8vo., 6s.

THE ANIMAL STORY BOOK. With 67 Illustrations. Crown 8vo., 6s.

Meade (L. T.).

DADDY'S BOY. With Illustrations. Crown 8vo., 3s. 6d.

Meade (L. T.)—*continued.*

DEB AND THE DUCHESS. With Illustrations. Crown 8vo., 3s. 6d.

THE BERESFORD PRIZE. With Illustrations. Crown 8vo., 3s. 6d.

THE HOUSE OF SURPRISES. With Illustrations. Crown 8vo. 3s. 6d.

Molesworth—*SILVERTHORNS.* By Mrs. MOLESWORTH. With Illustrations. Cr. 8vo., 5s.

Praeger.—*THE ADVENTURES OF THE THREE BOLD BABES: HECTOR, HONORIA AND ALISANDER.* A Story in Pictures. By S. ROSAMOND PRAEGER. With 24 Coloured Plates and 24 Outline Pictures. Oblong 4to., 3s. 6d.

Stevenson.—*A CHILD'S GARDEN OF VERSES.* By ROBERT LOUIS STEVENSON. Fcp. 8vo., 5s.

Sullivan.—*HERE THEY ARE!* More Stories. Written and Illustrated by JAS. F. SULLIVAN. Crown 8vo., 6s.

Upton (FLORENCE K. AND BERTHA).

THE ADVENTURES OF TWO DUTCH DOLLS AND A 'GOLLIWOGG'. With 31 Coloured Plates and numerous Illustrations in the Text. Oblong 4to., 6s.

THE GOLLIWOGG'S BICYCLE CLUB. With 31 Coloured Plates and numerous Illustrations in the Text. Oblong 4to., 6s.

THE VEGE-MEN'S REVENGE. With Coloured Plates and numerous Illustrations in the Text. Oblong 4to., 6s.

Wordsworth.—*THE SNOW GARDEN, AND OTHER FAIRY TALES FOR CHILDREN.* By ELIZABETH WORDSWORTH. With 10 Illustrations by TREVOR HADDON. Crown 8vo., 3s. 6d.

Longmans' Series of Books for Girls.

Price 2s. 6d. each.

ATELIER (THE) DU LYS: or, an Art Student in the Reign of Terror.

BY THE SAME AUTHOR.

MADEMOISELLE MORI: a Tale of Modern Rome.

IN THE OLDEN TIME: a Tale of the Peasant War in Germany.

THE YOUNGER SISTER.

THAT CHILD.

UNDER A CLOUD.

HESTER'S VENTURE

THE FIDDLER OF LUGAU.

A CHILD OF THE REVOLUTION.

ATHERSTONE PRIORY. By L. N. COMYN.

THE STORY OF A SPRING MORNING, etc. By Mrs. MOLESWORTH. Illustrated.

THE PALACE IN THE GARDEN. By Mrs. MOLESWORTH. Illustrated.

NEIGHBOURS. By Mrs. MOLESWORTH.

THE THIRD MISS ST. QUENTIN. By Mrs. MOLESWORTH.

VERY YOUNG; AND QUITE ANOTHER STORY. Two Stories. By JEAN INGELOW.

CAN THIS BE LOVE? By LOUISA PARR.

KEITH DERAMORE. By the Author of 'Miss Molly'.

SIDNEY. By MARGARET DELAND.

AN ARRANGED MARRIAGE. By DOROTHEA GERARD.

LAST WORDS TO GIRLS ON LIFE AT SCHOOL AND AFTER SCHOOL. By MARIA GREY.

STRAY THOUGHTS FOR GIRLS. By LUCY H. M. SOULSBY, Head Mistress of Oxford High School. 16mo., 1s. 6d. net.

The Silver Library.

CROWN 8VO. 3s. 6d. EACH VOLUME.

Arnold's (Sir Edwin) Seas and Lands. With 71 Illustrations. 3s. 6d.

Bagehot's (W.) Biographical Studies. 3s. 6d.

Bagehot's (W.) Economic Studies. 3s. 6d.

Bagehot's (W.) Literary Studies. With Portrait. 3 vols. 3s. 6d. each.

Baker's (Sir S. W.) Eight Years in Ceylon. With 6 Illustrations. 3s. 6d.

Baker's (Sir S. W.) Rifle and Hound in Ceylon. With 6 Illustrations. 3s. 6d.

Baring-Gould's (Rev. S.) Curious Myths of the Middle Ages. 3s. 6d.

Baring-Gould's (Rev. S.) Origin and Development of Religious Belief. 2 vols. 3s. 6d. each.

Becker's (Prof.) Gallus: or, Roman Scenes in the Time of Augustus. Illustrated. 3s. 6d.

Becker's (Prof.) Charicles: or, Illustrations of the Private Life of the Ancient Greeks. Illustrated. 3s. 6d.

Bent's (J. T.) The Ruined Cities of Mashonaland. With 117 Illustrations. 3s. 6d.

Brassey's (Lady) A Voyage in the 'Sunbeam'. With 66 Illustrations. 3s. 6d.

Butler's (Edward A.) Our Household Insects. With 7 Plates and 113 Illustrations in the Text. 3s. 6d.

Clodd's (E.) Story of Creation: a Plain Account of Evolution. With 77 Illustrations. 3s. 6d.

Conybeare (Rev. W. J.) and Howson's (Very Rev. J. S.) Life and Epistles of St. Paul. 46 Illustrations. 3s. 6d.

Dougall's (L.) Beggars All: a Novel. 3s. 6d.

Doyle's (A. Conan) Micah Clarke. A Tale of Monmouth's Rebellion. 10 Illusts. 3s. 6d.

Doyle's (A. Conan) The Captain of the Polestar, and other Tales. 3s. 6d.

Doyle's (A. Conan) The Refugees: A Tale of Two Continents. With 25 Illustrations. 3s 6d.

Froude's (J. A.) The History of England, from the Fall of Wolsey to the Defeat of the Spanish Armada. 12 vols. 3s. 6d. each.

Froude's (J. A.) The English in Ireland. 3 vols. 10s. 6d.

Froude's (J. A.) The Divorce of Catherine of Aragon. 3s. 6d.

Froude's (J. A.) The Spanish Story of the Armada, and other Essays. 3s. 6d.

Froude's (J. A.) Short Studies on Great Subjects. 4 vols. 3s. 6d. each.

Froude's (J. A.) Thomas Carlyle: a History of his Life.
1795-1835. 2 vols. 7s.
1834-1881. 2 vols. 7s.

Froude's (J. A.) Cæsar: a Sketch. 3s. 6d.

Froude's (J. A.) The Two Chiefs of Dunboy: an Irish Romance of the Last Century. 3s. 6d.

Gleig's (Rev. G. R.) Life of the Duke of Wellington. With Portrait. 3s. 6d.

Greville's (C. C. F.) Journal of the Reigns of King George IV., King William IV., and Queen Victoria. 8 vols., 3s. 6d. each.

Haggard's (H. R.) She: A History of Adventure. 32 Illustrations. 3s. 6d.

Haggard's (H. R.) Allan Quatermain. With 20 Illustrations. 3s. 6d.

Haggard's (H. R.) Colonel Quaritch, V.C.: a Tale of Country Life. 3s. 6d.

Haggard's (H. R.) Cleopatra. With 29 Illustrations. 3s. 6d.

Haggard's (H. R.) Eric Brighteyes. With 51 Illustrations. 3s. 6d.

Haggard's (H. R.) Beatrice. 3s. 6d.

Haggard's (H. R.) Allan's Wife. With 34 Illustrations. 3s. 6d.

Haggard's (H. R.) Montezuma's Daughter. With 25 Illustrations. 3s. 6d.

Haggard's (H. R.) The Witch's Head. With 16 Illustrations. 3s. 6d.

Haggard's (H. R.) Mr. Meeson's Will. With 16 Illustrations. 3s. 6d.

Haggard's (H. R.) Nada the Lily. With 23 Illustrations. 3s. 6d.

Haggard's (H. R.) Dawn. With 16 Illusts. 3s. 6d.

Haggard's (H. R.) The People of the Mist. With 16 Illustrations. 3s. 6d.

Haggard's (H. R.) Joan Haste. With 20 Illustrations. 3s. 6d.

Haggard (H. R.) and Lang's (A.) The World's Desire. With 27 Illustrations. 3s. 6d.

Harte's (Bret) In the Carquinez Woods and other Stories. 3s. 6d.

Helmholtz's (Hermann von) Popular Lectures on Scientific Subjects. With 68 Illustrations. 2 vols. 3s. 6d. each.

Hornung's (E. W.) The Unbidden Guest. 3s. 6d.

Howitt's (W.) Visits to Remarkable Places. 80 Illustrations. 3s. 6d.

Jefferies' (R.) The Story of My Heart: My Autobiography. With Portrait. 3s. 6d.

Jefferies' (R.) Field and Hedgerow. With Portrait. 3s. 6d.

Jefferies' (R.) Red Deer. 17 Illustrations. 3s. 6d.

Jefferies' (R.) Wood Magic: a Fable. With Frontispiece and Vignette by E. V. B. 3s. 6d.

Jefferies (R.) The Toilers of the Field. With Portrait from the Bust in Salisbury Cathedral. 3s. 6d.

Kaye (Sir J.) and Malleson's (Colonel) History of the Indian Mutiny of 1857-8. 6 vols. 3s. 6d. each.

Knight's (E. F.) The Cruise of the 'Alerte': the Narrative of a Search for Treasure on the Desert Island of Trinidad. With 2 Maps and 23 Illustrations. 3s. 6d.

Knight's (E. F.) Where Three Empires Meet: a Narrative of Recent Travel in Kashmir, Western Tibet, Baltistan, Gilgit. With a Map and 54 Illustrations. 3s. 6d.

Knight's (E. F.) The 'Falcon' on the Baltic: a Coasting Voyage from Hammersmith to Copenhagen in a Three-Ton Yacht. With Map and 11 Illustrations. 3s. 6d.

Lang's (A.) Angling Sketches. 20 Illustrations. 3s. 6d.

Lang's (A.) Custom and Myth: Studies of Early Usage and Belief. 3s. 6d.

Lang's (Andrew) Cock Lane and Common-Sense. With a New Preface. 3s. 6d.

The Silver Library—*continued.*

Lees (J. A.) and Clutterbuck's (W. J.) B. C. 1887, A Ramble in British Columbia. With Maps and 75 Illustrations. 3*s.* 6*d.*

Macaulay's (Lord) Essays and Lays of Ancient Rome. With Portrait and Illustration. 3*s.* 6*d.*

Macleod's (H. D.) Elements of Banking. 3*s.* 6*d.*

Marbot's (Baron de) Memoirs. Translated. 2 vols. 7*s.*

Marshman's (J. C.) Memoirs of Sir Henry Havelock. 3*s.* 6*d.*

Max Müller's (F.) India, what can it teach us? 3*s.* 6*d.*

Max Müller's (F.) Introduction to the Science of Religion. 3*s.* 6*d.*

Merivale's (Dean) History of the Romans under the Empire. 8 vols. 3*s.* 6*d.* each.

Mill's (J. S.) Political Economy. 3*s.* 6*d.*

Mill's (J. S.) System of Logic. 3*s.* 6*d.*

Milner's (Geo.) Country Pleasures: the Chronicle of a Year chiefly in a Garden. 3*s.* 6*d.*

Nansen's (F.) The First Crossing of Greenland. With Illustrations and a Map. 3*s.* 6*d.*

Phillipps-Wolley's (C.) Snap: a Legend of the Lone Mountain. 13 Illustrations. 3*s.* 6*d.*

Proctor's (R. A.) The Orbs Around Us. 3*s.* 6*d.*

Proctor's (R. A.) The Expanse of Heaven. 3*s.* 6*d.*

Proctor's (R. A.) Other Worlds than Ours. 3*s.*6*d.*

Proctor's (R. A.) Our Place among Infinities: a Series of Essays contrasting our Little Abode in Space and Time with the Infinities around us. Crown 8vo., 3*s.* 6*d.*

Proctor's (R. A.) Other Suns than Ours. 3*s.* 6*d.*

Proctor's (R. A.) Rough Ways made Smooth. 3*s.* 6*d.*

Proctor's (R. A.) Pleasant Ways in Science. 3*s.* 6*d.*

Proctor's (R. A.) Myths and Marvels of Astronomy. 3*s.* 6*d.*

Proctor's (R. A.) Nature Studies. 3*s.* 6*d.*

Proctor's (R. A.) Leisure Readings. By R. A. PROCTOR, EDWARD CLODD, ANDREW WILSON, THOMAS FOSTER, and A. C. RANYARD. With Illustrations. 3*s.* 6*d.*

Rhoscomyl's (Owen) The Jewel of Ynys Galon. With 12 Illustrations. 3*s.* 6*d.*

Rossetti's (Maria F.) A Shadow of Dante. 3*s.* 6*d.*

Smith's (R. Bosworth) Carthage and the Carthaginians. With Maps, Plans, &c. 3*s.* 6*d.*

Stanley's (Bishop) Familiar History of Birds. 160 Illustrations. 3*s.* 6*d.*

Stevenson's (R. L.) The Strange Case of Dr. Jekyll and Mr. Hyde; with other Fables. 3*s.* 6*d.*

Stevenson (R. L.) and Osbourne's (Ll.) The Wrong Box. 3*s.* 6*d.*

Stevenson (Robert Louis) and Stevenson's (Fanny van de Grift) More New Arabian Nights.—The Dynamiter. 3*s.* 6*d.*

Weyman's (Stanley J.) The House of the Wolf: a Romance. 3*s.* 6*d.*

Wood's (Rev. J. G.) Petland Revisited. With 33 Illustrations. 3*s.* 6*d.*

Wood's (Rev. J. G.) Strange Dwellings. With 60 Illustrations. 3*s.* 6*d.*

Wood's (Rev. J. G.) Out of Doors. With 11 Illustrations. 3*s.* 6*d.*

Cookery, Domestic Management, &c.

Acton. — *MODERN COOKERY.* By ELIZA ACTON. With 150 Woodcuts. Fcp. 8vo., 4*s.* 6*d.*

Bull (THOMAS, M.D.).

HINTS TO MOTHERS ON THE MANAGEMENT OF THEIR HEALTH DURING THE PERIOD OF PREGNANCY. Fcp. 8vo., 1*s.* 6*d.*

THE MATERNAL MANAGEMENT OF CHILDREN IN HEALTH AND DISEASE. Fcp. 8vo., 1*s.* 6*d.*

De Salis (MRS.).

CAKES AND CONFECTIONS À LA MODE. Fcp. 8vo., 1*s.* 6*d.*

DOGS: A Manual for Amateurs. Fcp. 8vo., 1*s.* 6*d.*

DRESSED GAME AND POULTRY À LA MODE. Fcp. 8vo., 1*s.* 6*d.*

DRESSED VEGETABLES À LA MODE. Fcp. 8vo., 1*s.* 6*d.*

De Salis (MRS.).—*continued.*

DRINKS À LA MODE. Fcp. 8vo., 1*s.*6*d.*

ENTRÉES À LA MODE. Fcp. 8vo., 1*s.* 6*d.*

FLORAL DECORATIONS. Fcp. 8vo., 1*s.* 6*d.*

GARDENING À LA MODE. Fcp. 8vo. Part I., Vegetables, 1*s.* 6*d.* Part II., Fruits, 1*s.* 6*d.*

NATIONAL VIANDS À LA MODE. Fcp. 8vo., 1*s.* 6*d.*

NEW-LAID EGGS. Fcp. 8vo., 1*s.* 6*d.*

OYSTERS À LA MODE. Fcp. 8vo., 1*s.* 6*d.*

PUDDINGS AND PASTRY À LA MODE. Fcp. 8vo., 1*s.* 6*d.*

SAVOURIES À LA MODE. Fcp. 8vo., 1*s.*6*d.*

SOUPS AND DRESSED FISH À LA MODE. Fcp. 8vo., 1*s.* 6*d.*

Cookery, Domestic Management, &c.—*continued.*

De Salis (MRS.).—*continued.*
SWEETS AND SUPPER DISHES À LA MODE. Fcp. 8vo., 1s. 6d.
TEMPTING DISHES FOR SMALL IN-COMES. Fcp. 8vo., 1s. 6d.
WRINKLES AND NOTIONS FOR EVERY HOUSEHOLD. Crown 8vo., 1s. 6d.

Lear.—MAIGRE COOKERY. By H. L. SIDNEY LEAR. 16mo., 2s.

Poole.—COOKERY FOR THE DIABETIC. By W. H. and Mrs. POOLE. With Preface by Dr. PAVY. Fcp. 8vo., 2s. 6d.

Walker (JANE H.).
A BOOK FOR EVERY WOMAN.
Part I., The Management of Children in Health and out of Health. Crown 8vo., 2s. 6d.
Part II. Woman in Health and out of Health. Crown 8vo., 2s. 6d.

A HANDBOOK FOR MOTHERS : being Simple Hints to Women on the Management of their Health during Pregnancy and Confinement, together with Plain Directions as to the Care of Infants. Crown 8vo., 2s. 6d.

Miscellaneous and Critical Works.

Allingham.—VARIETIES IN PROSE. By WILLIAM ALLINGHAM. 3 vols. Cr. 8vo., 18s. (Vols. 1 and 2, Rambles, by PATRICIUS WALKER. Vol. 3, Irish Sketches, etc.)

Armstrong.—ESSAYS AND SKETCHES. By EDMUND J. ARMSTRONG. Fcp. 8vo., 5s.

Bagehot.—LITERARY STUDIES. By WALTER BAGEHOT. With Portrait. 3 vols. Crown 8vo., 3s. 6d. each.

Baring-Gould.—CURIOUS MYTHS OF THE MIDDLE AGES. By Rev. S. BARING-GOULD. Crown 8vo., 3s. 6d.

Baynes. — SHAKESPEARE STUDIES, and other Essays. By the late THOMAS SPENCER BAYNES, LL.B., LL.D. With a Biographical Preface by Professor LEWIS CAMPBELL. Crown 8vo., 7s. 6d.

Boyd (A. K. H.) ('A.K.H.B.').
And see MISCELLANEOUS THEOLOGICAL WORKS, p. 32.
AUTUMN HOLIDAYS OF A COUNTRY PARSON. Crown 8vo., 3s. 6d.
COMMONPLACE PHILOSOPHER. Cr. 8vo., 3s. 6d.
CRITICAL ESSAYS OF A COUNTRY PARSON. Crown 8vo., 3s. 6d.
EAST COAST DAYS AND MEMORIES. Crown 8vo., 3s. 6d.
LANDSCAPES, CHURCHES, AND MORA-LITIES. Crown 8vo., 3s. 6d.
LEISURE HOURS IN TOWN. Crown 8vo., 3s. 6d.
LESSONS OF MIDDLE AGE. Crown 8vo., 3s. 6d.
OUR LITTLE LIFE. Two Series. Crown 8vo., 3s. 6d. each.
OUR HOMELY COMEDY : AND TRA-GEDY. Crown 8vo., 3s. 6d.

Boyd (A. K. H.) ('A.K.H.B.').—*continued.*
RECREATIONS OF A COUNTRY PARSON. Three Series. Crown 8vo., 3s. 6d. each. Also First Series. Popular Edition. 8vo., 6d. Sewed.

Brookings.—BRIEFS FOR DEBATE ON CURRENT POLITICAL, ECONOMIC AND SOCIAL TOPICS. Edited by W. DU BOIS BROOKINGS, A.B. of the Harvard Law School, and RALPH CURTIS RINGWALT, A.B. Assistant in Rhetoric in Columbia University, New York. With an Introduction on 'The Art of Debate' by ALBERT BUSHNELL HART, Ph.D. of Harvard University. With full Index. Crown 8vo., 6s.

Butler (SAMUEL).
EREWHON. Crown 8vo., 5s.
THE FAIR HAVEN. A Work in De-fence of the Miraculous Element in our Lord's Ministry. Cr. 8vo., 7s. 6d.
LIFE AND HABIT. An Essay after a Completer View of Evolution. Cr. 8vo., 7s. 6d.
EVOLUTION, OLD AND NEW. Cr. 8vo., 10s. 6d.
ALPS AND SANCTUARIES OF PIED-MONT AND CANTON TICINO. Illustrated. Pott 4to., 10s. 6d.
LUCK, OR CUNNING, AS THE MAIN MEANS OF ORGANIC MODIFICATION? Cr. 8vo., 7s. 6d.
EX VOTO. An Account of the Sacro Monte or New Jerusalem at Varallo-Sesia. Crown 8vo., 10s. 6d.
THE AUTHORESS OF THE ODYSSEY, WHERE AND WHEN SHE WROTE, WHO SHE WAS, THE USE SHE MADE OF THE ILIAD, AND HOW THE POEM GREW UNDER HER HANDS. With Illustrations. 8vo.

Miscellaneous and Critical Works—*continued.*

CHARITIES REGISTER, THE ANNUAL, AND DIGEST: being a Classified Register of Charities in or available in the Metropolis, together with a Digest of Information respecting the Legal, Voluntary, and other Means for the Prevention and Relief of Distress, and the Improvement of the Condition of the Poor, and an Elaborate Index. With an Introduction by C. S. LOCH, Secretary to the Council of the Charity Organisation Society, London. 8vo., 4s.

Dreyfus.—*LECTURES ON FRENCH LITERATURE.* Delivered in Melbourne by IRMA DREYFUS. With Portrait of the Author. Large crown 8vo., 12s. 6d.

Evans.—*THE ANCIENT STONE IMPLEMENTS, WEAPONS AND ORNAMENTS OF GREAT BRITAIN.* By Sir JOHN EVANS, K.C.B., D.C.L., LL.D., F.R.S., etc. With 537 Illustrations. Medium 8vo., 28s.

Gwilt.—*AN ENCYCLOPÆDIA OF ARCHITECTURE.* By JOSEPH GWILT, F.S.A. Illustrated with more than 1100 Engravings on Wood. Revised (1888), with Alterations and Considerable Additions by WYATT PAPWORTH. 8vo., £2 12s. 6d.

Hamlin.—*A TEXT-BOOK OF THE HISTORY OF ARCHITECTURE.* By A. D. F. HAMLIN, A.M. With 229 Illustrations. Crown 8vo., 7s. 6d.

Hampton. — *FOR REMEMBRANCE:* Wishes, Prayers, Thoughts. Compiled by the Lady LAURA HAMPTON. Small 8vo.

Haweis.—*MUSIC AND MORALS.* By the Rev. H. R. HAWEIS. With Portrait of the Author, and numerous Illustrations, Facsimiles, and Diagrams. Cr. 8vo., 7s. 6d.

Hime.—*STRAY MILITARY PAPERS.* By Lieut-Colonel H. W. L. HIME (late Royal Artillery). 8vo.

CONTENTS.— Infantry Fire Formations — On Marking at Rifle Matches—The Progress of Field Artillery—The Reconnoitering Duties of Cavalry.

Indian Ideals (No. 1).

NÂRADA SÛTRA: an Inquiry into Love (Bhakti-Jijnâsâ). Translated from the Sanskrit, with an Independendent Commentary, by E. T. STURDY. Crown 8vo., 2s. 6d. net.

Jefferies.—(RICHARD).

FIELD AND HEDGEROW: With Portrait. Crown 8vo., 3s. 6d.

THE STORY OF MY HEART: my Autobiography. With Portrait and New Preface by C. J. LONGMAN. Cr. 8vo., 3s. 6d.

RED DEER. With 17 Illustrations by J. CHARLTON and H. TUNALY. Crown 8vo., 3s. 6d.

THE TOILERS OF THE FIELD. With Portrait from the Bust in Salisbury Cathedral. Crown 8vo., 3s. 6d.

WOOD MAGIC: a Fable. With Frontispiece and Vignette by E. V. B. Crown 8vo., 3s. 6d.

THOUGHTS FROM THE WRITINGS OF RICHARD JEFFERIES. Selected by H. S. HOOLE WAYLEN. 16mo., 3s. 6d.

Johnson.—*THE PATENTEE'S MANUAL:* a Treatise on the Law and Practice of Letters Patent. By J. & J. H. JOHNSON, Patent Agents, &c. 8vo., 10s. 6d.

Lang (ANDREW).

MODERN MYTHOLOGY. 8vo., 9s.

LETTERS TO DEAD AUTHORS. Fcp. 8vo., 2s. 6d. net.

BOOKS AND BOOKMEN. With 2 Coloured Plates and 17 Illustrations. Fcp. 8vo., 2s. 6d. net.

OLD FRIENDS. Fcp. 8vo., 2s. 6d.

LETTERS ON LITERATURE. Fcp. 8vo., 2s. 6d. net.

COCK LANE AND COMMON SENSE. Crown 8vo., 3s. 6d.

THE BOOK OF DREAMS AND GHOSTS. Crown 8vo., 6s.

Miscellaneous and Critical Works—*continued.*

Macfarren. — *LECTURES ON HAR-MONY.* By Sir GEORGE A. MACFARREN. 8vo., 12s.

Max Müller (F).

INDIA: WHAT CAN IT TEACH US? Crown 8vo., 3s. 6d.

CHIPS FROM A GERMAN WORKSHOP.
Vol. I. Recent Essays and Addresses. Crown 8vo., 6s. 6d. net.
Vol. II. Biographical Essays. Crown 8vo., 6s. 6d. net.
Vol. III. Essays on Language and Literature. Crown 8vo., 6s. 6d. net.
Vol. IV. Essays on Mythology and Folk Lore. Crown 8vo, 8s. 6d. net.

CONTRIBUTIONS TO THE SCIENCE OF MYTHOLOGY. 2 vols. 8vo., 32s.

Milner.—*COUNTRY PLEASURES:* the Chronicle of a Year chiefly in a Garden. By GEORGE MILNER. Crown 8vo., 3s. 6d.

Morris (WILLIAM).

SIGNS OF CHANGE. Seven Lectures delivered on various Occasions. Post 8vo., 4s. 6d.

HOPES AND FEARS FOR ART. Five Lectures delivered in Birmingham, London, &c., in 1878-1881. Crown 8vo., 4s. 6d.

Orchard.—*THE ASTRONOMY OF 'MILTON'S PARADISE LOST '.* By THOMAS N. ORCHARD, M.D., Member of the British Astronomical Association. With 13 Illustrations. 8vo., 15s.

Poore (GEORGE VIVIAN), M.D., F.R.C.P.

ESSAYS ON RURAL HYGIENE. With 13 Illustrations. Crown 8vo., 6s. 6d.

THE DWELLING HOUSE. With 36 Illustrations. Crown 8vo., 3s. 6d.

Proctor.—*STRENGTH:* How to get Strong and keep Strong, with Chapters on Rowing and Swimming, Fat, Age, and the Waist. By R. A. PROCTOR. With 9 Illustrations. Crown 8vo., 2s.

Rossetti.—*A SHADOW OF DANTE:* being an Essay towards studying Himself, his World and his Pilgrimage. By MARIA FRANCESCA ROSSETTI. With Frontispiece by DANTE GABRIEL ROSSETTI. Crown 8vo., 3s. 6d.

Solovyoff.—*A MODERN PRIESTESS OF ISIS (MADAME BLAVATSKY).* Abridged and Translated on Behalf of the Society for Psychical Research from the Russian of VSEVOLOD SERGYEEVICH SOLOVYOFF. By WALTER LEAF, Litt.D. With Appendices. Crown 8vo., 6s.

Soulsby (LUCY H. M.).

STRAY THOUGHTS ON READING. Small 8vo., 2s. 6d. net.

STRAY THOUGHTS FOR GIRLS. 16mo., 1s. 6d. net.

STRAY THOUGHTS FOR MOTHERS AND TEACHERS. Fcp. 8vo., 2s. 6d. net.

STRAY THOUGHTS FOR INVALIDS. 16mo., 2s. net.

Stevens.—*ON THE STOWAGE OF SHIPS AND THEIR CARGOES.* With Information regarding Freights, Charter-Parties, &c. By ROBERT WHITE STEVENS, Associate-Member of the Institute of Naval Architects. 8vo., 21s.

Miscellaneous Theological Works.

** For Church of England and Roman Catholic Works see MESSRS. LONGMANS & CO.'S *Special Catalogues.*

Balfour. — *THE FOUNDATIONS OF BELIEF:* being Notes Introductory to the Study of Theology. By the Right Hon. ARTHUR J. BALFOUR, M.P. 8vo., 12s. 6d.

Bird (ROBERT).

A CHILD'S RELIGION. Cr. 8vo., 2s.

JOSEPH, THE DREAMER. Crown 8vo., 5s.

Bird (ROBERT)—*continued.*

JESUS, THE CARPENTER OF NAZARETH. Crown 8vo., 5s.

To be had also in Two Parts, price 2s. 6d. each.

Part I. GALILEE AND THE LAKE OF GENNESARET.

Part II. JERUSALEM AND THE PERÆA.

Miscellaneous Theological Works—*continued.*

Boyd (A. K. H.) ('A.K.H.B.').

OCCASIONAL AND IMMEMORIAL DAYS: Discourses. Crown 8vo., 7s. 6d.

COUNSEL AND COMFORT FROM A CITY PULPIT. Crown 8vo., 3s. 6d.

SUNDAY AFTERNOONS IN THE PARISH CHURCH OF A SCOTTISH UNIVERSITY CITY. Crown 8vo., 3s. 6d.

CHANGED ASPECTS OF UNCHANGED TRUTHS. Crown 8vo., 3s. 6d.

GRAVER THOUGHTS OF A COUNTRY PARSON. Three Series. Crown 8vo., 3s. 6d. each.

PRESENT DAY THOUGHTS. Crown 8vo., 3s. 6d.

SEASIDE MUSINGS. Cr. 8vo., 3s. 6d.

'TO MEET THE DAY' through the Christian Year : being a Text of Scripture, with an Original Meditation and a Short Selection in Verse for Every Day. Crown 8vo., 4s. 6d.

Gibson.—*THE ABBÉ DE LAMENNAIS, AND THE LIBERAL CATHOLIC MOVEMENT IN FRANCE.* By the Hon. W. GIBSON. With Portrait. 8vo., 12s. 6d.

Kalisch (M. M., Ph.D.).

BIBLE STUDIES. Part I. Prophecies of Balaam. 8vo., 10s. 6d. Part II. The Book of Jonah. 8vo., 10s. 6d.

COMMENTARY ON THE OLD TESTAMENT: with a New Translation. Vol. I. Genesis. 8vo., 18s. Or adapted for the General Reader. 12s. Vol. II. Exodus. 15s. Or adapted for the General Reader. 12s. Vol. III. Leviticus, Part I. 15s. Or adapted for the General Reader. 8s. Vol. IV. Leviticus, Part II. 15s. Or adapted for the General Reader. 8s.

Macdonald (GEORGE).

UNSPOKEN SERMONS. Three Series. Crown 8vo., 3s. 6d. each.

THE MIRACLES OF OUR LORD. Crown 8vo., 3s. 6d.

Martineau (JAMES).

HOURS OF THOUGHT ON SACRED THINGS: Sermons, 2 vols. Crown 8vo., 3s. 6d. each.

Martineau (JAMES)—*continued.*

ENDEAVOURS AFTER THE CHRISTIAN LIFE. Discourses. Crown 8vo., 7s. 6d.

THE SEAT OF AUTHORITY IN RELIGION. 8vo., 14s.

ESSAYS, REVIEWS, AND ADDRESSES. 4 Vols. Crown 8vo., 7s. 6d. each.
I. Personal ; Political. II. Ecclesiastical ; Historical. III. Theological ; Philosophical. IV. Academical ; Religious.

HOME PRAYERS, with *TWO SERVICES* for Public Worship Crown 8vo., 3s. 6d.

Max Müller (F.).

HIBBERT LECTURES ON THE ORIGIN AND GROWTH OF RELIGION, as illustrated by the Religions of India. Cr. 8vo., 7s. 6d.

INTRODUCTION TO THE SCIENCE OF RELIGION : Four Lectures delivered at the Royal Institution. Crown 8vo., 3s. 6d.

NATURAL RELIGION. The Gifford Lectures, delivered before the University of Glasgow in 1888. Crown 8vo., 10s. 6d.

PHYSICAL RELIGION. The Gifford Lectures, delivered before the University of Glasgow in 1890. Crown 8vo., 10s. 6d.

ANTHROPOLOGICAL RELIGION. The Gifford Lectures, delivered before the University of Glasgow in 1891. Cr. 8vo., 10s. 6d.

THEOSOPHY, OR PSYCHOLOGICAL RELIGION. The Gifford Lectures, delivered before the University of Glasgow in 1892. Crown 8vo., 10s. 6d.

THREE LECTURES ON THE VEDÂNTA PHILOSOPHY, delivered at the Royal Institution in March, 1894. 8vo., 5s.

Romanes.—*THOUGHTS ON RELIGION.* By GEORGE J. ROMANES, LL.D., F.R.S. Crown 8vo., 4s. 6d.

Vivekananda.—*YOGA PHILOSOPHY :* Lectures delivered in New York, Winter of 1895-96, by the SWAMI VIKEKANANDA, on Raja Yoga ; or, Conquering the Internal Nature ; also Patanjali's Yoga Aphorisms, with Commentaries. Crown 8vo, 3s. 6d.

10,000/10/97.